Desire leapt like a static charge from one to the other. . . .

She stared up into his handsome face, mesmerized by those laughing blue eyes, while her mind relayed the message to her that this man was, really and truly, her husband.

"Maggie," he said hoarsely, and then he was standing beside her on the bed, taking her into his arms. She melted, beautifully tender and warm, against him.

The next thing she knew, he was pulling her to her feet, smothering her face with kisses, as he ran his hands over her body. Then, without her even knowing he had done so, he pulled the ribbon on her gown, opening the neck wider and wider, until it fell over her shoulders and down to the floor to lie in a shimmering pool of cream silk.

Chills covered her, not from the cool air, but from the heat in his eyes. She moved to step out of the gown lying on the floor, and he must have thought she was going to pick the gown up.

"Leave it. I want to see you," he said.

# SO THIS IS LOVE

## Elaine Coffman

FAWCETT GOLD MEDAL • NEW YORK

*For Kamran, who came when I wasn't searching and loved my pilgrim soul, who gave me more than I can ever repay and makes me feel like Audrey Hepburn in ROMAN HOLIDAY.*

A Fawcett Gold Medal Book
Published by Ballantine Books
Copyright © 1993 by Guardant, Inc.

All rights reserved under International and Pan-American Copyright Conventions. Published in the United States by Ballantine Books, a division of Random House, Inc., New York, and simultaneously in Canada by Random House of Canada Limited, Toronto.

Library of Congress Catalog Card Number: 93-90091

ISBN 0-449-14860-2

For information contact: The Aaron Priest Literary Agency, 708 Third Avenue, 23rd floor, New York, NY 10017.

Manufactured in the United States of America

First Ballantine Books Edition: July 1993

*Take this sorrow to thy heart, and make
it a part of thee, and it shall nourish thee
till thou art strong again.*
                    Longfellow, "Hyperion"

# ❧ PROLOGUE ❧

*Scotland, 1856*

Maggie Ramsay folded the last of her husband's coats and placed it in the open trunk. She stared at the assortment of clothing, each piece recalling a memory, a happier time when the muscular frame of Bruce Ramsay had filled it to perfection.

She slammed the lid down and turned away.

Bruce Ramsay was dead now, and no amount of staring at his clothes would ever bring him back. She turned to the two servants standing quietly by the door. A tightness in her chest threatened to rob her of her composure, but she swallowed, forcing back the urge to cry. "This is the last one," she said. "You may take it downstairs."

She watched in a disjointed fashion, unable to feel much of anything as the two men lifted the great, humpbacked trunk by its worn leather straps and carried it from the room. Maggie was tired. Never had she felt so insignificant, so devoid of purpose or feeling. It was as if everything inside her had died. She wondered if she would ever be able to feel again, or would her life simply pass without her really noticing it had, just as it had this past year? Would she simply wake up one morning and look in the mirror and see an old woman looking back at her and wonder when it had all happened?

It was time to go now, but Maggie found it difficult to leave Bruce's room, knowing another link to him and the life they shared would be severed. She turned to go, then hesitated, wondering if she should take one last tour of Glengarry Castle, one last look at each room to commit it to memory. She had been so happy here. She had been married in the tiny family chapel behind the castle. Their three children were born here.

And now her husband was buried here.

No, she would not, could not, walk these halls again. The Glengarry she knew belonged to the past, to happier times. Best to leave it there. She sighed and picked up her muff, which lay in the tufted leather chair that had been her husband's favorite. Even now, the supple, worn leather retained the shape of Bruce Ramsay's beloved body.

*Oh, Bruce, what will I do now? What will become of us?* She buried her face in the muff. *Please let it all be a bad dream. Let me wake up now and see Bruce coming into the room, with Fletcher riding on his shoulders. He will laugh when I tell him—laugh at the silly idea that he had ridden his horse off the cliff. He, Bruce Ramsay, the finest horseman in the north of Scotland. Oh, how he will laugh. He will put Fletcher down and stand there, as strong and bonny and alive as ever, then he will take me in his arms and kiss the lingering residue of pain away. He isna dead. He canna be. Not Bruce. He was too full of life to die.*

But he had.

She looked at his chair and willed him to be there, then placed her hand in the seat, as if by doing so, she would feel connected to his life.

She gasped at the shock of cold leather, and jerked her hand away. The finality of it all swept over her with such force, she swayed upon her feet, clutching the back of the chair to steady herself against the dizziness, the weakness, that always came whenever she remembered. Despair and grief seemed too great a burden, and she fought to find a faint thread of the iron strength her husband always claimed she possessed.

Bruce Ramsay, the Duke of Glengarry, was dead. *They lied,* she thought. *They lied when they said time heals all wounds.* It had been a year ago that the splendid form of her husband had fallen, to be battered upon the sharp-fanged rocks at the bottom of the cliffs that ran along Scotland's bleak northern coast. One long year, but the pain of it was still with her. No explanation was ever given as to how the twenty-nine-year-old duke—an expert horseman—managed to ride his horse off the cliff, or how the horse—an intelligent animal—had been persuaded to go. In truth, Maggie had not been given much time to wonder at all, for the duke's bones had scarcely had time to settle in his grave when she was drawn into a lengthy court battle with a Lowlander by the name of Adair Ramsay.

Ramsay was no stranger to Maggie, nor was his claim unfamiliar—that her late husband's title was rightfully his. It had all started two years ago, when a small, bespectacled man appeared before the massive doors of Glengarry Castle, rapping soundly against the carved oak with the handle of his walking stick, demanding with brusque authority to see the duke.

Once sequestered in Bruce Ramsay's library, Adair Ramsay produced papers declaring that Bruce's claim to the dukedom was based upon falsified information—church records that had been forged, and marriages that had never taken place that had been recorded—things that had occurred during the times of Bruce's great-grandfather. He insisted that the title belonged to his own family, one that was, oddly enough, not connected to Bruce Ramsay's line, in spite of their common name.

Bruce declared the man an imposter and had him thrown out. But Adair Ramsay was as persistent as he was canny. Over the next year, he reappeared time and time again, and each time Bruce turned him away.

But the last time he came, he brought with him legally filed documents, and a summons to a hearing in Edinburgh. Maggie and Bruce made the journey to Edinburgh, and after two preliminary court hearings, the court ruled in Bruce Ramsay's favor.

After the last hearing, Adair Ramsay's face was mottled with rage. "I'll be back," he said. "You havena won yet."

"Keep your ain fish guts ta your ain sea maws," Bruce said.

After that, Adair seemed to disappear. For over two blessed months, things were quiet, causing Bruce to observe to Maggie one evening over a bowl of hotchpotch, "I dinna ken the fool has given up. He's a determined man, with a Scot's tenacity and stubbornness, and the cunning of an Englishman."

The gruffness in Bruce's voice couldn't hide the hint of intrigue the sudden silence of this man held for him, and Maggie picked up on it. "Do you ken we've seen the last of him?"

"He'll surface again, and I canna say that I'm no just a wee bit curious to see what his next plan of attack will be."

For some reason, Maggie never took the matter as casually as Bruce had, prompting Bruce to laugh at her on more than one occasion. "My overexcited little plover," he said, taking her in his arms. "You bristle at the sound of every approaching coach."

Maggie pulled away and wagged a scolding finger at him. "Laugh, if you please, but there is something about the man

I dinna trust. He has narrow, shifty eyes, and his lips snarl back, away from his teeth."

Bruce laughed. "You canna convict a man on the basis of shifty eyes and bared teeth."

"You may not, but I can. Have you no noticed how he willna look you in the face when he speaks to you? He'll no rest until he has your title, and all of us tossed into the loch."

Bruce took her in his arms. "Come here, my little cloker."

"Och! Dinna be calling me a broody hen," she said, giving his ears a box, "when you ken I am right."

"Aye, I ken you are right, lass," Bruce said, his tone turning somber. "He's a typical Lowlander, and I dinna trust him."

A week later, an urgent dispatch had come, summoning Bruce to Edinburgh.

He left immediately, but never made it there.

Two days later, the body of the Duke of Glengarry and that of his horse were found upon the jagged rocks that were hungry to devour anything that fell upon them.

One month after her husband's death, Margaret Sinclair Ramsay was taken to court in what proved to be a lengthy battle against Adair Ramsay, who hoped to claim the title now inherited by Maggie's young son, Fletcher.

"Dinna worry, lass," Maggie's father, the Earl of Caithness, had said. "I'll see what I can do."

In years past, a letter from the Earl of Caithness would have moved mountains. But times were changing in Scotland, and the old ways were dying out. The Earl of Caithness was old and almost blind, and because of that, he hadn't been to Edinburgh in over fifteen years. His name didn't carry the power it once had; in truth, not many in Edinburgh even recognized his name at all.

It was about this same time that Maggie learned her father was not only in poor health, but that he was virtually penniless and in danger of losing his vast estates.

Unable to count upon her aging father, and having no other family to turn to, she was forced to stand alone, aided only by a few loyal friends. In what was termed by many as "the most shameful case to ever be tried in Scotland," the title of Duke of Glengarry was stripped from young Fletcher Ramsay and awarded, along with the accompanying land and estates, to Adair Ramsay.

A shattered Margaret Ramsay was given notice. She had two weeks to vacate Glengarry Castle.

Alone, homeless and widowed, with no means of support, Maggie had packed all of her personal items, saving her husband's things for last. Now not even that task remained. Only minutes ago the footman had announced that her children and their nanny awaited her in the coach.

Her life at Glengarry had come to a sad, sad close.

She took a parting look around the room, if for no other reason than to make sure she hadn't left any of her husband's personal effects behind.

Maggie sighed and rubbed the chill from her fingers. She had done her job well; nothing but the furnishings remained, furnishings that now belonged to Adair Ramsay. There was nothing more to be done, yet she was reluctant to go. Perhaps this was because she really had no place to go, save her father's home. Yet, as she made the decision only this morning to return to the home of her girlhood, she couldn't help wondering just how long it would be before she and her children would be forced from there as well.

Hearing a discreet cough, she turned to see the minister David MacDonald standing just inside the door. Maggie seemed to recover, attempting, at least, to collect herself. "I'm sorry you came all this way for nothing, David. It's time for me to go. The children are already downstairs—waiting for me in the carriage."

"I ken that before I came up here. I spoke to them for a

moment." He stopped speaking and gave her a pleading look. "Maggie, I want a minute with you."

"I'm sorry. I dinna . . ." Maggie sighed and drew her wool shawl higher, covering her shoulders. "I dinna want to speak of religion right now. I canna. Perhaps later . . . when I've had time to heal."

"Now is the time you need God the most."

Maggie turned away. "My needs dinna seem to matter to God."

"God moves in strange ways, lass. He will be your refuge and strength. He willna turn His back on you."

"He already has." She turned back, but the light had faded from her eyes. "Do not speak of God so much. I fear He has all but forgotten me."

"You feel that way because there is too often strife between God's ways and man's ways. You must hold to your faith, lass. It willna desert you in time of trouble."

"Faith," she repeated slowly. "I canna hold to something that seems to contradict itself. I dinna ken if I even believe in faith anymore."

"That is your pain speaking, not your heart."

Maggie lapsed back into silence, staring at the Reverend MacDonald without really seeing him. Pain. Aye, she had plenty of that. It had been her constant companion of late. First with Bruce, and then with her youngest daughter, Ainsley.

Ainsley. One small girl, one small name, yet a powerful reminder. Maggie would go to her grave with the memory of the day Bruce was buried etched upon her mind. How she wished she could go back in time, to undo the damage that had been done that terrible day. If only she had known Ainsley had awakened from her nap and wandered down the stairs alone, seeking her mother, and stepping into the parlor, where the battered body of Bruce Ramsay lay. Never,

ever would Maggie forget the shattering scream that ripped from Ainsley's throat, the horror in her terrified eyes when she saw her father's body being placed in his coffin and the lid nailed shut. Tears burned in the back of her eyes and she swallowed against the pain of remembering how she had been forced to slap Ainsley.

The slap had stopped Ainsley's screaming, but the silence that followed was worse, much, much worse. Dear God, if only she had noticed her daughter, been aware of her tiny presence and taken her from the room before she saw the deed done. Perhaps, if she hadn't been so swallowed up in her own grief, she would have realized what it must have meant to a child to see what Ainsley had seen. But she hadn't—not until two days after the funeral, when the children's nanny remarked to her that Ainsley was strangely silent.

At first the doctors said it would pass, that the shock of seeing her father sealed in a coffin would gradually fade from her young mind. They said, too, that when it did, her speech would return.

The past year had been difficult for Maggie as well as Ainsley, and Maggie felt as if she had watched helplessly as her daughter lived in a world of silence. It was a level of existence that was neither Heaven nor hell, but a lost place that lay somewhere in between.

In time, the doctor's words had proven true. It had been over a year now, and Ainsley's speech had returned, but she was quieter than she had been, and she didn't laugh as much.

Maggie looked at the concerned face of her longtime minister and friend, David MacDonald. Somehow she did not find the comfort, the solace, in that face that she once had. It made her feel abandoned and hollow. God *had* turned against her.

There had been a time in her life when sorrow had been an impersonal thing. Now it had a name: loss.

She came out of her daze to find the Reverend MacDonald observing her. She gave him a look as direct as the one he gave her, then shrugged her shoulders and looked away, as if saying: *If God cares about me, He will have to show me. I hurt too much to cry out to Him anymore.*

Then, without a backward look, Margaret Ramsay walked from the room. Her composure was one of strength, but her eyes were quite, quite sad.

She started down the great staircase, looking out a window in the stairwell, noticing as she did that Adair Ramsay's coach was parked near her own in the driveway. He hadn't wasted any time in claiming what was now his. She quickened her step, not wanting to encounter the man if she could avoid it.

Her steps were rapid, and light as her slippers, skimming over the stone steps faster than the flutter of a bird's wing, but she was not quick enough to avoid Adair Ramsay's spiteful weasel face.

"A moment with you, madam, if you will," he called to her from the library as she passed. Whirling around, she saw him standing in the shadows of the room. The heavy damask drapes were drawn, but no candles were lit, and the gloom was broken only by the precious amount of light that seeped around the cloak of draperies. She stood in the doorway and peered into the long shadows.

"Come into the room," he said, motioning her in with his long, bonelike fingers.

Maggie took a few more steps and then stopped, her head held proud and high. As she looked at this man she hated above everything in life, her heart hammered with an unsteady beat. "You have everything I owned, you've destroyed the man I loved. What could you possibly want now?" she asked.

He seemed to throw himself around the desk, coming to

stand a few feet from her. "God's witness, madam, I can scarcely believe you would deliberately taunt me with your words when I only want to give you a bit of advice."

"What? That I should ease my sorrows with a glass of hemlock?"

"I have no desire to see you dead."

"No, I dinna suppose you do. Why should you? Only my husband was so privileged to receive your death wish."

He ignored her comment, but his expression turned even more cruel. Maggie took an involuntary step back and felt a shiver go up her spine at the grating sound of his laughter. "I would warn you, madam, to rid yourself of any fancy notions of regaining the dukedom or Glengarry Castle."

"Your warning is pointless. My husband is dead. The dukedom canna pass to me."

"Aye, but I speak of your son."

Maggie stepped forward, her hands in fists at her side. "Are you threatening my son?"

Adair took a step back. His face relaxed. "Not at all. I am merely giving you advice, madam. Leave things as they are. If you set about stirring up a hornet's nest, it might be you that gets stung. You may have nothing to lose, but your son has."

"How can he lose something a second time? *You* have his title now, or have you forgotten?"

"I wasna speaking of a title."

"You *are* threatening him," she said, feeling her heart pounding harder now.

"Start digging around in all these ashes again, and I will see that you regret it. There is no place you can go, no place you can hide, that I won't find you." He looked toward the coach. "The lad takes after his father. I would hate to see him follow in his footsteps."

Maggie felt a terrible sense of dread. She knew what he was saying, knew the threat he was making. How desolate this place seemed, how different from the memories of happier times when she and Bruce and their children were securely nestled here.

Once she was inside the coach, Maggie took one last look at Glengarry Castle through the window. She started to lower the shade, then changed her mind as she settled herself back against the hard seat. She looked at Maude, the children's nanny, who, with a typical Highlander's loyalty, refused to leave them, even when Maggie explained she had no way to pay her wages. Glancing up and seeing Maggie's eyes upon her, Maude leaned forward, patting her hand. "Why don't you try to get some rest? I'll tell the children a story."

Maggie closed her eyes for a moment, but it was no use. Her body might be tired, but her mind would not, could not, sleep. Opening her eyes again, she picked up a slim volume of *Hamlet* she had in her wicker basket. After reading for a few minutes, she paused, staring off into space. *Poor Hamlet, he had as many difficulties in life as I.* As the thought faded, she wondered if her own life would end just as tragically.

Here she was, at the lowest point in her life, as uncertain about the future as she had been a year ago, when Bruce died. Gathered around her were her weans, her three children, still no more than babies. She couldn't help wondering what would become of them.

*God never shuts one door that He doesn't open another. . . .*

For a moment she wondered where that thought had come from, then remembered that Reverend MacDonald had said as much the day he preached at Bruce's funeral.

"If you're planning to open any doors, I'd say it's about time," Maggie said, studying the overcast sky through the small window of the coach.

"Did you say something?" Maude asked.

"Do you believe in miracles?" asked Maggie.

"Of course I do. Dinna you?"

Maggie thought about that for a moment. "Aye, I suppose I do. There wouldna be much reason to go on if I said I didna."

"Dinna you go to worrying yourself sick over all of this. Things will work out. No matter how long and dark the night is, the sun always comes up in the morning."

"I know," Maggie said absently, resting her head against the wall of the coach. "It's just that I'm worried about making it through the rest of the night."

"You're troubling yourself over nothing," Maude said.

"Aye," Maggie said with a sigh. "I suppose you're right." She looked down at her book, finding her place, and began to read:

"When sorrows come, they come not single spies, but in battalions."

She paused to reread the verse, then read it aloud to Maude, who said, "That's nothing to worry yourself over. I'd say you've already had your battalion of sorrows. Now's the time to be expecting a miracle."

"A miracle is the only thing that could change our future," Maggie said. "I dinna mind telling you, Maude, I'm worried and just a little scared. My father's health isna good, and he's barely able to support himself." She looked at the anxious faces of her children and said, "Maude, what's going to become of us?"

"Hold to your faith and dinna worry. You've a lot to hope for."

Maggie shook her head. "My hopes died a long time ago. All I have left is doubt."

"Even doubt has a sunny side. We'll get on fine. You'll see. One of these days you'll be married to a good man and look back on all of this and say, 'Old Maude was right.' "

Maggie looked skeptical, then she leaned her head back,

closed her eyes, and said, "Any man who would marry a penniless woman with three children would have to be stark raving mad."

# CHAPTER
## ❧ ONE ❧

*Northern California, 1857*

When Adrian Mackinnon announced, with the same ease with which he poured syrup on his flapjacks, that he would soon take a wife, there were many reactions, none of them congratulatory.

"The man has gone stark raving mad," one logger whispered to another.

"I never thought I'd see the day," said another.

"It's what happens to a man when he spends too much time up here in these woods: He goes crazy. Not enough sunshine," whispered a logger called Clem Burnside. He was talking to another logger by the name of John Schurtz.

"I understand a man needing a woman," Schurtz replied, "but *no* man needs a wife."

"A wife?" Shorty Savage repeated, choking on the word. "Hellfire! If it's a wife he wants, I'll give him mine."

Dudley Dunlap hooted with laughter. "That goes for me, too. Criminy! I'll even throw in a dozen kids, just to sweeten the pot."

"We ain't talking about no poker game, Shorty," said Tom Radford.

"Aw, I don't know 'bout that," Shorty said. "Marriage or poker, they're both a gamble. Trouble is, when a poker game goes sour, you can throw in the cards, but when it comes to a wife, you cain't."

"Now, you ain't tellin' the truth, Shorty. You can throw in the cards when you're married. Ain't that what you did when you left *your* wife?" asked Dudley.

Shorty scratched his belly. "Well now, I ain't never thought of it that way, but now that you bring it up, I reckon it is." He shook his head. "Should've thrown them in a lot sooner—by the time I got around to it, I had to travel nigh on three thousand miles to get away from that woman. Lord-a-mercy! She had a nose like a bloodhound." He took another bite, then spoke while still chewing. "I can't imagine any man with his traces hooked up right actually *wanting* a wife, let alone going to all the trouble to go out *lookin'* for one. Wives and wisdom," he said, giving his head another shake. "The two don't mix. Don't mix *a-tall*."

"The only comfort I've had in life," said Hoot Howell, "is that I never had a wife."

"Me, too," said Ern Ingersoll. "Ain't seen a woman yet that would let you fall into her arms without tryin' to get you in her hands."

"You know what they say about marriage," said Clyde Bishop. "The bachelor is a peacock. The engaged man is a lion . . ."

"And the married man is a jackass," John Schurtz finished, as the cookhouse shook with laughter.

"Say what you will," Adrian said, casually waving a forkful of flapjacks in the air as he spoke, "I think it's high time I took a wife, so I'll be heading on down to San Francisco for a couple of weeks."

Fifteen forks hit the table. The room grew deathly quiet.

"A wife?" someone whispered, as if something terrible

would happen if the word *wife* was even spoken out loud. "Did he say a wife?"

"My wife is dead, so let her lie; she's at rest, and so am I," said Ox Woodburn, and the cookhouse shook with laughter once more.

"You must have been doing your thinking in a powerful hurry," said Big John Polly, "because two days ago you were doing everything you could to convince Tom Radford that a woman was the last thing any man needed in his life. Why the sudden change?"

Adrian exchanged his fork for a coffee cup. "I don't know. Maybe trying to convince Tom Radford that he didn't need a wife is what got me thinking that I did. Last night I was sitting in front of the fire, scratching my dog on the head and sipping a glass of brandy, when I began to think about everything I've built up here, and it suddenly occurred to me that I don't have anyone to leave it to. That seemed to rob me of the pleasure I've always found in knowing I made my dream into a reality."

"You've got three or four brothers that you can leave things to, and more nieces and nephews than you can count on two hands. Write a will," Big John said. "Save yourself a passel of trouble."

Adrian raised his brows in surprise. "Why, I thought you and Molly were happy."

"I didn't say I wasn't happily married, I said it's a passel of trouble staying that way, and it is."

Adrian laughed. "It must be worth it, if you've stuck it out this long. What is it now, thirty years?"

"Twenty-five," Big John said, just as someone shouted he deserved a medal for valor.

Laughter erupted, but in the midst of it, Adrian grew pensive. "I want sons to raise. I want to teach them to love and respect what I've built, to carry on after I'm gone. I don't want everything I've worked for to die with me."

"A man that talks like that will end up with daughters, sure as shootin'," Shorty said, "mark my word."

Adrian sent Shorty a look, and Shorty buried his face in his flapjacks, choking when Clem laughed and slapped him on the back.

"Let's go talk someplace else," Big John said, his chair scraping the floor as he pushed it away from the table.

" 'A woman, a dog, and a walnut tree, the more you beat 'em, the better they be,' " John Schurtz shouted, and everyone laughed.

"Schurtz, it sounds to me like you don't like a damn thing about women," Big John said.

"Aw, Big John, that ain't fair. I do. I do. I like their *silence*."

Big John looked at Adrian, and the two of them broke into laughter.

The two men left the crew of lumberjacks laughing and mumbling among themselves as they walked outside, ambling on down the hill toward the sawmill. "I don't know," Big John was saying. "Sounds to me like you're wanting a wife for all the wrong reasons."

"What makes you say that? Is there a *right* reason?"

Big John laughed. "Of course there is. Don't you believe in love?"

Adrian ignored that. "Children have always been a legitimate reason for marriage."

Big John laughed. "There's a heap of difference between what's legitimate and what's right, Adrian, but I don't reckon I know much about anything, so don't listen to me."

"But I am listening," Adrian said. "Go on, keep talking."

"Well, the way I see it . . . What I mean is . . . Aw, hell! What a man calls a legitimate reason and what a woman calls it ain't necessarily the same thing. You go bounding down to San Francisco telling every woman you meet that you're proposing marriage because you want sons, and you'll be finding a lot of doors slammed in your face. Women are scarce as a ten-cent steak in San Francisco, and the kind of woman you want isn't going to want to marry a man because he wants sons.''

''Don't forget, I'm a rich man.''

''Any woman that'll be swayed by money isn't the kind you want either. There are more rich men than there are respectable women in San Francisco. The kind of woman you would settle for will have a list of things she wants, and at the top of that list will be things like being loved—and courted.''

''Loved?'' Adrian threw back his head and laughed. ''A woman will know—if she's wise—that possessions and money will serve her far better than love.'' He looked at Big John, his brow drawn together. ''What makes you so certain you know the kind of wife I want, anyway?''

''Because I've known you for a long time. I've seen the way you've changed since your brother married and sold his part out to you. In the years since Alex and Katherine returned to Texas, you've become a hard, bitter man, Adrian. It doesn't take a smart man to understand that your bitterness came out of the hurt you felt, knowing the woman you loved preferred your brother over you. As for the hardness—I suspect it came when you set out to prove you didn't care, that you don't need anything. I reckon that's why you've become such a perfectionist—why you won't settle for anything but the finest and the best. I could be wrong, but I think that's your way of proving something to yourself.''

''I don't have to prove anything.''

''Then prove it by proving me wrong.''

''About what?''

''The kind of wife you'll go looking for.''

''Which is?''

"A woman as perfect and beautiful as the mansion you built for yourself. A woman every man will envy you for having. A woman who'll never be able to measure up to your standards, because the woman who can has never been created."

*But she has,* Adrian heard his mind say, *and her name is Katherine.*

The fact that the boss of the California Mill and Lumbering Company intended to take a wife swept over the camp like wildfire, and like the loggers in the cookhouse, the majority of the men in camp agreed that Adrian must have been out of his mind the day he made his decision. Not that anyone begrudged a lonely man like Adrian finding a little comfort and companionship. Besides, with women being as scarce as they were in these parts, it wasn't too likely that he was going to find himself one, anyway.

But, in thinking that, they all underestimated Adrian Mackinnon.

Over the past ten years, Adrian had become accustomed to getting what he wanted. If he couldn't build it or bargain for it, he would buy it. And he never settled for anything less than the very finest. He hadn't become one of the richest men in California by letting a few stumbling blocks force him into changing his mind or his direction. There were other ways to deal with obstacles besides backing up or turning away.

Adrian said good-bye to Big John and headed on down to the mill office, but once he arrived, he couldn't seem to concentrate on the work he had waiting for him. Today he couldn't keep his mind on his business—or even his future, and the taking of a wife. Today his mind seemed set on the past.

And the past meant Katherine Simon.

It had been a long time ago. What? Twenty-three years since the Comanches raided Parker's Fort and kidnapped his little sister, Margery. Adrian stared off into space, his fingers unconsciously toying with a pencil. He knew that the raid on Parker's Fort had somehow changed the course of his life, and left him with too few memories of the family he had lost because of it.

Margery. He could remember she had been six years old the day she was taken—but then, he and his twin brother, Alexander, had only been seven.

Seven years old, and terribly afraid. He remembered just how scared he had been that day, when his father, John, told his eldest son, Andrew, to stay with their mother while he took his remaining five sons with him to track the Comanche raiding party. When they returned, the first thing they saw was two new graves and a burned-out house.

Adrian's father was never home after that. He had spent the next year looking for Margery and the band that had killed Andrew and Margaret. Adrian and Alex were eight by the time the sheriff had ridden out to their farm in Limestone County, Texas, to tell the five remaining Mackinnon boys that they were orphans.

And then fate had scattered the five brothers like chaff: Tavis and Nicholas went to Nantucket to learn a shipbuilder's trade; Ross became a womanizer and a hell-raiser, finding himself on the receiving end of a shotgun wedding before hightailing it for Scotland to inherit a title; and the twins, Alex and Adrian, did a stint in the Texas Rangers, then signed up to fight in the Mexican War with Zach Taylor before hitting the gold-dust trail to California. After striking it rich, they headed up to Northern California to put their gold into lumber.

His life had gotten away from him after that. Alex had written that fateful letter back home, intending to ask the love of his life, Karin Simon, to come out west to marry him, and in a drunken stupor, had written the name of her sister, Katherine, by mistake.

Adrian had been afraid many times in his life, but he would never forget the gut-wrenching fear he felt the day he saw Katherine, the love of his life, walk off that ship in San Francisco. Something inside of him had died.

Looking back, he saw it had been for the best that Alex and Katherine had ended up back in Texas. Alex had never been able to get the farmer's dirt out from under his fingernails, and Adrian swore half of Katherine's blood had been made from that same blackland dirt.

Adrian leaned back in the chair and closed his eyes. He could never remember not loving Katherine Simon, from the moment he had first seen her down near Tehuacana Creek, crying from a bee sting. She couldn't have been more than five or six then, and he, not much older.

He sat up. There was nothing to be gained by thinking about Katherine now. She had never loved him, and now she was married to his brother. But the pain was still there, as well as the yearning. Since the day Katherine married Alex, Adrian had sworn he would never again be second best.

The pencil in his hand snapped in two.

The first thing Adrian did after deciding he wanted a wife was to leave his sawmill in the coastal woods of northern California and take the first available ship to San Francisco.

"Two weeks isn't giving yourself very much time to find a wife," John Schurtz said that morning as Adrian prepared to board the *Gold Rush*.

Aboard ship, Big John Polly was saying much the same thing. "A man would be hard-pressed to buy a prime piece of horseflesh in two weeks time, Adrian. You sure you don't want to stay in San Francisco a little longer, just to have time to . . .'' Seeing the way Adrian was glaring at him, he finished his sentence in barely audible tones, ''Just to give yourself a little more time?''

Adrian replied with mounting irritation, ''If I don't find a wife in two weeks, I'll have to resort to something else, won't I?''

Big John's bushy gray brows rose in surprise. ''Well, I don't know about resorting to something else, but if that's how you feel . . .'' He shook his head. ''I hear tell that some fellers take a shine to animals, although I ain't never had a hankering for that sort of thing myself.''

''I meant I would have to resort to another plan,'' Adrian said.

Big John laughed and turned down the gangplank. ''Have a good trip, and happy hunting.''

''I'm not going off on a bear hunt.''

Big John laughed. ''You might think differently the first time some sweet young thing sinks her claws into you.''

Adrian dismissed that with a wave of his hand.

The ship began pulling away from the dock. ''You gonna bring the little lady back with you?'' Big John called through cupped hands.

''I might,'' Adrian yelled back, apprehension eating at him. What in the name of hell was he doing? What would he do with a woman way up here in the middle of a lumber camp, anyway? Come to think of it, what would he do with a woman, period? He was out of touch when it came to women. He hadn't even *been* with a woman in over a year. He wasn't sure he remembered how to talk to one who wasn't a whore.

Adrian Mackinnon was the kind of man who didn't need women the way other men needed them. His business was his mistress. It was well known that he was too much of a perfectionist to ever marry. The men in camp went so far as to give reasons to back this up: Adrian would never find a woman he thought good enough, and no woman in her right mind would want to be married to someone who expected perfection all the time.

If a man like Adrian had a family, they said, he would run it like a sawmill.

# CHAPTER
## ❧ TWO ❧

Adrian Mackinnon was thirty-one years old. For the past ten years he had devoted himself to his prospering lumber business, building an empire, the towering California redwoods making him one of the wealthiest men in all of California. Two years ago his magnificent home had been finished, and yet the long loneliness had not lessened. He knew it would take more than wealth and possessions to ease the ache.

As the ship pulled out into the harbor, Adrian looked at the cluster of men gathered around the dock. He knew what they were thinking. His grin grew broader. He was about to prove them wrong. He was going to take a wife, and she was going to be a woman like no other woman the likes of these men had ever seen.

As usual, whenever his thoughts went along those lines, Katherine's rejection began to creep into his thoughts, and he began to feel the first tentative sprigs of fear and self-doubt—thoughts that gave way, after a time, to the feeling that he had to prove himself.

Adrian tried to remember how long it had been since he had felt this lost and lonely. Not for a long time, probably not since Katherine left Alex and returned to Texas. Then, as now, he felt lost and lonely and inadequate.

He looked at the rocky, tree-lined coastline, where the mountains rose to meet the sky in the distance. That was the place he called home, and there, he was in control. There, he was not plagued by thoughts of inadequacy. There, nobody turned his back on him or made him feel unworthy. But it was also there that he was lonely.

An hour or so out to sea, Adrian's mood began to grow darker, matching the cloudy sky. Rain seemed to obliterate the masts of the ship, and to absorb the skeins of thick, gray smoke. As if he could rebuff the pelting rain by doing so, he leaned over the ship's railing and stared down into the churning, foam-flecked grayness of the water below. Yet it wasn't the swirling foam of wind-tossed waves he saw, but the face of Katherine Simon Mackinnon. The face of his brother's wife.

He could not remember a time when he had not loved Katherine, the auburn-haired beauty his brother had married. Even now, almost ten years later, his recollection of her was as strong and vivid as it had ever been. Sweet, lovely Katherine, forever young and untouched by age in the pain-ravaged lair of his mind. Katherine, a standard of beauty no mortal woman could measure up to. Katherine, the only woman he ever wanted, the only woman he could ever love. Katherine, the one person in the world who could hurt him, and who had done so with a vengeance, by marrying his twin brother, Alexander.

There was, of course, a time when he had ceased to hurt; a time when he realized that his life with Katherine was over, as if it had been sealed shut. He realized the futility of grieving over a woman he had lost, a woman he never really had. For a time he had resigned himself to celibacy, telling himself he would never marry, that he needed nothing, not even sex. In time, even those feelings had passed, only to be replaced by the hard shell of the man he now was, a man determined not to let himself be vulnerable again.

The captain walked by and spoke. Adrian nodded, then turned to brace his arms on the ship's railing as he stared again at the churning water. He let his thoughts surface, knowing that afterward they would settle about him like feathers, ready to swirl in confusion at the slightest stirring.

Old feelings, old needs, the old bitterness, bubbled to the surface, and he closed his eyes against the memory of it, realizing then that it was too late. Thoughts of Katherine were always with him.

His thoughts spun backward, to the first time he had seen her after he and Alex had returned to the old homestead in Texas after the war with Mexico.

*We seem to have a lot in common, you and I,* Katherine had said.

*No, sweet Katherine, we don't. To have loved but been rejected is like being sent to bed with no supper; it's nothing more than a bee bite to one's spirit. But to love and be overlooked is to die slowly by starvation, like soap that wastes away, giving up a little of itself with each washing.*

*Oh, Adrian, why must life be so miserable?*

*I'm not sure, but I don't think even God goes through eternity without feeling some pain. Ahhh, Katherine, what a torment you've always been. Life's a road with one bump after another, but you're going to make it. Have no fear about that.*

*You'll make it too, Adrian. I know you will.*

*Of course I will. I've never doubted it. One of these days I'll be something to see, all right, a real sight for sore eyes, and then you'll look at me and say, I wish I had loved him when I had the chance.*

Only that day never came, for Katherine had married Alex, and she was happy. He doubted she ever thought of him anymore.

The frustrating sense of loss came back to haunt him, stronger, more acute, than ever. *Katherine. Katherine. Katherine.* Would he never be free of the pain of losing her?

He might never be free of the pain, but he could take away from it by filling his house with children. Children would be a part of him, something he could love without losing.

*It won't be long now,* he told himself. *Before long you'll have a wife and children, and the ghost of Katherine will be laid to rest. A wife will erase her from my mind. Children will give me what I need.*

*Won't they?*

He looked up at the overcast sky. "I'll get over you," he said. "I'll find a woman more beautiful, more refined, and more educated. She'll be everything you aren't."

Two days later, the weather was deceptively warm for the middle of October. His spirits rose with the temperature as he disembarked, taking a coach to the hotel. He remembered what Molly Polly had said to him when she came to cook his breakfast the day he left.

"You don't think much of my plan to go to San Francisco, do you, Molly?"

"Can't rightly say that I do, but to each his own."

"What is it about this trip that's bothering you? The fact that I'm going to take a wife? Or the way I'm going about it?" He paused, looking at her graying hair, with its precious few streaks of that pinkish orange color he had never gotten used to. "You think I'm wrong to go to San Francisco?"

"I never said that, but since you asked, I'll tell you what I think. I think you're wasting your time fishing in a herring barrel. That's a mighty dumb place to fish when you're looking for trout."

"You don't know what you're talking about."

Molly raised her eyes to Heaven. " 'Woe to them that are

wise in their own eyes, and prudent in their own sight,' "
she quoted solemnly.

It was so melodramatic, and out of character for Molly
Polly, that Adrian laughed. "I've found one more thing to
write on that list of wifely requirements," he said. "Something to go on the 'Don't Want' side."

"And what is that?"

"A Bible-quoting woman," he said.

"I would imagine *she* might have a few *don't wants* of her
own."

Adrian grinned at her. "Like what?"

"Like that wad of chewing tobacco you're always chomp-
ing on, spitting it here, spitting it there. It's enough to drive
a woman crazy. She'll never be able to keep her floors clean."

"I don't spit on the floors, Molly."

"You don't always *aim* to spit on the floors," she amended.
"Lord have mercy! The cookhouse floor looks like a bunch
of bugs have been squashed on it."

"I'm not the only man who chews," he said.

"No, but you're the only one I can't fuss at about it."

"You're fussing now," he said with a laugh, dodging the
sourdough roll she tossed at him.

One week later, Adrian was sitting in a barber's chair in
San Francisco, once again thinking about what Molly had
said. She was right. He had been fishing in a herring barrel,
looking for trout.

"You say you came all the way from Humboldt country
to find yourself a wife?" the barber asked.

Adrian nodded, then stared at the toes of his boots. He
regretted telling the man anything. He didn't want to discuss
his personal life with anyone. He watched the barber strop
the straightedge, waiting impatiently for him to lather his
face.

"Well, you've been here a week now. Got any particular woman picked out?"

"No."

"You might try the Silver Dollar. Most folks in these parts think the Silver Dollar has the best-looking women in San Francisco."

"I want a wife, not a whore."

"Lots of men in these parts see no difference. Most of them think nothing of taking a whore to wife. You got something against whores?"

"Not as long as they remain in a brothel, where they belong. I just don't want to take one for—"

He had been about to say, *for a wife*, but he didn't get to finish. At that moment the barber slapped a wide path of lather across his face, and he closed his mouth, a moment too late. He spit out a mouthful of soap and settled back in the chair. The barber cleared the two clean-scraped paths down the side of his face, then stood back. He pointed the razor at Adrian. "I hear tell a reformed whore makes a fine wife. Now, you take your whores, why, they don't have to be stoked like a stack of old, dry wood. They're like kindling, ready to burst into flame at the slightest spark."

"And they don't particularly care whose spark it is," Adrian said. "Now, can we get on with my shave before all of this lather dries on my face?"

"Well, if you're dead set against a whore, I hear tell the widow Peabody has a couple of daughters. . . ."

"I've had the pleasure," Adrian said, coming to his feet, the memory of the widow Peabody and her homely daughters following him. Heaven help him, but that woman and her daughters were as ugly as forty miles of bad road.

He removed the cape and wiped the lather from his face, tossing the cape in the chair he had just vacated. This whole absurd conversation was pointless. Just as this trip to San Francisco had been pointless. He reached into his pocket.

"Hey! I'm not finished."

"Yes, you are," Adrian said, flipping the man two bits.

An hour later, he stepped out of the Pacific Express Building on Montgomery Street and paused for a moment at the edge of the street. It took him only a second or two to search up the street and down, finding no hack he could hire to take him back to the hotel. Turning the collar up on his coat, he turned up the street and began walking. It was raining again. He was sick of San Francisco. He was sick of nosy people. He was even sicker of this asinine search for a wife.

Perhaps the rain was a godsend. Perhaps it was the cause of his morose mood, his loneliness, his sense of desolation, and if so, it must have accounted for his realization that the trip had been a futile one. It was as clear as glass to him now: No self-respecting woman was going to rush into marriage with a man she had just met, no matter how rich the man might be.

On top of that, he hadn't met one woman since coming to San Francisco whom he would ask to dance, much less take to wife. It was mighty slim pickings in San Francisco as far as women went. It was time to call it quits.

Shoving his cold fingers into his pockets, he increased the tempo of his steps, heading toward Portsmouth Square. He was hatless, and the rain darkened his brown hair.

He made his way back to the hotel, with his mind made up. Tomorrow he would head north, back to the country north of Humboldt Bay. He would forget all about this foolishness of taking a wife.

The clerk behind the desk looked up as he entered the lobby, his face lighting up as he smiled at Adrian. Adrian felt his cheek twitch. "I'll be checking out in the morning, Horace. Have my bill ready."

"It'll be ready and waiting for you, Mr. Mackinnon." Horace paused, his round, shiny face puckered in thought.

"Thought you were going to be staying on for another week."

"I wrapped up my business sooner than I expected," Adrian said.

"I hope you'll stay with us again . . . next time you're down this way." He handed Adrian a few envelopes. "These came for you today."

Adrian took the envelopes, not bothering to look at them. "It may be quite a spell before I'm back in these parts again," he said slowly as he tucked the envelopes into his coat pocket.

He went upstairs and paused in front of his door, inserting the key into the lock. Once inside, he removed his coat, tossing the envelopes on the desk. He remembered he was still half-shaved and debated finishing the job now. He decided against it, drawing the heavy damask draperies to shut out the light, feeling a dandy headache in the making. His head throbbed as he leaned over the desk to light the alabaster lamp, turning it low.

Then his eyes went to the letters. He frowned. He picked them up and sorted through the stack, opening them one by one. Invitations. All of them from a few overstuffed and overstarched matrons inviting him to dinner, trying to interest him in their silly daughters.

It hadn't taken him long to learn he wanted a mature, educated, refined woman for a wife, not some young featherbrain who giggled every time he looked at her. He shook his head, tossing the invitations back on the desk, then made his way to the bed. He couldn't help remembering one pleasant-looking young woman he had been seated beside at dinner two nights ago. She had actually fluttered her eyes at him and said, "My mama said I would make a perfect wife. Why, I have my whole future ahead of me."

Adrian wanted to ask her if there was someplace else she would rather have her future, but he decided it wasn't worth the breath to say it. He didn't remember much of the evening after that, for he had made a wager with himself to down a drink every time the young woman said something similarly stupid.

He woke up in his hotel room the next morning, having no recollection of how he got there.

Without another thought, he fell across the bed and stretched out, not bothering to remove his boots. Rolling over, he lay on his back, staring at the ceiling. Tomorrow he would get the hell out of San Francisco.

He looked at the envelopes still lying on the desk. The markings on one of the envelopes reminded him of his brother Ross's handwriting; slanted, large, and sloppy. He grinned at the thought and sat down in the chair, looking more closely at the letter, his thoughts finely tuned on Ross. Who would have ever thought it—all those years ago in that little house on the banks of Tehuacana Creek, back in Limestone County, Texas? Who would have ever thought that Ross Mackinnon would have grown up to go to Scotland to inherit a title? What was he, a duke? And married for several years now. With a passel of little dukes, or whatever they called them, running around. Adrian had stopped counting after the fourth one.

He rolled over and dropped his head into his hands. He remembered the letters that came infrequently from Ross and how proud he seemed to be of his aristocratic wife, Annabella. Best Adrian could remember, Annabella was the daughter of an English duke, and according to Ross, a real head-turner with a fine mind. She had been betrothed to a Scottish nobleman, and Ross had stolen her right out from under the man's nose. Yes, Ross was a man to be envied. He had himself a real, genuine lady, the daughter of an English duke.

*That's what I need,* Adrian thought. *A lady. A real lady.*

Only one drawback there, and that was that there wasn't a *real* lady in all of California, and Adrian didn't have the time to go gallivanting off to England or Scotland, hunting for a wife, making a fool of himself trying to pay court. He brushed the thought aside, but it kept coming back to pester him.

*A lady. A Scottish lady. One with a title.*

A woman like that would have to be the envy of every man in California. A woman like that would be the perfect jewel to set in the crown of his redwood empire. A woman like that would be harder than hard to find.

Adrian spit, and missed the spittoon. "Hell and double hell!" he said to the ceiling. "I don't have time to look for a wife right here in California, much less hunt for one in Scotland."

*No, but Ross does.*

The thought startled him at first. Let Ross find him a wife? "Naah," he said. "Ross wouldn't know what I was looking for."

*Maybe not, but you could write him.*

"Write him?"

*Write him. Tell him what you're looking for, the kind of lady you want. He did a pretty good job with those blooded horses he bought for you, didn't he?*

"Hell's bells!" he said, springing to his feet. "Those were horses. I'm talking about a woman . . . *my wife!*"

*So write him and tell him what you're looking for, just like you did with the horses.*

Adrian shook his head. He was thinking, but he just didn't know. No. He couldn't do it. A woman wasn't something you ordered from a catalog.

*Men in California get mail-order brides all the time. Some of them even marry women by proxy and have them sent out here as their wives.*

Adrian walked back to the desk. He stared at the envelopes as he sat down. For a while he simply rested his hand on the handle of the drawer. Should he, or shouldn't he?

He opened the drawer, taking out a piece of paper. Dipping the quill in the inkwell, he stared at the white paper for a moment, then scratched his way across the paper.

Dear Ross,
This letter may come as a bit of a surprise to you, since it came as quite a surprise to me. I've decided to take a wife, and I want you to find one for me. . . .

Adrian finished the letter and posted it. The moment he did so, he began to wonder what possessed him to do such an irrational thing.

With a muffled curse, Adrian left the post office. *What's done is done,* he thought. It's now in the hands of fate. *And fate has such terrible power.* Adrian didn't want to think about that, so he stepped up the pace of his walk. He would go back to the hotel.

An hour later, as he drifted off to sleep, Adrian was still thinking about that letter. He sighed. There was nothing to be done about it now—save saying a few prayers that Ross would find him the perfect wife. One like no other.

A moment before his troubled consciousness slipped into a deep sleep, he thought he could hear his mother's voice, coming to him as it had done so often when he was a child.

*Be careful what you ask for, Adrian, or you might get it.*

# CHAPTER
## ❈ THREE ❈

### Scotland

The horse had a fiery eye and ran like a demon from hell.

The rider pulled back on the reins in front of the baronial doors of Dunford Castle, swung one leg over the saddle, and dropped to the ground before the horse had come to a complete stop.

Slapping the horse on the rump, he sent the big, gray gelding trotting toward the stables before the groom could cover the distance between them, knowing as he did that it would irritate the dickens out of the groom and bring his hot Highlander's blood to a full boil.

Ross Mackinnon, Duke of Dunford, chuckled at the thought. There was nothing he liked better than to raise the ire of a Highlander. *Damn,* he thought. *It's going to be a fine, fine day.*

The laundress, talking to the gardener beneath the winter-bare boughs of a climbing rose, saw the whole thing and quickly crossed herself—something quite remarkable, considering the laundress was a staunch Presbyterian. "His Grace canna live too long and ride like that," she said, taking note of a finely turned leg as the duke took the front steps two at a time and burst through the heavy oak doors.

"Aye," the gardener said, blinking as the doors crashed back against the wall. "They say he's as wild as his horse."

"Wilder," said the laundress, giving her head a slow shake, "and spawned by the same devil."

Ross Mackinnon's spurs left a trail of sparks as they struck the stone floor.

"Ah-hem," a voice behind him said. "Your Grace . . . your spurs."

"What?" the duke said, turning to look, then following the butler's eye to his feet. "Oh, right," he said, pulling the spurs off and tossing them to Robert. "That should keep my lovely wife's disposition sweet," he said with a wink.

"Indeed it will, Your Grace," Robert said. "And might I be thanking you in advance for it."

The sound of the duke's hearty laughter could be heard all over the south wing of Dunford Castle.

Ross was still chuckling when he reached the library. He sat on the corner of his desk, swinging one leg as he sorted through his mail. He saw the letter from his brother, Adrian, and opened it before the others.

Reading the first few words, he paused, then backed up, to be sure he read what he thought he read. A grin began to spread as he went on, his eyebrows rising dramatically with each subsequent word. When he finished, he threw back his head and let roll with another hearty laugh. "Well, shoot me for an egg-sucking mule," he said, laughing so hard, he had to grip the side of the desk to keep his balance. "Adrian," he said, as if not believing it himself. "Who would have thought it?" He laughed for a full minute more. When exhaustion finally claimed him, he sent for his wife.

"Bella," Ross said, calling his wife to his side the moment he heard the rustle of her petticoats in the doorway. He smiled at the familiar scent of lemon verbena, turning to watch her walk toward him. As she drew close, a thoughtful, amused look on her face, he handed her the letter. "Take a look at this," he said.

Annabella took the letter, giving her husband a puzzled look.

"Read it," Ross said, settling himself. "Then we'll talk."

He watched as she read the letter, waiting for her comment.

Annabella's eyes skimmed the letter as Ross watched for her reaction—a smile, an elevated brow, a nod, a gasp of surprise, then a moment of stunned silence. When she finished reading the letter, she looked at Ross, a slow smile curving across her sweet mouth. The smile did not surprise Ross. Annabella loved intrigue. And why not? She was a woman, wasn't she?

*Aye,* he was thinking. *What a woman. And she's all mine.*

"He doesn't ask for much, does he?" Annabella said, then laughed and handed the letter back to Ross.

"Only the sun and the moon," he replied.

Ross glanced at the letter. He couldn't help laughing. Adrian asking for help? He would sooner believe snakes could walk. He shook his head. "I can't believe my self-sufficient little brother has come to me for help—and to find him a wife, at that." He turned to Annabella. "What in the blue blazes does Adrian think *I* know about finding a wife?"

"You found me, didn't you?"

"That was different," he said quickly, then added, "Don't forget that when I met you, I wasn't looking for a wife. I was just lucky enough to come barging into your life, too overworked about being told I had to wear a kilt to notice you at first. And when I did notice you, it didn't take me two shakes to realize you would tumble right into my arms."

Annabella scowled and crossed her arms in front of her. "Leslie Ross Mackinnon, you didn't know any such thing.

Tumble into your arms, indeed. You make me sound like a sack of flour.''

Ross grinned, but didn't let his wife's outburst deter him. "Of course, I was faced with one *slight* problem—getting you out of the clutches of that reprobate you were betrothed to.''

"That murderer, you mean,'' Annabella said.

Ross looked at Annabella and nodded, knowing the memory of her brother Gavin's murder was still as painful for her as it was for him. He didn't give her time to think upon it, but went on to say. "Of course, Adrian's case is much different.''

"Different? I don't see that it's very different. We are talking about marriage, aren't we?''

Ross didn't answer for a minute or two. After some consideration, he finally said, "Yes, it's different. Quite different.''

He paused and looked at Annabella, who took this for a cue to speak. "Go on,'' she said. "I want to hear this.''

"God's love, Annabella. You know what I mean when I say different.''

She busied herself with a close examination of her fingernails. "I'm not sure I do know. I *have* been known to be wrong a time or two.''

"Now I get humor,'' he said, his face looking grave. "Blast it, Bella. It's my brother's future that we're talking about, and it's suddenly resting upon my shoulders. Taking a wife is serious business.''

"Oh? I don't remember you being too serious when you chased me over half of Scotland, popping up every time I turned around. Causing me more trouble than I could ever imagine.''

"If I remember right, the trouble was the part you liked best.''

"Oh, posh!'' Annabella said.

He gave her a mischievous look.

"Now, I wonder why you are acting so sly," she said.

His face was the picture of innocence. "Sly? Me?"

"Does a Scot like whisky? Come on, tell me."

"Nothing, Bella. Honest. I was just trying to decide which is worse," he said, laughing. "A wife with no sense of humor or a wife who has one."

"Take my word for it; you're better off with a sense of humor," she said, "but we're straying off the path. Your brother has asked you for help in finding him a wife. Considering his circumstances, I don't find that a bit odd—or difficult either, for that matter. I would think you'd be highly flattered he's turned to you instead of Alex, considering how close twins are."

"In this case, they're only close enough for Adrian to know better than to trust Alex. Alex was always a lighthearted fellow, full of pranks and mischief. God knows what kind of wife Adrian would end up with if he wrote to Alex for help." Ross's voice stopped abruptly, as if something else had suddenly come to mind. "And there's the business of Katherine, or had you forgotten?"

"Yes, I had forgotten," Annabella said, the humor in her face replaced by an expression of serious contemplation. After a moment, she said, "I can see how Adrian wouldn't want Katherine to know he needed help finding a wife."

"Or want her help in finding one," Ross added.

"I still say you should be flattered that he wrote to you, but enough of that, for now." The ruffle at the edge of her skirt was moving, and Ross knew she was tapping her foot. "I am still waiting for you to tell me why you think helping Adrian is so difficult."

"Dash it all, Bella! It's difficult to find a wife for someone else, and just because Adrian is my brother doesn't make it any easier. I haven't even *seen* Adrian in over ten years. How do I know what he wants in a wife? I'm not even sure what I should look for.''

''A female,'' Bella said, collapsing with laughter at the expression on Ross's face. ''He did give a fairly complete list in his letter,'' she went on to say.

''And we both know that if I make a mistake, he'll be blaming me for the rest of his life—and mine.'' Ross paused again, then shook his head. ''This whole thing is too tricky. You know what makes it so difficult isn't finding a woman who fits the description—although that will take some doing—but finding a woman who would agree to marry a man she had never laid eyes upon.''

''I don't think it's *that* unusual. It's rather like an arranged marriage, and those have been happening for centuries. I've read that mail-order brides are quite the rage in certain parts of the world.''

Ross paused in reflection. ''You know the thing that surprises me the most about all of this isn't so much Adrian's wanting me to find him a wife as it is the fact that Adrian wants a wife at all.''

''You never thought he'd marry?''

''Never,'' Ross said, without having to give it a moment's consideration.

''Because of Katherine?''

''Precisely.''

''Well, I for one never thought his losing Katherine to Alex would make him swear off women entirely. I saw it as a temporary setback, nothing more.''

''Some setback. It's been over ten years.''

''I've never even met Adrian,'' Annabella admitted. ''All I know about him is from his letters, or the things you've told me. But from what I've learned, I don't think he's the kind of man to go through life without a woman—for that matter, *none* of you Mackinnons are.''

Ross laughed. ''I assume that's a compliment.''

Her laughter joined his. "It is."

Still, he looked skeptical. "Believe me, Adrian could withstand marriage, or anything else he put his mind to. He's too stubborn to die."

"I don't agree."

"Are you saying that just to disagree with me?"

Annabella flashed him her most wounded look. "How unworthy of you to say such a thing as that, Ross Mackinnon," she said, obviously fighting to keep her face seriously straight. "How could you even think such?"

Ross grinned. "Because I know you, lass. You like to fluster me."

"I don't!"

"Aye, you do."

She was the picture of coyness now, going so far as to exaggerate the fluttering of her eyes to the point that Ross laughed. "Well, don't blame me for that," she said, prissing away from him with a rustle of taffeta petticoats. "Women were born to fluster men," she said, fluffing a pillow on the sofa. "Besides, you do your best thinking when you're flustered."

"I do?"

"Yes, you do. However, we are getting off the subject again." She gave him a serious look, putting her hands on her hips. "I must say I don't know how you would ever muddle your way through a conversation and stay on course if you didn't have me to point you in the right direction."

When he started to respond, she held up her hand. "As I said a moment ago, Adrian isn't the type to go through life a bachelor."

"Bella, how can you say that when you've never even met him?"

She shrugged. "I've already told you." She narrowed her eyes. "Besides, he's *your* brother, isn't he?"

Ross laughed, his eyes gleaming with a special light that

could only be sparked by the pleasure he found in the woman he had married. "Point taken, love."

He picked up the letter, skimming the pages until he came to Adrian's list of desired attributes. Rereading them, Ross whistled and shook his head. Hearing the bubbling laughter coming from his wife, he looked at her and said, "Bella, this is serious. Now, stop laughing."

It was difficult, but she kept a straight face. "You will have to say that your brother can't be accused of not knowing what he wants. To the contrary, he has been quite explicit. Faith! I almost expected him to give her shoe size."

"Or her—"

Annabella sent him a chilling look.

"Never mind," he said.

"Aye," she said in her best Scots imitation, "never mind."

"Well, I'm not convinced he knew what he wanted at all. I think he simply listed everything he could think of, on the theory that if he left nothing out, he couldn't go wrong. After all, *he* isn't the one that's going to have to find a woman to fit this description," Ross said, giving the paper a thump. He glanced at the list again and said, "I don't suppose anyone came to mind when you read this list, did they?"

"Aha!" Annabella said, and wagged her finger at him. "Don't you go putting that task off onto me, Ross Mackinnon," she said, holding her hands up, as if to ward him off as she began backing toward the door. "You are the one saddled with the responsibility of finding him a wife." She was wagging her finger again, but she didn't stop backing up. Turning, she made a dash for the door.

Ross looked taken aback for a moment, then bolted. "That's a fine kettle of fish," he said, cutting her off at the pass and taking her in his arms. He kissed her soundly. "Behave yourself, wife." He kissed her again. "This is a family affair, my love, and here you are trying to desert me in the line of fire. Shame on you,'' he said, kissing her again.

Breathless from his kisses, Bella cocked her head to one side and said, ''You don't play fair.''

Ross shrugged and kissed her again. ''A man does what he has to do.''

''That's a pretty feeble way to drag me into this,'' she said, punctuating each word with a poke to his chest.

''Probably, but it's the best I could do on such short notice. Maybe by tomorrow . . . .'' He began, placing little nibbling bites along her neck.

''You'll never find your brother a wife if you keep this up,'' she said, pulling back to look at him.

''No, but I'll have more fun.''

''Ross, you're getting off course again.''

''I suppose you're right. This is no time to be distracted.'' Hearing the rumbling laugh Annabella was unable to suppress, he added, ''I still say this is no laughing matter.'' He looked down at her, his tone as serious as his face. ''You never did answer my question. Do you have anyone in mind, or don't you?''

Annabella tapped her cheek in thought. ''I might,'' she said. ''Read that part again . . . where he lists the qualities he considers most important.''

''All fifty of them?''

''Oh, Ross, there aren't that many.''

''There might as well be,'' he grumbled, and picked up the paper. He read the list to Annabella again, shaking his head as he did. He was right. His brother didn't want much, simply the sun and the moon, just as he'd said.

''She must be fair of face and form, polished, educated, from an excellent family of good breeding and high position—in other words, dear brother, a fair-haired milkmaid is not to my liking. But the daughter of a duke, or something like that, would be. And please, please, don't waste your time on some simpering nitwit who's only eighteen. I'm past thirty now. Maturity, grace, and poise appeal to me more than youth. A word of caution here, though. Children are the primary reason I seek a wife, so don't send a woman older than me and past childbearing. One more point. Since the time I can be away from here is limited, I desire you to select the right woman, then marry her—you standing in as proxy for me, of course. I have enclosed a draft to cover all expenses for her travel and anything she might wish to purchase and bring with her.''

When he finished, Ross looked at Bella, seeing her face puckered in thought. ''You're wasting your time, love. We won't be able to find a woman like this in a hundred years,'' he said, tossing the letter onto his desk. ''The women who fit the description best are the young *simpering nitwits* he doesn't want.''

''I suppose you're right. Any older, mature woman that would meet all that criteria would have been long married,'' Bella added.

''Or long dead,'' said Ross.

He opened his desk drawer. ''The biggest drawback here is the fact that a woman from a well-positioned family wouldn't be agreeing to marriage like this. Not unless she was desperate.'' Ross took out a sheet of paper, closing the drawer. ''I'll get a letter off to Adrian straightaway. He'll just have to understand that he's asking the impossible.''

Ross dropped into his chair, picked up the quill, and dipped it into the inkwell.

''Unless she was desperate,'' Annabella repeated softly, her expression one of deep thought. Then she made a sudden move, saying, ''Hold everything,'' which caused Ross to spatter ink all over the paper.

''Keep that up and I'll never get this letter—''

"Hold everything," she said again. "What did you just say?"

"I said I'd get a letter off—"

"No, before that."

"What? The part about a woman having to be desperate to—"

"That's it!" she said, clapping her hands together. "Oh, Ross, you are the luckiest man alive. You have just been saved by your clever, clever wife."

Ross looked at her blankly.

"I have the perfect woman," Annabella announced. "She is so perfect, I am simply amazed I didn't think of her right off." She rubbed her hands together like a child eyeing a sweet. "Oh, I have outdone myself this time." Then moving to Ross, she kissed him and said, "Count your blessings, husband. I have your brother's wife."

"You must be joking."

"Would I do that?"

"Aye, you would. Now, tell me who you've come up with. And no jokes."

"Margaret Ramsay," she said. Then, with more satisfaction in her voice, she added, "She is no joke, Ross. Maggie is everything he described and more."

"I'll say!" Ross said, his once hopeful expression wilting. "That something more numbers about three, if I remember right."

"You're being perfectly ridiculous."

"Bella, she's been married. . . . "

"To the Duke of Glengarry, don't forget."

"But—"

She silenced him with a wave of her hand. "Please, Ross, let me finish. Adrian didn't say the woman had to be a virgin or a spinster. You yourself said she had to be desperate, and Maggie Ramsay is the most desperate woman I know."

"Bella, if I sent Adrian a woman who had been married

before—one with three children—he would shoot me first and ask questions later.''

''It's because she's been married and had three children that she is perfect.''

Ross threw up his hands. ''I don't believe this.''

''Ross, listen to me for a moment. Adrian wants a family, and women have been known to be barren. Margaret is a proven breeder.''

''With three children, she's a bit overproofed, if you ask me.''

''Overproofed? You make it sound like we're talking about bread dough.'' Then Annabella added, ''Be sensible. She's perfect and you know it.''

''You can't be serious.''

''I most certainly am,'' she said. ''You know we could look from now till doomsday and never find a woman like Maggie Ramsay. She's intelligent and well bred, and she has more stamina and endurance than ten ordinary women— something she'll need if she's to become a member of the Mackinnon clan, I might add. Why, she's perfect for Adrian, I tell you. Her best asset is her calm, dignified manner, which would be a perfect foil for his blustery ways.''

''A calm, dignified manner would drive my brother to drinking.''

''So will remaining a bachelor. Maggie is the right woman for him. You know he could do worse. Maggie has a kindness of heart and generosity of nature you don't find in many people. A man like Adrian needs that in a woman. The last thing he needs is a hothead, a woman prone to outbursts and rages. Maggie is a woman of strong feeling and intense interest in the world around her.''

Bella went right on. ''She would adapt to Adrian's life beautifully—and well you know it. Moreover, she has a calm nature, a practical side, a keen wit, and sense of humor—all which she will need, I might add, *if* your brother is anything like you. Now, you tell me, Ross Mackinnon, just who would be a better match for him? Kate McNamara? Maura MacGregor? Jeanne Morris?''

Ross shook his head, shuddering more with each name she called.

''You see what I mean? She's too good to be true. If it weren't for her dire circumstances, I suspect Maggie would never even consider accepting such an offer, but desperate situations call for desperate measures. You know yourself, Maggie needs him as much as he needs her. California would be the perfect place for her, away from all the sorrow and pain she's faced here. It would be a new life, a new beginning. Can you just imagine what her life here would be like . . . how she would always be worried if that horrid Adair Ramsay would do something harmful to Fletcher?''

''I still don't know,'' Ross said. ''I have a feeling Adrian would gag at the thought of having a wife who had been married before. And one with children would probably anger him enough to commit murder.''

''Well, you're far enough away that his anger would have cooled by the time he got here,'' said Annabella. ''If not, you could always hide behind my skirts,'' she said, laughing at her husband's expression.

Annabella began straightening the lapels of Ross's coat. ''Maggie Ramsay is right for him, and you know it. It's almost as if fate put the two of them together. Praise be.'' She gave his lapels a final pat. ''And as for the children, don't be forgetting Adrian did say he wanted them. . . .''

''Bella, he wants to *sire* children, not get them ready-made.''

''What if we picked a woman who was barren? Wouldn't that be a fine kettle of pumpkins.''

''A fine kettle of fish,'' Ross said, amused by the way Annabella bungled his familiar expressions in the most delightful manner.

"Well, whatever," she said. "Now, let's don't argue about this any further. We need to put our differences behind us and think about convincing Margaret Ramsay to marry your brother."

"Why do I feel like a lamb being led to slaughter?" asked Ross.

"I'm sure I don't know," Annabella said, raising her brows. "I thought we merely agreed to put our disagreements behind us and join forces."

"I don't remember doing that," Ross said, "but I have a feeling you'll convince me it was my idea in a minute or two."

Knowing when he was outflanked, outmaneuvered, and outtalked, Ross didn't say anything else. When he looked at his wife, she was smiling.

# CHAPTER
## ❧ FOUR ❧

Two weeks later, the Duke and Duchess of Dunford, seated in their new traveling coach, bounced and rattled their way north, covering miles and miles of heather-covered moor, barely stopping to give their horses a rest, until they arrived at the home of Margaret Ramsay's father, the Earl of Caithness. Immediately upon their arrival, they made Maggie Ramsay an offer she couldn't refuse.

Her mouth open in astonishment, Maggie was too stunned to do more than stare at them. "Marriage?" she said at last. "By proxy?" She shook her head, the words of her friend Ross clamoring in her mind like a blast from the church organ.

The way Ross had spoken, it sounded as if he were offering a toast. *I would like to propose a marriage between you and my brother in California . . . a marriage by proxy. . . .*

Ross's brother was quite wealthy, she knew, and marriage to a man of means would be a godsend to any woman in straits as dire as hers, but marriage to a man she had never met? Marry an American and leave Scotland?

Ross frowned. "Well, Maggie, what do you say?"

She stared at Ross helplessly. "I . . . I'm not sure. I'm stunned. Speechless."

"A speechless woman," Ross said, then turning to Bella, he said, "You were right, love, she is the perfect wife."

"Oh, for Heaven's sake, Ross, give her time to breathe. You've just sprung the question. She needs time to think."

Then to Maggie she said, "Take all the time you need. Adrian has been a bachelor for over thirty years. A few days won't make any difference."

"I didn't mean she had to give me her answer straightaway," Ross said. "I merely wanted to know her initial response."

"Shock," Maggie said, her face white as paper. "I dinna ken what to say."

"Is the idea of marriage to my brother repulsive to you?" Ross asked.

Maggie stared at him helplessly, then she smiled. "I said I was stunned, Ross, not stupid."

"I think I can safely say Adrian has a more sensitive nature than Ross. . . . Aye, a *goat* is more sensitive," Bella said, giving her husband a quelling look.

Ross cleared his throat. "Now, Maggie, I didn't mean to scare you with my offer, but . . . well, what I meant to say was . . ." He looked helplessly at Annabella. "Perhaps you can put it better than I can, love," he said.

Annabella laughed, giving him a hug. "A two-year-old could do better," she said. Then, turning to Maggie, she added, "The Mackinnon men aren't known for their ability to express themselves."

Annabella went on to tell Maggie about Adrian Mackinnon, saying, when she finished, "And so you can see how it would make sense for a man in his position to enlist his brother's help in finding himself a wife," she said at last.

"Adrian is quite capable of giving you everything you could ever want," Ross said. "A bright future for your children, a grand home—anything you want."

*Except love*, Maggie thought, her heart softening toward

Ross. How like a man to think in terms of money and possessions, when what she wanted was the things money could not buy. The kinds of things she had with Bruce. "It's true, I dinna have a very bright future as things now stand, and I did hope to remarry. I've had one offer already. . . ."

"Your father told me," Ross said. "He said you had an offer from a man too old for you."

"Aye, he was too old," she said, "in his dotage, but I canna marry solely for money. I canna."

"Of course you can't," Annabella said, coming to sit beside Maggie and putting her arms around her. "That's why we felt Adrian would be the perfect man for you. He's young, and yes, it's true he is well off financially, as well as being handsome and quite the catch his brother was. But more importantly, he is a sensitive, caring man, capable of great depth in loving."

Ross raised his brows, but said nothing.

At last Maggie shook her head and said, "Marriage by proxy. I've never heard of such."

But before the duke and duchess ended their three-day stay, Maggie had not only heard of such, she had agreed to it.

The morning they were scheduled to leave, Maggie joined them in her father's study, going over details for the proxy wedding and the subsequent trip to San Francisco.

By this time, Ross was convinced Maggie was the woman for his brother. He felt he and Annabella had done a bang-up job convincing Maggie that she was making the right decision, but it wasn't in Ross's nature to be devious or manipulating, and he was certainly not one given to cheating. For these reasons, he laid his cards plainly on the table.

"As strongly as I feel you are the perfect woman for Adrian," he said, "I feel I must be completely honest with you, Maggie. To put it simply, you've got your work cut out for you. My brother isn't an easy man to live with. He's opinionated and moody, and cynical as they come, but his bark is worse than his bite. He's thirty-one years old and has never been married. He's wealthy, lonely, and bitter. He needs a woman like you in his life, someone to make him smile again."

At this last comment, Maggie glanced from Ross to Annabella. "The love of his life married his twin brother," Bella said. "Adrian never got over it."

"Don't let Bella mislead you. Katherine was Adrian's sweetheart in Adrian's mind only. She never had eyes for anyone but his twin brother, Alex. After Katherine and Alex married, Adrian replaced the need for women with a desire for success and fortune. He's one of the wealthiest men in California, with vast timber holdings. But he doesn't know beans from buckshot when it comes to women, and that's a fact."

"Darling, don't frighten Maggie with comments like that. Leave Adrian's letters with her. Let her read them, as I have."

Annabella leaned forward, the vivid green of her dress bringing out the rich black of her hair as the firelight danced across it. Looking at his wife, Ross forgot what he was about to say. How different her rich raven's coloring was from Maggie's wood thrush red and brown. When Maggie glanced at him, he thought, *She does have the loveliest eyes*—a point he reminded himself to mention in his letter to Adrian.

There were also a few other things he reminded himself *not* to mention, namely Maggie's marriage and her children.

That wasn't a decision Ross had reached easily. It was only after much thought that he had decided to withhold the information from Adrian. It wasn't as if Ross was trying to represent Maggie as something she wasn't. It was simply that Ross knew Adrian, and he knew the fact that Maggie had been married before—married and borne children—would not sit too well with his brother, at least not at first. There was little doubt in Ross's mind that Adrian had envisioned a woman who had never been married when he wrote his letter, and that was understandable. Not many men would consider being married—for the first time—to a widow with children, that is, unless he had fallen in love with her. And *that* was what Ross was banking on.

Ross knew that even as a boy growing up, Adrian had always felt he was in second place, running just a little behind his twin, the more sociable, outgoing Alex. As he reached manhood, it became apparent that Adrian was the ambitious one, the one determined to show the world that he could, and would, master his past. And he had done just that. Over the years, Ross had seen, through Adrian's letters, that Adrian was a man who expected and accepted only the finest and the best. It was only a hunch, but a strong one, that made Ross feel that Adrian wouldn't be so much upset over the fact that Maggie had been married before as he would be to discover he had, once again, come in second.

Only last night, he had lain in bed, talking to Annabella, who was, at first, shocked to hear Ross would even consider such deception. After a lengthy discussion, Annabella said, "I suppose you're right, but I can't help worrying about Maggie. What do you think will happen if Adrian finds out about her *before* he falls in love with her?"

"He will know what he has in Maggie the moment he meets her."

"You aren't answering my question."

Ross chuckled. "He won't shoot her, if that's what you mean."

"It's not, and you know it. Now, do be serious, Ross. This is, after all, Maggie's future we are discussing."

"You're right, love," Ross said, then with a serious tone, he added, "Adrian will be disappointed, and even quite angry, when he learns of her past, but he's no fool. It won't take him long to realize he could never find a woman to compare with Maggie—married or not." Ross rolled over in the bed and kissed Annabella. "Besides, it's *me* Adrian will be angry with. Now, if I was there, he would probably choose pistols at ten paces, but I won't be there, and my brother isn't a cruel man. He will know Maggie is innocent of all this."

Annabella lifted a skeptical brow. "Are you so certain?"

"Aye. Certain enough to put your pretty mind at ease. I promise I will write Adrian—in due time, of course—and I will confess, fully, to my sins of omission. Satisfied?"

"Only if you let me read the letter first." Annabella frowned. "I don't know," she said. "Perhaps you should at least tell Maggie."

"No. I've thought about that, but I've decided it would be best to keep Maggie in the dark about all of this."

"Why?"

"Because Adrian can't very well blame her for any deception when she had no idea one was taking place." Ross paused, then added, "And another thing; I don't think Maggie would go through with the marriage if she knew."

"I don't either, but you could wait until after the wedding. Once she is married . . ."

"I'm not so certain she would go to California even then," Ross said.

Annabella sighed. "I pray to God you know what you're doing, then."

"I do. As the saying goes, 'He can best avoid a snare who knows how to set one.' "

Because he felt in his heart he was doing the right thing, Ross felt no remorse over sending Maggie innocently on her way to California. God willing, Adrian would be too much in love with her by the time he learned of her past circumstances to ever consider ending their marriage.

At that moment, Ross looked at his wife and he gave his attention to what she was saying.

Annabella patted Maggie's hand. "You won't be able to

read Adrian's letters and not care for him. He needs you, Maggie. More than you need him, I suspect.''

By the time Maggie stood at the front door waving good-bye to Ross and Annabella, she was wondering just what she had gotten herself into. Once the coach crested the hill and disappeared from sight, she stepped inside the house, closing the door behind her.

She served her father a cup of tea and tucked his Shetland robe about his legs, knowing he would doze by the fire after his tea. Leaving her father, she made her way upstairs to find Maude reading to Ainsley. Taking Ainsley in her lap, Maggie kissed the top of her head. "Where is that brother of yours?" she asked.

Ainsley pointed toward the door and looked at Maude.

"He went with Barrie to the kitchen to have cook bring us a tray," Maude said. "We're having a tea party."

Maggie kissed Ainsley as she climbed from her lap. "I'll be in Father's study if you should need me."

Making her way downstairs, Maggie thought about the bundle of letters waiting downstairs, and the man they would reveal to her. She thought about Ross Mackinnon's honesty in telling her the truth about his brother, and her own dishonesty in agreeing to marry a man because she was so desperate. The only thought that eased her feelings of deceit was her determination to make it up to Adrian Mackinnon by making him a good wife.

Settling herself in the chair by the fire, Maggie took up the bundle of yellowed letters, pulling the string and taking the first letter from the bottom of the stack.

Three hours later, she placed the last letter on top of the stack and retied the string.

She had learned much about Adrian Mackinnon from the things he had written there. She had learned even more from the things he did not say. Feeling somewhat melancholy, she stared into the fire, wondering about this strange man who had revealed so much about himself, while writing so diligently about the redwoods and life in a lumber camp.

His letters were intelligent, well written, original, and crammed with a lot of facts and not too many feelings. What they told her was that Adrian Mackinnon was a proud man who had been hurt, and hurt deeply.

But it was his descriptions of the land and life he loved that gave Maggie the most insight into the man who was Adrian Mackinnon.

I suppose it's the vastness, the untouched wildness of this country, that humbles a man and brings him to his knees. You can't ride five miles into the redwoods and see the world's tallest trees towering two hundred and fifty feet over your head and not feel the hand of God upon your shoulder. There's a plant here with cloverlike leaves. We call it the redwood sorrel. Whenever a shaft of sunlight filters through the redwoods and touches it, its leaves fold up like tiny hands at prayer.

There's something bigger than mankind, bigger than even creation here—something I can only call the presence of God. It makes a man realize how insignificant he is; what a small part of the universe each of us occupies.

Adrian was a serious man, but there were touches of humor in his letters. Once, when describing himself to Annabella, he wrote:

I'm not as talkative as that husband of yours. Best I remember, Ross could talk the legs off a potbellied stove. As for me, I suppose you could say I don't use up all my kindlin' to get a fire started.

\* \* \*

From scraps of information she had obtained from Ross, Maggie had learned Adrian had brown hair and blue eyes, that he was tall and slender. But those things didn't interest her as much as other things, things like the sound of his voice, the way he held his head, the expression in his eyes when he looked at the redwoods he described so beautifully, the way his hands would speak to a woman he loved. Her thoughts turned toward more intimate things. What was he like as a lover? Was he slow, gentle, and understanding as Bruce had been, or was he quick and rough? Would he give as much as he took, or would he be demanding?

Only time held such answers.

The one fact about Adrian that kept surfacing—one she didn't want to think on—was the feeling that Adrian Mackinnon wasn't a forgiving man. Maggie's stomach twisted in knots at the thought, but she remembered herself. She had too much staunch Scot in her to be intimidated by an unforgiving man.

No matter what kind of man Adrian Mackinnon was, he was luckier than he knew to find a woman like herself to marry him, sight unseen, as she was about to do. She might not be the raving beauty that Annabella was, or even his Katherine, but the good Lord had seen fit to bless her with an abundance of common sense and an easygoing nature. It shouldn't take Adrian Mackinnon long to realize she married him to accept the challenge, not out of charity. She might be guilty of taking from him, but she was honest, and she gave as good as she got.

She supposed he could do worse.

That night she broke the news to her father over dinner. The old earl looked at her with cloudy eyes. "I ken what you're going to say, and you're wrong, Father. I would have accepted Ross Mackinnon's offer if you had been the richest man in all of Scotland."

Maggie came to her feet; moving to the sideboard and taking the crystal decanter in hand, she poured her father another glass of the red wine the doctor had prescribed for his stomach. "I ken a change of country is just what the children and I need. There are too many reminders of my life with Bruce here."

"I never thought you for a lass to run away from anything."

"I am no running away. I am simply starting over. From what I hear about life in California, it will be a wonderful opportunity for the children and a bright, new challenge for me."

"You always were a lass looking for a challenge," he said. "I ken you've decided against taking the children with you when you go."

"Aye, I'll be leaving them here, to come later with Maude. Fletcher and Barrie understand, but I worry most about Ainsley—because she is so young. We've talked about it, and I'm letting her help me pack. I've given her her own trunk, so she can begin packing her things as well. She knows Fletcher and Barrie will remain here with her and that they'll come later with Maude. We've already marked how long six months is on the calendar. Ainsley puts an X over each day when she arises. She knows how long it will be before they join me. Ross Mackinnon even hired a man in town to make a replica of the ship their passage is booked on, and Maude and I are reading to them about America from every bit of information we can get our hands on."

"Your mind is made up, is it?"

Maggie looked at her father. He had always been so tall, so strong, but now—now he looked bent and delicate. Old. He didn't need the added burden of worrying about her and her children. Much as she hated to leave him, she knew it would be best. "Aye," she said, "it is."

"And the marriage? I ken it will be soon, then?"

"Annabella and Ross will return in a fortnight. Ross has made arrangements for the wedding to take place then."

\* \* \*

It went exactly as planned, for a fortnight after the day she talked with her father, Margaret Sinclair Ramsay married Adrian Mackinnon, with his brother Ross, the Duke of Dunford, standing in as proxy.

After the ceremony, Maggie walked Annabella and Ross out to their carriage. After Ross handed Annabella into the coach, he hugged Maggie. "Welcome into the Mackinnon clan," he said. "You're going to make my brother a happy man."

"I hope your brother feels that way when he sees what you've sent him," she said, laughing.

The look in Ross's eyes faded. "He will. I know he will." Ross hugged her again. "Trust me, Maggie. Trust what I've done. Remember, it's better to have the last smile than the first laugh."

On her wedding night, she stood over the huge trunk in her room, packing the last of her belongings. When the final garment was tucked away, she closed the lid and sat down on top of the trunk. She looked around the room.

How strange it had been to come back home after being married for almost ten years. How strange to be married and the mother of three children, only to wake up one morning to find herself a widow, and shortly after that, to move back into the room she had lived in as a young girl.

The room looked bare now; the clutter she had accumulated over the past year was gone. For the second time in her life, she was packing her belongings and leaving this room, this house. Only this time she was married to a man half a world away. An American. A man she had never laid eyes upon.

She couldn't help wondering what it would be like. How would it feel to have another man's arms around her? Was he someone she could bear to have hold her close? Was he handsome? Strong? Clean? Would he give her time to become acquainted with him before he took her to his bed?

Would he come to love her? Would she come to love him?

She looked down at the gold band on her finger. It was wider than the band Bruce had given her. *Oh, Bruce, Bruce, why must I think of you now?* She pushed him from her mind. "Adrian," she said softly. "I must think of Adrian. Only Adrian."

She went downstairs, judging from the fragrant smell of sultanas, currants, and fruit peel that Jean, the cook, was baking a Dundee cake.

The kitchen was empty. Jean didn't make it a habit to linger in the kitchen when there was work to be done elsewhere. Maggie picked up the empty mixing bowl and sat on the table, as she had done as a young girl—only now her legs were too long to swing from the chair—and licked the residue from the spoon and scraped the bowl. She remembered the day her mother bought this bowl. They had been in Edinburgh. . . . She quickly pushed the thought away. Her mother had been dead for years, and thinking about it made her feel old.

She scraped the bowl again, licking the spoon. The taste of ground almonds and fruit peel reminded her of exotic places. She licked the spoon clean, then rubbed it in a circular motion over her lips. She wondered what it would be like to kiss Adrian Mackinnon.

Her heart fluttered and her stomach began to knot. It had been a long time since she had felt the warm, familiar curl of desire, and it was strange to feel it, thinking about a man she had never met. She looked at the ring on her finger. The feeling in her stomach was warm, but the ring she touched was cold.

She pushed herself off the table and left the bowl on the counter. She went outside, walking toward the barn. Cullen and Clootie, her father's sheepdogs, saw her and trotted to her side. Cullen licked her fingers, and she laughed, pulling them away.

She walked for a long time, so long that Cullen and Clootie gave up and turned away. But she didn't care. This might be the last time she walked these heathery, fragrant moors or passed by the dark, mysterious loch with its cold, haunted waters. She walked along the edge of the loch, staring out across its rippled surface.

Everywhere she looked, it was infinitely gray and infinitely silent, and most of all, infinitely dear to her. She sat upon a lichen-covered rock, watching the surface of the lake ruffled by a passing wind, and thought about her homeland. Scotland, so strong, so stoic, so staunch. Adrian's words came to her, words about the redwoods and feeling the hand of God upon his shoulder. God's hand might be in California, but surely his heart was here, in the Highlands.

She stood, her movement quick and so sudden, a grouse flung itself from the heather. Grouse and heather. They were a part of Scotland she would miss. Not deer and salmon perhaps, for Adrian's letters said they were both abundant in California. But the familiar flight of grouse and the lavender haze of a heather-covered heath—they would be as lost to her as the sound of the pipes. As she turned back toward the house, she wondered if she would pine for her Celtic heritage. Would she soon be as lost as the Gaelic tongue?

One month after her proxy marriage to Adrian Mackinnon, Maggie set sail for San Francisco.

Her first week at sea, she began a journal, writing in it each night after she re-read one of the letters Adrian had written to his brother. It was strange, how much she gleaned from his letters. She looked down at the list of things she had observed and written in her journal: "He's a proud man, and sometimes that pride makes him appear harsh and uncaring. He's built himself a powerful empire. He's one of the richest men in California, but he's lonely. He would not admit that, of course, but it's true just the same. He prefers to think he's self-sufficient, that he does not need . . . anyone.''

Judging from the things Ross had told her about his family, Maggie knew there had always been a tense thread of competition between Adrian and his twin, Alex. According to Ross, Alex had always been the outgoing one, the charmer, the one who always got everything he wanted, leaving Adrian to feel he was left in second place, always a step or two below. It hadn't helped those feelings any when Alex married the woman Adrian had fancied himself in love with since childhood.

Maggie closed the journal, feeling her heart go out to Adrian. There hadn't been much gentleness or softness in his life. She had a feeling he needed just that. As she leaned over and blew out the lamp, she was remembering something Ross had said the day of the wedding.

''Adrian isn't the kind of man to fall in love overnight. He's convinced everyone he loves leaves him, and he'll do everything he can to dissuade you, to send you running back to Scotland, so he can prove he was right. I've written to him about you. The fact that you've been married before is something that will take him a while to come to grips with. Don't push him to talk about it. Let him bring it up if he chooses. Don't badger him to discuss it or understand it. It will take time for all this to settle in with him. Remember, time is on your side.''

# CHAPTER
## ❧ FIVE ❧

It was voices that woke her.

She held her breath and listened, and knew there was no doubt. It was the soft voices of her daughters, Barrie and Ainsley, that stirred her consciousness; voices of the sweetest tone—clear, and high-pitched—that embraced, and surrounded her with comfort; childish voices, so careless and happy, singing nonsense. Or were they?

> *"Needles and pins, needles and pins,*
> *When a man marries, his trouble begins."*

Half-afraid, half-hopeful, Maggie opened her eyes. She searched the room, seeing everything in the tiny ship's cabin was just as it had been the night before. Her children were not here.

The sound of the wind and the sea surrounded her, yet the voices lingered, bright as a fairy tale, coming to her with the haunting strains of a nursery rhyme. Memories born of pain and desperation.

Never had she been away from her children more than a few days, and the wound gaped, as if something vital within had been ripped away. She missed them, and longed to hold

63

them. This separation, this being away from them, she knew, would pass, but there would always be the shadow of it upon her heart.

Maggie went to her trunk and took out the tiny miniature portraits of her children. Fletcher looked so manly, and Barrie's expression was one she had seen so many times. And little Ainsley, with her shy smile. A tear trickled down her cheek and splashed on Ainsley's picture. Maggie wiped it away. *My bairns*, her heart cried. *My bairns.* She regretted her decision to leave them behind, but how could she have known? How could she imagine the pain of being apart? She never dreamed it would be this difficult to be away from them. Never. The words of Dante seemed real to her now. *"Nessun maggior dolore. Che ricordarsi del tempo felice Nella miseria.* There is no greater sorrow than to recall, in misery, the time when we were happy."

She lay awake for what seemed hours, looking at the moon through the tiny porthole, consumed with memory and regret, not really aware when she drifted off to sleep.

It seemed to Maggie that she was no longer in her cabin, or even aboard ship, for she had the feeling she was lifted up, and transported, to a land of mist and stone. She stood alone on the moors in the darkness, the wind whipping her skirts and tearing her hair. Voices were all about her; then, in the distance and coming closer, the howling of many wolves. She saw her children and called them to her, but the wolves came between and surrounded her, snarling, their fangs dripping with foam.

Like a crack of lightning, a great bird swept down from nowhere, like an eagle made of light, melting the darkness and driving back the creatures of night, taking her up and away.

She was in a strange place, another land, one quite like Scotland, and yet it was not. She saw her children, but when she reached out to touch them, her hand passed through them, and their images faded from her sight.

She awoke with a violently pounding heart, her body drenched in sweat. She sat up, clutching the blanket to her breast, thinking she heard, or remembered hearing:

> *"When shall we three meet again,*
> *In thunder, lightning or in rain?*
> *When the hurlyburly's done,*
> *When the battle's lost and won."*

Macbeth's witches? Was her sanity slipping? Fear pounded, frantic as a beating fist, within her. What was happening?

A breath of sweet air stirred in the tiny cabin, and she felt strangely comforted. She lay back down again.

She had no more dreams that night.

The ship rolled and a shaft of sunlight spread warmly over Maggie's face. She rolled over in the bed and put her arm over her eyes. The memory of her dreams occupied her for a while, but not being the kind to lavish in self-pity or regrets for what is over and past, Maggie soon put her mind to the future.

The first task she set for herself was to decide what clothes to wear, knowing Adrian's first impression of her was bound to have some impact upon how things would go from there. She hurried to stand before the small mirror hanging from her cabin wall—a mirror she had attached with a lump of sticky black tar, something, she might add, that had taken a wee bit o' Scots ingenuity and a ton of patience. She posted herself in front of the mirror and surveyed what she saw with a critical eye, feeling the sticky residue of tar still upon her fingers.

Tapping her foot with impatience, she turned her head,

first to one side and then the other, lifting her hair away from her face. She had good clear skin, thick, glossy hair, and straight, even teeth. Her hazel eyes were large and determined, but a bit too large and wide-set by English standards. And by those same standards, her mouth was too full, her complexion too honey-colored, and her hair seemed destined to be lost somewhere between the shades of flaxen and red-brown. She had neither the pale Nordic coloring of her mother's Viking ancestors, nor the inky blackness of her father's Celtic ones.

There was something about Maggie, something that men enjoyed, for there was a challenge in having a battle with an educated woman with a quick mind and an even temper. On the other side of that coin, there was something within Maggie that put her in touch with her sharpest wits whenever the prospect of a confrontation with a man—any man—arose.

Before her marriage to Bruce Ramsay, Maggie had been one of the most sought-after women in Scotland, if not for her beauty, then because she was, simply put, captivating.

And now, God help her, she knew she was going to need all the captivating charm she could muster over the next few hours.

Whatever possessed her to marry a complete stranger and then embark, all alone, to sail halfway around the world to meet him? The calm, controlled picture she made standing before the mirror was clearly at variance with her feelings of jittery uncertainty.

A knock at her cabin door pulled her attention away. "Aye?"

"Captain wanted me to tell you that we'd be docking soon," a voice said.

"It canna be too soon for me," she said, thanking the man as she heard him chuckle and walk away.

After too much contemplation, in which her dresses all began to look the same, she chose a carriage dress of Pekin with satin stripes in green and rose. The three flounces on the skirt made her nineteen-inch waist seem no more than seventeen, the tight-fitting basque setting off to perfection a well-rounded bosom beneath slim shoulders. She swept her hair back from her face in a quiet coil before she stood in the center of the room pretending her cloak, hanging from the oil lamp overhead, was a stand-in for the husband she had yet to meet.

She held out her hand. "You must be Adrian Mackinnon," she said, then shook her head.

*Too formal.*

She extended her hand again. "Hello, I'm . . ." She paused.

*What should I call myself? Mrs. Mackinnon? Maggie Mackinnon? Margaret. Your wife?*

It was small wonder, then, that she suddenly whirled around and stomped her foot and said, "This is ridiculous," then, "Hang the introduction and all this rehearsing," and made her way out the door. "Damn the cannons and pray for wind," she added, turning down the long, dark passageway, without even bothering to retrieve her cloak from where it still swung beneath the oil lamp. A moment later she found herself on deck, bathed in sunlight, and saying to herself with a hint of relief in her voice, "This is ever so much better."

It was the first time she had seen the sun in several days, and although the clear patch of sky was surrounded by dark clouds, the sun was a spirit lifter. After spending all morning breathing the stale air below, she was quick to move to the railing, where the soft breezes caressed her cheek and the fresh, salty smell of the ocean was heavy in the air. Thankful the fog had lifted, she watched the *Stonehenge* drop her canvas and make her way through the maze of ships anchored in San Francisco Bay to slip, silent and sleek as a Scottish salmon, into her berth at the dock.

Maggie went below to get her cloak and bonnet, noticing

her trunks had already been taken out of her room. By the time she retied her bonnet three times to get the bow beneath her chin just right, and made her way topside, the sun was gone and the first hard drops of rain were beginning to splatter in dark circles upon the deck.

"Wonderful," she said, turning her head sideways and casting an eye toward the sky, seeing the dark rain clouds swirling overhead had completely obliterated the sun. "At least I dinna have to worry about standing on the dock like a fool wondering what I'm going to say."

*No, you'll be hurried into the coach, where you can sit there wet, and shivering like a fool, wondering what you're going to say.*

Half an hour later, she was still standing on the docks, wet and shivering, surrounded by her trunks and a few rough-looking strangers who hung around the harbor, the rain running in fat rivulets down her umbrella to splatter across her cloak. Looking about her, she saw that most of the ship's passengers who had lined the dock with her moments ago were now gone.

Alone and cold, her spirits as sodden as her clothes, Maggie bit her lip as she clenched her fists with anxiety. The suspicions and fears that ate at her were too terrible to contemplate. She was being ridiculous to feel abandoned and unwanted. After all, she had traveled halfway around the world, and Adrian was coming from northern California to meet her. Precise punctuality wasn't something she had a right to expect, and she was being childish to assume they would have made connections immediately. She would wait a few more minutes. If Adrian didn't arrive soon, she would simply find someone to deliver her trunks to a nice hotel and leave word with the ship's captain as to her whereabouts.

Scolding herself for being a bit melodramatic, she drew her cloak more tightly about her and sat down on her smallest trunk to wait, resting her folded arms across the wicker basket in her lap.

She refused to listen to the small voice in the back of her mind that said, *What if he doesna come . . . ever?*

Too practical to panic for long, she occupied her mind with two ideas: what to do if Adrian didn't come, and trying to find something positive about her situation. The positive thing about all of this was, she would have a home, a new beginning for herself and her children.

Her children.

She missed them. She vowed to never, ever leave them again. She suddenly realized that it was a blessing the children hadn't come with her, since she had no idea if she would ever get off this dock. That, in itself, was something positive.

Soaked to the skin, Maggie remembered her original decision and her intention of finding transportation to a hotel. Deciding it was time to locate some form of equipage to the hotel, she squared her shoulders, lifted her head, and was just rising to her feet when a shiny black coach pulled up across the rain-flooded street.

The man inside looked at her for a full minute or two before she noticed him. It was enough time for him to see as valiant a woman as he had ever laid eyes upon. He knew he had no right to say such a thing to her, and figured her to be the kind to give him a frank stare if he had had the audacity to even mention the word *valiant*. Yet his eyes told him a lot about her, and he knew she was the type to look life square in the eye and rely upon her instinct for survival whenever she encountered an obstacle.

*So that's the little Scot,* he thought, and chuckled to himself. She looked resilient enough to beat back a hurricane. Her kind would never recognize defeat.

Maggie looked up and saw the door of the coach come flying open as an enormous man stepped out. When his broad, tanned face broke into a wide smile, her heart fluttered and her stomach seemed to rise to her throat. Fighting back the swirling black cloud of faintness that threatened, she had a sudden vision of Bruce Ramsay's beloved face. Her mind screamed—*Oh Bruce, Bruce, my husband, my love, what have I done? How can I be this man's wife? How can I?* Yet even as her mind screamed its agonizing plea, Maggie breathed deeply and lifted her face into the cold rain, mingling the wet drops of heaven with the salt of her own.

She felt her disappointment like the thrust of a sword point as he closed the door and started across the street. He was a huge, lumbering hulk of a man, and although pleasant-looking, there wasn't an ounce of breeding or status in his overall appearance. *Surely this canna be my husband,* she thought, hoping above hope that the acute disappointment she felt did not manifest itself upon her face. *He's nothing like Ross. Nothing!*

She kept trying to tell herself he could have been worse; that he could have been like one of the rough sailors who made her so uncomfortable with their frank, assessing stares—or one of the men who had been leering at her while she waited on the docks. But try as she might, she couldn't prevent the slow, sinking feeling of acute disappointment. He was simply nothing like the man she had hoped for.

All she could do was try her best to look pleasant and hide her disappointment. After all, she was married to this man. She would have to make the most of it. With a labored sigh, she forced the heaviness from the corners of her mouth, giving her best go at a bright smile as she watched him make his way through the muck in the street.

He was close enough now that she could see the mud splatter on his pants and hear the suction of oozing mud with each step he took. Looking down, she saw that he had feet as big as a Clydesdale. She couldn't help carrying that vein of speculation a bit further. *Dear Lord above, dinna let the rest of him be in draft-horse dimensions*. Her face heated at the thought.

The two of them looked at each other for a moment. Maggie could see nothing but kindness in the man's eyes, while he seemed to be, as people often were, distracted by the unusual color of hers.

"You must be Miz Mackinnon," the redheaded giant said, extending a rough hand and giving her more delicate one a jarring pump.

When she didn't say anything, he looked up and down the dock, then turned a puzzled face back to her. "You are Miz Mackinnon, aren't you?"

Maggie remained silent, then nodded her head, her mouth moving, but the "Aye" she mouthed was inaudible. The man stared at her a moment, looking tremendously relieved when she nodded, but she hardly took any notice. This person was nothing like the tender, feeling man she had come to know through his letters. Even his voice lacked the power and strength, the educated refinement, she had come to expect. She watched him wipe his hands ineffectively with a dingy piece of cloth pulled from his back pocket, feeling the urge to cry as strongly as the day she had buried Bruce Ramsay.

*Think of something good, something positive.*

She saw immediately that he was an even-tempered, rather jovial sort of man. And healthy, too, judging from the size of him. He was broad as a Scots pine, with legs that looked as if they had been hewn from sturdy ship's timber. *He has nice eyes and he's probably kind to his livestock and the men who work for him—which doesn't amount to a hill of barley when speculating on how he will treat a wife.*

Her heart pounding, her hands trembling from distress, she lifted enormous hazel eyes to him and said, "Are you . . ."

The giant threw back his head and laughed.

Taken aback, Maggie was tempted to poke him with her

umbrella for his rudeness, but she was too thankful. The laugh, after all, was a nice sound. What he said was even nicer. "I'm not your husband, Miz Mackinnon. Lord-a-mercy, a pretty little thing like you deserves better than a coarse old war-horse like me."

Maggie smiled. "Thank you for the compliment, but you canna go so far as to say I'm pretty. I may be plain, but I'm honest. The truth doesna hurt."

If he was surprised by her frank honesty, he didn't let on. "Don't go expecting me to apologize none, 'cause I won't," he said. "You see plain. I see pretty. And pretty is in the eyes of the beholder, or so I've been told."

"Thank you."

Maggie looked at him. He cleared his throat and said, "We don't see many women in these parts, Miz Mackinnon, and when we do, they don't come dressed all fancy-like and smelling pretty. Truth is, you could put a dress and bonnet on a falling ax, and the men in these parts would tip their hats and gape at it."

Maggie decided she must have had the strangest look on her face, for the giant laughed again and said, "The name's Carr. Eli Carr. I work for your husband. I'm sort of his right-hand man, you might say. I'll be taking you north and . . ."

He went on talking, but Maggie didn't hear. Relief swept over her with such force, she swayed upon her feet. "Here now," Eli said, his big hands coming out to steady her. "I reckon you don't rightly have your land legs yet. Takes a while, it does. You just lean on old Eli and let me whistle up that driver. We'll have that coach over here in no time." He looked down at the flounce edged in fringe poking from beneath her cape and said, "I'll have him bring it up real close so you won't get your clothes muddy."

She was about to tell him a little mud didn't matter after the soaking she'd received, but he gave a shrill whistle and motioned the driver to circle around, putting her inside the coach as soon as it stopped, not giving her much chance to say anything. "Give me a hand with the lady's trunks," he said to the driver.

Her baggage loaded, Eli climbed inside, tipping his hat and taking the seat across from her. "Are we going to meet Mr. Mackinnon?" she asked.

"No, ma'am. We're going just around to the other side of the harbor. We'll be loading your belongings onto another ship, the *Wanderlust*. She'll be taking us north."

Maggie was bewildered. Here she had just experienced the biggest sense of relief in her entire life when she learned she was not married to this man, yet that news opened the way for a whole new set of disappointments—that her husband had not seen fit to meet her ship himself.

Apparently Adrian Mackinnon wasn't half as interested in making a good impression upon her as she was in making one upon him. It was chafing indeed to think she had spent the better part of her morning trying on this dress and that, worried about the way she would look, when he hadn't cared enough to even show up. It was just too much to ignore.

"My husb . . . Mr. Mackinnon isn't coming, I take it?"

"No, ma'am."

"Would it be rude of me to inquire as to why, Mr. Carr?"

"Your husband went up to Puget Sound last week, ma'am. Before he left, he made arrangements for me to come to San Francisco to fetch you back to camp, if he wasn't back in time. I'm sure he'll be there by the time we reach the country north of Humboldt Bay. He's been quite anxious for you to come." As if sensing her disappointment, he said, "Your husband arranged for you to have the best cabin on the ship. You'll be comfortable there."

"If it's out of the rain, I'll be comfortable," she said. "I'm fairly soaked to the skin, and I dinna ken Mr. Mackinnon would be too happy to welcome a wife with the sniffles," she said, looking out the window and missing the light of admiration in Eli's eyes.

Eli Carr didn't know it, but he had just received his first dose of Maggie Mackinnon's charm. "Mackinnon is going to be very surprised to find he's taken himself a wife with a dogged resolution and a cheerful, make-the-most-of-it nature. The little lady has bottom. Damn if she doesn't," he whispered.

Maggie glanced at him. "Did you say something, Mr. Carr?"

"Don't pay me no never mind, Miz Mackinnon. I was just thinking out loud, ma'am. Do it all the time."

Maggie smiled. "So do I, Mr. Carr. So do I."

The trip north was rough, a hellish journey through bellowing darkness where the ship was tossed and pitched about like a child's toy. The oil lamp swinging from the ceiling of Maggie's cabin threw eerie shadows across the room, its pale glow unable to cast the cabin in a more hospitable light. Everything about was dark, cold, and musty as a tomb. It was too dark outside to see anything, but she could hear the roaring protest of angry waves lashed by howling winds. The ship groaned and creaked as it struggled to inch its way northward, and Maggie thought surely she was getting her first glimpse of a cold version of hell.

Her feet frozen, her stomach unsteady, she made her way to her bunk. Sleeping was impossible with the ship pitching as it was, and all her attention and energy were needed just to hold herself flat against the thin mattress. Praying she wouldn't fall asleep and be tossed out on her ear, she could only brace herself for each coming swell and plunge, praying the journey to Adrian's camp would be a short one.

It took two days to battle their way north. Two days of cold food and a cold cabin. She would be lucky if she didn't come down with lung fever before the week was out. Maggie had never been so cold, and for a Scot, that was quite an admission.

They docked the next morning.

Seeing Maggie standing on deck, taking her first look at her new home, Eli came to stand beside her. "Nervous?"

"No," Maggie said, giving Eli a confident look. "I've made up my mind to like it here. Making your mind up is half the battle, you ken. It's been my experience that you can always find something good about any situation, if you tell yourself to do it." She looked away from him toward the lumber camp on shore. "This is my future," she said. "This is where I belong. I willna think about the past."

Deep inside, Maggie had never felt so lonely. She stood on the dock and watched the *Wanderlust* sail out of the bay, reminding herself that she had made up her mind to like it here, only she hadn't known just how hard that was going to be. Turning around, she took another look at Mackinnon's camp. It didn't seem any better than it had a moment ago. The camp was nothing more than a collection of humble buildings and dingy structures, piles of smoldering wood shavings, littered ground, protruding stumps, sawdust, staring men, unfriendly dogs, and scrap wood—a place as strenuous as the work. She stood as if someone had nailed her skirts to the dock, for she was unable to move, feeling a combination of gripping disillusionment, bitter disappointment, and a homesickness much worse than any she had experienced before. *I shouldna have come. I should have stayed in Scotland.*

But things hadn't gone too well for her in Scotland. The thought had barely come to her before she was reminded of Adair Ramsay. The vision of his face that day in the library of Glengarry Castle was a sight that would not go away. She put all thoughts of homesickness and wrongdoing behind her, chastening herself for allowing them to occur in the first place. As long as Fletcher lived, he was a threat to Adair

Ramsay and all that he so tenuously possessed. She had been right to come to California. Here, her children could start a new life with her. Here, Fletcher would be safe.

Safe. She shivered as the words Adair Ramsay had whispered came back to haunt her. For an instant she was surrounded by darkness and she felt herself sway upon her feet.

*Start digging around in all these ashes again, and I will see that you regret it. There is no place you can go, no place you can hide, that I won't find you. The lad takes after his father. I would hate to see him follow in his footsteps.*

But then Maggie thought about the long journey from Scotland to America. Now that she was so far away, Adair Ramsay would soon forget about Fletcher, realizing he was no longer a threat. That, in itself, was a fortifying boost to Maggie, one that reinforced all the reasons why she had married Adrian Mackinnon and sailed halfway around the world to become his wife. Fletcher *would* be safe here. The distance alone made it almost impossible for Adair to keep an eye on them. In time he would realize she had no intention of reclaiming Bruce Ramsay's title.

Eli's hand came out to take her elbow. "It don't look like much, but this is the worst part," he said. "After we leave the water's edge and get into the main part of camp, you'll see the place perk up a mite. And wait until you see your house. A real, genuine mansion, it is. Nothing like it in these parts."

"I ken it must be lovely, Mr. Carr, simply because you say so." Maggie watched silently as Eli directed two men to load her baggage on the back of a wagon.

"Take this on up to the big house," he said. "And handle them carefully. There's ladies' things in there—delicate things like teacups and such." Then, turning to Maggie, he added, "Ain't that right, Miz Mackinnon?"

"Aye. *Prize* teacups," she said with mock exaggeration.

Eli grinned. After the wagon rolled slowly away, he looked

at her. "If you don't mind waiting here for two shakes, I'll go fetch some sort of conveyance to carry you on up to the big house."

Maggie watched him trot amazingly fast for such a big man, crossing the timber-littered campground to a long, low-slung building across the way. A cold wind was blowing over the water, and the unfriendly clouds churned overhead. Already the sky was the color of dark, wet slate. The wind that assailed her whipped her skirts and carried the smell of rain. Maggie stood on the small wooden dock, waiting and struggling against the swell of disappointment rising slowly within her. Loneliness seemed all about her, and understandably so. She was in a strange place surrounded by strange people. Eli would surely come back before it started to rain.

It was sprinkling when he returned, a look of disappointment upon his face. "I should have put you on the wagon with your baggage," he said. "There isn't anything in camp right now that we can use. I'll have to get you on over to the office. You can wait there until the wagon returns. I'm sorry. It's the best I can do. Curse me for a fool," he said apologetically.

Maggie looked across the way, toward the building with the faded sign that said CALIFORNIA MILL AND LUMBERING COMPANY, then, in smaller letters below it, ADRIAN MAC-KINNON, PROPRIETOR.

It wasn't such a far distance, but the ground was saturated, and now it was raining again.

Eli followed the direction of her gaze, looking out across the muddy campground, lingering for a moment on the ruts that were up to the axle of a wagon. Seeing his discomfort and knowing he hated to ask her to walk through that, and knowing as well that he didn't exactly feel comfortable in asking her to let him carry her, Maggie took matters into her own hands. Opening her umbrella with a snap, she handed her wicker basket to Eli, and picked up her skirts. "My

father always said, 'If the Scots didna have enough sense to
come in out of the rain, they'd no get any exercise.' Shall we
go?''

He looked relieved. ''I'm sorry about all of this,'' he said.
''I guess I didn't think things through too much when I sent
the wagon on with your things.''

Maggie laughed. ''Mr. Carr, I will listen to no more of
your apologies. Believe me, I would crawl through all that
mud to get to a warm, dry place.''

Clutching her skirts, she took his hand for balance as she
stepped down from the dock. The mud was deep and oozing.
She felt the wetness soak through her morocco slippers almost upon contact. Two steps later, she lost one slipper.
''Here, let me,'' Eli said, coming to her side as she leaned
over to retrieve the lost slipper. Just as his hand slipped beneath her elbow for support, she lost her balance, falling on
all fours in the mud. Her head came up. Even from where
she was, she could see every eye in the camp was upon her—
there must have been about 150 men staring.

The deathly silence brought the burn of tears to her eyes.
She felt Eli's eyes upon her and she knew without even looking at him that he felt just as helpless as she did.

Never in her life had she gone down in a boggy mire on
all fours, up to her chin in mud. But one missed a great many
of life's experiences by never doing these things, she rea-
soned. Besides, mud wasn't anything that couldn't be washed
off, and the person who always did the circumspect thing had
a very dull time of it.

''You dinna tell me the mud here was so strong,'' she said
in a breathless way, then laughed and took Eli's hand as he
pulled her to her feet. ''I can see my first purchase will be a
sturdy pair of boots.''

Holding Eli's arm, she took three more steps, and the other
slipper came off. She paused for a moment, then continued
on, deciding to leave it where it lay. What good was one

slipper, anyway? "When I was a child," she said, "I envied horses for having four legs and being able to run as swift as the wind. Until this moment, I was never so thankful that God in His infinite wisdom saw fit to give us only two."

Eli laughed. "Miz Mackinnon, if you were a man, I'd slap you on the back."

Maggie laughed and released her hold on his arm. "Thank you, Mr. Carr. I ken I've got the way of it now."

She squared her shoulders and smiled, then stepped forth to conquer the hearts of every man in camp, as they watched Adrian Mackinnon's new wife walk toward them, barefoot and covered with mud.

# CHAPTER
## ❧ SIX ❧

The promontory rose up out of the ground like an angry fist thrust into heaven. Below, the great, swelling waves crashed against the rocks with all the fury of a battering ram besieged by an angry sea—then abating. Its rage diminished, the sea was reduced to nothing more than churning green water and white, frothy foam.

There was a savage wildness here that reminded Maggie of home, for, like Scotland, this was a place born of the violence of the earth. She had not expected it, and the kinship she felt with this wild and beautiful land was both welcome and maudlin, a bittersweetness that left her reflective. She clasped her hands over her knees and closed her eyes, inhaling deeply the smell of the sea, and thought of Scotland; then, opening her eyes, she felt a wave of homesickness she had not felt since leaving her mist-shrouded shores.

*Yes,* she thought, *this is Scotland. Before the sadness.* For there were no haunting echoes of the Gaelic tongue here, no dim visions of a brave piper, the kilt-clad warrior, the tragic saga of kings and queens. Sadness had not yet laid her hand upon this place. Feeling the pull of her homeland, the burn of tears behind her eyes, she looked quickly away. Sadness, it seemed, was Scotland's twin at birth. Was sorrow her sister as well?

Sensing her feelings, Eli pulled back on the reins, halting the team, his foot on the wagon brake. He stared out across the last stand of land buffeted by an unforgiving sea. "Sorta makes you feel like you're the only person left on the face of the earth, don't it?"

Maggie's throat was dry. She did not look at him. She didn't have to look at him in order to let him know that was exactly how she felt. Alone. Abandoned. Desolate. How could she speak of it? How could she put into simple words her feelings of this place, the mingling of far older illusions it evoked? How could she explain how it spoke to her of a place of remembered dreams, of visions sprinkled with bits of truth, chips of falsehood, fragmented strips of remembrance, and long, sad laments of what might have been?

*My God, my God, why hast Thou forsaken me?*

She climbed out of the wagon and stood, wind-whipped and chilled, halfway up a long, winding, narrow road, looking at the towering house she would soon call home. But would it ever truly be her home? A shudder passed over her, like a draft of frigid air. She sensed a presence here, a sadness.

The house on the point began to shimmer, and fade, and for the briefest twinkling she thought she saw the blurred countenance of a woman. Then, as quickly as it had come, it was gone. Was she going crazy then? Had her sorrow, the lengthy journey here, been too much? Perhaps she was simply manifesting her woman's intuitive side. Or was it the sight? She blinked to clear the dazed sense of possession that seemed to have gripped her, and looked at Eli, but even then, she felt its pull. Something about the house spoke to her. Turning back, she stared again at the house and saw it for what it was—a memorial Adrian Mackinnon had erected to the memory of his long-lost love, a woman she knew only as Katherine Simon Mackinnon. The tribute of a lonely, bitter man to his brother's wife.

The sight of the great house withstanding the anger of the sea was both awesome and frightening. There it stood, a reminder of a turbulent drama and grand romance of the past. She should hate it for what it stood for, for what it might come to mean, but she found she couldn't. It was both sad and maudlin, bittersweet and pitifully tragic, the last hapless stand of denial against pain. It was the Battle of Culloden Moor, the passing of the Gaelic tongue, the fading echo of the pipes. It beckoned to her with a flame of pageantry and the pride of the black Douglas. It called out to her to close her eyes and feel defiance and pain, to picture a desolate, treeless heath. It spoke to her in ways she could not express with words. Dear God, dear God, how it reminded her of home. Of Scotland.

"Are you all right, Miz Mackinnon?" Eli's voice cut through the silence.

"Aye," she said. "I'll only be a moment longer."

"Take all the time you need," Eli said as Maggie looked at him. She nodded and turned away.

Upon this jutting point, Adrian Mackinnon had built the crown of his empire, a house too magnificent to be called anything but a mansion. Huge and sprawling, it looked more like a hotel than a house. Homes of this size and magnitude were commonplace in Scotland and England, but out here, with nothing but ocean and trees and mountains for as far as the eye could see, it seemed odd and strangely out of place, as if she had stumbled upon the carcass of a giant whale bleaching in the middle of a desert with no explanation of how it came to be there.

She felt haunted by it. Her first instinct was to turn away and run, to leave this place, for she knew now, knew down to the very marrow of her bones, that always and everywhere there would be an eternal presence here, the shadowy memory of another woman.

What kind of man would build a house like this for himself in the middle of such a vast wilderness?

A man who had loved, and loved deeply. A man who could not forget. A man who built a monument to the past so he would remember. She shivered, and drew her cape more closely about her, but it did not help. The chill wasn't from the cold. It came from a premonition, a feeling that she was being inescapably drawn into the brooding passions of a romance long dead but not forgotten.

Maggie turned, and made her way back to the wagon. "I'm ready now," she said, and Eli helped her climb up.

The drive from camp had been a tedious one, and exhausting, most of her energy spent in keeping herself warm. Her feet, long ago too numb to feel much of anything, were tucked snugly beneath her skirts, in an effort to warm them. When, at last, the wagon topped the point and drew up in front of the door, she stood unsteadily, and clutched the back of the wagon seat for support.

Eli was already coming around the wagon toward her. "Excuse me, Miz Mackinnon," he said, and swept her into his arms before she could step down. Then, as if he wanted to explain away his bold actions, he said, "I should've done this back at camp and kept you from falling in the mud."

"You'll get your clothes dirty, Mr. Carr," she said.

"Don't mind that none, ma'am. Besides, you did a pretty fair job of cleaning the worst of it off yourself, and what's left is pert near dried."

He deposited her in front of the dark mahogany door. "I know you must be plumb wore-out . . . tired as a dog with eight feet," he said with a cheerful tone. "As soon as we're inside, I'll see what I can do to rustle you up some hot coffee."

Coffee. Maggie forced herself to smile. She liked tea. She

looked at the door, an inhospitable-looking barrier that stood between her and this house, and fought the urge to turn away, to run, before the doors opened and she was swallowed up in the shadow of another woman. She could not speak for the swelling tightness that came with the panic that clawed at her throat. Eli had mistaken her silence, her staid acceptance, as fatigue, or perhaps he knew, more than she, the ghost that awaited to greet her.

He opened the front door, drawing her inside with him. "Well, here you are," he said, looking around. "All brand-spanking-new and just itching for a woman's touch."

Maggie felt the dull throb of her own nails digging into the palms of her hands, and looking down, saw her knuckles were white and stiff from the tight grip she had upon the handle of her wicker basket. Nothing but silence greeted her; silence and long, eerie shadows that streaked across the glossy, unmarred floor. How different from the stone hallways of Glengarry Castle, worn smooth and dipped in the center from centuries of use.

"It's a bit much at first," he was saying, "catches you off guard, it does. It'll begin to feel like home in no time at all."

*Home?*

Maggie had never doubted anything more in her entire life. *You will like it here. You will. You will.* "Is there no one here?" she asked, finding her voice at last. "No one at home?"

"Only Wong, I suspect, but don't you go worrying none. He used to be the camp cook, but he's been taking care of the house good and proper since your husband hired a new cook. You won't have to fret about a thing. Wong does the cleaning, and Molly Polly helps out. Mostly she does the cooking."

Eli had moved out of the enormous foyer and into another room now, returning to the doorway and giving her a speculative look. As he watched her stand just inside the doorway, he saw a small, willowy figure in her mud-caked blue serge dress, clutching in her parchment-white hands a worn wicker basket, her face pale and smeared with mud.

Somewhere inside the house, a door closed. Footsteps approached. The light coming through the doorway was suddenly blocked, and Maggie looked up to see a woman of warriorlike proportions coming toward them. Her hair was thin and gray, twisted into such a small knot, it hardly seemed worth the effort. Her eyes were hazel, now looking almost yellow-green, and while not unkind, they were piercing and steady.

"This is Molly Polly," Eli said. "Her husband, Big John Polly, is the number two man here. She's the one I told you about, the one who does the cooking. Used to be the camp cook, along with Wong, but Adrian decided to keep her cooking for no one but himself."

"Only because I'm getting too old and too mean to get along with any of the kitchen help," she said. "Now, don't you go believing any of that whitewashing Eli's giving me. If I listened to him, I might start believing all that hoopla myself, and Big John says I'm hard enough to live with as it is."

"I'm pleased to meet you, Mrs. Polly," Maggie said.

"Saints above, I ain't been called Mrs. Polly since the day I was married. You can call me Molly, or Molly P., or even M.P., if you like."

Maggie noticed the way Molly was looking at her, not critical or unfriendly, but more like she was making a comparison. There was little doubt in Maggie's mind as to whom she was being compared with, and how she was quickly found to be lacking.

She looked around the room, seeing everything on the inside was as perfect and new as the stone and redwood exterior. "It's a lovely house. It seems quite new."

"It's not quite three years old. It took four years to build."

"Were you here then? When it was being built?"

"I've been here since Adrian and his brother Alex started their first camp."

A large yellow dog of dubious lineage came into the room, his nails clicking against the hardwood floor. He came up to Maggie and thrust his cold, wet nose against her hand, sniffing and inspecting until, apparently satisfied, he gave it a lick.

"That's Israel," Eli said. "He doesn't belong to anyone in particular, but he's sort of taken up with Adrian." He reached out and scratched Israel on the head. "We call him Israel because he's always wandering."

"Well, I didn't mean to keep you standing here in the middle of the floor like this," Molly said. "I can see you're pert near tuckered out. I imagine you'd like to rest." She looked at Maggie's muddy dress. "And maybe change for dinner."

"Aye, I wouldna like to come to dinner like this. It's been a long while since I've had a real bath," Maggie said.

"I'll put Israel out and see to dinner," Molly said.

"Oh, Israel is no bother," Maggie said. "I ken I'll find him to be good company."

Molly glanced at Israel. "He's company, all right, but I can't go vouching for how good he is." Looking back at Maggie, she said, "If he gets to be a bother, you can call me and I'll turn him out." She turned away, then paused. "I'll put some water on to heat for your bath, then I'll show you up to your room."

Molly left as abruptly as she had come.

Soon after Molly's departure, Eli exited, leaving Maggie standing in the hall. A moment later, Molly returned, showing Maggie to a bedroom upstairs.

Maggie bathed, changing into her dressing gown. The rest of the afternoon she spent unpacking. At half past eight she was summoned to dinner, and dined alone in the great dining room, where a table twenty feet long reflected the light of three massive chandeliers overhead.

After the dishes were cleared away, Molly came in. She stood silently for a moment, looking Maggie up and down. "I'll be heading on home now. Is there anything you need before I go?"

"No," Maggie said. "I think I can manage. Thank you."

"Well, Wong is about—if you should have need of him. Course, you'll have to go looking for him. Never in all my born days saw a body that could disappear like he does. Never know he's on the place. Moves through this house like a ghost, he does. Must be those little black shoes. They never make a sound. Nothing like these old clodhoppers of mine. You can hear me coming from a mile off." Molly paused, her eyes twinkling. "Well, here I go again, talking your leg off, and you so tired, you can't stand up straight. I'll be going on now."

She was left alone once again, in the great dining room, knowing that she and the Oriental man called Wong were the only two humans who remained in a twenty-room house.

Maggie sat at the table until the candles in the candelabra began to burn away, great masses of melted wax dripping down the base, hardening into strange shapes. She went to the sideboard and picked up a gold, two-branched candlestick. It was small and very heavy, but she could manage. She lit its two candles with one from the candelabra. After blowing out the candles on the table, she left the room.

Just before she reached the base of the enormous curving marble staircase, she decided to take a quick tour of the downstairs, finding the library and a room she could only think of as Adrian's study. Although each room was different, they all featured a great deal of what Eli had identified as primavera, the prized, honey-colored South American hardwood.

As she wandered around the great house, Israel padding

quietly at her side, she couldn't help thinking this would be her home for the rest of her life. Her children would grow to adulthood here, and here she would grow old, sipping tea in the quiet of the evening with the man she had married, a man she didn't even know. She reached down and gave Israel a good scratching behind the ears. He licked her hand eagerly. Her children would love him.

She continued on her tour, noticing a museumlike quality that made her uncomfortable. There was an odd, unused smell throughout, one that reminded her of a church on Sunday morning, when it is first opened after being closed over a long, wet week.

That didn't give her much bother. She would have pastilles burning, she told herself, just as soon as she unpacked her *cottage orné*. Then those musty smells would go away. From that moment on, the house would be aired and smelling fresh as the place it occupied, between the forest and the sea. She glanced around the room, imagining how it would all soon look with her own things scattered about.

In this room her children would play oranges and lemons in front of the carved mantel, and in the music room she could picture Barrie at the piano, her mouth held in that funny little grimace as it always was whenever she practiced her scales, while Ainsley pulled sheets of music from the rosewood Canterbury. In the library, her Staffordshire figure of Robert Burns and Highland Mary would rest upon the mantel, while her husband would prop his slippered feet on the richly covered needlepoint ottoman, patiently listening to Fletcher, whose hands were filled with an assortment of fishing poles, as he told about the big one that got away. And then later, at night, after she had put the children to bed, she would go up to their bedroom and take her gown from her chest, and after dressing and brushing out her hair, she would wait for her husband in a carved rosewood bed.

Her heart lurching at the thought, Maggie quickly pulled

her thoughts back, finishing her tour of the house, bypassing the dining room and kitchen, poking her head into the music room and then the parlor. Just before reaching the staircase again, she paused before two European-sized doors, distracted for a moment by the sonorous chimes of a long-case clock. The clock she recognized immediately as English, closer inspection telling her it was made by Joseph Windmills. Somehow, looking at its oak carcass covered with seaweed marquetry, she felt closer to home. How strange that she, a Scot to the core, and therefore not too enamored with anything English, would be comforted by the languorous ticking of an English timepiece.

Turning away from the clock, she opened the double doors and looked briefly at its panels painted with elaborate pastels of naked cherubs and clouds before stepping into the salon.

Holding the candlestick aloft, Maggie inhaled sharply. The room was breathtaking.

And so was the portrait of the woman in crimson velvet.

Immediately after she recovered from the shock of the enormous painting hanging over the fireplace, Maggie noticed something else. There was no musty, unused smell to this room as there had been to the library and other rooms of the house. This was a used room, a room someone had laid out and furnished with great care. This room was lived in and looked after, for already signs of wear were present in the scuff marks across the gleaming wooden floors and the stack of papers scattered across the top of a gateleg table, the familiar aroma of a gentleman's cigar. Her gaze rested for a moment on the box of cigars lying open on the table.

Maggie put the candlestick down and lit a nearby lamp. Taking the lamp in hand, she went to stand beneath the portrait. The sudden burst of light brought the painting to life, and the effect was electrifying. The colors were magnificent. It was as though the artist had just placed his brush upon his palette and stood back to survey his final touches. The pig-

ments burst forth with a riot of fairy-tale tints, where irides-
cent flesh tones were radiantly fresh against shades of auburn
hair blazing with copper fire. The marvelous flow of an exquisitely clinging red velvet gown swirled, light and vapor-
ous as gauze, around a body pulsing with life.

Out of the shadows of supposition, out of the mystery of
wonder, appeared reality. Katherine. A woman standing in
a regal pose, her hands resting on a table strewn with flowers,
as if she were about to touch them and give them purpose
and meaning. Her dress was red, but a deep, breathing red
that became dark as claret as it melted into wine-dark shadows; a dress that revealed a gently curved nape and the hollow at the base of her throat, then sloped gently over the
feminine curve of her breasts. The woman was beautiful, yet
her beauty was subtle and somewhat sad.

Who had painted this portrait and brought her to such
unexpected life?

Israel, who had been sitting quietly at her side, stood and
crossed the room. Suddenly she felt the presence of someone
in the room with her, and Maggie's attention was drawn away
from the portrait. Turning, she saw the huge, hulking figure
of Molly Polly standing in the doorway behind her.

Maggie's hand flew to her chest. "Och! You frightened
me."

"I'm sorry for that. I came back to check the candles in
the dining room. I had forgotten to tell you to blow them
out."

"I've already done that," Maggie said.

"Yes, I saw. I just came in here to tell you I was leaving
again. Didn't want the sound of me rustling around in here
to frighten you none."

Israel whined and went to Molly, sniffing her hand and
circling her twice before coming back to sit beside Maggie.
Molly looked at the portrait, but said nothing.

"Can I get you anything before I go?"

"No, nothing, thank you."

Molly looked at her for a moment, then slowly let her gaze glide back to the painting.

"It's a lovely portrait," Maggie said. "I was just admiring it."

Molly looked at it for a moment. "Yes," she said at last, "it is lovely. But not nearly as lovely as she was."

Maggie felt a catch in her heart. "You knew her."

"Yes. Quite well. She was a beautiful woman, inside and out. I was proud to call her my friend."

Maggie looked up at the portrait. Strangely, she felt no dislike, no hostility, toward this woman. "Aye, she is beautiful. I ken the artist is exceptional. He seems to have captured the fire and spirit of her."

"Yes, he has."

"Was it painted by someone well known?"

"It was painted by someone I know well . . . your husband."

There was no way to hide the jolt of surprise that registered on her face, or the paleness Maggie knew was left when the blood drained away in defeat. Her heart began to pound. "I didn't know. . . . I had no idea he was such an exceptional artist. His brother never mentioned it."

"Well, that's because Adrian isn't an artist—at least not in the sense you mean. That," she said, nodding toward the portrait, "is the only thing he ever painted."

Maggie studied the painting again. "It's hard to believe he's never painted before. The color, the detail . . . it's perfect, down to the exact hue of the draperies over the window. I knew immediately just where she was standing in this room when he painted her."

"Everyone feels the same way, yet, hard to believe as it is, Katherine was never in this room. She had been gone for quite some time when this house was built. And the painting was done before it was even started."

"He must have built it as a tribute to her."

"Katherine would have hated this house. It's nothing like her."

"Yet he built it for her."

Molly shrugged. "Perhaps. Adrian never knew Katherine, not really. He fancied her, thought himself in love with her, but he never knew her."

Maggie studied the portrait. "For a man who didn't know her, he certainly seemed to capture a lot of her on canvas."

"Superficial," Molly said, and the words poked at Maggie like the point of a knife. "He painted what he saw. Beauty. He didn't know Katherine's heart. If he had, he wouldn't have loved her so stubbornly all those years. Katherine was never meant for him. Those two would have never suited. If Katherine had married Adrian, they would have been like two mules hitched together, one straining to turn right, the other, straining just as hard to go left. She would have never been as happy here as she is in Texas. She's a lover of the land, just like Alex. She isn't a woman of visions and dreams."

"And Adrian is?"

Molly gave her a frank look. "He is. Are you?"

Maggie smiled at her candidness. She and this woman would get on well. "I'm a Scot, and Scotland is a place of visions and dreams. Although we love to wallow in the glories and moan about the tragedy of the past, we are a forward-looking people. We're born inventors, and astute in the sciences. We cling like lichen to the words of James Boswell. '*Spero meliora*, I hope for better things.' "

Before Molly could respond, Maggie swept her skirts aside and sat down, indicating with a sweep of her arm for Molly to do so as well. Leaning forward, her arms folded in her lap, she spoke with her customary frankness. "Tell me about my husband, about the visions and dreams that brought him to California."

Molly, looking reluctant, sat down. At first Maggie had to extract each bit of information, but before long, Molly was telling her about the days of the gold rush, and how Adrian and Alex came west, inflamed with the passion of promise, and how they struck it richer than they ever imagined. "It was Adrian that had his heart set on building an empire here in these redwoods. He saw his future here. Alex never wanted anything more than to be a farmer. He always planned on returning to Texas."

"To marry Katherine."

"No. To marry her sister, Karin."

Apparently the shock of surprise was well written across Maggie's face. "You don't know about Karin?" Molly asked.

"No. Ross didn't tell me much about Katherine, just that Adrian had always been in love with her, and his twin brother married her."

"Well, that much is true. It was a strange twist of events, and complicated as all get-out. Alex had his heart set on Karin. Adrian was in love with Katherine. Katherine fancied Alex."

"And Karin? Who did she fancy?"

"Herself, mostly. She married some wealthy man, one a lot older than she was, but from what I hear, she's happy with the choice."

"And with Karin married, Alex turned to Katherine."

"No. Alex married Katherine before all that." Molly sighed. "I can see you're primed to go the full distance, so I might as well tell you now, if I'm to have any peace." She shifted her large frame into a more comfortable position. "Alex and Adrian always fought like dogs and cats—something I suppose is quite normal for twin brothers—but one night they had a real knock-down, drag-out, and Alex, nursing his wounded pride, went off and got himself wasted. . . ."

"Wasted? You mean drunk?"

"Worse than drunk." Molly paused, her look reflective.

"Lord-a-mercy! I'll never forget the way they fought that night. I had to break them up with a chunk of kindling. After Alex got himself wasted, he wrote Karin a letter, asking her to come out here to marry him, only he wrote Katherine's name by mistake."

"And Katherine came."

"She did."

"Did Alex tell her what happened?"

"No."

"Why not?"

Molly sighed. "Partly because of Adrian and his threat to kill him if he did—although that wasn't the real reason, since Alex was never one to back down because of Adrian's threats. I s'pect this time it was because, deep in his heart of hearts, Alex knew Adrian was right. Katherine didn't deserve the humiliation and hurt that would be inflicted by telling her the truth."

"So she's never known. . . . After all this time, she's never known."

"Oh, she found out, all right, and it damn near cost her life. She went streaking out of here like her bloomers were afire. Alex went after her, but a grizzly got to her first." Molly paused. "You ever hear of a grizzly?"

Maggie shook her head.

"It's a bear, particular to these parts, and not like any bear you've ever seen. Some can reach over eight feet tall when standing. They're easily provoked and deadly when they attack. I've heard tell of them fighting when they've been hit with as many as twenty slugs of lead. It's almost impossible to bring one down unless you hit him in the right spot."

Maggie winced and turned her head away. "How dreadful."

"Yes," Molly said, her tone reflective. "There wasn't much we could do for her here, so they took her to San Francisco. Adrian and Alex stayed with her for a while there.

Alex knew he was in love with her by that time, of course, but he was too muleheaded to admit it. Katherine returned to Texas as soon as she was well enough to make the trip.''

"Alex didn't go?''

Molly shook her head. "He didn't know Katherine was leaving. But Adrian did.''

"And when Alex discovered Katherine was gone? Did he go after her then?''

"Not exactly. He hung around here for a while, looking as sad as a locked-up hound, before he decided to go after her. I've never seen a happier man in my life than Alex the day he sold his part out to Adrian and lit out for Texas.''

"Perhaps it was for the best, then.''

"Oh, it was that, all right, for things would have never been the same between Adrian and Alex after that. Alex was too resentful toward Adrian for knowing Katherine was leaving him and not trying to stop her.''

Maggie glanced at the lovely woman in the portrait. She could see why a man would follow her to the ends of the earth. She could see, too, how easy it must have been for Adrian to love her.

The immense room had grown uncomfortably warm. Suddenly Maggie wanted to be away from this reminder of another's love. She wondered what Molly would think if she were suddenly to spring to her feet and run from the room as fast as her feet could carry her. Then she wondered what had gotten into her for allowing her thoughts such liberties. She wasn't a woman to run from anything. She had always had her feet planted firmly on the ground and was mindful to keep her head out of the clouds. It shouldn't matter what Adrian's feelings for this woman had been in the past. He had married her, Maggie Mackinnon, and she intended to see that he did not forget, or regret, it.

As if reading her thoughts, Molly said, "I wouldn't worry none, if I were you. Like Adrian, Alex married a woman he didn't fancy himself in love with. In Alex's case, he found out later that he had married the right woman after all. God does that to us sometimes—doesn't give us what we want, but what we need.''

The quiet pensiveness of the room seemed to pervade her thoughts as Maggie said softly, ''Perhaps that is true, but I canna help wondering if I'm what he needs.''

''Only time will tell that,'' Molly said, matter-of-factly. Then she came to her feet and said, ''Here I've been blabbing my fool head off again, knowing all the while that Big John Polly is sitting at home wondering where in tarnation his supper is. What time would you like your breakfast?''

''Oh, please, there's no need to go to that much trouble for me. I can make my own breakfast.''

''It's what I'm paid to do,'' Molly said. ''If you don't have a preference, I'll have it ready at the usual time.''

''What time is that?''

''Five.''

Molly turned to leave, and Maggie cleared her throat. ''Is the option still open to choose a time?'' she asked. ''Because if it is, I'll settle for eight.'' As she spoke, she could swear she saw the curve of a smile wrapping itself around Molly Polly's mouth.

''I'll have scones and hot tea ready at eight.''

Surprised at those words, Maggie said, ''I would have never expected scones and hot tea to be your usual fare for breakfast here.''

''It isn't. This will be the first time.''

With that, Molly nodded her head curtly and left. It was the first indication Maggie had that Molly Polly went out of her way for anyone or anything.

Maggie turned back to the portrait. So she had been right. This never-ending feast for the eyes in crimson velvet was Katherine. Katherine, ghostly and yet so very real. She was just as Maggie would have imagined her, a woman of extraordinary elegance, a being of beauty seen in a tender light by the man who had loved her. A dream whose voice haunted and robbed him of sleep.

"This," she said softly, "is what stands between us. This is where it all begins."

# CHAPTER
## ❦ SEVEN ❦

Apparently Adrian Mackinnon was not very well versed in the Highlander's way of looking at things, for if he had known that his failure to return to camp for two weeks after Maggie's arrival was adding fresh peat to a well-stoked fire, he would have returned sooner.

It was early afternoon by the time Adrian and Eli rode up the narrow, winding road toward his house. Summer had come at last to redwood country; the sky was clear, and the sun overhead was bright and warm. Not one to become engrossed in his surroundings, Adrian would have never looked across the grassy, flower-strewn slope at all if something out of the corner of his eye hadn't caught his attention. Glancing toward the distraction, he saw a woman in white, her dress billowing out around her as she stood on a sunlit point, a summit of rusty-pink earth and sweet spring grasses, looking out across the haze of blue, sun-dappled ocean. He pulled up, ignoring the nervousness of a high-strung horse snorting and pawing the earth in his impatience to be home, and the jingle of bridle as he lowered his head and rubbed the throat latch against his foreleg.

Adrian felt as if he were seeing this particular patch of earth beneath a clear blue sky for the first time. His eyes

went to the woman, and he felt there was something funda-
mental here, something remindful of God and creation, of
the heavens and firmament, of Adam and his helpmate, Eve,
of the beauty and wonder that was woman.

He pondered his feelings for a moment. What was it about
this woman that evoked such a strong reminder of creation?

Feelings along this vein weren't such strange things for a
body to be thinking, but it was past strange if that body
happened to be Adrian Mackinnon, for he was not one to
ever have thoughts such as those. Adrian simply was not the
sort of man to dwell long upon a woman's appearance. God
created man and woman, and Adrian accepted it as fact.
What good did it do to think upon it? He had more important
things on his mind, and his philosophy was: If it doesn't
make money, it doesn't deserve much attention.

Intrigued, both with the woman and the strange feeling
that, at least for the moment, some of his shrewdness was
being superseded, he watched the woman make her way
down the hillside, her back slightly to him as she angled off
in the opposite direction.

He was both relieved and disappointed that she had not
seen him; disappointed that he could not see her face, relieved that his presence would not disturb and interfere with
her freedom, her almost uninhibited way of moving. He had
no way of knowing just how long he sat there, or even why
he did, captivated by a woman, slender, elegant, mysterious;
a gust of wind fluttering the gauzy thinness of a long veil
trailing from her hat, his attention on the way the wind
molded the fabric of her dress against a shapely length of leg
that went on forever, as she seemed to skim across the grass.
She looked soft and feminine. She was loveliness itself. She
was woman. His woman.

She also happened to be his wife.

His wife. The thought sobered him. His brows drew together in his customary way, one of a bold, almost contemp-

tuous, scrutiny. There was no doubt as to who this woman was, for he had known her immediately, as if she were something, some part of himself, that had been lost or misplaced, a part of himself he had suddenly discovered. He found that feeling strange. But even the strangeness of knowing who she was did not lessen the effect of surprise, the way she had suddenly appeared, her long, white dress trailing behind her, as if she had stepped out of a dream with all the unexpected charm of a childhood apparition. It struck him as strongly as the memory of Katherine.

"Uh . . . you still want me to come on up to the house?" Eli asked, clearing his throat and shifting uncomfortably in the saddle.

"What?" Adrian turned dazed eyes upon Eli, for until the moment Eli had spoken, Adrian had forgotten about him.

"The house. You still want me to come with you?"

"No," Adrian said, looking back at the woman. "We can go over those accounts another time. Seems I have more pressing business now."

Eli followed Adrian's gaze. "Yep, I'd say that you have at that. But don't you worry about meeting her none, about being nervous over her being a real, genuine lady and all of that. She's just like plain, ordinary folk, she is. Never met myself a Scot before, but I've been thinking they must not be so different from us, except for the strange way they have of saying things. You'll get a kick out of it, when you hear her talk. It's English, but then again, it ain't." Eli shook his head. "She's a wiry little thing. Kinda reminds me of a little terrier I had once. He weren't very big, but he didn't know that. Amazed me every time, how he could stand his own against dogs three times his size."

Adrian shot him a quelling look. "Surely you could find a better comparison for my wife than a dog," he said.

Eli laughed. "Well, maybe I could, although I don't think it would bother her none."

"It bothers me," Adrian said. "That should be enough."

"Well, at any rate, I think you'll like her. She's got what it takes. Came right in here and made up her mind to fit in, and by golly, she's done just that. Fell flat on her face in the mud, she did . . . her first day here, mind you, but that didn't stop her none. Pulled herself right up and marched on like nothing happened, bogging down in the mud, up to her elbows. Lost both of her slippers." He chuckled. "Must've weighed a ton, with all that mud, but she never said a word. Had every man in the outfit admiring her spirit. She's got what it takes," he said, nodding his head, as if agreeing with himself. "Yessir . . . she's got bottom, that one has. Real bottom."

"To hell with her bottom," Adrian said, not bothering to look at Eli, but keeping his eyes on the woman. "My interest lies in another direction entirely."

"Well, maybe you'll get that, too. . . . They say the squeaking wheel's the one what gets the grease."

Eli's words ringing in his head, Adrian turned back to look at his wife. Possessing a nature that was strictly business at best, he knew his first impulse was to confront her, to make her immediately aware of his arrival, to catch her off guard and gain control of the moment by doing so. Yet he could not compel his body to move with the same urgency that prompted his mind. He found himself oddly content to observe her—even more closely than before, as if he had only this moment in time to capture the essence of her, dreading, almost to the point of fear, that like an apparition, she would be gone all too soon and he would be left with nothing but a memory and the aftertaste of something sweet that had once lingered on a tongue accustomed only to tartness and vinegar.

Some yards behind her, she had abandoned an ivory-handled parasol, and her arms, he could see even from here, were filled with spring flowers. He felt inadequate and frustrated at his lack of knowledge, his inability to interpret each movement, each gesture. There was nothing out of the ordinary about her behavior that should intrigue him so; no throaty laughter, no cavorting, no frisky capers, no graceful arabesques, no whirling around until dizzy—nothing but simple, straight, fleeting lines of extraordinary elegance, the gentle and unexpected purity of beauty and woman, the sensitivity and mystery of God's gentler side. Her loveliness was delicate and disturbing and just a little terrifying. It was strange how bleak nature looked beside her, and it crossed his mind that Mother Nature should be jealous.

For the first time, he understood what Ross had meant when he had written, "She was born a lady—one look at her defines the word."

Here truly was a woman who would stand out, and she did so, even against the fleecy luster of a cloud.

For as long as he lived, he would never forget his first glimpse of her, the way he was overwhelmed by the lines of a woman's supple body graced by a simple dress of brilliant white, his sudden awareness of blended reflections, gentle shadows, and vivid, vivid light.

Captivated, he watched her turn slowly and walk farther down the grassy slope, gathering wildflowers, still quite ignorant of his presence. Life was such a realist painter, for in observing her for only a short time, he seemed to see and feel all the emotions of existence.

"Well," Eli said, clearing his throat again, "I guess I'll be moseying on back toward camp. I'll bring these figures by the office tomorrow."

"Right," Adrian said. "Tomorrow will be fine." When Eli made no move to leave, Adrian said, "Was there anything else?"

"No, I guess not."

Adrian opened his mouth, but Eli broke in. "I know, I know," he said, "it's time for me to make myself scarce, but I shore do hate to. Confrontations are something I don't like to miss. Especially the good ones.''

Adrian was looking at him strangely now. ''You expecting a confrontation?''

Eli chuckled. ''I do, but it won't last long, I suspect.''

''No,'' Adrian said, ''it won't.''

Eli laughed. ''I'd watch myself if I were you. The bigger a man's head, the bigger his headache.''

Eli turned his horse around, and put his hand respectfully to the brim of his hat. ''Good day to you then, Mr. Mackinnon,'' he said dryly. ''I'll be seeing you tomorrow . . . if you're up to it.''

Then, with a laugh, he urged his horse forward and rode out of sight.

Adrian watched Eli leave, then turned his horse off the road, feeling himself drawn toward her, imagining as he rode what her face would look like up close. He was frustrated at his inability to learn more about her just by watching her, as his shrewd, businesslike nature had taught him to do. The woman intrigued him. The charm had taken hold. As he drew nearer, momentarily blinded by the brilliant burst of midday upon the whiteness of her dress, he could not help but wonder how she would look naked, and turning toward him in the violet shadows of night.

His body stirred at the thought, and he curbed it. Adrian did not give in easily to emotion, and even less to passion. Control was his trump card, and he always held one in reserve. He studied the woman with a hard, arrogant glance, the same he used to intimidate when he felt vulnerable. One look at the woman on the hillside, and Adrian knew he was like an open wound.

Although still a few yards away, he could see she had been painting, her canvas still on the easel, an opened paint box filled with mixing pots, paints, and brushes sitting on the ground. He wondered if she had any talent for painting. Or was she one of those of little talent who took up the brush to wile away the hours of boredom?

Remembering she had been here for over two weeks made him feel just a little responsible for any boredom she might be experiencing, so he reminded himself that he was a busy man with a company to run, and it was best for her to learn early in their relationship that there were parts of his life that came first, before her.

He nudged his horse forward, knowing it was intimidating to those on the ground to be looked down upon from a superior height. By the time he rode up behind her, she was gathering her brushes. He pulled his horse up, thinking she was a daring little thing, painting as close to the edge of the cliff as she was, but he was too intrigued by her canvas, her almost naive attempt to paint the noble efforts of nature on a tiny square of cloth, to make any comment.

She hadn't noticed him yet, and he decided to wait, to see how long it would take her to feel his presence. He studied her canvas. He was certainly no judge of art, but he had seen enough, and purchased enough for his home, to know the pictorial quality of her work was no accident. Her painting possessed the potent charm of a child; simple and honest, unmarred by perplexing detail. With remarkable fidelity, she reproduced what she saw on canvas: a field of spring flowers, sunshine, waves breaking against dark, jagged rocks, all against the never-ending blue of the sky.

His study was broken by the clattering of a tin pot against rocks, and he looked toward her in time to see one of her pots go bouncing and rolling across the rocks, dangerously close to the edge, where it teetered for a moment.

She moved quickly, so quickly that he didn't at first realize she intended to go after the tumbling pot. He reacted with instinct born of desperation, leaping from his horse and moving behind her with a swiftness that surprised even him, one arm lashing about her waist and jerking her against him as he turned them both away from the edge of the cliff as the pot, caught by a sudden gust of wind, tumbled over and vanished from sight.

For a blurred instant, Maggie had a glimpse of the jagged rocks and pounding surf that lay below, then she felt herself wrenched backward, the breath slammed from her as she contacted with something solid.

Adrian swore swiftly. This wasn't exactly the kind of meeting he imagined for their first encounter. He felt the weight and warmth of her in his arms and became uncomfortable. He found this woman unsettling, almost annoying. He wanted to shake her until her teeth rattled. He wanted to hold her closer than he held her now. He felt angry and he didn't understand why. Was it because of the way she felt in his arms, the feelings her closeness brought to the surface?

Adrian had never known fear like this before. The fear of losing her before he came to know her caused him to react more harshly than he intended. He knew he should be gentle with her. She was, after all, a woman, and more than likely, terrified. And she *had* come damnably close to going over the cliff with that paint pot of hers. She would probably burst into tears any moment. The thought of tears did not sit too well with him. It also removed any thought of gentleness. Anger was a good foil for tears, and anger was something he was feeling right now. It was also something he was comfortable with. He had no experience with the softer emotions. "God spare me a foolish woman," he said. "Were you intending to kill yourself? Or were you hankering to spend the rest of your life in bed, an invalid?"

The moment he spoke the words, he gritted his teeth. Why had he spoken as he had? He had no reason to be so hard on her. She was his wife. What was he trying to do, run her off? He searched his mind for something to say, some soft sentiment, the kind a woman would love, but he had no skill with either.

He might have gone on, feeling this bumbling inadequacy, but she picked that moment to turn her head, looking at him, and he released her abruptly. What he saw staggered him.

She was not beautiful.

But she was angry. "What I wasna hankering for was to spend two weeks here, alone," she said, pulling away and setting her clothes right. "You may be a wealthy, important man, Mackinnon, but you dinna have any manners."

That drew him up short. "If you wanted manners, you should have stayed in Scotland," he said, then cursed himself for letting her bait him.

"Aye, or married a butler."

Adrian blinked a time or two at the way she spoke. This was a woman to be reckoned with. He was accustomed to always being in control, if not having the upper hand, and he didn't exactly like the fact that this new wife of his was not only holding her own, but causing him to make a fool of himself in the process. Her very presence bothered him. She made him feel odd, even awkward, unsure of himself, unsure of what to say, or how to say it. *Manners*, he thought. Of all the things he expected a woman to want, it never occurred to him it would be manners. She was a real, genuine lady— with a title. Where in the world would he get the kind of manners she wanted? He had never felt so bungling and ill suited for the task at hand. Loggers, he could talk to. Or even Molly or Israel. But a genuine lady? "We haven't time for such niceties as manners here," he said in his defense. "California is rough and uncivilized."

"Aye, I ken it's a lot like the people."

He almost smiled at that. She had a sharp mind and a keen wit. She wouldn't be boring. That pleased him more than he could say. He felt his anger drain away, and even some of his initial disappointment over the fact that she was not beautiful. "You're quite outspoken for such a little thing."

"Aye, it's a family trait."

"Mmmmmm," he said thoughtfully. "That surprises me."

"Why?"

"For some reason, I thought a well-bred lady would know how to control her tongue."

This was said with such an overtone of infuriating amusement that she felt her irritation mount. She opened her mouth to tell him what she thought of him, then closed it. But she couldn't restrain herself for long. "Don't you appreciate honesty, or is it that you don't like a woman who speaks her mind?"

He looked her over, up and down, quickly. "I have an appreciation for honesty. As for the other, I can only say . . . Never mind. I suppose I have Ross to thank for it. Our tastes always were different."

"If you ken that, why did you ask him to find you a wife?"

"It was a sudden impulse—as a man who drinks poison, or shoots himself."

There it was again, that maddening tone of amusement in his voice, as if he were intentionally provoking her. "Perhaps you should have tried poison."

His smile was like a Highland winter. "You've a sharp tongue," he said. "I trust you know how to control it." He said nothing further, but stood looking down at her, a brown-haired stranger with penetrating blue eyes and a hard mouth. She shivered at the impact.

"You're chilled." His eyes swept over the thinness of her dress. "You shouldn't have come out here in such light clothes. The wind is brisk here."

"Like the conversation."

He lifted a dark brow, but said nothing, his eyes going over her slowly, as if reassessing what they had seen earlier. The woman was no beauty, but the realization did not seem to matter. The short time he had held her had been enough to burn the memory of a superbly slender figure, curved and swelling in all the right places, upon his mind, and *dear God! What eyes!*

They weren't the clear green he remembered so vividly from Katherine, but a strange hue—neither green nor brown, but somewhere in between—alive and flashing, intelligent, and certainly not in any way soft and tender, as a woman's eyes should be. Her nose was small and slender—too small and slender to be considered classic—and her mouth was too full and too wide.

That same mouth was too set, too firm, too resolute, for a woman. He had seen that kind of mouth often in men he had business dealings with, and they were always the most difficult to deal with, to get off center, and always the most reluctant to see things his way. This was a face to do battle with, a face composed of too many strong angles that blended into a determined chin. There was too much honed strength there, he realized, too much understanding, too much patience, and more than enough willpower to see things through. It was a face too dauntless to be beautiful—*and he had requested a beautiful woman.* He made no effort to hide the fact that he was surveying her critically, nor was he concerned that his disappointment was so obvious.

"You are disappointed," she said. "You expected beauty."

"It doesn't matter. I'll get used to it. It isn't the first time I didn't get what I wanted."

He saw the gleam of humor deep in her oddly colored eyes. "Well, the devil's bairns have the devil's luck," she said.

If Adrian had not been taken so off guard by her plainness and the odd way she said *well*, so that it sounded like *wheel*, he might have come back at her, but this woman had him coming and going. He didn't know which end was up. Completely flustered now, all he could do was stare.

He did not like this woman. She was too outspoken by

half, and yet the image of her on a wind-swept hillside stayed with him.

She was most assuredly not what he had in mind when he wrote that letter to Ross. Yet something about her reached out to him. *Her eyes*, he thought, they were the eyes of a stranger, the kind of eyes a man could lose himself in, for to look at them was like stepping through a mirror into her very soul. He saw so much there, determination, understanding, gentleness, goodness, a cloudy residue of pain—things he did not want or need from her.

Anger rose within him, tingling like an itch on the end of his fingers—something that wanted release, or at least retribution. His look turned cynical and hard, and when she looked back at him, he saw the wide-eyed stare of awareness and he knew he had his retribution. His thoughts were astonishing to him. She might be graceful and lovely to watch. He might be married to her. He might even go so far as to say he desired her.

But he did not like her.

He wasn't a very experienced man as far as women were concerned, but it didn't take an experienced man to know about women like this. Even with his limited exposure to the fairer sex, he knew about women who looked for a man to attach themselves to like a leech; women who would drain the life from a man; women who gained strength from a superior position, from the vantage point of being able to lord it over a man; women who had that sly, knowing smile. He had never admired this kind of strength in a woman. With open frankness, he let his eyes roam over her.

The sound of her voice startled him, coming out of the silence that had enveloped them, for the world seemed to quiet and go still, save for the sound of the wind whispering and dancing through tall, silky grasses.

"It's a little late to change your mind, Adrian, if that's what you're thinking."

Adrian was taken aback. The sudden use of his name had caught him off guard. She turned those devilish eyes upon him and smiled, the stubborn angles of her face melting into enchanting softness. The corners of her mouth lifted with amusement. She might be smiling, but he knew the strength that lay temporarily passive within her, ready to spring with sudden ferocity at a moment's notice. She lifted her brows slightly, as if waiting for him to make a further fool of himself. The way things had been going, she wouldn't have long to wait.

She shook her head, as if disbelieving what was going on here. And why shouldn't she? He didn't believe it himself. Things were definitely not off to a good start, but he'd pay hell knowing how to back things up a bit and start over. They weren't exactly off on the wrong track here; it was more like the whole damn train had been driven off a cliff.

Adrian watched her, feeling a powerful rush of blood to his head that left his mind muddled.

"I'm afraid I'll have to disagree. It's *never* too late. Not even in marriage." He paused a moment, expecting her to respond. When she didn't, he went on. "The fact that you are my wife doesn't necessarily signify permanence, does it?"

He thought he saw a spark of anger flare in her eyes, but if he had, it was quickly overridden by a gleam of humor. "Aye," she said with infuriating calmness, "it doesna—no more than drawing a breath implies you will live long enough to draw another one. All we can do is hope."

"Hope? Is that what you were doing? Hoping to draw another breath by flirting with death at the edge of these rocks? If it was, then you have a muddled sense of reasoning."

"Aye, and it brought me here to be your wife," she said, as if feeling a pinch of anger over the way he came blundering into her life like a well-meaning sheepdog, tripping over his big feet.

"I am as fond of life as anyone," she went on to say. "I was trying to catch my paint pot before it rolled over the edge," she said, her voice clear and strong. Then, looking at him squarely, she added, "I would have had it, too, if you hadna interrupted me with your rescue."

Adrian frowned. "What you would have had is your head split on one of those rocks below," he said. "No pot of paint is worth that risk."

"My home was among cliffs such as these. I played around them as a child. My father always said I was a surefooted lass. I never came close to falling."

Adrian felt as if he had just ridden full speed into a rock wall. She disappointed him. She angered him. She made a fool out of him. She was not what he wanted, yet looking at her, he felt a quickening, a rapid surge to his pulse that he knew did not belong there. He couldn't be feeling desire for her.

He couldn't.

He gave her another one of his unpleasant smiles. "Although I admire your overstoked sense of confidence, I should remind you that there's always a first time."

His eyes swept over her. A sudden urge to jerk her into his arms and kiss her silly made him come back at her harder than he intended. "I can see that aside from being different, my brother's taste in women is also less . . . particular."

"Aye," Maggie said. "I know all about your taste in women." Her words were a reminder that she could mention his thwarted desire for his brother's wife and cut him to the bone.

"I should warn you," she was saying, "that one can be particular to the point of obsession."

He flinched. A hot flush spread across her cheeks. "I beg

your forgiveness," she said, her voice laced with genuine regret. "I canna always control my tongue."

"I've had plenty of proof of that," he said, then his tone softened and he sighed. "The fault was mine, I suppose. I had no business provoking you. I shouldn't be surprised you retaliated with anger. I seem to have that effect upon most people." His apology struck her as hard and bitter.

"Having no knowledge of your surefooted past, when I saw you dangerously close to the edge of the rock, I feared for your safety. I didn't mean to be so rough. Are you all right?"

She smiled, the smile fading when he did not return it. "I dinna break anything . . ." she said, then noticing the jagged edge of a torn nail, she added, "major."

"You're fortunate in that, at least. You shouldn't be out here, this close to the rocks. This is no place for a woman. If I were you, I'd gather up my play-pretties and get myself home before I did something really foolish."

"It's a little late for that now." Her eyes swept over him. "Fools rush in," she said, and started to laugh.

He did not share in the hilarity of it, and Maggie thought about that. The suddenness of his appearance to jerk her away from the cliff's edge had momentarily stunned her; the force of his anger, his curt castigation, left her a bit confused. Here she had been at his home for two weeks, much of that time spent in a brown study, where she played out the dramatics of their first meeting. In all the instances of her imaginings—where she saw herself perfectly groomed and draped upon a piano bench, or some other equally sublime setting—she had never, not once, considered that she would be greeted by an ill-tempered man who had jerked her by the scruff of the neck from what he thought to be the jaws of death, then rounded on her reproachfully, ordering her home with all the ire of an aggravated schoolteacher.

It had been some time since she had been ordered home

in punishment, and the almost theoretical aspect of it was more than she could contain. She bit her lip and reminded herself it would not do to raise the ire of her husband on the occasion of their first meeting—at least not any more than she already had. That reminder produced a valiant effort to stifle the urge to laugh outright.

He looked at her hard, the clenching of his jaw telling her he was well aware of her urge to laugh again, but his eyes never softened toward her. In spite of his aloofness, his coldness, she was unable to dismiss him and look away. There was something arresting about his face; something besides the fact that he would have been a devilishly handsome man if it weren't for the cold, cynical expression he directed at her.

"We aren't getting off to a very good start, are we?" she asked suddenly. "Shall we try again?"

"Leave it be," he said sharply. "We might do worse the second time."

She laughed. He had a nice, masculine voice, but the tone was one to make a banshee shudder. She wasn't daunted, however. To a Highlander, time took care of all things, and by tomorrow this first meeting, unpleasant as it might be, would become another matter entirely.

"Aye," she said, smiling in spite of herself, "I ken we might at that." His nearness, and the knowledge that he had been watching her, made Maggie's heartbeat flutter with an oddly unsteady beat.

She watched the way his deep-set eyes moved over her, missing nothing.

"Do I pass muster?" she asked quite frankly, not hatefully, not with spite, but simply as one would ask a straightforward question.

"Does it matter what I think?" He watched her closely, as if looking for a look of contempt, but she gazed at him with gentleness.

"Aye, it might," she said, feeling the spread of something warm and distracting, something she could only akin to pity— not so much pity for him, for a man of his looks and wealth deserved none, but pity for the loneliness she sensed inside of him, the things that were missing in his life that left him cynical and hard and unfulfilled. But most of all, pity for the thing in him that drove him to fill his life with wealth and possessions, not knowing these things never made their way into a human heart.

"Are you fishing for a compliment?"

"Would I get one, if I was?"

He laughed. "Probably not. What is beauty anyway? I always heard a little powder and a little paint made a woman what she ain't."

This man might have never set foot on Scottish soil, but it was apparent he had a Scot's fine sense of the value of provocation and the overwhelming tendency to proceed to the logical extreme and then take a stand. Too bad he didn't understand what she had been through, her very fight for existence, her ability to survive on precious little and be glad of it without expecting more. Self-sufficiency and independence were bred into her. And to top that off, she had never thought of herself as beautiful, so his similar feelings were neither surprising nor shocking.

She could tell it surprised him when she laughed.

"Aye, I ken I'm no beauty, as you said. But that could work to your good. Beauty in a wife, I'm told, terrifies a husband. At least I willna be in danger of being stolen away." Then, with abject honesty, she said, "I'm sorry if you're so verra disappointed."

Maggie took advantage of his bewildered pause, using the time to study him as critically as he had been observing her. He was taller than his brother Ross, and more slender. She saw none of Ross Mackinnon's glossy black hair and pale eyes, but a thick head of golden-brown hair and the darkest blue eyes she had ever seen.

From the moment she had first looked at him, she had known him as stubborn, obdurate, and staunch and sturdy as the ancient redwoods that lay beyond them. He struck her as remarkable, and quite unlike any man she had ever met. He was hard as Grampian stone and brooding as a Scottish mist.

She liked him immediately.

She was wise enough to not let him know that. She was also wise enough to know it would not be easy for her. She willed herself to be calm, to hold back her anger over his churlish disregard for her by not coming sooner, for there was no doubt that his two-week delay had been intentional. Like the wind, he threatened, hoping to buffet her and send her scampering on her way like a leaf driven. She tilted her face into the breeze and inhaled, feeling the wind's strength in her lungs. Then, turning, she faced him squarely, as her ancestors had faced peril countless times in the past—steady, decided, unswayable, unwilling to concede defeat, impervious to wind, the angry battering of the sea, the gloom of mist, the loneliness of the moors, the cunning of the English, and the ravages of time.

Maggie regarded him in confused silence. Never would she have pictured the man who wrote those letters to be so ruggedly male, so powerfully built. Such sensitivity belonged to a smaller man, a man of more meager looks. How could a man write such sensitive, caring letters and then appear so hard and callous?

She eyed him critically. There was nothing, absolutely nothing, either gentle or caring about this blue-eyed brute. By the wife of Job, she had never seen a more cynical man. His mouth was tight and aggressive. His look was one that could freeze a boiling pot. From where she stood, he seemed hard, arrogant, conceited, self-sufficient, and bossy. She sighed. It was too much. She had had too much to do, of late, with brokers, bankers, advocates, and the Presbyterian aristocracy, and now she was having to deal with this sour-faced American. It was just too much.

From out of nowhere sprung her father's voice, the memory of something he said coming to her so vividly, she could have sworn he was standing beside her. "We Scots can be a cantankerous race. Our intellectual pleasure seems to lie in disagreement."

If that was true, then here truly was a man who, although he had never set foot on Scottish soil, was Scot to the core in personality and attitude. If this man wanted to hold to his own loyalties of the past, then she wasn't one to stand in the way. He wasn't the first to draw attention to his divided self, and how could she chastise or condemn a man for exhibiting myriad-mindedness and being essentially Scottish?

She turned away from him and began gathering up her paint pots.

"Where are you going?"

She turned back toward him, her hands busily screwing the lid on a pot of carmine red. She wondered if she should tell him she was merely exercising another Scottish trait, practical judgment. "I believe I was ordered back to the house a few minutes ago."

That drew him up short. He glanced around, taking in all the paints, the canvas, the easel, her discarded parasol. "You came out here alone?"

"No," she said, sweeping an errant strand of hair from her face. "I had that faithless dog, Israel, with me."

Adrian surveyed the area. Israel was nowhere in sight.

"He's a fickle one," she said, closing the lid on her paint box, "abandoning me for the first rabbit he saw."

He smiled, and she suddenly saw why he didn't do it too often. Women wouldn't be able to stand it if he did. He had a smile that would melt butter, a smile women would fight over. Suddenly she felt warm all over. The blood drummed in her veins. Tension crept into her muscles. At first she thought it to be anger, but some tingling sense of awareness reminded her that the irregular fluttering of her heart, the slight tremor in her hand, was not due to her irritation, but to his nearness.

He stood towering over her, his dark blue eyes alert and watching. The collar of his shirt was open, the skin beneath lightly tanned. *And probably warm.* The hot glare of afternoon caught glints of gold and red in the soft layers of his hair, now ruffled by the wind. He looked composed and in control, but there was something about him that called out to her, something that told her he wasn't as he would have her believe, something that she called sad, and, too, perhaps, lonely. Maggie looked quickly down, rubbing at a smudge of paint on her hand, all too aware that she had been looking at him quite frankly, knowing he had not missed the hot flush of color that rose to her face.

Her husband had a manner that was rough, even caustic, but he was strong and vital and virile, and all warm, living man. She felt a wave of loneliness that left her almost dizzy. His presence reminded her of too many things she had been without. She missed the closeness of marriage. She missed the warm contentment that comes with living with a man, of sleeping with him. She missed the intimacy, the soft looks, the gentle caresses. She missed the sleepy, sated feeling that comes after making love.

She almost missed his next comment.

"Israel has never been trained for obedience. He doesn't know the first thing about what's expected of him," he said.

*A lot like his master* . . . She was positive there was never a man to douse the ardor of a woman quite so completely as this man had just done. Here she had her thoughts on intimate things, and he was talking about a dog. *If* she and this man were to ever understand each other, the first thing they had to do was find a way to have their minds in the same pony cart. As things stood now, they were miles and miles apart. "Then Israel and I have a great deal in common," she said.

His mouth tightened, growing white at the corners. "Do you always say exactly what you think?"

"Aye. Does it bother you?"

"Frankness isn't something I can say I've exactly admired in a woman."

"From what I've seen, you don't admire much of anything."

"Oh, I have an eye for beauty," he said, turning slightly. "Take this horse here. Now, that's beauty."

She smiled. She wouldn't fash herself, or draw her claymore over that comment. She was too smart to be lured into something as obvious as that. Her father had always taught her not to show all her troops, to keep some in reserve. "Like we decided earlier, we don't seem to be doing very well. I ken it's time for me to go. Perhaps we can try again at dinner. I am invited to dinner, aren't I?"

He saw the humor dancing in her eyes. This woman was irritating enough to throttle. Hell's bells. She had him all fidgety. He stared at her hard, as if, by doing so, he could send her running, terrified and screaming, back to the house. Then the strangest thing happened. As he stared, he became distracted—something Adrian never did—by her eyes, of all things. A moment ago he had called her eyes green. Now, her face turned toward the sun as it was, they looked golden brown. She had to be a devil. No human could change the color of her eyes. She tilted her head around, her face suddenly in shadow. The eyes were green now. *Just what the hell color are they anyway?* Confused, he said the first thing that popped into his head. "Humor in a woman isn't a virtue."

"Neither is rudeness in a man."

*Thunderation.* Was she always so quick with back talk? If she was, she wasn't going to be as easy to live with as he'd hoped. He hadn't been with her more than a few minutes, and already he was questioning his wisdom in taking a wife. He'd better say something to shock the ruffles off her drawers, something to put her in her woman's place, a place he called submission. His eyes swept over her. "You aren't what I expected."

*There, that ought to do it.*

She laughed. "I must confess you are no what I expected either."

*What kind of woman is this?* "Ross neglected to write that you were so outspoken. I don't—"

"Like outspoken women," she finished for him. "Would you be attracted more to a liar? A woman who practiced deceit? Do either of those hold any appeal for you?"

He grinned slyly. He had her now. He would play with her a little, the way he played with salmon before he brought them in. "Are you asking me, or warning me?" he asked softly.

"Neither," Maggie said, and turned away, folding up her easel and tucking it under her arm, her canvas in her hand. "That's the one thing I canna do anything about." She picked up her paint box just as he reached for it.

"I'll take that," he said, his hand brushing against hers. The contact startled them both. He jerked his hand back. She dropped the paint box. They leaned over simultaneously. Their heads bumped. He straightened and looked at her. She did the same.

He felt caught off guard. Adrian never liked for anyone to best him, or have the advantage, not even by a slight edge. He was a wealthy, powerful, and influential man who ruled his empire like a king. He never came in second.

At least not anymore.

All his life he had taken a backseat to his brother. Alex was born first, and somehow that one quirk of fate had set the pattern for the rest of their lives. Alex was the stable one, the twin who always laughed. He was the one who was noticed, the one who demanded respect and got it, the one who had the even temper, the easygoing nature, the brand of looks that turned a woman's head. He was a looker and a teaser, and women adored him. He was a charmer and a flirt, and women loved it. He had said he loved Karin Simon, and yet he had married her sister Katherine.

And Adrian had sworn he would never come in second again. From that moment on, he would be first. He would be the best, the richest, the most powerful. Whatever he owned would be the finest, the most expensive, the envy of all who came his way. Never again would he be given the scraps, the leftovers. He had loved once, and loved powerfully, and losing her to his brother had almost destroyed him. Even now, after so many years, the memory of Katherine burned like a brand upon his mind; Katherine in her innocence, her purity, the way she had been before Alex had taken her.

And that had been the way he had painted her.

Adrian lifted his head and gazed somberly at the sun dropping slowly into the ocean. He continued to do so, even after he knew Maggie had trained her gaze full upon him and now had her damned changeable eyes locked on him.

"If you and I are going to get on and live together as man and wife, we're going to have to do better than we're doing. Perhaps we might talk again tonight, at dinner, after you've had a chance to rest and clean up."

He looked down at his clothes, then turned on her. "Do you detest the sight of honest labor, madam?"

"What I detest is the way this conversation is going. I merely thought to suggest another time, hoping it might be more to your liking." She leaned forward and snatched up her paint box, turning to leave.

"I'm not through talking to you."

"Then we have a problem, for I'm no in the habit of being dismissed."

"You're my wife," he said, as if that one fact should make her submissive.

She paused, turning. "Aye, I am your wife, but I came with a marriage certificate, *not* a bill of sale."

Maggie knew when there was a storm brewing, and the idea of crossing broadswords with this accomplished man was both terrifying and exhilarating. But something told her that jumping into a fight with him now wasn't the wisest way to go about things. He was cynical and a bit of a hothead. If she gave in to her temper, she would be a hothead as well. Two hotheads never resolved anything, as far as she knew. One of them must be calm and levelheaded. Thanks be to God that He had seen fit to give her a liberal dose of both. Patience and understanding would serve her far better than a temper and hostile words.

When her thoughts gradually wandered back to him, she noticed he was looking at her strangely. She also noticed some of the bluster had gone from him. When he spoke, his tone was almost cordial. "My brother wrote that you're a titled lady, and educated."

"Aye, I willna disappoint you there, I ken."

"And your father is a duke."

"My father isna quite that high on the peerage charts. He is an earl."

"You don't seem to be the sort of woman who would marry a man by proxy and sail around the globe to live in a wild, savage land with a man you've never met."

"And you dinna seem to be the kind of man to order a wife through the mail."

"How did my brother find you?"

"He didna find me. I've known Annabella and Ross for several years. After reading your letter and the list of things you were looking for—quite a *long* list, I must say—they decided I was the perfect choice. They came together, to my father's home, and made the offer to me.''

''And you accepted.''

She dipped low in a curtsy. ''Aye, as you can see, for I am here.''

She turned toward the house and began walking. He took the easel and the paint box from her and walked at her side, leading his horse.

''I didna accept right away,'' she went on to say. ''That isna the sort of thing a lady would accept right off, you ken.''

''I wouldn't think it was the sort of thing a lady of your breeding would accept at all. What softened you to the idea? My brother's convincing persuasion, or the fact that I'm a very wealthy man?''

''Neither. It was your letters, some twenty or thirty of them written over the past ten years. After reading them, I felt I knew more about you, knew you as a person, understood you.''

He stopped, not looking at her, but staring out over the rippling expanse of water. ''If you understood me, madam, you would have chosen not to come.''

''If you understood me, you would know that is precisely why I did.''

His eyes returned to her, probing her face, the depths of her eyes. ''Something isn't right here,'' he said. ''I'm not sure what it is, but something isn't right.''

''Is that to be your excuse then, your reason for sending me back?''

''I won't have to send you. Sooner or later, you'll choose to leave of your own accord.''

Maggie locked eyes with him for a moment. There were so many thoughts of him running through her mind. Her heart began to hammer.

''Are you so certain?''

''I am.'' He turned away, walking briskly.

Her heart went out to this man, and she suddenly understood that she would be good for him. She would be something constant and permanent in his life, someone he could depend upon. Although she shuddered at the comparison, Adrian did remind her of a little dog she had found and brought home with her as a child. It was a small terrier that had been so abused that it growled and snarled whenever anyone came near. For weeks Maggie had fed the dog, sitting on the stoop, watching him eat, speaking to him in soft tones. Gradually the dog had allowed her near him without baring his teeth at her. Over a period of weeks, her persistence, her gentle care and loving hand, had proven stronger than the memory of pain and abuse. From the moment he had first licked her hand, he had been a devoted friend, loyal and protective of her for sixteen years until his death.

With a flood of tender understanding, she followed him, keeping the pace. "I'm no a quitter, Adrian." Her hand came out to touch his sleeve. He stopped abruptly, turning only his head to stare at her. She dropped her hand. "I willna leave unless you ask me to. I dinna go back on my word, and I willna break my vow."

He watched the way she regarded him, the dying light from the sun fanned around her like an aura, her eyes searching his questioningly, as if she had been mistress of the big, sprawling house on the bluff for years, and he was being considered for hire. He remained quiet.

That didn't seem to bother her, for she smiled, her teeth even and white. "It's a pity you dinna have the same privilege I did, that you couldna have a bundle of my letters by which to know me."

"My brother wrote me all I need to know of you."

Her face changed, but she maintained her composure. "Aye, Ross said he would post a letter to you. What did he say? That I fulfilled your requirements for a wife?"

"He said you would be able to give me children. I have

built an empire here. I want someone to leave it to. *That* was the reason I sought a wife. I put that in the list Ross showed you, so it should come as no surprise. You would do well to remember that and refrain from trying to embellish it.''

''There is nothing wrong with wanting children, Adrian.''

Her voice was low. He felt a stab of desire. ''Perhaps you misunderstood,'' he said after a pause. ''That was my *sole* purpose for wanting a wife.'' He didn't know why he was persisting as he was, why he wanted to jar her composure. Unless it was to ruin the sense of peace that surrounded her.

He needn't have concerned himself. She wasn't jarred. ''It's an honest reason, I ken, and a valid one. I love children and I greatly admire honesty.''

''Then if it's honesty you want, I'll tell you now not to expect any of the ordinary things from me that go along with marriage. I have no intention of falling in love. Ever.''

''Why?''

His eyes narrowed and his voice was cold, hurtful. ''Because I'm still in love with my brother's wife.''

She flinched from his mention of his brother's wife. It suddenly occurred to her how happy she should be that he was being completely honest with her. A visible foe was much easier to defeat than an invisible one. Besides, she had known all about Katherine before she agreed to marry Adrian.

''Does that shock you?'' he asked, feeling the urge to choke her when she smiled up at him.

''No, it doesna,'' she said. ''Is it supposed to?''

He shrugged. ''You take it the way you take it.''

''Then I canna say I'm shocked. Ross told me about Katherine,'' she said softly, ''before I came.''

The look of incredulity on his face made her heart leap with joy. ''And still you married me?''

''Aye.''

''Then you are a fool.''

"Perhaps."

"Why?" he asked. "Why would you marry a man you knew to be in love with someone else?"

"I had my reasons."

"I'm sure you did," he said, "but I can't help being curious to know what they were."

"They were basically the same as yours."

"Children?"

"Loneliness."

About that time, Israel, winded from his chase, came loping over the hill toward them, running and barking.

Maggie drew up short, her hand resting on Israel's warm, golden head as she watched Adrian lengthen his stride and pull ahead of her. He was a strange one, all right, with more layers than an onion.

*Hout! Onions could be dealt with.*

*An onion made you cry when you cut it, but there were no tears when you peeled it, layer by layer.* She almost laughed outright at the thought that she was comparing her husband to an onion.

Yet, there were worse comparisons.

*Aye, there are, at that.* Her eyes rested on the hind end of Adrian's horse.

Clapping her hands over her mouth, she stood and watched him walk away, unable to find anything but humor in his sudden display of almost childlike anger.

It wasn't anger that spurred Adrian on, but the shock of reality. For over ten years he had been his own man, organizing his life in such a way that no one would ever be instrumental in guiding the course of his life as Alex and Katherine had once done. By the time they had returned to Texas, Adrian had come to realize that being in control of his own life was of utmost importance. The sudden shock of reality had come just moments before, when he realized abruptly that by his marriage to this determined yet soft-spoken woman, he had enlarged the sphere of his life to include another person, that now he had to consider another being when making the decisions that affected his life.

Once he reached the steps of the house, he turned to find she was no longer following him, but had propped her canvas against a boulder, so she could give her attention to Israel—throwing a stick, then laughing as he bounded after it, only to come loping back to her, dropping the stick at her feet, barking and jumping his encouragement to throw it again, which she did.

She was an accommodating creature, one who could be riled, but not easily so, with, it seemed, infinite patience and a forgiving nature. He could have done worse, he supposed.

Again and again, he watched her throw the stick, laughing at Israel's antics.

*She will be good with children.*

His eyes blazed a deep cobalt blue, dark and brooding with the shadows of pain and regret. He sought Maggie, taking in the fiery blond of her hair against the red-gold tones of evening sun that streaked the sky.

He hated reddish blond hair.

As far as Adrian was concerned, hair should be blond or it should be red, and not just red, but the rich, coppery red that was Katherine's hair. This woman's hair was neither.

He watched Maggie pick up her easel and run toward the house, Israel barking at her side. Breathless, she stopped beside Adrian, just as he turned to open the door.

"Will you be coming down to dinner?" he asked, knowing, after the way their first meeting had gone, that she would plead a headache, or exhaustion, and request a tray to be sent to her room.

She laughed. "Aye, of course I am." She wanted to say, *You foolish, foolish man. You are no going to scare me away with such outbursts.* She didn't say that, of course. But she did marvel a bit at the weakness of the stronger sex. For such a spirited, masculine man, he was using tactics that a child wouldn't fall for. She wanted to laugh.

If he wanted to keep her at arm's length, he was going to have to do a lot better than this. Too bad for him that he had stayed away these past two weeks, for it had given her enough time to dig in, to become familiar with her surroundings, and to learn a great deal about the man she had married, enough to begin to feel a part of his life.

In other words, if Adrian Mackinnon wanted to drive her away, he should have been here from the beginning, when she was new and less certain of herself. Like an animal preparing for winter, she had had enough time to stock up her supplies. She was prepared, and because of this, winter, when it arrived, wasn't much threat.

She looked at his dark scowl and felt a gush of delight. She knew him. She knew this man, and her heart flooded with the joy of it. He was like Scotland to her—hard, harsh, shrewd, skeptical, inhospitable to outsiders, prejudiced, proud, resistant to change, and oh, so touching.

Once this man loved, he would be loyal, fiercely protective, cherishing—a love for all time. His harsh exterior, his hard looks, the cynical twist to his mouth, no longer disturbed her. His rages, when they came—and they would come—would not be against her, but what she stood for, yet they would be no more ruthless than a lashing by fierce winds that would soon blow over. Love would not come easily to him, but when it came, it would be sweet and well worth the wait. She was willing to wait for the rarely seen pleasure of loving and being loved by a strong, uncompromising, and very difficult man.

Taking her paint box from his hand, she smiled up at him as she passed, stepping inside the house, her image fading to a blur of paints, easel, petticoats, and big yellow dog.

# CHAPTER
## ❧ EIGHT ❧

Eli and Big John Polly were waiting in the office when Adrian arrived the next morning. "Pope and Talbot are building another mill at Teekalet," Big John said.

Eli looked at Big John. He looked at Adrian. "We just got word from Captain Kline when he dropped anchor this morning," he said.

"Damn," Adrian swore, throwing his gloves on his desk. "Then the talk in San Francisco wasn't all hearsay after all." He braced his hands flat against the desk, leaning forward and staring down at the scattered papers. That bastard Pope was going to be the death of him, or at least the ruination. Ever since he and Talbot followed Adrian's lead and ventured into the northern timberland, they had been nothing but trouble. Not content to make their own fortune, they were dead set upon stripping Adrian of his.

"Damn," he swore again, moving to the window and looking out at the mill yard, "that's what I was afraid of."

"I don't understand why he waits until you build a mill, and then he wants to build one close enough that he could spit on us if he tried," Eli said.

"Oh, I understand it, all right," Adrian said. "Pope is the

culprit here. Talbot just goes along with whatever Pope decides.''

"What can he hope to gain?" Eli asked. "There's enough timber in these parts to keep us all in lumber for years. Why does he have to set up right in our back door?"

Adrian turned away from the window. "He isn't just after the timber. He wants to drive us out of business."

"That's what I don't understand," Big John said. "There's room for all of us."

"We've spent years setting up our foreign markets. Our contacts and agents are the best to be had. It wasn't something that just happened overnight. Their Puget Mill Company needs foreign markets. Pope wants to drive us out of business and take over ours. It's as simple as that." Adrian was silent a moment. "I had word over two months ago that Pope had someone sniffing around Valparaiso, then I heard the same thing from Sydney." He picked up a letter lying on his desk. "Three weeks ago I received this letter from Hong Kong."

"Same thing?" asked Eli.

"Same thing," said Adrian, tossing the paper back on the desk.

Big John moved to the map on the wall, studying it for a minute or two. "Then we'll probably get the same report from Manila and Shanghai," he said, pointing to each place in turn.

"And don't forget Honolulu," Eli said, moving to the map and poking a finger in the general vicinity of the Hawaiian islands. "They won't overlook that one either."

"No, they won't overlook a thing," said Adrian. "You can count on it."

After another half hour, they carried their discussion outside to stand on the porch for a spell, so Adrian could have himself a chew without having to worry about where he spit.

After the two men left, Adrian went back to his desk, his

forehead resting in his hand, thinking about Talbot and Pope—at least he *tried* to think about Talbot and Pope, but after a few minutes, thoughts of the Puget Mill Company were superseded by thoughts of another nature entirely.

There was no way around it. He had taken a wife, and his life had changed. He hadn't expected this to happen, but it had. The question now was, what could he do about it?

This whole marriage business wasn't going according to plan. He wanted a wife to give him legitimate heirs, not to fill his head with thoughts like a swarm of gnats. Of course, it wasn't his wife's fault he was spending too much time thinking about her, time he needed to attend to more important things like his business.

In his earlier years, Adrian thought women were people you tipped your hat to, or gave your seat to, or stood up for when they entered the room. As the years had passed, Adrian learned that a certain part of his anatomy did just that: it stood up whenever a woman entered the room. And that was when his penis, heretofore used for the sole purpose of relieving himself, became the source of another kind of stress, one that he couldn't as easily relieve himself of—at least not in certain places, say, church, for instance. He also noticed that this particular kind of stress came whether he was around women, or when he lay in bed at night, thinking about them.

He had been around men all his life and had never spent more than five minutes talking to any woman other than Katherine Simon or her sister Karin. Whores, he decided, did not count, most especially since he wasn't given much to talking to whores anyway.

All this thinking reminded him of his first meeting with his wife yesterday. It was then that Adrian decided he would have been a whole lot better off if Alex had been there to do the talking for him. He had to admit he was awkward as hell around women, and he had never before been near a real, honest-to-God lady before. Each time he remembered talking to her down by the cliffs, he cringed. It didn't take a wise man to realize he had not only put both feet in his mouth more times than he would like to remember, but that he had managed to wedge his boots in there as well. It was amazing to him that this strange-talking woman was speaking to him at all.

He thought about the way she had seated herself across from him at dinner last night, her body outlined in perfectly exquisite detail by a dark blue dress trimmed with rose, her waist so small, everything above and below seemed to blossom. Fighting the desire to drag her across the table and make love to her on the spot, he was feeling a little put out because of the discomfort he was feeling.

She, apparently, was feeling no such discomfort, for she went on smoothly ladling her soup, asking him first one question and then another about life around a lumber mill. He was finding it distracting to talk about business when his mind seemed bent on reminding him of the way she smelled, all clean and sweet like, when he had leaned close to her to push in her chair. Katherine had always smelled clean, like soap. Whores suffered the opposite affliction, bathing themselves in toilet water and steering clear of soap and water. Maggie was the first woman he had ever known to smell like both.

By the time their salmon steaks arrived, he had begun to think about what he wanted to do with her. If he was going to have those heirs he wanted, then he was going to have to do something about getting her out of the bed she had been sleeping in and into his.

*Running a lumber mill was never this hard.*

It was apparent to him during the length of the meal that he had not given the matter much thought before taking a wife. This woman was going to be here night after night, sharing the same house. He might be randy, but even he couldn't spend all his time for the next thirty or forty years in bed, making love. What would they do in the meantime? And what in the hell could they find to talk about, day in and day out, over the course of three meals and for the duration of the evening? There were just so many things about his business he could tell her, so many sights he could take her to see. And then what? He tried to remember what Alex and Katherine had done during the short period of time she had lived here, but the memory of anything except his feelings for her escaped him.

Over and over, all evening long, he couldn't help wondering if it would shock her if he simply rose to his feet and asked, matter-of-factly, "Just what kind of things do you expect of me?"

The thought was there, but he never told her about it.

It was half past six when Adrian wound things up at the mill and returned home. Nothing but a profound silence greeted him, a silence that seemed to expand his feeling of restlessness. He strolled through the downstairs rooms, seeing nothing out of the ordinary—and that was odd, since he considered a certain Scotswoman to be something out of the ordinary.

He went to the salon and stood in front of the fireplace, staring blankly at the picture of Katherine, his thoughts on Maggie. During all those months since he had written that letter asking Ross to find him a wife, he had envisioned a sweet-faced woman doing her stitchery by the window who put it quickly aside and rose to greet him the moment he came home. Never, not once, had he imagined walking into a dark, silent house. Turning abruptly away from the portrait, he walked briskly down the hall.

As he was about to put his foot on the first step of the stairway, a voice behind him said, "She takes a walk with Israel every day about this time. You'll probably find her down near the rocks that run along the shore."

Adrian turned. At least Molly was still here. "What makes you think I'm looking for her?"

Molly was stone-faced, but her eyes held a peculiar light. "What makes you take me for a fool?"

"What indeed," he said, and left.

Just as Molly said, he found her wandering along the edge of the rocky shoreline, not far from the place he had seen her the day before. She was alone.

As he had done yesterday, he paused to watch her, seeing her standing among the reds, pinks, and yellows of a Pacific sunset, on the brink of a place where earth and sea seemed to collide. She had stopped to look out over the water. It was a study of contrasts: she standing immobile against the brilliant rainbow colors brought to life in a shower of misty surf breaking around sharp rocks. Here, the very earth seemed alive with color and energy, the sunset a perfect backdrop for a dark blue ocean of frothy breakers capped with white. She was a solitary creature, all alone in a wilderness of sea stacks and rocky inlets, where a dense forest maintained a foothold, however tenuous, along a steep, rock-edged coast.

He wondered if she had ever painted this particular scene, if she had ever captured these colors, this energy, on canvas. He wondered why he was even concerned with the fact. He urged his horse forward and rode directly toward her, pulling even with her before he dismounted, noticing the far-off look in her eyes, the almost pensive air about her.

"Hello," he said, thinking it sounded stupid.

"I dinna hear you come," she said, as she looked up at him and smiled.

She was hatless, her hair braided and twisted low on the nape. Her dress was a soft yellow, edged with white and rose. She blended with the red and yellow sunset, and he found it difficult to see where the red-gold tones of her hair stopped and the vivid colors of late evening began.

Adrian looked at her, wondering what she was thinking

about, his hand twisting tightly in the reins. The sun was setting, but the warmth of it seemed to surround him. Dryness sucked at his breath. He could feel the irregular pounding of his heart. The collar of his shirt flapped in the wind. She was watching him now, still, silent, no show of emotion upon her face. "Were you looking for me?" she asked.

"No," he said, dismounting. He tried to make his tone believable, but the word sounded contrived even to him.

"I thought you came from the direction of the house."

"I did. I often take a ride out here after I get home."

He looked into the huge pools of yellow-green that were her eyes, not missing the way they widened at his lie. How smoothly she mocked him, how effortlessly she let him know she knew he never walked among these rocks. Yet she said nothing to contradict him, but turned away, gazing out at the profound color. He felt anger swell in his throat, choking back his words. She, however, seemed perfectly at ease. "I should like to paint this," she said.

"Why don't you?"

"Oh, I could never get the colors right. I'm far too much the novice for that."

"Is that why you left your paints at home?"

"No. I didn't feel like painting today. I just felt like walking."

"I thought perhaps you had come down here looking for your pot of paint."

She turned toward him and smiled. "I'm afraid it's halfway to China by now. The current is very strong."

*Yes it is*, he thought, feeling his heart pound. He didn't say a word, for the warmth of her smile had disturbed and distracted him. He was unable to think past the fact that she was his wife, and anything . . . *anything* he wanted to do with her was his right.

*Come to bed with me.*

*What in the hell is the matter with you, Mackinnon? If you want to make love to your wife, go to her room and do it.*

"Shall we walk together?" she asked. "Do you have a certain route you prefer to take?"

"No. I don't really pay much attention to where I'm going."

"Oh, that's a pity," she said, "for it's so lovely here, and there are many beautiful things you are sure to miss."

He had expected her to be angry, or at least withdrawn, considering his obvious rudeness the day before, and the way he had left before dawn without bothering to tell her. But if his early departure disturbed her, she didn't let on.

She turned away from him, looking out over the rocks to the endless stretch of water beyond.

"You're thinking about Scotland."

She turned those unbelievable eyes upon him. Today they were like cat's eyes, almost yellow, tinged with green. "Yes, I was."

"Homesick?"

"I dinna ken if that's what I feel. I'm no too sure of my feelings just now." She looked around her. "There are so many things about this place that remind me of home."

"Surely not the redwoods."

She laughed. "No, not the redwoods—we dinna have anything so magnificent—but the coastline is quite the same, and the fury of the sea battering the rocks." She closed her eyes and inhaled. "I love the smell of the ocean. I grew up with it." She was looking over the water now. "Sometimes I feel such a kinship to this place . . . as if I had no left Scotland at all, but had simply stepped back in time. I ken there is a newness here, an untamed wildness that was the Scotland of old." She turned toward the trees that ran like fringe along the coastline. "Sometimes, when I'm sitting here, I can hear the thunder of running horses, the clang of broadswords, and for the briefest moment, I can see a band of kilt-clad warriors ride out of the forest, as if they were tramping over the moor and down the burnsides.''

"Imagination plays strange tricks on everyone from time to time.''

"It's no my imagination," she said. "I saw them and I heard their pipes, too. Not the modern pipes with three drones, you ken, but the old pipes—the ones of centuries ago—with two drones.'' She stirred and turned from him. "I know you must be thinking me a puir daftie.''

"No. I find you intriguing, not daft, Margaret.''

"Margaret," she repeated. "Och! It's been so long since anyone called me Margaret.''

The corners of his mouth tightened. "Ross wrote that was your name.''

"Aye, it is. No one close to me calls me Margaret. I've always been called Maggie.''

"A name more suited for a barmaid than a lady,'' he said, cursing himself for being so hard. *What is wrong with me? Why can't I talk to her like I long to? Why can't I tell her the things I feel inside? Why must everything I say or do be something that will drive her away, when I might just want her to stay?*

She dipped her head. "Thank you," she said quite musically, then she laughed. It was clear, and happy, and quite, quite sincere. "Perhaps I am more aptly named than I thought.''

"Or perhaps you aren't.''

She laughed again, and he had never itched more to take a woman in his arms. *Maggie, Maggie, would you kiss me?* His heart sprang forward at the thought. He almost felt the soft weight of her in his arms, the heat of his palm against a softly rounded breast. Dizziness swept over him, the effect of too much blood, aroused and gushing into his heart—and another place, lower down. He stepped closer to her, taking her chin in his hand. The humor in her eyes faded. Her expression was now watchful. Wary. Adrian ached to hold her, to kiss her. He wanted to take her clothes off and see what she was like beneath all those gauzy layers of dress and petticoat. His thumb stroked the mouth he found too full for fashion.

Strange how it looked so perfect for kissing.

He needed no further prompting. His body was rock-hard and trembling. His arms felt like lead weights as he drew her against him. There was no further thought as his lips slid over hers in a hard kiss.

Maggie's arms went around his lean frame, her fingers gripping the hard muscles of his back. He thought of another place he would like to feel those hands, and groaned at the sudden leap of his body's response.

Maggie held her breath as his hand came up to touch her breast, the heat of his fingers touching her through layers of clothing as if none of it existed. Her breasts tingled and a slow ache spread across her belly. She sighed and leaned closer to him, responding to the intensity of his kiss with an intensity of her own.

He pulled away from her, his hand dropping down to take hers. "Come over here," he said, "behind these rocks."

Maggie's first impulse was to shove him into his beloved rocks and tell him to rut whatever he found there, but she knew part of his brazen assumption that he could toss her skirts outside like a common strumpet was her fault. She had responded to him. She had enjoyed kissing him. She had found pleasure in the feel of his hand upon her breast. And she *had* let him know it.

The look she gave him was filled with confusion and shame, and she turned her face away, feeling the tension of the past few days grip her body. She contemplated leaning her head against the comforting strength of his shoulder, letting him lead her behind the rocks. And then she remembered Ross's words. *Go easy. He won't fall in love overnight. Remember, time is on your side.*

She pulled away from him, but she didn't look into his eyes.

"Who are you?" he asked.

Her head tilted back and she looked at him, her face full of surprise. "You know who I am."

"I know nothing, save what I'm told. And that, at times, can be confusing. Margaret . . . Maggie, you leave me flustered. You see visions, you hear sounds, you speak in riddles. Your name isn't your name. I find you past plain and then see you so beautiful, I ache. You're a lady to the core, and I find you melting in my arms like a woman who has done this sort of thing before. You are the daughter of an earl, and yet you have given up everything to come to me, a man you don't even know. You're open and honest, and at the same time, shrouded in mist and mystery. And even your goddamned eyes change color. Who in the hell are you?"

"Perhaps I am all of those women you described, but more importantly, I'm your wife."

"I know, but I can't help wondering why." His voice was thick now, his finger stroking the curve of her cheek. "What are you running from? What is the real reason you chose this path?"

He saw her eyes widen. The sun filtered through long lashes to leave a fringe of shadow upon a porcelain-smooth cheek. "Tell me," he said, "tell me why you came here. It couldn't be because you had no other offers."

"No, it wasna. I did have another offer, but I chose you."

"Why?"

"I told you," she said, turning her face away and gazing out over the water. "I came because of the man I came to know through your letters. Your life here was intriguing, of course, and I had never been to America, but it was the man in the letters that drew me, that made me choose the unknown over the familiar.''

''What did I put in those damn letters that interested you so much?''

''I read about a lonely man, a man with needs, and I knew I could have understanding, a partnership with a man like that. It is important for me to be needed, to feel I am contributing something.'' She turned toward him, her eyes steady as they looked into his. ''My life may not have looked very promising, but I still had a choice. I wasna forced to come here by my circumstances—unfortunate as they were. To have accepted the other offer and remain in Scotland would have been to choose the easier way. Whatever you might think of me, Adrian, I want you to know I *chose* to marry you and come here.''

Adrian could tell by the honesty he saw in her eyes that she was telling the truth, yet something about all of this didn't sit right with him. It pricked at him constantly, this need to dig deeper, to find the real reason she chose to marry him.

''You said you received only one other offer. That intrigues me. I would have thought the daughter of an earl would have received more offers—and a lot sooner. How old are you?''

''Old enough,'' she said with a laugh. Then, her voice turning serious, she said, ''I'm twenty-seven.''

''Twenty-seven,'' he repeated. ''What made you wait so long to marry?''

''How old are you, Adrian?''

''Thirty-one.''

''What made you wait so long?''

He laughed at that. ''I told you. I was in love with someone else.''

''As I was,'' she said, her voice turning soft and wistful.

Before he could ask her anything more, she spun away from him and ran back toward the house.

He watched her go, unable to think beyond the fact that she had loved someone else. It never occurred to him that it might be equally hard on her, knowing he had loved another.

And loved her still.

# CHAPTER
## ❧ NINE ❧

Every candle in the dining room threw golden images on the windows, where mullioned panes reflected the light back into the room. Over the dining table the three chandeliers glittered like a thousand lights upon a gleaming floor. But the man standing before the windows, swirling a snifter of brandy in his hand, seemed not to notice. Obviously irritated, Adrian frowned, a pulse beginning to throb in his forehead.

He was waiting for her, and she was late . . . again. He intended to tell her just how annoying he found it to have her always late, but when he heard her coming down the hallway and he turned to tell her, the words died in his throat.

The moment she stepped into the room, the light from the candles struck her. She wore a gown of the deepest moss green; velvet, clinging, daring. Her pale shoulders were bare, the hue of creamy pearls. The bodice was tight, molded like a hand over perfect breasts, high and full above a slender waist. The gather of folds looked almost black as they fell away from the waist to be caught up in the back in a bustle that cascaded like a waterfall behind her. A pair of antique emerald earrings surrounded with diamonds glittered in her ears. Her throat was bare. Her hair, pulled back into a low cluster of curls, made her large eyes appear even larger.

"I'm late," she said.

"Yes," he said, "you are . . . again."

"Perhaps in time I will get more punctual."

"Perhaps."

As she came toward him, he watched the way she moved, fluidly and in control, like a slow-moving stream following a course it has known for centuries. Everything about her was regal: her walk, her bearing, the way she held her head, and most of all, her composure. There was no sign anywhere that this was the same woman who had found herself overcome with emotion and fled his presence a few hours ago.

She stopped just inches away, turning her eyes upon him. Tonight they were amber—pale and glittering with the light of a million golden candles. He looked at her face, his eyes following the smooth lines of her beautiful white shoulders, lingering at the swell of half-covered breasts. He didn't want to be distracted by her eyes, or her breasts. He did not want to feel drawn to her. "It's a bit chilly in here. Do you think you need a shawl?"

She looked up at him and saw the angry clench of his jaw. She also saw the hunger in his eyes. "I dinna think it's a shawl I need. From the way you're looking at me, I think I need a bodyguard."

At that, he threw back his head and laughed.

She stood beneath his scrutiny feeling ridiculous. He had never looked at her as he did now—a look that went beyond mere curiosity or familiarity. And because of it, there was an awkwardness between them now that had not existed before. It was the first time she dreaded being alone with him, and she hated herself for the feeling.

Her heart beat strong and rapidly, and her breath seemed too great for her small throat. This wasn't the way things were supposed to be between them. She had been married before; she had known the intimacy, the assurance of warm familiarity. This wasn't the way she imagined being with her new husband. He made her conscious of herself, made her aware of her shortcomings. Most of all, he made her aware of the instability of her marriage, the delicate state of her tenure here. There were problems that existed between them. Some spoken, some that remained unsaid. Her father always taught her that problems were messages, some sort of a good thrashing life had to give one sometimes, in order to teach a lesson. Experience had taught her it was easier to learn the lesson the first time around, for the thrashing had a tendency to get more severe when repeated.

At last her common sense took over. They couldn't stand here all evening like a couple of doorjambs, facing each other, each of them thinking private thoughts and imagining what the other was thinking. With an almost pleading look, she broke the strain of silence.

"I must apologize for this afternoon. It wasna like me to turn my back and walk away as I did. I—"

Amusement danced in his eyes. "You didn't walk," he said, remembering vividly what she had said and how she had turned away from him.

"Aye," she said, smiling, "it was a fast walk." When he didn't smile, her mood turned serious again. "I dinna make a habit of running away. It willna happen again."

Adrian was surprised by her apology, especially since he knew it wasn't entirely her fault. He had goaded her, though he couldn't bring himself to apologize. His curiosity about the man she had been in love with was still there, but it wasn't a topic for discussion over dinner. He would ask his questions later.

"Don't make any promises," he said. "Promises seem to be made for breaking. Let's try to have a pleasant meal tonight. After receiving ear strain the last time we dined, I asked Molly to move your place closer to mine. It's damnably hard to talk to you when you're sitting half a mile away.''

Determined not to break the fragile thread of truce that stretched between them, Maggie said, ''It will be much easier on my voice as well, I ken.''

''Shall we sit down?'' he said, pulling out a chair for her.

''Aye, thank you,'' she said, dropping into the chair with one graceful movement, feeling her nerves stretching with tension. How stiff they both were. How terribly formal.

He took the chair at the end of the table, which was to her right. He poured her a glass of claret from an exquisitely cut decanter. She picked up the glass and took more than a ladylike sip. Over the rim of the glass she caught his amused look. She put the glass down. ''I like claret.''

A half smile played around his mouth. ''Apparently.''

''I suppose you think I took a rather large swallow.''

''You *did* take a large swallow,'' he said, laughter in his eyes.

''Aye,'' she said, laughing. ''But I had a good reason, you ken.''

He was about to ask her what that reason was, but at that moment Wong brought in the first course, and Maggie gave Adrian a surprised look. ''I gave Molly the evening off,'' he said. ''But don't worry. Wong is only serving the salmon soup. He didn't cook it.''

She laughed, feeling more relaxed ''I'm glad you gave Molly some time off. She deserves it. Besides, she is a married woman.''

The humor faded from his eyes. ''More often than not, that's a reason for keeping apart.''

''Aye,'' she said, feeling the strain between them again, ''it can, but it doesna have to be that way.'' She looked down at her soup and picked up her spoon.

*She even eats like royalty.* He picked up his glass, annoyed at himself for even noticing. He didn't care if she picked up the bowl and drank from it, or crawled on the table and lapped it like a dog.

"How did you come to be so interested in building a lumber mill?"

The sound of her voice startled him, pulling him back from his thoughts. He studied her for a moment before answering. "I thought Ross told you everything there was to know about me."

"Not everything," she said, then smiling, she added, "I ken he wanted to leave us something to talk about."

Actually Ross had told her a little bit about Adrian's background—his years in the Mexican War, his attempt and failure at farming, and how that led to his coming to the gold fields with Alex. She knew about Katherine, of course, and that Adrian had bought his brother's interest in the mill. But she didn't know where Adrian's interest in a lumber mill had come from.

Adrian began to tell her—slowly at first and then more freely when he discovered her interest was genuine. Her questions were intelligent, well phrased, and thought-evoking. Not at all the kinds of questions he would have thought a woman would ask.

Before long he was telling her of his love for this lonely, majestic land, the thing he had achieved, the goals he still had, the places he had succeeded in doing what he set out to accomplish, the disappointment over his failures. She had a way of listening that made him want to talk, and he found that talking gave him a renewed vigor, a sense of excitement he had not felt in a long time. It was one thing to have a dream. It was another thing to share it. Before he was even aware that he was doing it, Adrian was telling her about the problems with Pope and Talbot, and how they wouldn't stop until they had ruined him, or at least taken over his foreign markets.

By the time dinner was over and Wong had removed the

last of the dishes, Adrian had been talking for almost two hours, and the two of them had finished the bottle of claret.

In a state of mellow companionship, they fell into silence, each regarding the other.

*I didn't know it would feel so good to talk like this.*

*I had no idea he had so much on his mind, lived with so much responsibility.*

"You obviously are accustomed to discussing topics normally reserved for the men's smoking room. Your father must be quite a man."

"Aye, he is. I was born late in my parents' life, the youngest of three boys and two girls. Because of the age difference between myself and the others, it was like being an only child. My father didna rear me to think of myself as inferior to a man. He saw to it that I was well educated in the traditionally feminine areas, and in many areas normally thought to belong to men. I helped him with his accounts, with the running of our estates."

As she talked, it was apparent she had the knowledge and ability many a man would covet. He folded his hands in front of him, thinking about this new side of her he had not realized existed. But while he admired the things he had discovered, he wondered if these things had something to do with the fact that she had been so long to take a husband. Had her father depended upon her so much that she felt compelled to stay with him, giving up her future prospects of a husband and family? Was he the only man of importance in her life?

The stirring to life of these questions reminded him that he had some other questions to which he wanted answers. He came to his feet, coming around behind Maggie to pull out her chair. "Do you play the piano?" he asked.

"Aye," she said, then added lightly, "I play the bagpipes, too, but I dinna think you would want to hear me. My playing is dreadful at best. Whenever I played, my father's dog would howl."

An odd expression came into his face and he almost smiled, then checked himself, but when he spoke, his voice was laced with humor. "Piano, I have. Thankfully, we're out of luck on the bagpipes—unless you brought some with you. Dare I hope . . ."

She laughed. "You're safe for now. I had enough baggage to accommodate several bagpipes, but none found their way into my belongings. I ken it's just as well. I'd run off all your help if they heard me play, especially if they've never heard anyone play the pipes before. The first few notes can be quite dreadful to the unexperienced ear. I've heard it likened to the screeching of a cat and the wailing of a banshee."

She turned her face toward him, and once again he was aware of the surge of lust for her that had prompted him to kiss her as he had on the cliffs this afternoon. He looked down into her upturned face, seeing no residue of anger, no lingering remorse over his sudden display of passion with her. He had never known a woman so completely capable of putting things behind her. He realized suddenly that she was looking at him with obvious interest in what he was thinking. "So the bagpipes are out," he said.

"Yes, and devilishly happy you should be that I have only your piano to prove my skill."

"I'm sure you must play quite well."

"Of course I do. Have you ever known a Scot to admit he could do anything in a bad way?" When he shook his head, she smiled and said, "However, I have been told I am quite an accomplished pianist, but of course, that was when I was standing in the room. What else could they say?" He paused by the door, waiting for her to pass through. As she did, she said, "I ken you will have to judge for yourself. Would you like me to play for you?"

"I would."

As they walked to the music room, Maggie said, "I must admit I've already taken the liberty of playing your piano."

He didn't say anything, but she went on to explain. "Dinna forget I was here for two weeks before you arrived. I ken you expected I would do a little snooping. It's a woman's nature to be inquisitive, after all. I'm surprised you haven't discovered that before now."

"I am not all that experienced with women, as you will soon learn."

"That is probably to your advantage—and mine," she added with a laugh.

All this talk about women made him uncomfortable. It also made him remember the way she felt in his arms, the way her mouth felt beneath his. She had the mouth of a courtesan, meant to pleasure a man. All over.

He imagined what it would be like to have her make love to him, to pleasure him with her mouth. He ground his teeth in frustration, forcing his mind back on the piano. "How do you like it?"

"The piano?"

*No, making love.*

He nodded and said, "Yes."

Maggie didn't know the direction of his thoughts, but she knew they didn't lie in the music room. *The bedroom, more than likely*, she said to herself, careful to keep her voice light when she answered his question.

"It's a lovely instrument," she said, "but slightly out of tune." She was going to add that was to be expected any time something was shipped a great distance, but he spoke before she had a chance.

"If the piano isn't good enough for you to play on, I won't force you," he said, his jaw clenched. His anger flared to rise quickly to the surface. "I bought the most expensive piano to be found. It's brand-new, so there shouldn't be anything wrong with it. Perhaps it was your playing."

Maggie had never known anyone so sensitive. She tried to remember that as she spoke in the calmest of tones—firm, but calm. "New or most expensive doesn't always mean best, but I dinna say there was anything wrong with your piano, Adrian. I said it needed tuning—something any piano would need after being shipped such a great distance."

She contemplated responding to his last statement implying she didn't know how to play. She decided to ignore it, when the next thing she knew, she was saying, "I began playing the piano when I was four. My father was an accomplished pianist and taught me himself. I learned to play on a Cristofori made in 1720."

His voice was as hard as his look. "I know nothing about pianos or their makers, so I've never heard of Cristofori—but I know a great deal about those who flaunt their superiority over others. People of that ilk have never been held in very high regard by me."

"I daresay they are not held in high regard by anyone, save a woodenhead. When I said what I did, I didn't mean to imply your piano was inferior, or that I considered myself to be your superior. I only mentioned Cristofori because he invented the piano. Yours is a Stein, built much later and possessing a lighter, sweeter tone. It is far advanced over the Cristofori." She remembered the way she had run her hands over the polished rosewood of the piano the first time she had seen it, remembered the thrill of playing on such an instrument. "I've never had the privilege of playing such an instrument before. To own one would be any pianist's dream."

Adrian couldn't remember ever being so angry over something so trifling, so simple. All this jabber about pianos and their makers with fancy names made him feel inadequate, and that made him angrier still. He was sorry he mentioned the piano, sorry he asked her to play. He had no way of knowing that to do so would give him such a crushing feeling of imperfection, or serve to remind him of his humble beginnings. She had been born into wealth and splendor, while he had been born into a family as poor as piss and potato peelings. Well, he might not be the son of a fancy Scottish earl, but by God, he was the grandson of a duke, and he had a brother who was a duke as well.

It occurred to him then that the only thing he had to impress this new wife of his was his wealth, and a woman like her was little impressed by that.

He didn't speak as he walked her into the music room. She was silent as well. When they reached the piano, he waited for her to seat herself at the bench before turning away. He went to a small table and poured himself a glass of brandy, then took a chair across from her, one that gave him an unobstructed view of her face.

"What would you like to hear?" she asked.

"Suit yourself," he said.

*What would you like to hear?* his mind mimicked. She knew, of course, that he didn't know anything about music. Anger boiled in his veins and increased the tempo of a heart already beating too rapidly. How many times had he wished he were more educated? His hand closed tightly around the fragile glass he held. He wished it were her educated neck. The frustrating feeling of impotence grew stronger. *Stupid. Stupid. Stupid.* It was what he deserved, requesting a cultured, refined lady for a wife. One who had a title. What was he thinking? That some of her refinement and her fancy learning would rub off on him? He would have pushed his thoughts further along this line, but she began playing, and he found himself distracted.

*Music to soothe the savage in the beast.*

Even that thought angered him.

Maggie chose three lively pieces by Mozart, then settled into a slower tune.

"You've changed composers," he said, hoping to God that was true so he would be spared further humiliation at the hands of this woman. "What are you playing now?"

"Chopin," she said. "Prelude, Opus Twenty-eight, Number Fifteen in D-flat Major, commonly called 'Raindrops.' "

The desire to throttle her was growing stronger. "I prefer 'Raindrops' over—" he coughed "—the other."

She laughed, a lively, musical sound that seemed to compete with the beautiful melody she played. "That's what my husband always said."

The glass in Adrian's hand shattered, sending fragments tinkling to the floor.

*That's what my husband always said?*

*Bitch! Goddamn bitch!*

*She had been married before. Some other man had been before him.* Fury, red-hot and intense enough to kill, exploded within him. His chair scraped, then fell over with a deadening crack as he sprang to his feet. Maggie stopped playing and turned to look at him. Her hand flew to her throat, a look of complete surprise upon her face.

For a moment that seemed longer than eternity, they stared at each other, neither of them speaking. The room grew deathly silent. Her heart thudded so loudly, she was certain he could hear it across the room. If she had ever seen a face angry enough to kill, it was his.

"Adrian, what—"

He held his hand up. "Don't say another word."

"But—"

Through clenched teeth, he said, "If you know what is good for you, you'll keep quiet."

She never took her eyes off him, but simply sat there, frozen in time, watching him struggle with himself. What had she done?

At long last, he spoke, and when he did, her skin crawled and her blood ran as cold as his tone. "Your husband," he said, crossing the room to where she sat pale and still, her hand spread against the pounding in her chest, her eyes wide and staring up at him.

He stood looking down at her, his eyes sharp and deadly as a sword point, the muscle in his jaw working. His hand trembled as it came out to lift one of two curls that lay over her shoulder, rubbing the silky texture, then letting it sift, painstakingly slow, through his fingers. The tension was palpable. She felt like tearing her hair and running from the room. *Say something, damn you! Anything! Only speak to me! What in the name of God have I done?*

"How strange," he said, speaking too slow and too calmly to be anything but the voice of utter and complete rage. "I wonder why you waited until now to tell me you have been married before."

His hands came up to fasten around her slender throat, his thumbs caressing the hollow where her blood pounded as if desperately trying to escape.

Her eyes never left his face, nor did his leave hers. Fear tingled throughout her body. She knew he was going to press now, press on the hollow of her throat until he cut off the flow of precious air to her lungs, or snapped her neck. She inhaled deeply and closed her eyes. *I'll make it easy for him,* she thought. *I won't make him remember the fear in my eyes.*

He released her throat, his hands dropping lower to grip her upper arms. Her eyes opened slowly. He drew her to her feet.

"Tell me, sweet Margaret, just how the matter of your being married before escaped my attention. Didn't you think it was important? Something I had a right to know?"

Her face was pale, colorless, her eyes a bit too bright and sparkling. "Of course you have a right to know," she whispered, unable to control the trembling of her lips. "I thought you did. I never dreamed you didna."

"And how would I know, since you've never seen fit to tell me?"

"Ross," she whispered. "He said he wrote to you. He said he told you all about me, so naturally, I assumed—"

"Ross," he said thoughtfully. "Of course, it's just the sort of thing my dear brother would do—leave out anything pertinent, anything that might have made a difference."

Her breath sucked in sharply. She drew back to look at him. "And does it? Does it make a difference?"

"It's a little late to be asking that now, don't you think? The marriage is legal and binding."

"Before," she said, "if you had known before, would it have made a difference?"

"Of course," he said, his words calm and cold and shattering. He lifted a finger to trace down the curve of her throat. "If I had known before, sweet Margaret, I would never have married you." His hand dropped away.

"I see," she said, her voice breaking and unsteady. She closed her eyes and inhaled deeply, feeling her composure slip away. She had never felt so close to crying in her life. She looked at him and felt her heart crack like an eggshell. She felt guilty and full of shame, guilty because she left something to Ross that she should have seen to herself, shame for knowing how the news must have shocked him and knowing he had a right to have a virgin for a wife if that was—as it was to many men—important to him. There was so much pain in his face, pain she understood.

Even as she understood his disappointment, she couldn't help wondering why. *What is so horrible about my being married before?* She decided it was because he thought her to still be in love with her husband, because he saw her previous marriage as a threat to their happiness. But then she remembered that he was in love with Katherine, and you couldn't threaten something that did not exist.

She opened her eyes. The urge to cry had passed. "I'm sorry about the mistake. . . ."

"Deception," he corrected.

"It wasna intentional."

"I don't give a damn about intentions. I'm interested in the facts."

In spite of his anger, his harsh words held an element of promise. He wouldn't be hurt if he didn't feel something. She was sorry for what had happened, sorry she had been misrepresented, sorry that it had mattered so much to him, sorry enough to want to do the right thing. *I'm sorry. I'm sorry all we seem to do is hurt each other. I'm sorry we can't seem to feel anything for each other except lust and anger. I'm sorry we don't seem to be right for each other.*

"So," she said at last, her breathing deep, and sounding remarkably in control of herself. "What do we do now?"

"I don't know," he said. "Understandably, I'm not in the best frame of mind to be making any decisions of importance right now."

*Understandably?* Maggie stiffened, wanting to point out that he hadn't come into this marriage with his hands exactly clean either. He was, after all, still in love with his brother's wife, and he still had her portrait in the house. Maggie couldn't think further. She was too shocked, too stunned, to be rational.

At last the stunned feeling began to lift and reality returned. "The marriage was never consummated," she said, feeling suddenly tired of all of this and as anxious to end this disastrous mistake between them as he was. "It can easily be annulled."

"We've lived in the same house together for some time," he said, his eyes sweeping over her, lingering on her breasts, then dropping lower. "I doubt anyone would believe we hadn't been together as man and wife before now." His eyes hardened accusingly. "And since you've already been used by a man, there's no way to prove the validity of my claim."

"How dare you," she said, fury exploding in her. Without even realizing it, Maggie swung at him, pain wrenching a gasp from her as he caught her wrist and squeezed. *Break it,* she thought. *I don't care.* She turned to face him squarely. "I was married," she said, her breath coming so fast, her chest heaved, "legally, and in the church. Contrary to what you think, I was never *used*. I was loved," she said, tears shimmering in her eyes. "What a pity you don't know there's a difference." She twisted, trying to pull away from him.

He was still holding her arm, and he applied pressure, jerking her against him. "Come here. Let me see just what I've purchased," he said, his mouth coming down hard upon hers. His kiss was savage, brutal, making her lips numb. He drove his tongue into her mouth, digging his fingers into her perfectly arranged hair. He held her head in place, wanting to master her, to show her she held no power over him, that she was capable of doing only what he wanted.

He released her suddenly. "Take off your clothes."

She stood, not moving, or even breathing, staring up into his face, into those fathomless blue eyes that glowed like the pits of hell. The only awareness she had at all was the terrible constricting pain she felt each time she took a breath.

"What's the matter, goddess? Didn't you understand me? There's no need to be shocked, or even embarrassed. You'll only be doing the same thing you've done a hundred other times—stripping for your husband."

"Adrian, please listen . . ." Her voice sounded far away.

His hands shot out and jerked her against him, close enough to feel how she fought for each sharply drawn breath, to feel the cool flutter of her breath across the heat of his face. "The time for listening was before, not now. Now, drop your clothes, sweetheart. Show me those breasts that have been tantalizing me all evening. Let me see if your nipples harden when I touch you, like I imagined they would. I want to see how much you know."

She inhaled sharply, trying to break his hold.

He held her fast. "Don't stand there like a simpering virgin. When I think how many times I've wanted to do this and didn't.'' He paused a moment as if questioning the sanity of what he was doing. "We both know how experienced you are. Show me!'' he said, shaking her. "Damn you to hell, show me how good you are!''

"I can't,'' she said softly, her arms going around him. "I can only show you how I feel.'' She came up on her toes, placing her trembling mouth against his.

It was the sweetest mouth, and the most tempting. And he *was* tempted. He closed his eyes, fighting the urge to kiss her back, to give in, but when he opened his eyes, the shattered look on her face told him she knew he wasn't moved. Removing her arms and pushing her away, he said, "I asked you to take off your clothes.''

"I can't. Not like this.''

"What's the matter, love? Don't you think I have the right to see what I've bought at such a great price? Don't I have the right to bed my wife?''

"I dinna think you have the right to rape me,'' she said, sounding strangely in control, "wife or no.''

The tension between them shattered. He released her so abruptly, she stumbled back. She watched him turn, shoving his hands into his back pockets, his head thrown back, his eyes closed, as though there were some powerful, raging thing within him he was trying to hold back. He struggled with himself, and the agony of it reached out to her, but she remained motionless.

*Rape? Dear God.* Was that what he intended? Was it possible? The thought disgusted him. His stomach twisted. Inside, Adrian felt as if he were bleeding from a dozen wounds. He was beginning to care for her. He thought things between them would really work. *Why?* his mind screamed. *Why? Couldn't you see I was beginning to care, that I wanted you? Why couldn't you have told me?* The moment the thought escaped, another followed on its heels. *Maybe she didn't because it was just as she said; she thought I knew.*

His heart pounded painfully. Each breath was a laborious task. *I don't know what to do. I can't bear being made a fool of. . . . I'm not ready to let her go.*

*You'll have to, unless you believe her—unless you believe that she thought you knew. Believe her, or send her back. It's as simple as that.*

*Send her back? Not on your sweet life.*

At last, without moving, he opened his eyes and said, "Annulment is out of the question."

"Why? Is that to be your way of getting even with me, your way to punish me, by reminding me every day for the rest of my life that I'm no what you wanted?"

His eyes locked on her. "Think what you will, you're in the habit of doing that anyway, but remember what I said before. No one would believe we hadn't been intimate." *That's not the reason, and you know it. Why can't you tell her the truth? Why can't you tell her how you feel?*

"I dinna really care what anyone would think," she said. "What difference could it possibly make? Your reputation isna at stake. Nothing in your life would be harmed."

"No, but yours would."

"How odd; I would no have thought it to be your nature to be concerned for anyone. Please dinna change yourself for me," she said, then added, "My reputation will survive. I've faced worse battles and prevailed. My name and my word of honor is still respected in Scotland. I ken we willna have trouble having the marriage annulled by mutual consent."

She turned back to the piano and closed the lid with an ominous thud, the chords humming in response, then she turned away.

"Where are you going?"

She stopped, but she did not turn to face him. "I ken we've

said enough hateful things to one another for one night. I dinna wish to make it more. I'm going to retire now. It's been a long day and I have some packing to do."

"I haven't asked you to leave."

She turned slightly, her eyes drilling into him. "Nor," she said softly, "have you asked me to stay."

It was a standoff, each of them eyeing the other, waiting to see who would give in first. At long last, Adrian sighed and crossed the room, standing before the wall of windows that looked out over the ocean. He did not look at her as he spoke. "I have to go to Puget Sound tomorrow. I have another logging camp there. I'll be gone for a couple of weeks. That will give us time to think this through, to see what we should do, time to adjust to the fact that I'm not your first."

"I have no adjustments to make," she said. "I never assumed I was *your* first. I was married. In most circles of society, that makes a difference. It isna as if I were a common woman of the streets."

"I never meant to imply that," he said. "It's just that—"

"It makes little difference to you that it was my husband. One man," she said. "But that doesna matter. To you it's the same, isn't it? One man or a hundred, it's the same." She shook her head sadly. "You would marry *her*, would you not? If something happened to Alex, you would marry her in a second, *used* or not."

"Don't bring Katherine into this," he said. "You know nothing about her. There is no need to mention her name."

"I ken there is. She's always in your thoughts, isn't she? Much more, I'll wager, than Bruce is ever in mine. It's no the fact that I was married that has come between us, is it? It's the fact that you never were. What kills you, Adrian, is no so much that Bruce was my first. It's because you couldna be hers."

He took a step backward, as if she had struck him, and perhaps she had. "That isn't true," he whispered.

"Aye, it is. She dominates our lives as much as her picture covers the wall in the salon."

His voice sounded weary now. Unsure. "Why can't you leave Katherine where she belongs, in the past?"

"Why canna you?"

"I told you Katherine isn't the issue here. You are. Maybe I shouldn't expect you to understand that. After all, you aren't the one who was deceived."

"No, I suppose I wasna. At least I *knew* about Katherine. In your eyes, that makes your daily worship of her all right, doesn't it?"

"How like a woman to confuse the issues. If you wish to discuss Katherine, by all means we will. At a later date."

"We have several issues that seem confused. It isna entirely my fault. I no had a way of knowing. I am no a deceptive person, Adrian. I thought . . . I assumed because Ross knew that—"

He interrupted her. "My brother seems to have known a lot of things he forgot to tell me. Things that he knew would be important. I wonder why."

She sighed, her body slumping in weariness. She rubbed her temples where a headache threatened. "I dinna ken why." She looked at him. "Is it so important?" she asked. "Being first?"

"Yes," he said, "it is."

"Why? Why is it so important to you?"

"Because . . ." He stopped, turning his head away, as if he couldn't look at her and say what he had to say, "because I don't know how to be second."

His words brought back the old torment, the old pain of losing, of being second choice, second best. Would there never be a time in his life when he would be first, when he wouldn't have to settle for what was left?

The thought faded, and he went on. "I have the biggest lumber empire in America. I produce more lumber than all my competitors put together. My house is larger, as is my bank account. I came here from the gold fields, and my brother and I cleared this land with our bare hands. We barely had a toehold when he sold his part to me and returned to Texas. For over ten years I've lived like a hermit, driving myself and those who work for me to carve a life out of nothing, working against men who connive to take it from me, or Mother Nature, who has her own ways to destroy. I've succeeded here—far beyond even my expectations. And you know why? Because I never, not once, settled for second best.''

Maggie now saw clearly it was time. Time to speak of things that should have been addressed long before now. He knew about Bruce and he condemned her for it, yet they had never really discussed Alex. It took more self-control than she knew she possessed to speak in normal tones, for in truth, she was trembling with apprehension.

''Now that we seem to be speaking honestly to each other for the first time, there's something I've been wanting to know. Ross told me about you and Alex. He said the two of you were always inseparable. Why did he sell out to you? Why did he leave? Was it because of Katherine?'' she asked with biting sharpness. ''Did you ask him to leave?''

Color rushed to his face, and for a moment she thought he would refuse to answer. ''He left of his own choosing,'' he said, then added, ''Alex knew it would never have worked out between us.''

Maggie's brilliant eyes narrowed, boring into him with great intensity. ''Why? Because of Katherine?''

The muscle in his jaw worked. Then he nodded and said, ''Partly. Partly because he wasn't cut out for this kind of life. He's a man of the land, not a man of visions. Texas is the best place for him, and he realized that. And since Katherine had already returned, it made his going much simpler.''

Then she looked at him, almost feeling something akin to

pity. Was there never to be any hope for them? *Not until he rids this house of Katherine.* Maggie grew quiet, contemplative. She felt as if a door to Adrian's mind had suddenly opened and she could see inside. He seemed to be carrying so much pain, and it was this pain that made him strike out, that made him so hard. At last she spoke, her voice laced with understanding. "Alex always came first, didn't he?"

When Adrian didn't answer, she said softly, "I can see how that would influence you, why you can't bear to be second."

Her words struck too close to his raw places, to the open wounds he carried inside. His words were a reaction to the pain, and he found a way to hit back, as a wounded animal will bite a loving hand. What was sadder still was his knowledge that even as he spoke the words, it wasn't Maggie he wanted to hurt. It was himself. "No," he said, "you don't see. You don't see at all. My feelings have nothing to do with Alex—or even Katherine, for that matter. I'm sorry to disappoint you, Maggie. It is simply because I don't relish eating after another man."

Like a queen walking to her own beheading, Maggie turned, and walked from the room.

*Don't let her go like this. Say something.*

As Maggie walked through the door, Adrian called out to her. "I suppose it could have been worse," he said. "At least you don't have children."

"Dear God," she whispered, and fled the room, running all the way up the stairs.

# CHAPTER
## ❧ TEN ❧

Maggie closed the door to her room and leaned back against it, closing her eyes and breathing heavily. Her pride seemed to shrink away, a little more each day, and for what?

Squeezing her eyes tightly, she tried to hold back her tears, but tears, it seemed, have a will of their own.

She felt a heaviness settle over her, and a deep, bone-penetrating weariness seemed to hold her in its grip. Her muscles ached. Her eyes were tired, as if they had seen far too much of the misery in the world. Her heart twisted and she felt consumed by a great, aching sadness.

She raised her voice to God. "What have I done?" she cried. "What have I done? Was I so wrong to marry a man I didna know? Was I so wrong to want? To want a new beginning for myself and my children? Am I wrong to care if we live or die? I dinna want to see my family destroyed. *That* is my crime!" she cried. "Unheard-of, I ken. Something that should be punished, wouldna you say? Oh, I am a foul and wretched woman, am I not?" She began to beat her chest, then bringing her hands to her face, she sobbed into them as her body slid to the floor.

She must have cried herself to sleep, for she awoke on the floor to an aching cold. The room was icy and dark. She came to a sitting position, drawing her knees up and resting her elbows upon them, her chin in her palms. She felt infinitely better. There was nothing like a good, gut-wrenching cry.

*What a pity Adrian can't do the same.*

The events of the past two years had proven one thing to her. She was utterly and completely alone, and her marriage to Adrian Mackinnon had in no way changed that. After Bruce's death, she felt abandoned, forced to depend upon her own resources. She had erroneously thought this new marriage would be her salvation, but she could see now that she was being called upon again to save herself. And saving herself meant she could not succumb to this wicked twist of fate that had put her off on the shores of this new country and into this new life, on the wrong foot. Ross Mackinnon had made a decision to withhold information from his brother, and in spite of the pain it caused her, Maggie knew that Ross had both her and Adrian's best interests at heart when he made that decision. Of course, she would have loved to tell Ross just what she thought about his decision and all the grief it was now causing her.

Maggie's first instinct was to write Ross Mackinnon a letter that would scorch the paper it was written on, but even as she thought it, she knew in her heart she could not bring herself to blame Ross. She had no doubts that Ross and Annabella were her dearest friends, and that neither of them would do something to intentionally cause her pain . . . unless, of course, there was a greater gain to be had because of it.

Thinking about that, Maggie remembered Ross's last words to her. *Trust me, Maggie. Trust what I've done. Remember, it's better to have the last smile than the first laugh.* Maggie's heart wrenched. Would she ever have either?

Her eyes reflective, her thoughts went back to Adrian, reliving the short time they had been together. He was such a complex person, a complete contradiction to himself—kind one minute, harsh the next. The man she had met in person was nothing like the man she had come to love through his letters, and she could not help wondering just which one was the *real* Adrian.

Maggie was never certain just why it was that she knew the real Adrian was the one who expressed his inner self so beautifully whenever he took pen in hand. Thinking about those lovely, revealing letters, she now saw them as a guiding star, a point to keep in her sights so she would not lose her way. She thanked God that Ross had had the insight to give the letters to her; that it had been such a long voyage; that there had been time enough to read and reread those letters until they were inscribed upon her heart. She saw it as a blessing that she had been given the opportunity to know this man before she met him. She now recognized, with sudden clarity, that Adrian was completely different from any man she had ever known. This was a man to be conquered only by understanding, loving faithfulness, and subtle strategy. Adrian closed doors and sealed his heart away. Perhaps that is what Ross realized, and perhaps, by withholding the fact that she had been married before, he was hoping to give Maggie a chance to get her foot in the door.

Well, she had, and now Adrian was squeezing that foot for all it was worth. She couldn't very well accomplish much with just a foot in the door. She felt a smile light up her heart. All wasn't lost. Her next strategy would simply have to be the wedging of something else in that tight space—a shoulder perhaps?

She shook her head, feeling it was almost funny, really, to be comparing love and marriage to squeezing oneself through a closing door, but in this case it did have its merits. After all, it did enable her to see things from a different vantage point. Adrian would not be conquered at once. She would have to lay siege and batter down his defenses. She prayed she wouldn't find herself battered in the process.

She rubbed her eyes. All this thinking made her sleepy. She did not want to think about Adrian anymore right now. A calmness and a peace had settled at last over her, and she looked toward the window, seeing the stars glittering brightly against a blue-black backdrop of velvet sky. "Thank you," she whispered. "Thank you for always being there."

There was no doubt in her mind that God, in His infinite wisdom, had seen fit to bless her with a moment of solitude, and she wasn't about to spoil it by making herself miserable over thoughts of Adrian and her plight. Whatever the problem was, it would still be there in the morning. There would be time enough then to think about it.

Maggie went to bed that night telling herself not to make any hasty decisions she would regret. Tomorrow would be soon enough. She would talk to Adrian tomorrow, and that would be time enough for them to decide what to do.

But Adrian was gone the next morning when Maggie came downstairs.

"He left before daybreak," Molly said. "Lit out of here like a ruptured duck in a hailstorm, he did. Never in all my born days have I seen that man acting so strange. You must have him tied in knots," she said with a laugh. "Probably do him good."

Maggie tried to smile, but she knew it failed miserably. Afraid Molly might decide to ask questions, she took Israel for a walk along the cliffs, trying to sort out the shattered pieces of her life. She tried putting herself in Adrian's place. Ross had neglected to tell him of her marriage. He had every right to be shocked, even angry.

She remembered the night Ross told her that he had written to Adrian, telling him all about her. He had even counseled her to give Adrian time to come to grips with the fact that she'd been married before, telling her not to discuss it unless Adrian brought it up. It was obvious now that Ross hadn't written Adrian about *everything* as he had claimed. Why? A chill swept over her as she remembered the cold, calculating words he spoke when she left the room.

*At least you don't have children.*

She shivered. *Children.* That bit of news would further complicate a relationship that was difficult already. It was beginning to make sense now just why Ross was so eager to advise her to leave the children behind. Not to give her time to be with Adrian, as he had said, but to trick him. Why? Because Ross knew children would be a bone lodged in Adrian's throat? A bone he could not possibly swallow?

She watched Israel sniffing a trail, then, turning, he came loping back to her side. "Come on, you rogue. I canna have all my men running off and leaving me, can I?"

Her trust in Ross made her feel a wee bit more optimistic. No one knew Adrian better than his brothers, so if Ross thought this was the way to go, then who was she to decide otherwise? She would trust Ross's judgment in this. She had no other option.

She resolved that problem, and another cropped up. She had to tell Adrian about her children sometime. *You might as well clear the air of that glaring fact as soon as he returns*, she told herself.

Molly Polly was in the kitchen when Maggie returned. She gave Israel a final pat on the head and closed the kitchen door behind her, pausing and looking back at the door when she heard his mournful whine.

"He only does that with you," Molly said.

"He had me pegged for a softie right from the beginning," Maggie said.

"He has a knack for that," Molly said. "Must get it from Adrian." She laughed.

"Aye," Maggie said, trying to keep her voice light. "He must."

After washing her hands, Maggie poured herself a cup of tea and sat down at the table, absently stirring to dissolve the sugar. Molly, who had been peeling carrots and potatoes, stopped her work. "You want to talk about it before it festers anymore?"

"What?"

"Whatever it is that's bothering you. You've been stirring that one spoon of sugar for fifteen minutes. When are you going to stop? When you've rubbed a hole in the bottom of the cup?"

Maggie dropped the spoon, turning to look at Molly. "Sometimes I would swear you were a Scot."

"Because I'm outspoken?"

"Partly. Partly because you're a woman of few words and deep wisdom. And because you are so verra canny."

"Well, I'm putting some of that *deep wisdom* to good use. What's bothering you?"

"Is it that obvious?"

"Written all over your face, it is. The two of you ain't gettin' on too well, I gather?"

"It's worse than that, I'm afraid."

"Two newly married people that don't get on is about as bad as it can get in my book. I didn't know it could get any worse."

"It can when one of them has been married before, and the other didn't know about it."

Molly dropped the knife, and Maggie watched absently as a carrot round rolled across the floor, thumped against the opposite wall, and wobbled on its edges a few times before coming to a stop. "Up jumped the devil!" Molly said. "You say you've been married before?"

"Aye. For several years."

"What happened—You aren't a runaway wife, are you?" Molly shook her head. "No, you have to be a widow."

"Aye, I'm a widow."

Maggie went on to tell Molly about Bruce and his death, and the hearing that stripped the title and estates from him, leaving her homeless. She didn't tell her about her children or Adair's threat the day she left Glengarry Castle. She liked Molly and she trusted her, but she wasn't certain Molly was above going to Adrian with a tidbit or two if she thought Maggie might be in any kind of danger. The less Adrian knew about her affairs in Scotland, the better. She didn't want to involve him in her life there—especially if there were problems with Adair later on. Her marriage was off to a bad start as it was. Any additional strain would stretch to snapping the few threads holding it together. Lost in thought, she almost missed Molly's next words.

"Ross should've told Adrian," Molly said. "But I can see how he might have decided to hold that little bit of information back, to give the two of you a chance to be together some, to get better acquainted. I suppose he meant well. He must have been hoping Adrian would come to care enough for you that it wouldn't matter that you had been married before."

"Well, he missed it on that one," she said. "But you're right. That's the same conclusion I reached. It wasna right of Ross. That wasna his decision to make."

"No, it weren't, but I reckon he meant well by it." Molly dried her hands and poured herself a cup of coffee. Joining Maggie at the table, she said, "Is he sending you back?"

Maggie laughed. "You make me sound like a sack of rotten Irish potatoes about to be tossed into the garbage heap. One doesn't return a wife as easily as a bolt of cloth."

"I know, but did he *ask* you to leave?"

"Why? Is that important? His asking me?"

"It's important. Adrian is a man who says what he thinks. If he was upset, he wouldn't have hesitated to pack your bustle onto the next ship out of here."

"I ken he's hoping I have enough sense to go on my own

so he can save himself the trouble. He said he would be gone for two weeks. I would imagine he expects me to be gone by the time he comes back.''

"And will you?'' Molly asked, coming to her feet.

Maggie thought about that for a minute, then she looked Molly squarely in the eye. "I'm a Scot,'' she said with a smile. "Scots don't run, and they don't quit. I'll see this thing through, and I willna make it easy for him. If Adrian wants me to leave, he will have to tell me.''

"Good for you,'' Molly said, giving her a slap on the back that came close to sending Maggie out of her chair. "Adrian has needed someone like you in his life for a long time.''

"I dinna think Adrian would agree with you on that.''

"Men,'' Molly said with a snort, "they don't know what they want until a woman gives it to them.''

Israel whined again, scratching at the door with his paws. Molly looked at Maggie and laughed. "He knows you're in here. He's playing on your sympathies, just like a child would.'' Molly grinned. "Or a man.''

Maggie groaned and dropped her face into her hands.

"What's the matter? Did I say something wrong?''

Maggie looked up. "Speaking of children . . .'' she said, her voice drifting off to nothing. Slowly, ever so slowly, Molly stared at her with new awareness dawning. Her brows lifted, not in question. "You trying to tell me you have some younguns?''

*Younguns?* Maggie laughed. "Aye. I have children.''

"Holy heaps of trouble,'' Molly said. "Children . . . more than one?''

"Two more than one,'' Maggie said. "A boy and two girls.''

"My, my, you Scots may have a lot of good qualities, but I'll say one thing for you, you sure do know how to complicate things. I'll have to hand you that.'' She gave Maggie a frank look. "You sure you don't have a husband floating around out there somewhere that might just decide to turn up on our doorstep some fine afternoon? Packin' a gun?''

"No. He's dead.''

"So, what are you going to do now?''

"I have to tell him, of course, but—''

"You don't have to tell him straightaway.''

"That's being deceptive, dinna you think?''

Molly shrugged. "We get it from Eve,'' she said matter-of-factly, "so we can't be blamed.'' She winked at Maggie. "Don't fret so. He's already been deceived. As I see it, he can't rightly get any more angry if he hears about it now or a month from now.''

"My children will be here in a month or two. I can't wait too long.''

"Just wait long enough for Adrian to get this thorn out of his paw before you go jabbing another one into it. No need to heap more coals on a roaring fire. It's kinda pointless. Just take it one thing at a time, as my pa always said.'' Molly crossed the room, putting her cup away, then went back to chopping vegetables, and Maggie knew the subject as well as their discussion of it was finished.

"Molly, do you think Big John would mind showing me around the mill tomorrow?''

Molly didn't answer, but she did give Maggie a mighty strange look. "You feelin' all right?''

"Yes, but I need to get out of the house. I need to do something besides paint and play the piano, or take Israel for a walk and weigh my mind down with my problems. I'd like to know more about Adrian's business. Then perhaps I could talk to him when he comes home in the evening. I could discuss what he does all day. I'm frightfully ignorant of the kind of life he and the others here lead.''

"I'll speak to John tonight. I can't think of any reason why you couldn't go down to the camp and have a look-see. Like you said, it would get your mind off other things.''

Maggie carried her teacup to the cabinet, putting it into the big enamel dishpan before she turned and leaned against the cabinet, looking at Molly steadily. "You willna mention any of this . . . the things we've discussed, I mean, to Big John or Adrian?"

"Your secrets are as safe with me as they are with Israel," Molly said.

Maggie laughed. "How did you know I talked to Israel?"

"Don't take no smarts to know that. Anybody what loves animals talks to them, same as with children. . . . Sorry. Didn't mean to bring that up again."

"Thank you," Maggie said, placing her hand over Molly's and giving it a squeeze. "I dinna ken what I'd do if you werena here for me to talk to."

For a moment Molly looked like she didn't know what to say, then she said, "You know, I was prepared to not like you, seein' as how I was so fond of Katherine and all."

Maggie looked surprised. "What was she like?"

"Reminds me of you in some ways—levelheaded, good-natured—but Katherine can be riled a mite faster than you can."

Maggie laughed. "Aye, I believe it. I saw the red hair."

"You've got a speck or two of red in your own hair, but you do have the dad-derndest knack for holding yourself on an even keel. That's why I think you're better suited to Adrian than Katherine was. It'll just take Adrian a spell to realize it, that's all. He's as stubborn as Alex was for not realizing all those years it was Katherine he loved, not her sister, and now here comes Adrian, following stupidly in his brother's footsteps. It's enough to make a body scream. Course, you may not believe that . . . and you might be feeling just a little miffed that I had the gall to compare you to Katherine."

"I'm not offended, Molly, and I'm not Katherine's enemy. Quite the contrary. Judging from her picture and the things I've heard about her, I think the two of us could become quite fast friends if given the chance. Adrian loved her. I dinna hold that against either one of them. How could I? I was in love with another man as well.''

''You're a wise woman, Maggie Mackinnon. That in itself will get you far. I 'spect Adrian will see the way of it before long. He's a mite shocked and hurt right now. His pride has been given a dent or two, but it'll polish up good as new. You've got a strange way about you. Calm as a moonless night. Doesn't anything ruffle you?''

''Aye, I've been known to have my moments.''

''We all do, but you seem so dad-blasted calm about everything. I can't help wondering why.''

''Perhaps it's because I've been through a lot. You know the Bible says, 'Tribulation buildeth patience.' ''

''Lord-a-mercy, and don't I know it,'' Molly said, and they both laughed.

Big John Polly came for Maggie the next morning.

A heavy fog groped its way along the ground, so heavy that droplets condensing on the evergreens overhead fell on the brim of Maggie's green bonnet. Silence was everywhere. Not even the horses' hooves clipping over a soft carpet of damp fir needles made any noise. Over to her right, coming from someplace deep in the trees, came the sudden and steady hammering of a woodpecker grubbing for insects beneath the bark of a massive tree. The hammering stopped, and Maggie smiled. Evidently the woodpecker got what he was after. The smile faded when she wondered if she would be able to do the same.

Big John glanced at the young woman perched at his side like a bird. According to Molly, this bird was one of a different feather. He watched her for a moment and couldn't help smiling. She was so small and finely put together, not much bigger than a minute, and because of that, she kept sliding around on the leather seats, though she braced herself with her hands splayed on each side of her.

Whenever the wheels dropped into a chughole, or bounced over the stump of a log, she bounced in the air, pushing that funny-looking green bonnet back out of her face as she came back down. She was as prim and properly put together as any picture he had ever seen of a lady, but she wasn't the kind to make the lesser folk, like himself, feel one bit uncomfortable. He could talk to her as easily as he talked to Molly.

Suddenly a loud clanking sound broke the silence, and Big John pulled the team up, pointing over the side of the bluff. Looking down, Maggie saw a wide trail paved with timbers laid crosswise. She turned questioning eyes back to Big John.

"It's called a skid road. We build them so we can get the trees further up the mountain down to camp. That clanking sound you hear is the sound of the bullwhacker bringing a load of logs down. They'll be passing by here any minute now."

A moment later, eight yokes of oxen lumbered into sight; a thin man in a floppy hat, galluses, and calked boots walked at their side. Instead of cracking a whip—something she was accustomed to seeing done with coach horses in Scotland— this man carried a long stick with a sharp piece of metal driven through the end. She gasped when he jabbed the oxen in the rump.

"The bullwhacker doesn't poke them hard enough for the goad to break skin, Mrs. Mackinnon. Oxen are fat, lazy beasts, and they need a little prodding."

"Like some people I know." Maggie had been about to respond that there was surely a better way to prod when a series of loud words brayed by the bullwhacker rent the air.

"Move on there, you lazy beast! Move on now! Hump up there!"

In openmouthed horror, she watched the man hop up to

the beasts' backs and walk on them in his calked boots. Big
John said this was to prod them to move along, which they
did, but Maggie's sympathy lay with the oxen, straining and
grunting as they pawed for footing on the next timber, their
feet sinking into the mud between each one. As the oxen
moved forward, a string of at least ten or twelve enormous
logs, chained together, inched its way forward, coming into
view around the curve of mountainside.

"There's close to ten thousand pounds of lumber being
moved down there," Big John said. "There'll be another
load along before too long."

As they drew closer, the clanking of chains and metal, the
grunting of the oxen, the shouts and curses of the bullwhacker, grew so loud, Maggie considered putting her hands
over her ears. But the slow-moving train gradually passed
and disappeared around another bend, and the noise faded
and the forest returned to quiet.

Big John slapped the reins against the horses' broad backs,
and the wagon moved forward. The hum and buzz of the
massive saws was faint at first, growing louder as they drew
closer. By the time they reached camp, the whine of the huge
saws drifted over the treetops, carried by the steady breeze.
Overhead, the sky was patchy, the fog already growing thin
from the heat of the sun. Following the direction of her look,
Big John glanced heavenward. "It'll burn off and we'll have
a fine summer day on our hands." He glanced at the long-
sleeved green outfit she was wearing. "You sure you won't
be too hot in that dress?"

"I can remove the jacket. The sleeves beneath are short,
and the neckline is easier to live with."

Big John nodded and pulled the wagon to a halt in front
of the office. Over the door was the familiar red and white
sign that said simply: CALIFORNIA MILL AND LUMBERING
COMPANY, ADRIAN MACKINNON, PROPRIETOR.

Big John left her standing there on the porch. "You wait

right here for a minute or two. I've got some work to attend to, but I'll send Tom Radford over to show you around.

Tom Radford came for her a minute later, a tall, lanky man with coal black hair. "Big John says I'm to show you around," he said, and before the next two hours had passed, he had done just that.

A week later, Maggie was riding down to the camp on one of Adrian's smaller, gentler geldings. There were no sidesaddles, of course, but Ox Woodburn, the blacksmith, had fashioned one for her from an old youth's saddle. It was an odd-looking contraption, but it served the purpose, and Maggie found she liked making her way to camp by herself ever so much better than having to rely on Big John or one of the other men to come after her with the wagon. They were busy men, and although they had always been accommodating and courteous, she knew that spending their time entertaining a woman wasn't something any man could honestly say he really took a liking to.

After almost two weeks of daily treks to the camp, Maggie decided that loggers, besides having marvelous strong bodies, had undeniable wit and charm. Of course, there were times when their fun-loving side got the best of one lumberjack or the other and caused a few hard feelings.

Ox told her one such story. "They took a lumberjack known only as Dirty Shirt Jim—they called him that, you see, because no one ever saw him change his shirt or take a bath during the six months he'd been here. The other lumberjacks decided it was time for Dirty Shirt to have a bath, and they tossed him in the river and followed him in, washing him and his shirt at the same time. Scrubbed him raw, they did, and him a-howlin' his fool head off."

Maggie couldn't help laughing when Clem Burnside told her, "Old Dirty Shirt Jim was madder than a widder woman at a wedding. He skipped camp the next morning, and no one has heard from him since.''

The loggers had their superstitions and their loggers' quirks, which blended well with Maggie's own brand of Scottish superstition. It was John Schurtz who informed her that lumberjacks don't start lumbering in a new area on a Friday because it's bad luck.

He also said, ''A fat man in the woods means three accidents are about to happen.''

When she asked Eli Carr about the copper band he wore like a bracelet, he said, ''Copper bands worn around the wrists and ankles keep you from getting rheumatism.''

Since there was no doctor in camp, Maggie began spending an hour or two each day in the small hut set aside for medical purposes. She swore she didn't know much more about doctoring than they did, but each man who visited the small hut with a cut or bruise or twisted muscle would have vouched she was an angel of mercy.

More than one man who visited the medicine hut came to ask her about her Scots superstition, and before long, she was passing out dozens of small crosses made from the wood of a rowan tree, which she said kept evil away from any house that displayed the cross over the front door.

Big John learned from Molly that a similar cross had been neatly tacked over the front door of Adrian Mackinnon's mansion. The two of them placed private bets as to just how long that tiny rowan cross would stay there once Adrian returned.

Two days before Adrian was due back, Maggie made her customary trek down to the camp. She found, as always, that the camp was a busy place, with teams of oxen dragging in the never-ending supply of logs, the saws in the mill whining, and the ring of the smithy's hammer riding on the currents of the ever-present wind.

Dudley Dunlap was busy in the office, his head bent over

the well-thumbed time book, scribbling figures and chewing on the end of a stubby pencil, when Maggie poked her head in.

"Hello, Dudley," she said, and Dudley looked up, giving her a wave before going back to his figures again.

She closed the door, finding Tom Radford a few minutes later, but Tom, who was in charge of the Ayrshire oxen, was busy working a new team. Maggie sat on a stump for a while and watched Tom. Because he was the man who engineered the skid roads that moved the logs down the mountains and trained the oxen, he was called a bullwhacker. At first Maggie had mistaken this to mean he whacked the oxen, but it didn't take Tom long to set her straight.

"I wouldn't whack one of these valuable beasties," he said. "A pair of 'em goes for three hundred dollars or more. Handle 'em with kid gloves, I do."

She decided he spoke the truth, for a moment later, she watched him rub arnica into the raw neck of one ox, and give another pair a good bath.

Soon it was obvious to her that Tom was busy—too busy to spend any time teaching her anything more today about a bullwhacker's job—and Maggie, being too proud to let him see she was lonely, left, heading for the cookhouse, stopping to talk to John Schurtz for a minute along the way.

Actually, the cookhouse was a favorite place of hers, for she enjoyed the company not only of Hardtack, the cook, but that of his two teenage helpers as well. The two young men, Oscar Price and Olley Page, were not more than sixteen and full of good-natured teasing and boyish pranks.

Although not related, the boys did, in fact, resemble each other, both being tall, rather gangly, and slender, and both possessing a mop of curly hair. Oscar had red hair, a liberal dose of freckles, and a cherubic face, while Olley's hair was berry brown, like his eyes.

Hardtack, on the other hand, was an institution of sorts in

the camp. Hardtack had gotten his name from the fact that he had once been a sailor. He had grown up in a fishing village on the coast of Maine and spent the early years of his life on a whaler. His hair was as white as Father Christmas's, and his blue eyes were just as merry. In fact, he reminded Maggie a lot of Father Christmas, aside from the fact that he had seemingly traded a protruding stomach for a tattoo of a dragon that curled from his shoulder down to his hand. "I got another tattoo of a snake coiled around my—"

Thankfully, he caught himself just in time, but not soon enough to stop the sudden burst of red that seemed to explode upon his face. Maggie pretended not to notice. It was enough that she had seen the coiling, scaled body of the dragon that ran from his elbow to where the tail came to a point over his knuckles. The fire-breathing head, he kept covered up.

When he offered to show it to her, Maggie tactfully declined.

Wondering what mischief Hardtack and his helpers were up to today, Maggie made her way to the cookhouse. It was large, airy, and relatively tidy for this part of the country. It was filled with organized clutter that ran the entire length of the large, rectangular building. Dishes, pots, utensils, hanging lamps, barrels of flour, tins of spices, and kegs of sugar lined the shelves and floor.

Dozens of tin cups and coffeepots hung from the beams overhead, and five long tables that sat thirty men apiece ran the length of the room.

When she entered the cookhouse, Hardtack was up to his elbows in biscuit dough, cursing oaths and shouting directions to Olley and Oscar, who were lost somewhere behind a thick column of smoke and steam rising from the stove.

"How many times do I have to tell you to turn your head when you sneeze? Cripes! You think anybody wants to eat soup with slime floatin' in it?"

He wadded up a ball of dough and threw it through the

smoky haze. Beyond the haze a voice yelled, "Hey! Whaddaya hittin' me for? He's the one that done it."

"Then I'm hitting you in advance," Hardtack said, catching sight of Maggie.

"Come in, come in," he said, picking up the rolling pin. "You ready for a hot cup of coffee?"

"I dinna think so, if it's been sneezed in," she said, and cook laughed.

"I think Oscar is through sneezing now," he said. "He knows how much biscuit dough I have left."

"Hey!" a voice behind the steamy curtain called out. "I told ya it weren't me that was sneezin'. It were Olley that sneezed."

"Open yer mouth again, and I'll close it with this rollin' pin. See if I don't," Hardtack said. "Blasted boys are a pain in the arse."

Maggie smiled, knowing how fond Hardtack was of the two boys. "Why dinna you get rid of them, then, if they're such a nuisance?"

"Well, the way I see it, they're kind of like my old bunion here—a real aggravation, for sure, but a whole lot less painful than cutting it off."

Maggie smiled at him. "You aren't saying, in a roundabout way, that you've become attached to the two of them, are you?"

Hardtack cut the last biscuit and placed it in the pan. Moving to a dishpan, he washed the dough from his hands. "I s'pose I am—in a roundabout way, you understand," he said.

Maggie sat on a stool, listening to Hardtack tell about his seafaring days as he fried enormous slabs of bear steak. Maggie, who had never seen a bear, much less tasted one, inquired, "Do the men *like* bear steaks?"

"They like anything that's dead and smothered in gravy," he said, forking the last steak into a platter. He opened a tin next to him and began spooning flour into the hot grease left from the fried bear.

"Need more flour," he said, then looking at Maggie, he asked, "Could you hand me that crock of flour there on the top shelf?"

Maggie slid off the stool about the time Olley and Oscar both shouted in unison, "Don't touch it!"

But it was too late.

Maggie, standing on her tiptoes, had just reached for the crock and was taking it down when she discovered there was no lid.

Hardtack, hearing the boys shout, knew they had been up to mischief again and looked up about the time a white sea of airborne flour showered down upon Maggie. Hearing her muffled cry, followed a second later by the sound of a shattering clay crock, he picked up the rolling pin and started after Olley and Oscar, who narrowly made it through the cookhouse door before he sailed the rolling pin at them. It hit the door and fell to the floor with a clatter.

Maggie, by this time, was gasping for a flour-free breath. Hardtack came to her aid with a towel and began wiping the mess from her face, but in the end, he said, "I think you're gonna need a good dousing in the crick to get this off."

Maggie spent most of the next day pulling clumps of dried paste from her hair. A bath had removed most of the flour, but it had turned large quantities of it in her hair to glue. Later that evening, Hardtack, with Olley and Oscar in tow—one on each side of him, held in place by his fingers wringing their ears—came to offer their most humble apologies.

Maggie offered them tea in the kitchen and graciously accepted their apology, laughing afterward to Molly that "I wasna certain which amused me more. The expression on the two boys' faces when they saw me wreathed in a cloud of flour yesterday, or today, when I invited them into the house for tea.''

''That's because they all know you're a real lady with a father that's royalty.''

Maggie laughed. ''I ken my father would say being royalty isna worth a muckle.''

''You'll have to translate that one,'' Molly said.

''A muckle means not much. And an earl is hardly considered royalty.''

''Well, it's probably as close to royalty as those two younguns will ever come. They'll probably live to tell their grandchildren that they had tea with a real, genuine lady that had manners like a queen and the disposition of an angel.''

''Oh, Molly, you're exaggerating, for sure. Why, I ken I've never heard such fummery in all my life. It's a good thing we Scots dinna pay verra much attention to flattery.''

''It's not flattery. You don't have no way of knowing, but I hear tell from Big John that the men in camp have placed you just a mite below angels. Seems you've won even the hardest hearts in camp.''

''I've done nothing to deserve any such comments.''

''Yes, you have. You've given these men something no one has ever bothered to give them.''

''What's that?''

''Attention. Recognition. A dose of human kindness. A feeling that they amounted to something. Most of these poor devils have never seen a lady such as yourself. It would not have stunned them more if the Virgin Mary had put in an appearance down at the camp, and you not only put in an appearance, you've made it a point to do it on a regular basis. You've learned their names. You've asked questions about their families, and their health. You've listened to them tell you about their jobs here, and made suggestions for improving their lot. You've made them feel important, and they hold you in very high regard for it.''

"I had no idea. . . ."

"I'll tell you something else, too. There are other stories circulating about camp, too. Stories about the way you fell in the mud the day you came here."

Maggie cringed and said, "Och, I hoped they wouldna remember that."

"Well, they have, and it's proud of you they are for the way you picked yourself up and went right on like nothing happened. And you did the same thing when you found yourself on the receiving end of that prank in the cookhouse yesterday. Every man in camp knows about the way you took it all in a good-natured way."

Maggie fell silent for a moment. She had never considered her small visits with the men as being something special to them. For her, it was commonplace to speak to the workers, just as she had done with her father when he made his rounds of the crofters' huts. Being a lady in Scotland didn't mean sitting down to tea parties on a daily basis. As the daughter of an earl whose wife was dead, Maggie had taken her mother's place when it came to dealing with the people who worked for her father. With these men, just as she had done with those back in Scotland, she offered her assistance wherever it was needed: showing them how to mix turpentine and camphor to remove lice, writing a letter to the family back home, or reading one that had just arrived.

She glanced up at Molly, who was just standing there looking back at her. It wasn't very often that Maggie found herself unable to think of anything to say.

At her usual time the next afternoon, Maggie was finishing up her rounds in camp and was about to mount her horse when Doc Arnenson walked up. He wasn't really a doctor, at least not that anybody knew. Doc was saying to Big John, "We've got ourselves a mighty big problem in the tool shed."

"What sort of problem, Doc?"

"Mice and rats. Lots of 'em. Big enough to carry off an

anvil, some of them are, and they're eating their way through the burlap bags and gnawing on the wooden handles.''

The next morning Big John Polly's laughter could be heard clear over to the cookhouse, and timberbeasts came running from everywhere to see just what all the ruckus was about. Finding Big John standing in front of the tool shed with a crowd behind him, the men saw him point to a piece of paper nailed to the wall, not more than three or four inches from the floor. Not a man breathed a word as Big John read what it said.

> *"Rat and mouse,*
> *Away from this house;*
> *Away over to Talbot's mill*
> *And there take your fill."*

The men laughed, and Big John told them how the Scots were a superstitious lot, believing in magic and holy wells and amulets and charms and the like.

"All right now, enough of this," Big John said. "You're clustering worse than a gaggle of geese. Now, back to work with the lot of you."

The men turned away, but more than one of them was heard to speculate upon what old Talbot would do if an army of rats and mice showed up at his mill, way up in Seattle.

# CHAPTER
## ❧ ELEVEN ❧

The day Adrian returned, he looked out the window of his office and raised his brows. "What in the blue blazes is Maggie doing here?" he asked, catching a glimpse of his wife going into the medicine hut, where ten or so men formed a line outside the door.

With a sense of dread, he watched Big John tally the last column of figures for the previous week's production, then lay the pencil aside.

Adrian braced himself for Big John's reply.

"Maggie has been coming down to camp every day since you left," Big John said. "Contrary to what you'd think, it hasn't caused any problems from the men. In fact, it seems to be quite a morale booster. The men look forward to her coming. . . ."

"Oh, I'm sure of that," Adrian said.

"She's an intelligent woman, Adrian. She has made some suggestions that have merit."

"And?"

"And she has gone further than to suggest on a few of them."

"What are you trying to say, Big John?"

"That your wife has made a few changes during your absence."

Instead of flying into a rage, or sending immediately for his wife, as Big John fully expected him to do, Adrian simply went to his chair behind his desk and sat down. Leaning back, he propped his feet up, made a tent of his fingers and placed them over his stomach, and said simply, "Go on."

Those two words and the way Adrian looked ready to hear almost anything prompted Big John to go ahead and get it over with. "Before I go into the details, I want you to know there has been a marked increase in production since Maggie began spending a little time here in camp. It's all here in the production reports from the previous two weeks," he said, waving his hands over the stack of reports.

"And you attribute *that* to Maggie's presence here in camp?"

"I do."

"Well, go on. I'm listening."

"Maggie has not only made some changes that have been instrumental in making the men's lives easier and healthier, but in doing so, she seems to have put a little spark of purpose in their lives."

"Give me the specifics," Adrian said, "and stop talking like you're at a ladies' church social."

"First off, I want to tell you that Maggie has learned, in a remarkable amount of time, just what it means to own a lumber mill. She has carried account books home at night to read, only to come back the next day with a detailed account of things she wanted to question or suggest."

"We can't run a lumber mill like a household account."

"I know that, but honest to God, Adrian, some of her ideas have real merit."

Adrian looked bored, and Big John went on. "I'm not talking about hanging frilly curtains on the doors, Adrian. I'm talking about the notes she made in regard to shipping."

"Shipping?"

"She has a point, Adrian. We've already got the lumber, and right now we own ten ships. We both know we could easily use ten more. Maggie has suggested that we build them."

"I'm not a shipbuilder, and I have no desire to become one."

"But you could be."

"What in the hell has been going on here? I'm gone for two weeks, and my wife has turned my business upside down. My brothers build ships. I don't know the first thing about it."

"Then give the business to your brothers. With them building the ships for you, instead of you buying them outright, you'd still save a passel of money." Big John sorted through some papers, locating one and bringing it to Adrian. "Take a look at this," he said. "She's put the pencil to it, and it makes sense. She also said your brothers could design ships that were better for carrying lumber than the ones we're buying, and that they could be built much cheaper than they can be bought. The idea of sturdier, better-designed ships makes sense. You know how many ships are lost on these shifting sandbars—if not by us, then the others. She even mentioned steam-powered tugboats."

"Enough about her blasted ideas. You mentioned changes. What changes?"

"Opening the medicine hut on a daily basis. Teaching the men about cleanliness. She's set up a laundry area behind the cookhouse and has been lecturing the men on boiling their clothes to get the lice out. She's ordered lye soap. We now have a steam hut."

"And what, may I ask, is a steam hut?" Adrian asked, listening with mounting irritation as Big John explained how Maggie had the steam engine hooked up to the bathhouse so the men could steam themselves and shed their lice.

"The next thing I know, you'll be telling me she's opened a goddamn social parlor. What are you getting at?" Adrian asked, giving him a mixed look of irritation and impatience.

"I'm trying to point out a few things to you, if you weren't so blockheaded where your wife is concerned."

"I don't want her meddling in camp."

"Her ideas are sound."

"To hell with her ideas. I don't want her down here. Is that clear?"

"Yes," he said, "it's about as clear as your stubborn refusal to admit she might be an asset to this establishment."

"Whatever changes my wife has made, I want things put back the way they were before I left."

"The changes are for the good of the men. To go back to the old ways will cause trouble."

"Then there's no problem, is there? I've had nothing but trouble since the day she arrived."

Although Maggie had been in the medicine hut the day Adrian returned, and one of the men came running in to tell her, she didn't actually see him until that evening at dinner.

Sitting across the table from her, Adrian was silent. The way he watched her made her think all her secret thoughts were being read by him. There was little doubt that he had heard about her visits to camp while he had been away; little doubt that he wasn't pleased with what he had heard. The fact that he might be displeased with her trips to camp did not bother her in the least. It was time Adrian learned he had not married a woman who could do nothing but whine, breed, complain, and run an efficient household. She had, after all, a perfectly good mind, and by all the saints in heaven, she intended to use it. Adrian would save himself a lot of trouble by realizing it.

Maggie felt an additional strain all through the meal, knowing Adrian had not forgotten about the words they had exchanged before he left, and wondering just when he would choose to bring it up again. Neither of them spoke much, but the tension in the room seemed to relay its own message. Maggie knew the worst was over, as far as her previous marriage went, for Adrian had been away for two weeks, and that was enough time to at least soften the blow. Instead of worrying herself into a state for no reason, she managed to smile and converse lightly on a wide assortment of subjects.

"I hear you've been learning your way around the mining camp," he said at last.

She felt disappointed. "I have been, but shame on the person who told you. I wanted it to be a surprise."

His blue eyes locked on her. "Oh, it was a surprise, all right. I come home to hear my wife has been taking flour baths, tacking bits of enchanted wood to doors, and filling the men's heads with ideas of cleanliness—going so far as to have the bathhouse converted into a steam hut."

"The men are covered with lice. . . . "

"As men in every logging camp are. It's something they are accustomed to, and they learn to live with it."

"But they dinna have to. Lice can be controlled."

"I don't want you hanging around camp, Maggie. It's too distracting for the men to have a woman about."

"I've been meaning to ask you why there are no women here. I know some of the men are married."

"Some are, but most of them are single. Their work is dangerous, and it requires the agility that comes with youth. Most of them haven't had time to court a woman. The ones that have wives aren't allowed to bring them here."

"Why?"

"Because I forbid it."

She looked astounded. "But why?"

"It's a responsibility and a distraction, and I have neither the time or the inclination to waste my energy on it. Women and children mean stores and doctors and schools. Before I knew it, this place would be a town, not a mining camp.''

''But—''

''Leave it alone, Maggie. You have full run of the house, but leave the mining camp to me. And that includes the medicine hut. I don't want you going there.''

''I don't understand.''

''I don't expect you to understand. I expect you to obey me.''

Maggie came to her feet. Having a conversation with Adrian was like playing a game of wordy battledore and shuttlecock—keeping a feathered bird in the air by batting words about. No matter how well she played, now and then a bird was bound to fall to the ground, and when the inevitable happened, Adrian seemed to gain strength from it, like Samson gained strength from his long hair.

Still, she wasn't one to give up, or to keep her thoughts to herself. ''I'm afraid the word *obey* isna in my vocabulary.''

''Then add it.''

Still sitting calmly, Adrian watched and waited to see what she would do. With as much detached interest as he could muster, he studied the complex woman before him.

Wrapped in yards of rose taffeta with her hair piled softly upon her head, diamond earrings in her ears reflecting the light from the chandelier, she looked beautiful, inexperienced, and yielding—though he knew her appearance was an illusion. She looked beautiful, but she wasn't. She looked inexperienced, but she had been married before. She appeared to be yielding and submissive, but in truth she was both stubborn and determined.

Were these the things that drew him to her? ''It shouldn't be so difficult to add one word to your vocabulary,'' he said at last.

''I canna,'' she said softly. ''Not that word. It would make me feel like an animal. Humans respond, Adrian. They dinna obey.''

*Humans respond.* . . . Dear God, didn't he know it. That was what he had thought about for two weeks now, making her respond to him, making her writhe beneath him until she cried out his name and he drove himself into the very heat of her, erasing forever the memory of another man from her mind. It wasn't supposed to be like this. He wanted to keep his thoughts of Katherine fresh and alive, but already this woman was supplanting the memory he had harbored for years.

He wanted Maggie. He did not want to want her, but he did. That was more than enough reason to hate her, but even then, he couldn't bring himself to feel anything for her save desire.

*Go ahead*, he told himself. *Fuck her and get it over with.* His crudity surprised him. He knew why he used such a word. He wanted to degrade her to make her less than acceptable to him. But it didn't work. Not this time. Because he knew in his heart that Maggie wasn't the kind of woman a man fucked. You made love to a woman like Maggie. Exquisite love. Long and drawn out. To the point of exhaustion. He felt himself swell with the thought.

While Adrian was lost in his own musings, the silence in the room was stifling to Maggie. *Go ahead*, she told herself. *Tell him. Tell him about the children. Get it over with. Don't live with this deception any longer.* This wasn't a good time. He was still hurting over the news of Bruce. *Give him a little while to get over that before you dump another load of bricks over his head.* No, now wasn't a good time, but when would there be a good time? Perhaps tomorrow? Perhaps next week?

At last, Adrian glanced up. ''Sit down, Maggie,'' he said, and looked her over slowly. ''You know as well as I, we have a lot to discuss. Leaving won't do anything but postpone it, and I think we both agree that won't do either of us any good.''

He watched her sink slowly into her chair. He wanted to tell her he was aware of her discomfiture, and remembering the things he had said the last night they had been together, he searched for some way to broach the subject. *Go ahead*, he told himself. *Put her mind at ease. Tell her you know it wasn't her fault that Ross didn't tell you about her marriage. Tell her you're willing to give it a try.*

"I'm not . . ." she said.

"I want . . ." he said at the same time.

They both stopped.

"Go ahead," he said. "What were you going to say?"

"It can wait. You go ahead."

"I wouldn't be much of a gentleman if I did."

"We willna have much to discuss if you dinna," she said. "I seem to have forgotten what I was going to say." *Coward*, a voice inside her said.

*I'm not a coward. I'm just shy.*

*Ha!* said the voice.

Maggie willed it away.

"I was going to say," Adrian began, "that I wanted you to understand that I didn't mean to be so hard on you that night before I left. It wasn't you, Maggie. It was simply the shock."

"Aye, I ken that. It was a shock to me as well."

"A shock? Now, that *does* surprise me," he said, his eyes sparkling with humor. "Here I was thinking you *knew* you were married."

She laughed and seemed to relax. "You are'na angry with Ross, are you?" She flinched when she saw his knuckles go white, the tight clench of his jaw.

"Not as angry as I was." Adrian inhaled deeply. "Two weeks ago I could have beat that pretty face of his into a living, bloody pulp, but time has taken some of the edge off my anger.''

''I'm glad to hear it. I know he thought he had good reason—that he meant well.''

''I'm sure he did,'' Adrian said, in a tone that dismissed any further talk about his brother.

For several seconds they simply sat there, each one wondering what the other was thinking. At last Maggie spoke. ''What happens now?''

''I don't know, Maggie. Take it one day at a time, would be my best guess. I can't promise that it will be easy from here on out, but we've both come this far. I hate to see it end before we've even given it a try. I suppose what I'm trying to say is, you are locked in here for a while longer, regardless. Even if you wanted to, you couldn't leave. It's almost winter now in South America. Going around the Cape this time of year is too dangerous.''

She wanted to tell him that she didn't want to leave, but his mention of the Cape reminded her again of her children, who would be coming soon. *Tell him. Now.* But Maggie told herself she had a little time, and time with Adrian was something she sorely needed. A moment later, Adrian stood, coming around behind her to pull out her chair.

''Would you play for me again?'' he asked, his breath warm and stirring upon her neck. *Oh, Adrian, will it always be like this between us? Strained. Artificial. Me afraid to talk. You afraid to let me.*

Maggie's face darkened with distress. Well she remembered the last time she had played for him. What if she forgot tonight? What if she found herself carried away and said something about the children? A choking pain swelled in her throat. *Dearest God*, her mind screamed. *Tell him. Tell him.* She *wanted* to tell him, but she was afraid. It wasn't like her to keep secrets, to present herself as something she was not. But as she thought this, she knew it was too soon. Adrian was just recovering from the news of Bruce. Their marriage would not stand the shock of children. Not yet. She needed time. But the children were on their way here. Time worked against her. The fear of revealing it weighed her spirits down. The fear of losing out on this marriage forced her to be jovial.

Maggie felt herself lost somewhere in between. She had never felt so desperate, so alone. She glanced at Adrian. He was looking at her strangely, waiting for her answer. For a moment, she had forgotten the question.

*Would you play for me again?* Thankfully, it came to her. With a sigh of relief, she forced a smile and nodded, unable to do any more than gather her skirts gently in her hand and turn toward the doorway. He walked to the music room with her, and like her, he was silent.

She sat at the piano, her fingers skimming over the keys, her mind unaware and unconnected from what her fingers did. Once or twice she looked up to see his eyes upon her, deep and brooding, and she wondered about what he was thinking. Three times he got up to pour himself another brandy, yet during it all he never said a word, never took his eyes from her.

At last the strain was too much. Her composure snapped. Her fingers froze on the keys and she came to her feet. "I'm sorry," she said. "I can't play anymore. Not tonight. Please . . ." she said, looking at him as if there was some great burden she wanted him to share, but she quickly looked away and, collecting her skirts in one hand, said, "I'm sorry, Adrian. Please excuse me."

He watched her go in silence. After she had gone, he continued to stare at the place he had seen her last, wondering why everything concerning Maggie was so intense—whether it was his anger or his desire.

And it was intense.

Did that mean it was lust then, after all? He knew he had never felt this sort of intensity in his feelings for Katherine, and yet he knew he loved her, and it was nothing like his feeling for Maggie. What he felt for Katherine was like a pond, still, silent, reflective. But his feelings for Maggie? They were like a waterfall, turbulent, swift, and churning. And like a man going over a waterfall, he knew how it would all end up. By destroying one or both of them. No one could live with such intense feelings of passion. He could not eat. He could not sleep. He couldn't even work for thinking about what it would be like to make love to her.

*So why don't you?*

He didn't know the answer to that, but he sure as hell was going to find out.

Downing the rest of his brandy in two gulps, he left the glass on the table and made his way upstairs. He fully intended to go to his room. He told himself it would serve no purpose to stop by hers. But somehow he found himself standing in front of Maggie's bedroom door. The hand that reached out to knock locked around the doorknob instead, turning it slowly and pushing until the door opened.

Maggie stood in a cream satin dressing gown, next to her bed. His eyes went from her to the bed, seeing the covers turned back like an invitation.

It was all he needed. He pushed the door shut with one foot as he stepped farther into the room.

Maggie turned to face him, making no effort to hide herself from him, in spite of the fact that he could see clearly that her breasts were full and high and pointed, and that her nipples were hard and thrusting against the lace-trimmed fabric. He felt response between his legs.

"I dinna hear you knock."

"I . . . I guess I was a little too nervous about coming in here. I didn't think." The moment the words were out, Adrian wanted to slap himself. *Nervous? How could you? Fool. How could you say something like that? Why don't you tell her some more stupid things, like how awkward you feel around a lady like her, or how much you want to make love to her? Go on. Why don't you make a bigger fool of yourself?*

She seemed to relax, her face lighting up with a smile. "Aye, I can understand being nervous. I'm nervous now."

He felt the urge to smile back at her, but he was afraid, afraid of showing her too much. "I came by . . . that is, you were upset when you left. Sometimes it helps to talk about it."

"You came in here to *talk*?"

He made a half shrug and rammed his hands deep into his pockets. "It seemed like a good idea at the time, but now I wonder if I have the confidence for it." *Shut up, Adrian. You're digging your own grave with your big mouth.*

Maggie looked off for a moment, as if collecting her thoughts. The stretch of silence was more than Adrian could bear. "Tell me about your husband," he said, thinking as he did, *God strike me dumb if I open my mouth again.*

"You want to know about Bruce? *Now?*"

He nodded. "It's as good a time as any, and I've had enough fortification, so I'm sufficiently mellowed to hear it."

"I wonder," she said, then added, "What, exactly, do you want to know?"

"I want to know what he was to you, how you felt about him, and what happened—how he died."

She looked at him for some time before she spoke. "I dinna think that's what you want to hear. I dinna think that at all."

"What makes you say that?"

"I'm not sure," she said, looking at him. She smiled faintly and shook her head. "Perhaps it's because you don't look like a man that's in a talking mood."

That brought a lifted brow and words spoken in a slow, lazy way. "What kind of mood do I seem to be in?"

"Argumentative, perhaps, or maybe . . ." She stopped, the loveliest blush of color rising to her face.

"Or maybe what?"

"Nothing. I don't think this is the time to talk."

"I think it's the best time. I've had two weeks to think about it, and all that thinking has raised a few questions. I want answers to them tonight."

"I ken what you're about, Adrian. You've nursed the idea of another man making love to me, of another man doing the things you want to do. You want me to tell you my husband was a bastard, or that he was a weakling, that he beat me, that I despised him. But I canna say those things because they are'na true. Bruce Ramsay was the kindest, most loving man I've ever known. I adored him. We had the perfect marriage. It almost killed me when he died."

"And there's no room for another man in your life?"

"I never said that. I couldna. Not to you. Bruce is dead. I've done my grieving for him. Whether or not I love again—well, it all depends on you, you ken?"

He gave her a blank look.

"If it's your goal to replace him in my heart, you are doomed for failure before you start. There are many things I admire about you, Adrian. I ken I could come to love you for yourself, for who you are, if you give me the chance. But dinna think you can replace Bruce. Dinna even try. You will have to carve your own place in my heart. You aren't Bruce. You aren't a branch of him . . . you aren't his replacement. I will grow to love you for a hundred different reasons that have nothing to do with Bruce Ramsay or my life in Scotland."

She turned to her dressing table and picked up a satin ribbon. He realized she intended to tie back her hair. He had been so taken with the way her body responded to the clinging, smooth fabric of her dressing gown, he hadn't noticed her hair was down.

She had beautiful hair. And the color—he must be becoming accustomed to it, for it didn't chafe him as it had at first. Yes, her hair was beautiful—a woman's crowning glory. It belonged down. Or entwined in a man's hands . . . his hands. The lamplight turned it to the color of a red sunset, throbbing with fire and life. Down, her hair softened her strong features. He felt the confusion return. Tonight she was beautiful. He wanted to step closer, to take her in his arms, to look down into her face and see the color of her eyes.

She slipped the ribbon beneath her hair.

"Leave it down," he said. "It becomes you."

She shrugged and tossed the ribbon back onto the dressing table. "You asked me about Bruce. I'm not sure I can explain it. It's a chapter of my life that has been read, not one that has been taken out of the book. You canna compete with the ghost of Bruce any more than I can compete with the ghost of Katherine." She looked at him squarely. "The difference between us is that I dinna want to try."

He crossed the room swiftly, coming to stand before her, his gaze one she had never seen before. His arms came around her as he drew her against him, pressing her head against his chest, stroking her hair.

"I can make you forget him," he whispered into her hair. "I can, and I will." His hands came up to press against her temples. "Even if I have to crush his memory from your mind."

"You can try," she said with that infuriating calm he found so antagonizing.

He held her tightly as his mouth slammed down upon hers, as if he could kiss the memory of another man away. "If you're going to make love to me," she whispered, "at least do it for honest reasons. Do it because you are a man who desires me as a woman."

He drew back, his hands gripping her arms. "What is that supposed to mean?"

"Dinna make love to me for the wrong reasons, Adrian. Dinna do it to prove something to me, to show me you are just as good in bed as my first husband was, that you can bring me as much pleasure. I can pleasure myself, but it isna the same."

His body stiffened. He pushed her away.

"Why are you angry?" she asked. "Is it because of what I said, or because I spoke the truth? Is that why you came in here tonight? Or was it to prove to yourself that you can feel something for another woman after loving *her* for so long?"

"I told you before to leave Katherine out of this."

"Why? You have no qualms about dragging my past out in front of me. Is yours more sacred because you never made love to her?"

The veins on his forehead stood out. His face darkened. "Maggie, I'm warning you."

But Maggie would not be stopped. Not tonight. She was running out of time. "Warn all you like. It willna do any good. I'm no afraid of you, Adrian, no matter how hard you try to frighten me."

"Keep talking like that and you may change your mind."

"What are you afraid of?" she asked.

"I'm not afraid of anything," he said, coming closer. "Want me to show you?"

"Which ghost are you trying to stifle, Adrian?" she asked calmly. "Mine, or yours?"

His heart lurched. The shock of her words stopped him. Was Maggie right? Was that what he was doing?

Adrian was feeling just a little annoyed with himself now, for pushing her, for trying to get her riled, knowing that even if she had lost her temper, it would have been his fault. What was it about her that made him lose touch with himself like this?

He sighed and ran his fingers through his hair, not certain what direction he should take from here. "Has it ever occurred to you," he said at last, "that maybe, just maybe, I want you because it's been a long time since I've had a woman? Maybe it's for no other reason than the fact that I need a woman, and you happen to be convenient. You are my wife." He wanted to kick himself the moment the words were out, for they sounded hurtful and childish, even to his ear.

"At least those would be honest reasons," she said, her hands going down to the sash at her waist.

Adrian watched, his heart in his throat, as she untied the satin sash, then pushed the robe from her body, first one shoulder, then the other.

When both shoulders were bare, she dropped her arms to her sides, and the fluid fabric slid like water over the perfect lines of her body to puddle around her feet on the floor. She stood before him now, proud and humble, and so gloriously naked, he hurt. It occurred to him that in humbling herself, she had humbled him even more. Yet even then, he could not take his eyes from her, from the way she stood there, pale as a moonbeam, slim and white as a narcissus, the lazy red-gold curls of her hair nearly covering her lovely breasts.

Turning to the bed, she lay down.

Adrian didn't move. He couldn't. His throat was bone-dry. His muscles were hard and frozen in place. His heart pounded painfully in his chest. The blood gushed in wild, runaway rivers to his head.

He had never seen anything so lovely.

He had never desired a woman so much.

She lay as still and quiet as a marble statue; pale and smooth and cold. There was no coyness, no flirtation, no frank gaze that wandered hotly over his body, or stared blatantly at the swelling between his legs. Nothing. She was as impersonal as stone. He felt his desire shrink away; felt his penis grow limp.

He hated her.

"What are you waiting for?" she asked. "It's what you wanted, isn't it? After all, I am your wife. If you need a woman, why not take me? I am, as you said, convenient. We women are all made the same, aren't we? Go ahead. What you want to do is legal and morally right, recognized by the laws of man and the church. What more could you ask for?"

"I don't want this!" he said. "If I did, I could poke a goddamn statue."

"Perhaps," she said, drawing the sheet over her body, "you need to decide what it is you do want before you come in here again."

"Damn you," he said, opening the buttons of his pants. "Goddamn you to hell!"

He joined her in the bed, ripping the sheet from her glorious body before taking her into his arms, kissing her, feeling no response, and kissing her harder because of it. He wanted to drive her as insane as she was driving him, wanted to make her feel the same smoldering, gut-twisting churning in her belly that he felt. He kissed her and kept on kissing her, rolling over on top of her and grinding himself against her.

His mouth still on hers, he tore at the fastenings of his pants, and his penis sprung free. He was hard, and hot, and straining with need. With a groan of defeat, he eased himself inside her, surrounding himself with exquisite peace, and wet, wet warmth.

His body took over when he became too mindless to function. His need was primitive now and without a thought, save one. He came quickly, the throaty groan of deeply felt rapture mingling with the harsh sound of his breathing. He felt his heart pound within his chest, the blood racing at a dizzying speed through his veins as he groaned and felt his release.

Slowly consciousness returned. He hated himself more than he hated her at that moment. She felt small and warm and soft beneath him. She had challenged him and won. He felt lousy and filled with shame. By giving in, by feeding his hunger, she had bested him. He despised what she had made him do, yet he couldn't leave her. He lay there, waiting, desperately wanting her to communicate with him, to save his soul from this humiliation, his mind from despair. But she lay statue-still beneath him. He couldn't even hear her breathing. Not even whores were this impersonal. He cursed softly and pushed himself away from her.

"No," she said, her hands coming up to hold him in place. "Dinna go," she whispered against the dampness of his chest. "Come to me again, Adrian."

She was kissing his throat now, and he closed his eyes against the agony of it. "Only this time make love to me, and leave Bruce and Katherine in the past, where they belong."

# CHAPTER
## ❧ TWELVE ❧

Maggie didn't sleep well. What little sleep she got was fitful, nothing more than brief little snatches where consciousness never really left her. The most delicious memories and irreverent ideas kept coming into her head. Adrian had made love to her last night.

It hadn't taken her long to realize that he was not an experienced lover. Not that he wasn't adept, for he was. No, it was simply that he was too eager and too hungry. He made love with a trembling sort of uncertainty, an almost clumsy eagerness that was both touching and highly arousing. For a man past thirty, he had the exuberance and almost awestruck devotion to duty that reminded her of youth.

The moment he entered her, filling her with himself, a bridge had somehow been crossed. A bridge that led her from her first marriage and her old life into the new. With the swiftness of an unexpected kick, she realized Adrian was far more real to her than any memory of Bruce. Surprisingly, she found she no longer thought of Bruce as her husband.

Adrian was her husband now. Her reality. And he filled her life and her consciousness so completely that she had little time or desire for anything else. His lovemaking last night had proved that, and her heart turned over at the thought.

Maggie looked at the window. It was still dark outside. She turned over and closed her eyes. It was no use. Her mind was full awake. Shortly before sunrise she gave up. If she couldn't sleep for thinking about last night, then she might as well get up and get dressed and give those bedeviling thoughts her undivided attention.

She dressed and went down to breakfast. Afterward she was feeling happy, mellow, and very domestic. It had become a habit with her to wake up feeling all wifely and homespun the morning after making love. It had started when she was married to Bruce. Apparently that same warm, buttery domestic feeling was going to continue with Adrian. She smiled, remembering how Bruce had always dreaded those fits of wifely exuberance, when, with a sudden burst of energy, she turned all helpful. "It's no that I mind your being happy, Maggie, but it's the way you go about showing it," Bruce had said to her one afternoon after she had dismissed his valet, and taken it upon herself to clean out his wardrobe. "Please, love, dinna put starch in my drawers again. Today I played the worst game of golf I've played since I was a boy. I couldna bend over, and when I got hot, my drawers stuck to me." He had started from the room, paused, turned back to her, and said, "One other thing. Dinna dye my handkerchiefs saffron yellow . . . or any other color. In fact, just stay out of my clothes altogether."

Maggie had learned her lesson. She wasn't about to touch Adrian's clothes . . . but that desk of his . . . the one in the study . . . now, that surely could use some help.

Papers were everywhere, sticking out of books and ledgers, wedged in between a pipe stand and lamp, sitting beneath a polished chunk of wood, or just plain scattered. They were folded, stacked, tossed, held down by paper weights, bound by wire clips, and tied together with string.

Sitting behind Adrian's desk, Maggie began to sort through the papers. It was a lot of work organizing and putting them in some semblance of order. Why, it was a wonder to her how Adrian ever found anything.

Three hours later, she had cleared his desk, and polished the mahogany top to a soldier's boot shine. It was about this time that Molly came looking for her. "Uh-oh, trouble," Molly said, coming into the room. "What have we here?"

Maggie blew a strand of hair out of her face and gave the desk one last swipe before coming around it to stand beside Molly, viewing the change—for the better, she might add. "I've straightened this mess," she said, with a tone of satisfaction. "Won't Adrian be surprised?"

"Oh, he'll be surprised, all right. I should have warned you—I would have, if I had known you were thinking about this," Molly said, looking at the desk and shaking her head. "I don't suppose you could put it back the way it was, could you?"

"Put it back?" Maggie asked. "What do you mean, put it back? It took me three hours to straighten it. Why, for Heaven's sake, would I want to put it back?"

"Because Adrian is going to kill both of us if you don't."

"That's absurd. He should be happy that this has been done."

"Maybe he should," Molly said, "but you can take my word for it, he won't be. I've been given strict orders not to touch anything on this desk, not even to dust."

"Well, there you have it," said Maggie.

"Have what?" said Molly.

"*You* didna touch it. I did."

"That only means he will kill you first," said Molly.

Adrian did not come home for dinner, so Maggie ate alone. After dinner, she spent some time in the library with her knitting, but soon she grew weary of that. Going to her room, she dressed for bed. Sitting at her dressing table looking through her ribbon box, she came across a raven's feather Fletcher had given her. She picked the feather up, absently stroking its sleek, glossy surface. How well she remembered the day he had given it to her, along with two plover eggs. The plover eggs were gone now—where, she did not remember—but the feather . . .

She wrapped her hand tightly around it and clutched it to her breast, feeling her eyes burn with the sudden swirl of recollection. She wanted to cry, and fought the urge by closing her eyes, but not even that could shut out the memory of her beloved children: Barrie sitting in the nursery, toiling over an alphabet sampler she was stitching, the sunlight turning her red hair to flame. Ainsley bouncing on her rocking horse, telling it to go faster. And of course, Fletcher, as sturdy and sensible as the brown color of his hair, a Scot to the core, and so like his father. She couldn't help wondering if he was still trying to coax his sisters outside to play Harry Racket or hoodman-blind, or if there was even any room to play such games aboard the ship they were now on.

She remembered afternoon tea parties spent with her daughters, sitting in miniature tufted chairs, sipping tea from a tiny china tea service, and the precious, intimate moments during the evening bath, when Fletcher always forgot to wash behind his ears, and the girls made beards for each other from soap bubbles. She recalled Barrie and Ainsley sitting on the kitchen stoop, blowing bubbles in Bruce's favorite clay pipe, and Fletcher fishing in the fishbowl with a tiny hook tied to the end of a piece of string, Ainsley crying when he told her he was going to eat all of her fish for dinner. There were happy times flooded in sunlight, and crisscross days, when nothing seemed to go right, and convalescent days for sore throats and bowls of steaming leek soup. There were winter afternoons just made for sledding, and warm summer mornings spent riding in a flower-bedecked pony cart, and dreary days when the mist turned to rain, keeping the children indoors to wile away the hours cutting snowflakes from paper and making crumbly oatcakes in the kitchen with Maude. There were sunny spring afternoons spent walking on the moors, gathering mallow blossoms and violets, or lying beneath the cool shade of a rowan tree making gowan chains and finding animal shapes in the clouds overhead.

She opened her hand and smoothed the tiny feather, placing it in the botom of her ribbon box. Then she picked up a button that she had meant to sew on Barrie's dress. Putting it back, she picked up a pale blue satin ribbon, seeing a few strands of Ainsley's red-gold hair still tangled in the knot. She left the knot there, putting the ribbon back where it was, knowing there would be other times she would take it out, for these memories were like stones that were too heavy to be washed away at will, stones too heavy to do anything but sink to the bottom of her mind and wait.

She closed the ribbon box and picked up her hairbrush, her thoughts now on her children as well as Adrian, her mind busy imagining the ways she could break the news of them to him.

What had happened last night had complicated things, to be sure.

She drew the brush absently through her hair, looking at herself in the mirror. Her face was a pale oval lost in a frame of red-gold hair. She pinched her cheeks and was rewarded with a faint blush of color.

Hearing a soft knock on her door, she was about to answer when she heard her name called.

"Maggie?"

It was Adrian's voice.

"Aye. Come in," she called, turning toward the door. "It isna locked."

He opened the door and stepped inside, closing it behind him. She smiled tentatively.

He greeted her with a curt nod.

*Trouble*, her mind warned. She had been so lost in the luxurious after-haze of his lovemaking that she hadn't stopped to think about *what if*.

What if Molly was right? What if he didn't want his desk touched? What if he was angry that she had?

One look at him told her that he was more than angry.

They stayed that way for a minute, him looking at her, her looking back at him, both of them busy mentally circling each other like two wolves—cautious, on guard, wary—each of them looking for an opening, a way to move in with a killing lunge, a way to catch the other with his guard down, a way to be victorious without suffering any wounds. Kill or be killed. A ritual, a dance, that was old as man.

*Why must men and women drive each other crazy before they settle in?* she wondered.

Here was a man pulled between two forces, his expectations and his desires. Clearly what she had done in his study wasn't sitting too well with him.

"I suppose you've come about the papers on your desk," she said, seeing her directness had surprised him.

"What are you talking about? What papers?"

"The papers on your desk," she said. "The bills and things. The ones I straightened today and put away."

"You what?" he shouted.

"I straightened your papers and cleaned your desk."

"Tell me you didn't," he said. "Tell me this is some kind of joke."

"I canna," she said softly, understanding now that Molly had been right. He would kill her first.

"What else did you do in my study?"

"Why, nothing. Havena you seen it?"

"No, I haven't, and now I'm sure as hell afraid to. Let me tell you something, Maggie. Don't ever touch anything on my desk. Better yet, stay the hell away from my study."

She looked puzzled. "But if you havena seen it, why did you come here?"

"I came here to tell you that last night . . ."

*Was wonderful . . . the second time.*

He paused, looking off for a moment. When he looked back at her, he said, "I want you to know that what happened last night . . . I'm sorry I forced myself on you. It won't happen again."

The brush trembling in her hand, Maggie rose to her feet. He was watching her with an odd expression on his face. "Why?" she asked, fighting for her lost composure.

He shrugged. "What difference does it make? What happened, happened. It was a mistake that can't be changed. There's no reason to try."

"I wasna," she said, matter-of-factly. "Unlike you, I canna say I am sorry it happened. And it wasna force." She began to laugh.

"What do you find so amusing?"

"Us," she said simply. "It is something to laugh at, you ken."

"Only if you're mad," he said. "Are you?"

She laughed harder. "Aye. I ken I must be verra mad to find the way we always seem to see everything through such different eyes so humorous."

His gaze was direct. He clearly did not understand. He held her eyes with his, waiting. Her first thought was to look away, but something prevented it.

"Last night," she said reflectively. "I canna help thinking about it, and apparently neither could you. But no for the same reason, I ken. You come into my room after a night of undeniable brooding, telling me it willna happen again—" her voice dropped now, low and husky "—while I have been sitting here counting the hours until it did."

For the craziest moment she felt like laughing at the look on his face. She shook her head instead. "How different is truth from fancy," she said, then glanced at him with a look that she hoped burned right through him. She saw the red, bloodshot eyes, the stubble of a beard, the weary stance. "I ken you didn't sleep much?"

"None," he said.

"Aye," she said, "I ken that. I couldna sleep either. I lay awake most of the night thinking."

He seemed to relax a bit, as though he was a little interested in hearing just where she was headed with all of this.

"I spent a great deal of time thinking about our next meeting, only now I ken just how very far apart our thoughts have been. You were thinking stop. I was thinking go."

"You don't make sense."

"Aye, it's a peculiar habit of mine." She smiled sadly. "You canna imagine what I thought about all night, the things that filled my mind and kept me from sleeping."

"Things like what?"

"I thought about what you would look like without your clothes." She paused.

Maggie watched as his body seemed to jerk in response. "Thoughts have no place in this," he said curtly.

"Neither has reason, apparently," she said, her voice lower.

The muscles in his jaw worked. "Reason has nothing to do with it."

"Aye, it does. By reasoning we arrive at conclusions."

"I am not an idiot."

The corners of her mouth lifted. "I've seen no proof of that," she said, then realizing how he resisted even humor, she sighed. "Then tell me you dinna reach the same conclusions I have. Tell me that after last night, you can say there is nothing between us. Tell me that when you touch me, you feel nothing."

She paused, looking at him. Waiting. Pleading.

He remained as he was. Resistant.

Last night he had made love to her. Twice. The first time she would have to toss out, of course, but the second time . . . A man who made love to a woman like that did not harbor thoughts of never doing it again, and yet he was telling her it wouldn't happen a second time, that he was sorry. What was he afraid of?

She sighed, turning her face away, feeling suddenly shy about what she was going to say. "You made love to me last night, Adrian, and I . . ."

She turned back, knowing she had to say the words to him, to his face. "What I want to say is that I enjoyed it." She doubled her fists in frustration. "No, not enjoyed," she said, her hand coming up to her forehead. "It was more than that, but I canna find the right words." She stepped toward him, her hand coming out as if she were going to touch him, then it dropped to her side. "When you touch me, Adrian, I feel as though I've been touched by fire."

She looked at him. He was leaning against the door, watching her. The air was heavy with his discomfort.

"It wasna force, Adrian. No matter what you believe."

He shrugged. "It was, but it doesn't matter now," he said.

She started to speak, but he said, "Leave it be, Maggie."

"Why? I dinna understand. Why are you so hopelessly disillusioned? Is it because I was a disappointment to you, because I wasna the woman you had in mind, the woman you described to your brother?"

"I said leave it be."

"Why? So we can both hide behind excuses? I canna be anything but honest, Adrian. I'm a real person. I can only be myself. I canna be something I'm not—not even to make you feel safe and happy. You try to blame me, and you do, but it willna work, do you ken? I willna be made to feel guilty."

For a moment he simply stood there, looking at her; then, without responding to what she had said, he simply nodded his dismissal and left, the door snapping shut behind him.

For a long, long time, Maggie stood there, staring at the door, her heart wrenching for him. He hadn't forced her. Why couldn't she make him see that? How could she make him understand? How could she help him to stop being so hard on himself? Maggie had never felt so frustrated. Strange, but the thing she found most frustrating wasn't that she had lost, but that she had come so close to winning.

Blinking back tears, she thought there was nothing simple about it. She cared for him. Aye, more than she would have thought possible in such a short time. Even more frustrating was knowing Adrian had come to care for her as well. And he did. She felt it more with their every encounter. He was simply too stubborn for his own good, and when it came to matters of the heart, he wasn't overblessed with common sense.

There were so many wonderful things she admired in Adrian, but his moodiness, his lightning-quick shifts of emotion, were too difficult to deal with. Just as she was wondering what she could have done to prevent this new life of hers from slipping away, it suddenly occurred to her that she had already taken a chance on this man and lost. There was nothing else to lose.

Something her father said to her after Bruce's death came suddenly to mind. "Once you've been knocked to the ground, lass, you canna be knocked verra much further."

A slow smile stretched itself across her face. Her children would be here in a few weeks. A lot of things could happen in two months' time.

*Aye,* she said to herself, *all isna lost yet.*

It was strange to Maggie how things sometimes work out, for once everything was out in the open, a calm seemed to settle over the stormy state of affairs that had existed between herself and Adrian.

Over the course of time, Maggie came to understand how

demanding Adrian's life was. Sometimes she would see him slumped over his desk going through a sheaf of papers, or drawing circles on a map pinned to the wall. At other times she didn't see him at all, learning later he was deep in the woods, working with the men or staking out a new location.

At home, their life began to settle into some sort of a pattern. After dinner they would retire to the library, where Adrian would work and Maggie would take up her knitting, or they would go to the music room, where she would play for him.

Maggie much preferred the library. She felt at ease there, away from the painful reminders the music room held for her. As they sat together, he bent over his papers, the smell of his pipe filling the room, she felt comfortable, married. And she had time to study him, time to wonder what he thought about her.

Often she would hear his leather chair creak and look up to see him lean back in a weary stretch, his eyes upon her, and she would wonder what he was thinking. More than once she used this as an opportunity to talk to him about the mill. Tonight was no different.

Hearing Adrian's long, drawn-out sigh, the sound of his pencil hitting the desk, she looked up as he stretched, then stood, moving to the table to pour himself a brandy.

"What's bothering you?" she asked.

He finished pouring and took a drink before giving her a soft look. "What makes you think something is bothering me?"

She smiled. "You're restless. You keep running your hands through your hair. You tap your pencil. You beat your fingers on the desk. You've chewed three plugs of tobacco. Those are the signs that you have something on your mind."

His smile was tentative, almost shy. "I don't know if I like knowing someone has privy to my thoughts," he said.

"I dinna have privy to your thoughts, you ken. But I do

know how to read your actions. Are you going to tell me or no?''

"Or no," he replied with a chuckle. "Maggie, it's not important enough to bother with."

"It has caused you considerable thought, so it must be important."

Adrian grinned. "Stop standing there blinking at me like an owl." She blinked again, and he said, "Maggie, if I tell you, you'll be down at the mill at first light tacking bat wings to the bunkhouse door, or sprinkling spiderwebs over the bunks. I know you—*do you ken?*"

He mumbled something when she laughed at the way he tried to mimic her. "I know your odd Scots ways, your superstitions and your idiotic cures." He threw up his hands. "What in the name of God is happening to me? To my life?"

"I dinna understand what you mean, but you canna blame it all on me. Being Scot, I canna help, but if I promise to keep my idiotic cures to myself, will you tell me?"

Adrian raised his hands in surrender. "All right. Have it your way. Sometimes I forget that reasoning with a Scot is like trying to talk sense with a grizzly. One encounter leaves you bleeding from a dozen places." He paused a moment, and she realized he was looking full at her.

"We have a problem with lice," he said calmly. "It's as simple as that. There's a bad outbreak of them in the bunkhouse. Much worse than we've had before. It's gotten so bad, the men are having trouble sleeping. We've tried the usual remedies—even sending the men to your steam hut—but nothing seems to work. The minute they go back into the bunkhouse, they are covered with lice in a few hours. Their beds, their clothes . . . the whole bunkhouse is crawling with lice. They're even in the walls."

Maggie frowned. "What if you ran a pipe of steam into the bunkhouse?"

Adrian shrugged, treating her question with his customary

taciturn indifference, but Maggie wasn't about to be deterred.

"You could seal the windows and door, then fill the bunkhouse with steam just like you fill the steam hut." She nodded to herself. "Aye, that's it. The men hang their laundry in there, so everything could be left in place. They wouldna have to move a thing."

Adrian pondered that for a moment. He didn't appear too enthused, but then, Adrian rarely appeared enthused about anything. "I'll talk it over with Big John tomorrow," he said at last, and Maggie nodded.

Molly was clucking about the kitchen like an old broody hen the next day when she informed Maggie that the men were sealing up the bunkhouse in readiness. "Do you want to go watch?"

Maggie considered what Molly had said. At some other point in her life, she would have found anyone who invited her to a delousing a wee bit daft.

With a nod of her head, Maggie said, "Aye, I'll go, though I canna think of a single reason why I should."

"Well, come on then. You can think of reasons on the way."

When Maggie and Molly arrived at the mill, the steam was already being pumped into the bunkhouse. After disconnecting the steam pipe, the men waited for the bunkhouse to cool down a bit. When they opened the door, they saw the last, hard-line stragglers of lice crawling out of the walls to die. Clem Burnside let out a whoop, and the rest of the men followed with a cheering roar.

The cheer died when a big blond lumberjack named Jock Halverson mumbled something about not having any more louse races on Sundays.

The grumbling about the loss of contestants for the Sunday louse races subsided a bit when Eli Carr stepped inside and pointed grimly at the loggers' crude furniture, which had been warped out of shape by the steam, leaving it completely unusable.

"Well, we can make new furniture," Dudley Dunlap said. "Shorty, you and Clyde go on in and see if you can find any lice that ain't dead."

"And then what, club 'em?" Clyde asked.

"Club 'em or stomp 'em," Dudley replied.

Shorty and Clyde stepped inside. A few minutes later, they came back out, Shorty holding his red wool shirt up in front of him, and Clyde holding a pair of long johns. Both items had shunk down to a child's size.

Molly and Maggie hurried back to the wagon, where they could laugh in private. "I ken Adrian won't be confiding in me anymore," Maggie said at last.

"He might be confiding," Molly said, "but he may not be taking your advice."

Molly slapped the reins against the horses' backs, and turned the wagon up the hill. "Did Adrian ever say anything to you about that fit of cleanliness you had with his study?"

"No, he didna say verra much," Maggie said, remembering the reason why.

Molly shook her head. "Now, *that* surprises me. It surely does." She shook her head again and slapped the reins. "I just don't understand it. Adrian never lets anything slip by. He's so thorough with everything he does."

"Aye," Maggie said in agreement. "He would burn down a house just to kill a rat."

Dinner had been over for what seemed hours, and Maggie was just putting away her knitting when she yawned, thrusting her arms out in a lazy stretch. Pausing midstretch, she felt Adrian's eyes upon her and she looked up and met his glance. Everywhere his eyes touched her, she felt burned, consumed. Her response was immediate. Their recent compatibility, their comfort around each other, his handsomeness, even the memory of his lovemaking, lay forgotten. Nothing had any effect upon her, save his look—an open, hungry look that devoured. Her heart thundered painfully in her chest. There was something about that look that was deep and searching, and yet pessimistic. It reminded her of the way he viewed everything, with cynicism and distrust. Even now, he was probably putting a motive to something as natural and innocent as her yawn.

Any other woman might have dismissed him as spoiled and childish, or at best a cold, uncaring man with a cruel streak wider than a loch, a man with nothing better to do than to make those around him miserable and uncomfortable. But Maggie did not. She bore the scrutiny of his dark gaze without flinching.

When she looked at him, she saw not spoiled childishness, or coldness, but a look of dull withdrawal, a suspicious look in his blue eyes, a mouth that was hard and wary. If there was any childishness to his behavior at all, it was infinitely touching.

"Are you tired?" she asked.

"No, are you?"

"No," she said, glancing at the fire, letting the conversation die, slipping once again into silence. She looked back at him. He was still looking at her in that devouring, hungry way.

The last time he had looked at her in that way, he had made love to her. Did he want to do so again? He looked as if he were about to say something to her. *Say it,* her heart cried. *Say it!* But he looked away. The room seemed to fill with a foreboding silence. *Say it, damn you,* she cried inwardly. *Say what I've waited for weeks for you to tell me. You can say it honestly, and without fear, for I've seen the feeling you have for me in your eyes, and I willna turn away. You care for me, Adrian. You have only to say the words . . .*

*you've only to tell me how you feel. Dinna make us both
suffer any longer. End the agony, I pray you.*

She did not realize that she had spoken his name, or that
she had looked at him with such yearning. She was unaware
that she had raised her hand toward him in silent entreaty.
She only became aware when his face darkened. His face
told her how he hated the way he felt so helpless against her.

Maggie closed her eyes, then stood, rubbing her arms as
she crossed the room. Taking up the poker, she stirred the
quiet coals to a crackling blaze. "Perhaps we could just go
on pretending," she said without turning to look at him.

"What?" he said blankly.

"I said, perhaps we could just go on pretending."

"Pretending what, Maggie? You're talking in riddles."

She turned now, and was looking straight at him. "Pretending that we like each other. Pretending that we're married."

He didn't flinch, but his face turned red. "We *are* married," he muttered, then in lower tones, he added, "And I
do like you . . . sometimes."

"You *do*?" she asked, her face flushed.

He laughed. "If you think I'm going to answer that with
you standing there waving that red-hot poker in my face, you
don't know me very well," he said.

How dare he laugh when she was serious. "Och! I ken
you well enough, Adrian Mackinnon . . . enough to see your
brain rests at the bottom of dullness. I dinna ken why I try
to reason with you, to be civil. You're incapable of it. When
will I realize it, that you are nothing but a gowk?"

Throwing the poker into the fire, she quit the room, hearing his rolling laughter as she did.

Always a busy place, the logging camp was a beehive of
activity on payday. Loggers came and went all day, dropping
in and out of the office. Some came just long enough to pick

up their wages; other used the few free moments in camp to stop by the medicine hut to have a new injury or infection looked after.

Despite Adrian's order to stay away from the camp, Maggie went anyway. Starched in a white cotton apron, she was the picture of efficiency visiting with the loggers, giving advice on keeping a wound clean, or sewing up a deep cut. Whenever there was a slump in the number of patients, she would drift over to the window and lean her elbows on the sill to watch the activity going on outside.

" 'Scuse me, ma'am."

Maggie turned to see a young boy of fifteen or so. His hair was as white as flax, and his eyes were as blue as a Viking's. Her eyes dropped to the right leg of his trousers, which was soaked in blood.

"Och, laddie, this is no time to be polite," she said. "Dinna stand there bleeding to death." Grabbing an armful of bandages, she patted her working table. "Up here with you, now," she said, taking his arm and helping him.

He winced as he sat down, but Maggie was too busy cutting away the leg of his pants to pay that much mind. "What have you done here, lad? It looks like you've got six inches of splintered wood gouging into your thigh."

"And there's at least six more inches below that," the boy said, leaning back, his voice quivering and unsteady.

Maggie looked up. His arms were trembling. "Here now," she said softly, cradling the boy's head. "Take a sip of this, lad, then lie down while I'm seeing to your leg." She gave him a few sips of opium diluted in water, and when he had finished, she held his head until he was lying flat. While the opium eased him, she busied herself by gathering the things she would need.

"You ain't gonna cut off my leg, are you?" he asked, coming up on his elbows.

Maggie stopped beside him and shook her head. "No, lad,

I willna do that.'' She smoothed his unruly hair back from his face. "I ken you couldna be chasing the lassies if I did that, now could you?'' She pushed him back down. "Now, you stay there, you ken?''

He nodded and smiled weakly. "Thank you, ma'am.''

"What's your name, lad?'' she asked as she began washing the blood from the wound.

"Will Watkins.''

"Well, Will Watkins, tell me how you feel now.''

"Sleepy.''

"Then you sleep a bit, lad, and let me see to your leg.'' She picked up his hands and placed them over the edge of the table. "If it hurts, you squeeze the table, you ken?''

"Yessum.''

Maggie looked at the huge shaft of wood imbedded deeply in the muscle of Will's leg. Blood oozed around it. Packing the area beneath it with cotton sheeting to absorb the sudden flow of blood that would come when she removed the splinter, she grasped the piece of wood with both hands and began to pull.

Will's hands gripped the table. Beads of sweat collected in the peach fuzz over his lip. His breathing was short and gasping.

"Breathe deeply, lad. Dinna be ashamed to cry out if you need to.''

With one tremendous burst of strength, Maggie pulled again, this time using all the force she could muster. About the time she decided she would have to send for Adrian or Big John, the splintered chunk of wood gave, and Maggie fell back with the force of it.

Half an hour later, she had the wound cleaned of smaller splinters and neatly closed with black thread. Will was sleeping when Clem Burnside came to carry him back to the bunkhouse.

"I'll need to remove the stitches in a week," she said, holding the door open for Clem.

She barely had time to put things in order when Big John poked his grizzled head through the door and announced it would be getting dark soon.

"If you hurry, you can go up to the house with your husband. He quit the office no more than two minutes ago," he said with a wink, and then he was gone.

The following Sunday afternoon, Maggie was in the library, writing a letter to her father, when Molly came in. She handed Maggie a small doeskin pouch drawn together with a rawhide string. Maggie took it, giving Molly a questioning look.

"Big John asked me to give it to you. Seems Will Watkins was too shy to do the honors himself."

Maggie opened the pouch and poured a necklace of shells into her hand.

"They're dentalium shells," Molly said. "Dentalium means little tusks. They're a measure of wealth among the Yuroks."

Maggie examined the pale-hued shells. "I've never seen shells like these before."

"They're found quite a ways north of here, fished out of the water by the Indian tribes up there." Molly reached out and lifted part of the strand in her hand. "A strand this size could buy a wife for a Yurok brave," she said.

Maggie held the strand aloft, admiring the shells and remembering the flaxen-haired young boy called Will Watkins.

The week that followed seemed to erupt with a rash of minor accidents. Walking back from the cookhouse after lunch one afternoon, Maggie gave an accounting to Big John and Adrian.

"Why, just this morning I've seen five mashed hands,

one broken finger, a rope burn, a broken nose, four saw cuts, and one foot badly bruised by a clumsy ox.''

''Which clumsy ox was that?'' Big John asked. ''John Schurtz?''

Maggie laughed. ''I dinna ken Schurtz was a clumsy ox, but the one I was thinking of had four legs.''

Big John laughed, and Maggie joined him. She looked up, her face bathed in sunlight, to find Adrian watching her with another one of his odd expressions. This one lay somewhere between contemplation and curiosity.

''Dinna fash yourself. It's called laughter,'' she said to him, disappearing through the door of the medicine hut as Big John gave a great guffaw.

For the rest of the afternoon she treated patients intermittently, for it always seemed the small room was either very full or empty, but never in between. During one lull, Maggie was leaning against the window, looking outside, when she noticed that everything in the camp seemed to come to a standstill.

Opening the door, she stepped out onto the porch, suddenly aware of the deadening quiet coming from the woods, where there was no sound of whistles, axes, men shouting, or the creaking groan of massive trees as they fell. The men in the camp had noticed it, too, for they had stopped milling around and were standing in small groups, whispering, making speculations when they saw a group of loggers coming down out of the woods, carrying something. When they drew closer, Maggie saw it was Will Watkins, the flaxen-haired skid greaser who swabbed the skids with dogfish oil to make the logs slide easier.

She started toward the men when a hand came out to stop her. ''He's dead, Maggie,'' Adrian said gently. ''There's nothing you can do for him now.''

Maggie stood motionless. It seemed that somehow Will

had tripped into the path of the skid road and was crushed beneath ten thousand pounds of timber.

"He never did come back to let me remove the stitches," she said, her voice faltering.

"He was just a boy," Clem Burnside said, tears running down his face.

With a strangled cry, Maggie covered her mouth with her hand and turned away, stumbling back inside the medicine hut to cry.

She didn't hear the door open and shut, or Adrian's footsteps as he entered the room, but she did hear the steady rhythm of his heart when he took her in his arms, and held her head against his chest while she cried.

After that day, a cloud of mysterious sorrow seemed to hang over the camp. It wasn't long before Maggie was convinced that Will Watkins's death was a herald of things to follow.

Late one afternoon, two weeks later, just before Adrian was due home for dinner, Maggie took Israel for a walk along the cliffs to watch the sunset. Only a few minutes before, he had wandered off with his nose to the ground, and Maggie had walked on alone. Sometimes Israel seemed severely lacking in character.

She smiled as she remembered her father telling her once, "You can't castrate character into a dog." She would not try castrating Israel, but there was someone else who might benefit from it.

She walked on until she reached an outcropping of rocks and found one that looked perfect to sit upon. She sat down, staring out over the water, wondering if she would be able to see any of the gray whales that Adrian said wintered along the coast, often swimming quite close to shore.

She was running out of time. Her children were due soon, and still things between herself and Adrian weren't as she wished them to be. Oh, he was no longer angry about her previous marriage, but . . . Maggie paused. But what? What was it about their situation that frustrated her so? *Because you're falling in love with him, and he hasn't come close to telling you how he feels. What would it be like*, she wondered, *if Adrian loved me?*

She thought about that for a moment. *To love, and be loved, is to feel the sun from both sides.*

"Well," she told herself, "you canna sit out here all day moping about the way things are. Worries are like bread crumbs in the bed. The more you wiggle, the more they scratch."

Maggie turned her thoughts back to the gray whales, but soon she gave up on them and began watching the sun sinking into the ocean. It made her wish she had brought her canvas to capture the Pacific as it looked now, tinged with lavender and gilded with gold.

She heard Israel come up behind her and turned to give him a scolding, but it was Adrian who approached.

"What are you doing out here?" he asked. "It's almost dark."

"I was looking for the gray whales," she said, turning away from him and staring out over the water.

"And did you see any?"

"No, I didna, so I began watching the sunset. It's beautiful this time of day. There are colors at gloaming that you canna see at any other time."

"Gloaming?"

"Twilight," she said absently.

"Hmmm," he said, coming around to sit down beside her, giving her a studying look. "Are you becoming maudlin?"

"Aye," she said softly, then with a shot of humor, she said, "and hungry, too."

"Why didn't you come back to the house if you were hungry?"

"I'd rather watch the sunset."

"And leave me to eat alone?"

"Aye," she said, laughing and giving him a sideways look. "I ken how you dote on my absence," she said, her eyes brimming with humor.

Adrian did not smile.

"You dinna smile even out of politeness, do you?"

"I smile only when there's a reason to."

She shook her head. "There's always a reason to smile," she said.

"Even when you're thinking of Will Watkins?"

"Aye," she said, her voice breaking. "He touched my life, and I am richer for it. I canna smile now, when I think of him, but I ken there will be a time that I can wear his necklace of shells and smile."

"Maggie . . ."

"Dinna," she said. She turned her head toward him, and he saw her eyes sparkled more than before. "Sometimes I think the only brightness in your life at all is the sunshine reflecting on the whites of your eyes."

"That's what I love about Scottish humor—its sarcasm," he said.

"Aye, and well you should love it. It's a lot like you, bitter and caustic."

He looked at her, and she sighed. She had spoken more sharply than she intended. Her steady gaze softened. "I'm sorry. I was thinking about Will Watkins before you came, and the mention of his name like that . . . I was a wee bit maudlin, as you said, and unsettled as well, but I ken it's no reason to be angry with you."

He didn't reply, only leaned forward, bracing his elbows on his knees and staring out over the water. "Will's death was only the beginning," he said after a while.

She turned her head to stare at him. "I dinna ken what you mean, only the beginning. The beginning of what?"

"Death," he said slowly. "Accidents."

"There have been more?"

"Too many more. Too many to be just accidents," he said. "In the past week we've had three men injured, two killed. The week before, there were two accidents, one death."

Maggie leaned forward, putting her hand on his arm. "Why dinna you tell me?"

"I didn't want to worry you."

She didn't believe that for a minute. "What kind of accidents?"

The usual kind—falls from trees, somebody being careless. You know how accidents lie waiting at every stage of the lumbering process. We have accidents in the mill or in the woods all the time, but never this many in such a short time. The men are starting to talk."

"About what?"

"They think someone is causing the accidents, and I think they're right."

"Pope and Talbot?"

"More than likely."

"But nothing you can prove?"

"Nothing we can prove," he said tiredly. He looked at Maggie and shook his head, coming to his feet. He gave her one of his rare attempts at a smile. It was a rather helpless gesture. "I didn't mean to unload all of this upon you."

"You couldna keep it from me forever," she said.

He must have been thinking the same thing, to judge from the look on his face and the hasty way he changed the subject.

"It's almost dark," he said. "We'd best be getting back. Molly will be waiting dinner, and she needs to get home to feed Big John."

"Aye," she said, coming to her feet. "The gloaming colors have all gone anyway."

The walked along in silence until they reached the house. Adrian opened the door, following her inside. "I canna go to dinner like this," she said, looking down at her dress, "or Molly will be sending me to eat in the kitchen. I'd better change," she said softly, turning toward the stairs.

She started up the steps, and not hearing the sound of his footsteps, knew he must be watching her. The thought turned her legs to jelly, and she felt wobbly-legged.

She had almost reached the landing when he called out to her.

"Maggie?"

"Aye," she said, turning to look down at him. He was smiling, and she thought surely the stars must be dancing in the heavens.

"What's a gowk?"

She smiled, but she turned her head so that he couldn't see it. "A cuckoo bird," she said. "And I havena changed my mind about it."

# CHAPTER
## ❧ THIRTEEN ❧

Maggie asked Adrian to go on a picnic.

Adrian said he did not go on picnics. "I don't have time."

"Sometimes it's easier to give in than to fight," she reminded him.

"Are those the only two choices I have? Give in or fight?"

"Aye, and I'll warn you now, I'm a bonny fighter."

Adrian looked at her and threw back his head, laughing.

As it turned out, the picnic wasn't such a bad idea. Maggie had chosen a place for their picnic where the forest gave out and the land gradually sloped down to the sea; a lonely stretch of beach lay sprinkled with driftwood below wave-eroded cliffs. The weather was mild, the sun was warm and mellow.

And so was Maggie.

Adrian leaned back on the quilt, resting on his elbows, his legs stretched out and crossed at the ankles, and thought about that as he watched Maggie out of the corner of his eye.

Maggie was unaware of his scrutiny. She was busy exploring a tidepool, stooping to pick up something here, bending over to look at something else there; glancing skyward intermittently, whenever a gull circled overhead.

Adrian watched her make her way back up the beach, angling off toward him, stopping for a moment by the buggy to deposit a few shells before coming to the quilt. Dropping down beside him, she dusted the sand from her skirt and hands, then began putting the leftovers back into the basket.

She offered him the last of the blackberry wine. He shook his head, wondering if the Scot in her would let the small amount left go to waste.

It wouldn't, and he felt as if a shaft of sunlight had fallen only on him as he saw her glance at him, then at the bottle. With a shrug, she started to pour what was left into her glass, then thinking better of it, put the bottle to her lips, tilted back her head, and finished it off.

His eyes went to her throat, lingering there, watching her swallow. He was thinking he would like to put his lips there. Feeling lazy and as mellow as that circle of sun overhead, he observed her put the empty wine bottle and glass back into the basket and close the lid.

The wind stirred, wrapping the lightweight fabric of her gray skirt around Maggie's legs as she stood up. The breeze caught the ruffled edge and gave it a flirtatious flip, giving him a view of a well-turned ankle. He closed one eye, as if he were taking a bead with his rifle. She had a nice backside. He liked a woman with a nice backside. Funny, he had never realized that before. He tried to remember if Katherine had been so endowed, but couldn't seem to remember much about Katherine at that moment.

Even when he tried to conjure up a vision of Katherine, his gaze never left Maggie. He recalled how she had looked the night he had gone to her room to tell her that he wouldn't force himself on her again. The shocked, hurt look he had seen briefly—before she had carefully masked it—had been enough to make him feel remorseful.

A slow curve of a grin formed as he remembered the mess she had made of his desk that same day. Damn if it hadn't taken him a week to get his papers in order. Filed everything in alphabetical order, she had. Now, who in their right mind would have put a receipt for forty bags of flour in with a receipt for a falling saw?

Maggie would.

And who would have torn up his order for chewing tobacco?

Maggie would.

*Ah, Maggie, Maggie, I could grow old with you.*

The thought shocked him. *Well, what's so strange about that? She is, after all, my wife. Why shouldn't I think of growing old with her?*

Because you led her to believe you wouldn't make love to her again. *I was angry and hurt, and that often makes people say things they don't mean. Things have gotten better since then. I'm beginning to become accustomed to her.*

Adrian stopped thinking when Maggie picked up the basket and returned to the buggy. Without giving it much thought, he came to his feet and picked up the quilt, folding it in quarters as he followed her. She must have heard him coming, for just as he drew close to her, she turned, reaching for the quilt.

Their hands brushed, and for a moment their eyes met and held, then she whispered, "Thank you," and turned to put the quilt on top of the basket. His gaze raked her over good, from the gleaming red-gold of her hair to the tips of her shoes, thinking it must be hard for a woman to go through what she was going through—to travel halfway around the world to marry a man she had never seen, only to be sent back again. Was it guilt, then, that made him say what he said? "I'm going over to the old millsite tomorrow. If you'd like to go, you're welcome to ride over there with me."

She turned back to look at him, neither of them realizing at first just how close they were. Instinctively her hand flew to her bosom as her eyes grew wide with surprise. For a moment he was mesmerized by those eyes. Today they were as golden and mellow as a mess of butter stirred with molasses.

She eyed him dubiously, and he had no trouble reading what she was thinking. Still, he supposed it wasn't odd for her to be wondering what he was up to, considering . . .

"The old millsite?" she said, her voice uncertain.

"It's about a three-hour ride from here—in the buggy. There isn't much there now. We use it mostly for storage. There are some ledgers I can't locate, and I thought they might have been left there."

"I ken I would love to go," she said. "Wouldna it be faster on horseback?"

"Yes, but if the files are there . . ."

"Aye," she said, giving her head a thump. "I ken you couldna bring them back on a horse. I wasna thinking."

It was early the next morning when they left, Maggie too sleepy to do much talking, Adrian too self-conscious to try. Adrian found it odd that he was feeling a bit shy around her. Just what in the name of hell was he doing going off like this, as if they were a happily married couple who enjoyed each other's company?

Strange thing was, he really *did* enjoy her company. She was a very charming woman. And there had been times, right after her arrival, that he had found her so desirable that he had walked around for days with his penis standing as straight and rigid as a tent pole. For a while he was afraid it was going to become a habit to wake up each morning and see a pyramid rising out of the bedcovers.

He slapped the reins, urging the gelding forward, wishing he knew how to recall the warm intimacy they had shared on the picnic yesterday. He stared off in the distance, fishing around in his mind for a neutral topic—something in safe waters for them to discuss. Unable to locate one, he remained silent.

The longer they rode along in silence, the more Maggie was afraid he might want to talk about her marriage, her past, and in so doing, she feared she might forget and say something about her children.

At last she decided the best way to get him talking about something other than her past was to get him talking about his.

"Ross told me your mother and father were killed by Indians."

"And my brother Andrew."

"I've never seen an Indian. What are they like?"

"I can't speak for all Indians, but Comanches, I know pretty well. They're savage and wild, and about ten times braver than brave. They're foolish, as well, clinging to the past, fighting a battle that's already been lost."

"They sound a lot like Scots."

"Yes, I suppose they do, and in some ways that's probably a good comparison. The whites are to the Indians what the English are to the Scots. They don't trust the whites. And they probably have a good reason not to."

"You sound almost sympathetic."

He looked at her. "They killed three members of my family, kidnapped my sister, and orphaned five young boys. I can't say I'm sympathetic, but I can say we haven't always dealt right by them."

"Have you ever thought about looking for your sister?"

"I used to, but not anymore. She's been gone too long. Even if we did find her, she wouldn't be white—not anymore." His face took on a faraway look, then he shifted his position, transferring the reins to his other hand. "She's better off left where she is. She's a Comanche now."

He had withdrawn again. They rode along in silence until they reached the old mill.

It took Adrian more time than he thought to find the ledgers. "I had intended to show you around a bit," he said, putting the ledgers into the buggy. "But we've been here longer than I planned."

He looked at the sky.

"We'll have to head on back, and at a fast pace at that," he said. "We can't travel at night. Not in a buggy over these rough trails."

She felt more relaxed with him on the way back, and oddly enough, the more relaxed she felt, the more silent she became. She sat more comfortably on the seat next to him, content to take in the magnificent scenery, asking him enough questions in the beginning that he took it upon himself to point things out to her after that. He stopped once to point out a cougar. It had emerged from the trees on the other side of what he called a gorge. The mountain sloped away from the forest where the cougar stood upon a large boulder. They sat in silence watching the cougar, who seemed not to notice them, until he turned away and disappeared into the trees.

Adrian slapped the gelding, urging him into a steady pace. Maggie clamped her hands over her knees and felt as if she were smiling from her insides out. She removed her bonnet, noticing Adrian gave her a curious look, but he didn't say anything, and neither did she. She was too relaxed and too content, and she didn't want to spoil it by talking. She realized for the first time just how happy she was here, how free she felt, how safe. Adair Ramsay and the pain he had inflicted was behind her now. She had a husband—a strong man, a man who could and would protect her from the likes of Adair . . . if it came to that.

Feeling deliciously happy, she settled back into watching the countryside, noticing how the shadows from the trees stretched long and thin across the road. Glancing at the sky, she saw mist collecting on the mountains, but there was none to be seen along the bottom of the gorge. She remembered a little phrase she had taught her children, one that her mother had taught her.

*Mist on the hills*
*Brings water to the mills;*
*Mist in the hollows—*
*Fine weather follows.*

She didn't realize she had spoken the words aloud until Adrian looked at her. "Although I would prefer mist, it smells like rain to me," he said.

"At least the buggy has a top on it," she said cheerfully. "I ken I'm glad we didna come in the wagon."

He nodded and shifted his position, giving her a quick glance. "If it rains, we won't make it back before dark."

"What will we do?"

"We'll spend the night in the buggy," he said, giving her a soft look that he soon covered. "Pray it doesn't rain," he said quickly, casting an eye heavenward.

"I dinna think that will do any good," she said a moment later. "It's raining now." She looked at the dark spots appearing on the gelding's brown back, noticing how little puffs of dust rose around each splatter.

A short time later, the gelding's back was glistening black, and everything around them was a flat, dull gray. Twice the horse had slipped—once dangerously close to the edge of a steep drop-off.

Adrian cursed, calling the horse a clumsy bastard, then fell silent. Maggie said nothing.

They moved slowly down the mountainside, reaching a small clearing just about the time they lost the last traces of daylight. "We'll have to stop here," Adrian said, climbing down out of the buggy. "There aren't many clearings where we can wait away from the trees, in case there's any lightning."

The wind was picking up now, and the air smelled heavily of rain and pine. Maggie scooted closer to the center to keep the rain from blowing on her skirts, tucking the lap blanket around her, suddenly feeling chilled from the lower temperatures the rain had brought. Her chin propped in her hands, she watched the dim outline of Adrian as he unhitched the gelding and hobbled him.

It was dark now, and Adrian was nothing more than a dark shadow when he climbed back into the buggy.

He removed his slicker and placed it over her legs, covering the blanket. "Here," he said, "this should help keep the blanket dry."

"Thank you," she said, lifting the corner of the blanket for him.

"I'm all right," he said, remaining where he was.

She shrugged, then leaned down, rummaging around beneath her seat in the dark. After a few minutes, he asked, "What in the name of hell are you doing?"

"I'm looking for the napkin," she said. "I ken I wrapped the rest of the chicken in it. Are you no hungry?"

"No."

"Good. There wasna much chicken left, and I'm starving." She rummaged some more, giving a yelp of pleasure when her hand closed around the napkin. Joining him on the seat, she unfolded it, offering him the first piece. "Are you sure you dinna want any?" she asked, thrusting it toward him, thumping him on the nose in the dark. At least she supposed it was his nose, since he made some remark about not wanting any "goddamn chicken," and then proceeded to enlighten her further.

"I don't think you want that piece either," he said rather snappishly.

"Why dinna I?"

"Because you rammed it halfway up my nose."

"Then you better eat it," she said, slapping it in his lap. He picked it up and threw the piece of chicken as far as he could send it, then leaned back in the seat, pulling his hat low over his eyes and crossing his arms in front of him.

It was going to be a long, long night.

Maggie finished off the chicken, making an inordinate amount of noise, then licking her fingers, she began rummaging around beneath the seat again.

He pushed his hat back and gave her a glare, which was wasted in the dark. "Now what?" he said with supreme irritation.

"I ken there was one apple. . . ."

"Son of a bitch!" he said, and began searching for the apple, bumping heads with her as he leaned down. At last he found it. "Here!" he said, thrusting it toward her. "Now will you go to sleep?"

*Sleep?* She blinked her eyes. "Are we sleeping, then?"

He made a disgruntled sound. "Yes, we are. What else is there to do out here in the middle of nowhere?" he said.

*Make love.* "Hout! If you have to ask me that, Adrian Mackinnon, you have a better store of idiocy than brain."

She shook her head and took a bite. *CRUNCH!*

"Will you be quiet?"

"Aye," *Crunch . . . crunch . . . crunch.*

"Maggie," he said after a few minutes.

"Aye?"

"You're doing that on purpose," he said. "And I know it."

"What? Being hungry?" she said. She was pleased that it was too dark for Adrian to see her satisfied smile.

"No, eating that goddamn apple."

"Och! I canna get it into my stomach if I dinna eat it," she said.

"Never mind," he said, giving her his back.

*CRUNCH! Crunch . . . crunch . . . crunch . . .*

He gritted his teeth and listened to her chomp.

"There's one bite left," she said at last. "Do you want it?"

"No!"

*CRUNCH!* She finished it off.

He ground his teeth again.

She tossed the core from the buggy, then settled back into the seat. "Good night."

He said nothing.

"Adrian?"

Nothing.

*"Adrian?"*

He half turned toward her. "What the hell is it now?"

"I said good night."

"Good night." He gave her his back again.

She changed positions. It wasn't comfortable, so she changed again. The seat springs creaked.

"What in God's good graces are you doing now?"

"Settling in."

He gritted his teeth again. If this kept up, he wouldn't have any teeth left. "How long does that usually take?"

"What?"

"All this goddammed settling in."

"I dinna ken. I canna remember ever having to settle in when I was in a buggy before."

"For the love of God," he shouted, "will you shut up and go to sleep?"

"Aye. Will you?"

The urge to throttle her was strong. But she was such an unorthodox mixture of practicality and sentiment that she would probably wiggle out of his hands like a trout.

Adrian wasn't sure how long he sat there listening to the sound of the rain tapping on the top of the buggy and the noise she made trying to settle in, as she called it. She was worse than a damn pig with all her rooting around, and she made more racket than a coon in the attic.

He was so busy thinking about how much she irritated him that he didn't notice she had settled down. He thought perhaps he might have dozed off, for when he became aware of where he was, he slowly realized that the rain had stopped.

And so had Maggie.

The moon broke between the clouds, bathing the small clearing in moonlight. He saw the dark shadow of the horse, then looked down at her, seeing the faint outline of her barely visible in the moonlight. She must have been asleep, sitting straight up, her head dropped forward. She looked uncomfortable as the devil.

But she was still.

And she was quiet.

He hated to wake her up, purely for selfish reasons.

Still, she didn't look too comfortable—and she would probably get a crick in her neck or a catch in her get-along, and he would have to listen to her complain. He felt a little guilty about that, when he was reminded that Maggie did precious little complaining. In all fairness, he would have to give her credit. He hadn't exactly made her short time here pleasant, yet she had made the most of it, and most of the time, she was optimistically cheerful about it.

While he watched her, she shifted and stirred in her sleep, moaning something he couldn't understand, then tilting toward the left, farther and farther, she came to a stop when she thumped up against him. He wasn't about to touch her. He was no fool. He might not love this woman. But she *was* a woman. And he sure as hell wanted her. She was warm and soft in all the right places, and it was damnably fresh upon his mind what it had been like to hold her, to make love to her. He looked down, knowing he should take her in his arms—if for no other reason than to see she slept comfortably.

His old feelings toward her warred with these newer, more tender ones that began to emerge. He pushed her upright and back against the seat, then turning his back toward her, he settled himself into a comfortable position and went to sleep.

Some time later she moaned again and turned toward him, her face and her breasts pressed against his back, and something hot and liquid stirred within him. He closed his eyes. He couldn't sleep. Not now. Not like this, with her so close, so warm.

With a frustrated oath, he turned toward her. Before he could finish saying, "Oh, for God's sake, come here," she had tumbled into his arms.

He held her against him, setting his back against the corner of the seat, stretching his legs out toward the opposite corner, bracing them against the dashboard. She adjusted to his change in position, rolling half across him. He didn't close his eyes. He knew it would do no good. She was lying across him, *that* part of her dangerously close to touching *that* part of him. He groaned, feeling his body was ready and stiffly alert.

Damn. It was going to be a longer night than he first thought.

He wasn't sure when he began to rub her back, or when he first rested his chin on the top of her head. But he was dead sure she realized it, because he felt her body go suddenly rigid and tense. He could feel her eyes upon him, and looking down at her, he could see she was watching him, her eyes wide in the moonlight. He didn't think about his sending her away, or that she had known another man before him. He was only conscious that she was a very desirable woman and she was his wife, and she was damnably close, and she felt as if she was where she belonged.

In his arms.

Slowly, ever slowly, the hand that had been caressing her back began to climb higher, until it settled around the back of her neck, his thumb coming up to stroke the soft hair where it curled near her ear.

The intimacy of it shattered her. She knew as well what could happen here if this continued much longer. The rigid length of him pressing against her hipbone said his body had started some plans of its own. A tremor rippled over her when Adrian's head lowered and she felt him kiss the top of her hair, her forehead, her eyes.

She could have resisted him, and for a while intended to, but this gentler, tender side of him was something she had never seen before.

When she looked up at him, she saw his beautiful, full, inviting mouth. His expression seemed to ask whether she would accept him or push him away. Slowly he lowered his head and pressed his lips lightly against hers.

Adrian had his answer when her arms came up, locking around his neck.

For a moment he felt frozen in time, uncertain which he wanted most. To touch her. Or to have her touch him. He felt consumed by the aching, the need to have her want him. Dangerous thing, this wanting, this needing. It made a man just a little crazy.

He felt her weight shift against him as she raised herself, her arms coming up to take his head between her hands, pulling him down so she could kiss him.

"Maggie," he warned.

"Aye?"

"You're making it hard," he whispered against her lips.

She laughed, a deep, throaty sound. Her hand came down between them. "I can make it harder," she whispered, her hand closing around him.

"Dear God in Heaven!" he whispered, his breath sucking in sharply.

"Relax," she said.

*Relax?* He leaned back a bit and looked at her. "Relax? I'm supposed to say that, aren't I?"

"Aye, but I could grow old waiting for you to do it," she said.

"Maggie . . ."

She smiled and said nothing, but she caressed him just a little harder through his breeches, nuzzling his throat as she did so. "Relax," she said, with laughter in her voice. "Just lie back and think of England."

"England!" he said with a start.

"Aye."

His arms came around her. "I can't think of England at a time like this," he said.

"Why not?"

"Because I've got my mind on Scotland."

"Well, you—"

"Maggie, will you shut up and kiss me?"

"Aye," she said. "I will."

And she did, placing her hands to each side of his face. Then she planted a kiss on his mouth that had enough heat in it to fire up an extinct volcano. Adrian had never known his body could react so violently to a woman's aggression. Then he reminded himself that it hadn't reacted to a woman's aggression before, only to Maggie's. There was a difference.

He shifted their position in the buggy, turning her to lie beneath him, taking control of the kiss as he did so. He groaned, pressing himself against her softness, feeling his penis grow hard in response to her own groan. Her hands were in his hair now, as if she had to hang on to him to keep her sanity. He could understand that. He was feeling a little crazy himself.

She whispered a frantic "No," clutching at him, when he pulled away, but he only left her long enough to open his pants, and to pull her skirts up and her drawers down. A moment later he was back, his mouth searching for hers.

She whimpered in frustration, and his breath came hard in response. His mouth searched hers, and she groaned when he used the weight of his legs to nudge her thighs. She parted them readily, her hands rubbing his back frantically, then cupping his buttocks, urging him on. "I want you," she whispered, her breathing coming in short gasps.

"It's a good thing," was all he managed to say before he drove himself into her. She was so ready, and he was, too. A few hard, sure strokes and he heard her pant.

"Too fast," he whispered. "I didn't want it to go so fast."

"We can be slower next time," she said, then he felt her body convulse, his own coming a split second later.

His mind drifted between contentment and thoughts of making love to her again. *It can be slower next time.* He felt himself growing hard.

"Adrian?" she whispered.

"Hmmmmm?"

"We have to stop now."

"Stop? Are you crazy?"

She laughed, pulling away. "No, but I think he is. I dinna ken I have ever seen a horse eat a felt hat before."

Adrian whipped his head around, and there in the moonlight he could make out the shape of the hobbled gelding with his neck stretched out, the rippled brim of Adrian's hat protruding from his mouth.

She was doing it again. She was driving him crazy. "Stop laughing," he said. "That's my favorite hat."

"It's only a hat," she said, "and I canna be blamed for laughing. It is funny."

"It wouldn't be funny if it was one of your hats."

"Dinna be angry at me, Adrian. *I* dinna eat it."

"No, but you sure as hell distracted me, or I would have heard that son of a bitch before he did any damage."

"Distracted you?" she said in a surprised voice. Then with a throaty laugh, she said, "Aye. I did at that." She snuggled closer to him and closed her eyes. She could sleep now.

But Adrian sure as hell couldn't. Too much had happened tonight, too much had passed between them. It seemed like a long, long time before the sun began to peek over the mountains, but Adrian was ready to go when it did. He glanced over at Maggie. *Now she sleeps.* He hitched up the horse and headed for home, pulling Maggie toward him, a smile curving across his face when she took some time to settle in. Eventually she ended up in his lap. Oddly enough, it was exactly where he wanted her.

About the only complaint Maggie had about her marriage was that there were times that she didn't see much of Adrian. Often he was gone when she arose, or he was late for dinner—sometimes both. Whenever she mentioned it, he had the audacity to look surprised. "You wish I didn't work so hard? Why?"

"Because I enjoy your company."

He looked at their cold dinner. "You should have eaten," he said. "I'm too tired to be good company to anybody anyway." After dinner he announced he had some work to do, and something about the way he said it made Maggie think he wanted to be alone. Once he was gone, she went into the kitchen and told Molly to leave.

"I will, as soon as I've cleaned the kitchen."

"I'll do it tonight. You go on home and feed that husband of yours."

"He's used to waiting. He always sleeps for a spell when he comes home. Doesn't wake up until I stick a plate under his nose."

"Then go home and wave that plate. I feel like cleaning the kitchen tonight. I might give the floor a good scrubbing as well."

Molly looked her over. "You're either with child or having a fight. Have you missed your monthly?"

Maggie laughed. "If I didna have it, I ken I wouldna miss it."

"Then you and Adrian must be at it again." She gave the

strings of her apron a yank. "Never saw the likes of it in all my born days. It's amazing to me that two people who would rather be making love find so many other things to do. Are you two having a fight?"

"If we are, he forgot to tell me," Maggie said.

"Well, he didn't look too happy when he came home tonight. If you two aren't fighting, then what's wrong with him?"

"I dinna ken. Something must be bothering him."

"Maybe he's sorry he was so hard on you about being married before. Has he said any more about that?"

Maggie's expression turned pensive. "No. But I dinna ken that is a problem for him any longer."

Molly didn't even try to hide the surprised look on her face. "You don't mean he's falling in love with you?"

"I wouldna go so far as to say that. Do you ken it's possible?"

"Not if that fool persists in being a fool," Molly said. "And you know *which* fool I'm referring to."

"Aye," Maggie said, taking the apron from Molly and tying it around her own waist. "You're developing a fine sense of Scottish humor, Molly."

"You didn't think you could come into our lives and not make a few changes, did you?"

The two of them stood there looking at each other, as if they both had something to say and neither of them could find the words. Before Maggie could think of something lighthearted, Molly turned through the door and was gone.

After cleaning the kitchen and scrubbing the floor—rinsing it twice—Maggie felt better. Tired, but better. Hanging her apron on the peg, she picked up the lamp and made her way down the hallway, noticing the rectangle of light coming from beneath the library door.

Adrian looked up when she opened the door and stepped

inside. "It's late," he said. "I thought you would have been in bed by now."

"I thought the same about you."

"I've got two letters to write to families of the two men killed this week." He rubbed the back of his neck and closed his eyes. "I'm tired," he said. "Tail-dragging, moon-howling tired."

Maggie put the lamp down and came around his desk, stopping behind him to rub his neck. The muscles were hard and tight, forcing her to massage deeply. "No wonder. You haven't had much sleep these past weeks. I wondered what was bothering you. You should have told me about the accidents. I could have helped."

"We were able to handle things. Like I told you, I didn't want to worry you," he said, and Maggie's heart lifted.

"I worry more when you keep things from me."

"I know," he said, and reached up to pat her hand. Then, almost shyly, he pulled his hand away, clearing his throat. "Well, I guess I better be seeing to those letters now," he said.

"I could write them for you," she said, turning back toward him.

For a moment he simply stared at her. "It's late. You should go to bed."

"I can rest tomorrow. You canna. Besides, I ken I have a gentler way with words."

She could see the battle going on in his mind. He was tempted, she could tell, but still he didn't want to let her into his life. She held her breath, standing quietly, afraid to move, as she waited to see what he would say. She expelled a breath of relief when he spoke at last.

"All right," he said, and stood.

Maggie took a seat, picking up the pen and dipping it in the inkwell.

"The names of the men are here, along with their next of

kin. Say whatever you like. Include these vouchers for the pay they had coming and something extra from me. Tell them it isn't much. . . ." He stopped and looked at her. "You know what to tell them," he said gruffly.

"Aye," she said, "I ken what to say."

Maggie sat down and began writing. When she finished the first letter, she looked up, finding she was alone.

The next evening, a worn and weary Adrian returned home, and although he arrived earlier than usual, he was more exhausted, the signs of worry and strain etched deeply in lines that seemed to have suddenly appeared on his face.

When Molly announced dinner was getting cold, Maggie went to find Adrian, locating him in his study, his long legs stretched out over the length of the leather sofa, his feet dangling over the massive rolled arm. His boots were lying on the floor, and as she looked at him sleeping in his stocking feet, he appeared younger and more vulnerable. This was a strange thought, she decided, for Adrian was not the kind of man to give off any hint of vulnerability. She found the discovery curiously uplifting.

Without waking him, she took a seat across from him, content to sit quietly and watch him sleep. Adrian's senses must be acute, even when he was asleep, or so she decided when, after a few minutes of observation, he opened one eye and looked at her.

She was sitting in the chair, her elbow crooked, her chin resting in the palm of her hand. When he opened the other eye, she said, "Hello. You must have a clean conscience. You slept like a bairn."

"And what makes you so knowledgeable about babies?" he asked, coming up to a sitting position and stretching.

Her heart cracked like an acorn.

He reached for one of his boots and his words skittered across her nerves like nails scraping ice, but she smiled, so he wouldn't know just how close he had come to uncovering another secret.

"I was a bairn once myself," she said, coming out of the chair and picking up his other boot, handing it to him.

He reached for the boot and their fingers grazed. They looked up at the same moment and their eyes locked. He broke the contact, looking down to pull on his boot. "Are you sure you're a duchess?" he said, without bothering to look at her.

She raised her brows and tilted her head curiously to one side. "Why would you be asking a thing like that?"

He scowled, and she threw back her head, consumed with laughter. He was distracted for a moment with the white, pearly luster to the skin of her throat.

"Tell me," she asked, her hands on her hips. "How does a duchess act, then?"

"Dignified," he responded without having to think upon it.

"And I'm not . . . dignified?" She dropped into the chair across from him.

"Sometimes you are. Sometimes you aren't. You sure as hell don't know how to eat apples. Makes me wonder if you can serve tea."

"Then you must tell me how a dignified duchess should behave and I'll try to amend my ways."

His frown was so deep now, she wanted to reach out her hand and smooth the line away from between his eyes. "All I know is what Ross wrote me."

"And what was that?"

"He said they made odd little bows and served tea," he said, allowing his sarcasm to dismiss the subject.

She laughed, knowing what he was about, and refusing to dismiss such an interesting topic. When she spoke, there was a bubble of humor in her voice and her eyes sparkled with amusement. "I ken I can give you an *odd little bow*," she said, dipping gracefully to the floor, her skirts billowing about her. "If this is what you had in mind." When he didn't respond, she said, "Well? Is it, my lord? Were you thinking of a curtsy?"

"Something like that," he grumbled. "But not here. Not right now."

"Well, come and eat then," she said, and the merry sound of her laughter followed her from the room.

The next evening Molly met him wandering around the house, dazed as a duck in thunder. "Are you lost?"

"No," he said with surprise. "Do I look lost?"

"You do," Molly said, then added, "She's in the salon."

Molly wasn't being too friendly, but Adrian figured she would come around in time, whether he said anything to her or not. So he decided to remain silent and let her anger run its course, figuring he could handle almost anything she dished out. As long as she didn't poison his food. He went to the salon and found Maggie there, wearing a gown of the deepest shade of rich sapphire blue. She was seated at the sofa, behind a lavish silver tea set. She indicated a chair with a wave of her hand, and Adrian, curious as to what she was up to now, dropped silently into it, his feet thrust out in front of him. "Shall I pour?" she asked.

"If you want to put any tea into those tiny cups, you'll have to. My aim isn't that good."

She poured and handed him a cup and saucer. He gave her a blank look. "It's tea, not poison," she said, offering him a smile.

He took the cup, glancing up at her when the cup rattled, but she seemed to take no notice. He followed her lead and took one sip, before deciding he looked like a complete and utter fool, and what was worse, he felt like one. *Why am I such a clumsy oaf around her? Look at me, Maggie. Hear what my heart speaks. Don't listen to my foolishness.*

Coming to his feet, he dumped the saucer and cup back

on the tray. "I liked you better the other way," he said with a growl, and left the room.

He collided with Molly as he came out the door. "What in the hell are you doing? Eavesdropping?"

"If I was, it would be a mighty lonely occupation. You sure never say anything worth listening to."

Adrian felt his temperature rise. "It's hot in here," he said, going around her. "Why don't you open a window?"

"You might as well get used to it," she said. "It's hotter where you're going."

Once she was in her room, Maggie fell backward across her bed, not even thinking to remove the moiré dress or to at least lie down in such a way as to not crush the fragile roses that held up her bustle. For a long time she lay there thinking about the way Adrian had reacted tonight. Why had it upset him when she served the tea? She had only meant it as something funny, a reminder of the day before when he had asked her if she was sure she was a duchess. Was his memory of rejection what made him toss his cup of tea on the tray and leave the room with such abruptness? Had there been so much pain in his life, then, that he suffered from it still?

*It couldn't be,* she thought. It couldn't be because he was beginning to care for her, that he was afraid of falling in love. But she knew, even as she denied it, that seemed the only explanation. *Dear Adrian.* Was he so unlucky at love that he was either hurt by those he loved, or hurt the ones who loved him? Was she such a terrible threat to him, then? Her mind was in an emotional upheaval, but she felt somewhat relieved. She smiled wryly, her heart beginning to race. A shiver rippled across her when she remembered their lovemaking. He cared. He had to care.

Didn't he?

The strain of it had her nerves close to shattering. She

would rather face the English on a battlefield than to go through many more days of this.

Coming off the bed, she began pacing the floor, removing her clothes as she did. When she was stripped down to her chemise, she began pulling the pins from her hair, then taking up the brush, she brushed in unison with her pacing the floor. One, two, three, turn. Brush, brush, brush, change.

Adrian was coming around. She knew it, as well as she knew that was the reason for the rise in tension. He was coming around, and he was resisting her all the more because of it. All she needed was more time.

Putting on her gown, she climbed into bed. Her prayers were for more time—time with Adrian she knew she needed. Just a little help from the Almighty. Adrian was coming to care for her. She was certain of that, and while she wasn't so foolish to call it love, he did care for her. He did.

It wasn't much, but it was a beginning. The thought of this almost savage stranger, whom she shared a life of desire and suspicion with, coming to love her still seemed as incredible as it ever had. Incredible, but at least it now seemed possible.

She fell asleep thinking about tomorrow. Tomorrow was a brand-new day that hadn't been touched yet. Tomorrow she would try again to show him he could trust her. The thought of it washed over her like laughter. She felt as excited as a schoolgirl.


Downstairs, Adrian sat in his study eyeing a bottle of brandy. He was angry with himself for losing control as he had this afternoon in front of Maggie. What was he afraid of? Why did he want to get close to her, only to run the other way when he had the chance?

The way he saw it, he had two choices. He could drink himself into a stupor and pass out, thereby eliminating, for a time, the desire he felt for Maggie, or he could go to her now and make love to her.

He liked the sound of the second one better.

He thought about that. Maggie frustrated him. The only way he could get the memory of making love to her out of his mind was to think about making love to her again. He looked at the brandy. *Drink or make love,* he told himself at last. Put that way, there was precious little thinking he had to do.

A few minutes later, he was knocking on Maggie's door, wondering if she would notice that he hadn't opened the door and walked in, as he had that time before. He knocked again, and heard a soft "Come in."

He opened the door and stepped into the dark room. Making his way to her bedside table, he lit the lamp, turning it low, before looking down at her with amusement dancing in his eyes. He had only one word to describe the way Maggie looked right now. Soft. The perfectly groomed hair he was accustomed to had been replaced by a cloud of unruly curls that fanned about her like a golden cape. Somehow the refined, elegant woman she was, was gone, and in her place was a ravishing creature whom he felt an uncontrollable, irrational need to bend to his will and make her respond until she was mindless with wanting him.

"Did you come in here to fight, or to make love?" she asked, her voice husky with sleep.

His body lurched at her words.

"Which would you prefer?"

She smiled and stretched. "That depends. The last time you came into my room to make love, we ended up fighting anyway, and then you disappeared for two weeks. Have you ever thought what people around here must think?"

"About what?"

She wiggled back into the bed, stacking her pillows one on the other, then pushed herself up to sit upright. "First you leave me waiting for two weeks after I arrive here, before you come to meet me. A short while later, you leave again for the same length of time. I ken this is an uncivilized part of the world, Adrian, but even so, your men must be wondering what's wrong with me that you dinna want to be around me.''

"I don't think anyone would ever *wonder* about anything we did," Adrian said, his voice laced with amusement. "Anyone who would have his brother pick him a wife and marry her by proxy would have already given them plenty to talk about.''

It suddenly occurred to Maggie how that must have looked to the men around camp, and just how much teasing Adrian must have taken because of it. He had to have been embarrassed by all the joking these men were so fond of—and knowing these men as well as she did, she knew it was probably quite a bit, and quite funny. A slow, creeping smile came out of nowhere to match the bubble of amusement that seemed to have popped inside her.

"You wouldn't laugh at a man simply because he made a fool of himself, would you?''

"Aye, I ken I would, if the man was you.''

"Laugh all you like," he said, while watching her try unsuccessfully to keep a straight face, "but it wasn't funny at the time.''

"No, I'm sure it wasna.''

"You should have seen the way the men looked at me the morning I told them—over breakfast—that my brother had picked me out a wife and married her for me. I never knew so many forks could hit the table at the same time.''

"You surprised them, that's all.''

"And perked up their interest a bit, too, I think. If I had one, I must have had fifteen men ask me if I found you in a catalog.''

"What did you tell them?''

"I asked them what kind of fool they thought would order a wife out of a catalog."

"And?"

"And John Schurtz said, 'A smarter one than would let his brother pick one out for him.' "

Maggie couldn't hold back the burst of laughter. "Well, I ken he was right."

"Exactly, and that's why I felt like such an ass. All I could do was laugh with them."

A wellspring of admiration flooded her heart. Anyone who could laugh at himself, in spite of great embarrassment— well, that showed promise. All the obstacles between them seemed to disappear, and he was simply a commanding, powerful man who had married her and offered her a new life. Unaware, at first, of what was happening between them, of the current of desire that leaped like a static charge from one to the other, she stared up into his handsome face, mesmerized by those laughing blue eyes, while her mind relayed the message to her that this man was, really and truly, her husband.

He must have realized it about the same time she did, for the next instant, she heard him whisper her name. "Maggie," he said hoarsely, and then he was standing beside the bed, taking her into his arms. She melted, beautifully tender and warm, against him.

The next thing she knew, he was pulling her to her feet, smothering her face with kisses as he ran his hands over her body. Then, without her even knowing he had done so, he pulled the ribbon on her gown, opening the neck, wider and wider, until it fell over her shoulders and down to the floor to lie in a shimmering pool of cream silk.

Chills covered her, but they weren't from the cool air, but from the heat in his eyes. She moved, to step out of the gown lying on the floor, and he must have thought she was going to pick the gown up. "Leave it. I want to see you," he said. "Don't cover yourself."

"I wasna," she said, stepping away from the gown.

Leaning away from her, Adrian reached for the lamp, turning it up until her body seemed to glow. Maggie's heart pounded and her breath was coming in short, panting gasps. His hand came out, and he placed it with the palm flat against the place where her heart beat so wildly between her breasts. "Your breathing is off. Are you nervous?"

"No."

"Are you certain? Your heart is pounding. I can feel it."

"Aye, it is, but I canna say it is from nerves."

"What then?"

"You. The way you look at me."

His eyes traveled over her slowly, his fingers tracing the slow-fading welts left from the bones of her corset. He placed his hands around her waist, his thumbs almost touching. Then he dropped them lower, his thumbs gliding over the sensitive hollow beneath the bones of her hips. She shivered. "You have a beautiful body, Maggie," he said, taking her in his arms and kissing her.

When she looked up at him, he was smiling. It was an honest smile, the kind she thought he might smile when no one was looking. There was a softness, a gentleness, to it that made him look younger, almost boyish. Gone was the customary cynicism, the hardness, the man who went to such lengths to hide what he was feeling. If she didn't know he loved another woman, she would have sworn what she saw in his eyes was love.

"I dinna—"

"Shhhh," he said, placing his fingertips over her mouth, then drawing her close, he kissed her forehead, each of her eyes. Then moving lower, he placed kisses along her throat, dropping down to kiss a fiery trail along the line of her shoulders. She shuddered, sucking in her breath when he began to kiss her thoroughly, and with such attention to detail, as though he could take the rest of his life to finish. She found herself wishing he would. He might be a man of few words, but his actions spoke volumes. She had no idea a kiss could be so agonizingly slow—or so well placed. Methodically he moved from her shoulders to her breasts, taking her into his mouth.

Maggie groaned and leaned her head back, wanting him with a desperation that consumed her. Her mind racing, she didn't, at first, realize he had picked her up until he stood her on the footstool in front of the chair. He was kissing her belly now, and her hands curled in his hair from the exquisite pleasure of it. There had to be another word for what he was doing, for *lovemaking* seemed far, far too tame. Adrian wasn't making love to her, he was . . . what? Frustration mounted, until it came to her at last. Adrian didn't love, he worshiped, and her whole body tingled at the thought.

Over and over, he kissed her, his hands touching, caressing, all the places his lips missed—and there weren't many. She almost smiled at the thought. How like Adrian to be so thorough. He kissed her as if he would never tire of it, first her thighs, then her knees, her calves, the tops of her feet.

"That's about it," she said in a breathless way, and heard his chuckle.

"Oh no," he said, "we've just begun."

"Good."

He chuckled again, and she felt her stomach knot in response.

"This isna fair," she said. "I'm naked as the day I was born, and you still have all your clothes on. You have me at your advantage."

"You have no idea how long I've wanted just that," he said softly.

His hands came up to her waist to hold her as he buried his face between her legs.

"Holy Mother of God," she said, her breath sucking in sharply. "Adrian . . . please . . ."

"Don't talk," he said, then did something with his mouth that made her dig her nails into his shoulders.

"Please. No more. Make love to me. Now."

"I'm not finished."

"You will be when I . . . get . . . my hands on you."

"They're on me now."

"Aye, but they're busy holding me up."

He stopped talking, and she felt the reason why. "You're driving me insane," she said, feeling a trail of sweat trickle down, between her breasts. "How much further can you go with this?"

He didn't answer.

"Adrian, for the . . . l-love . . . of God," she cried, then felt her body shatter like fragile glass before she collapsed, feeling his arms come around her.

"I'll get even with you," she said weakly as he carried her back and placed her on the bed.

"That," he said, "is my dearest wish." He began removing his clothes.

Maggie stretched like a sleepy cat, gasping when she felt his bare skin cover her own. "Adrian," she whispered.

"Slowly, love, slowly. I know what you need."

"Aye, but it may not be what I want," she said, wishing he would go faster.

He groaned, and entered her.

Maggie did not speak after that. She couldn't, for Adrian began making the longest, slowest thrusts, and she could only follow the urging of her body to begin moving with him. Her hands on his buttocks, she could feel the flex of solid muscle, the curve of his flanks. How perfectly his body fit against hers, as if they were made from the beginning for this purpose, this joining, and perhaps they were.

All thought left her, for at that moment, her body convulsed, Adrian following her a second later. For a long time they lay together, neither of them moving. At last Adrian rolled to one side, pulling the blanket over both of them, and taking Maggie into his arms, they slept.

When Adrian awoke some time later, Maggie was looking at him. "Couldn't you sleep?" he asked.

"I could, but I'd rather look at you."

"Why?"

"Because I like looking at you. You're a handsome man, Adrian. Any woman would be a fool not to look at you all she could."

"I'm not interested in what *any* woman does, Maggie. Only you."

She watched him for a long time, then she glanced away. "You confuse me."

"I confuse myself." His hand came out to stroke the baby-soft skin on the inside of her arm. "I'm not very good at expressing myself, Maggie. I feel the words here," he said, putting his hand over his heart, "but it's hard for me to get the feeling from there to here." He touched his lips.

She rolled toward him. "Oh, Adrian, that's not true. Your letters . . . they were beautiful, written with such expression, such tenderness, such emotion."

"I can write what I feel, Maggie. I can put it on paper. I just can't *say* it."

"Why?"

"I don't know. Maybe it's because I've kept so many things bottled up inside for so long. I feel like I've lost the ability to communicate. I feel one thing, but I seem always to show something else. I haven't meant to hurt you, Maggie, but that seems to be what I do best."

"But you can learn again if you try. It always lightens your burdens to talk about it."

"I wouldn't know. I've never had anyone I could talk to."

"So you kept your feelings, your emotions, to yourself?"

"I suppose I did. It's understandable, I suppose. What man in his right mind would go baring his soul to four brothers? Can you imagine the teasing I would have taken if they had known what I was feeling?"

Maggie looked at him, her hand coming out to cup his cheek. "What are you feeling now?"

"Like I have a lot of things I should tell you . . . things I *want* to tell you, but I don't know how."

"You dinna know how?" she asked. "Or are you afraid?"

He stared at the ceiling, his hands coming up to fold behind his head. "Maybe I am afraid. I don't know."

"I think you are. I won't laugh at you, Adrian, and I won't throw your feelings back in your face. Why is it so hard for you to trust?"

"Because trust hurts," he said, squeezing his eyes closed.

"And that is why you hold yourself back."

"I learned a long time ago that if you trust in yourself, no one else can betray you."

"You feel those you've loved have betrayed you?"

"Yes," he said, almost shouting. "Yes. Yes. Yes. And it's true. You want to know why?"

She nodded.

"Because *every* person I have ever been close to, *everyone* I've ever loved, has either died or turned away from me. My parents died and left me an orphan, my brothers scattered . . ."

"But Alex came out here with you."

"And left, taking . . ."

"Taking Katherine with him," she said. "Another rejection."

"It doesn't matter now. After a while, you get used to it. Better a quiet death than a public humiliation. My heart seems to gain its strength by being wounded."

Adrian wasn't at breakfast the next morning, and he didn't come home for dinner that night. Maggie spent the morning alone, taking Israel for a long walk along the beach, sitting for a long time on the point, staring out across the water, thinking about last night. *One fire burns out another's burning; One pain is lessened by another's anguish*. How true the words of *Romeo and Juliet* now rang, for in truth, Adrian's anguish had all but extinguished the memory of her own pain. He suffered, and she suffered with him. How strange it was that she had always thought laughter was so easy to share, but pain was something private to be shared alone.

She stood, calling Israel, and walked back to the house. Her step was lighter, the look on her face a bit brighter. Adrian hadn't gone so far as to say he loved her, but he had opened his heart to her, and that had a brightness all its own.

She spent the afternoon in the house, adding the finishing touches to a painting she was doing, one of Adrian and Israel: a large canvas with Adrian in a relaxed pose, his features softened and gazing out over the Pacific, his hand resting on Israel's yellow head.

Maggie dabbed her brush in yellow ocher and blended it with a little sienna brown, pausing before stroking the darker color along Israel's muzzle, thinking that this was the only time she had ever seen Israel still—unless, of course, he was asleep.

Finishing touches were always tedious and time-consuming, but it was a good way to spend a lazy afternoon. Long shadows of late afternoon streaked across the floor when she began to clean her brushes in turpentine.

A door suddenly slammed down the hallway and she could hear shouting, peppered with a few well-placed curses. Maggie quickly put the painting and her supplies away, then hurried as she heard all manner of stomping and grunting coming from the vicinity of the kitchen.

She stepped inside in time to see Adrian and Big John dragging in a large, burlap-covered carcass. Over at the sink, Molly was dwarfed by a mountain of salmon.

Stopping in the middle of the room, she looked from Adrian to Molly, then back to Adrian.

"Where have you been?"

"Fishing," he said, without looking up.

"We were running low on meat, so we took time off to go salmon fishing. On our way back, we came upon a herd of elk, and Adrian here shot one," Big John said, in way of explanation.

"Well, you could have told me," Maggie said. "I worry about you. I was afraid there was some problem down at the mill." *Look at me, Adrian. Act like I exist. Dinna turn away from me. Dinna be embarrassed about last night. I won't hurt you. Trust me.*

Adrian didn't look up. "I thought you'd find out from Molly."

"She didn't ask," Molly said with a shrug, "so I saw no reason to tell her. I don't go about blabbing everything I know."

Adrian looked at Big John, and Big John said, "I'm sitting on the middle of the fence, and that's where I'm staying. I have to keep peace in the family."

Adrian and Big John laughed, then seeing the look of disharmony on Maggie's face, Adrian laughed some more, and said cajolingly, "Don't be so disgruntled. What if your face froze that way?"

"I'm no disgruntled," she snapped, "but I'm no gruntled, either."

While Adrian and Big John collapsed with laughter, Maggie promptly left the room, going upstairs to change clothes. She didn't want Adrian to see that paint on her apron, or he might begin to ask questions, and she wanted to keep her work a secret.

A few minutes later, she returned, wearing an old dress. Adrian, Molly, and Big John were up to their elbows in blood, fish skin, and elk hide when Maggie came back into the room.

Finding the bloody scene totally unexpected, she gasped, taking a step backward when the three of them turned to stare.

"Don't come in here," Adrian said, giving her a frown. "The room's a big enough mess without you throwing up all over it."

Maggie stopped, giving him a strange look. "I willna throw up, and as for me not coming in here, I dinna ken why not. You're in here."

"This isn't a pretty sight for a duchess," he said, "but it's good honest meat for the men."

"Taking a salmon from the river, a tree from the forest, and a deer from the mountain are three things no Gael was ever ashamed of," she said, rolling up her sleeves and searching for an apron. Tying it around her, she added, "I ken I've gutted more salmon than you have goose bumps."

Adrian looked at her with a sour expression.

"That isna a face I'd advise you to make too often," she said. "What if your face froze that way?"

When she joined them, Big John and Molly were laughing, but Adrian didn't say anything. Never one to let an opportunity pass, Molly wasn't so shy. "Don't feel so bad, Adrian. At least she didn't come after you with the business end of a claymore."

"What do you know about a claymore?" he snapped. "Business end or otherwise?"

"Only what Maggie tells me," she said with a laugh.

"Which, I take it, is plenty," he said.

Shortly after lunch the next day, Maggie arrived at the mining office. Adrian had been avoiding her, and she wanted to spend some time with him, time to let him see the baring of his soul to her the other night hadn't changed anything between them. It had only made her feelings for him stronger. But before she could say anything, Big John rushed through the door to face Adrian.

"Did you know Matt Greenwood worked for Talbot and Pope before coming here?" Big John asked.

"No, I didn't," Adrian said, coming to his feet, his eyes going to Maggie as she removed her cape and bonnet. "How did you find out?"

"That new man, Saunders, just told me. He tried to get on with Talbot and Pope, but they wouldn't hire him."

"So he saw Greenwood working there," Adrian said. "It doesn't necessarily mean anything. You know as well as I do how these timberbeasts move from outfit to outfit."

"But not when they're the bull of the woods."

"Greenwood was their top man?"

Big John nodded. "Makes you wonder about all these little accidents we've been having, don't it?"

"Yes," Adrian said, "it does."

"You want me to fire him?"

"No, I want you to catch him red-handed. Find someone we can trust to keep an eye on him. I want to know every move he makes from here on out."

"I've already done that," Big John said. "A fella named Burt Haywood. He's honest as the day is long."

"I don't give a damn whether he's honest or not. Just as long as he's good." Big John nodded and slipped through the door. Adrian looked at Maggie, noticing the basket she picked up.

"I heard you dinna have lunch, so I brought you something."

"I don't have time to eat, Maggie. Now now. But thanks anyway."

"Then I'll feed you. And dinna be telling me you don't have time to open your mouth, or the men will ken you for a fool,'' she said, and Adrian noticed for the first time how she pronounced *fool*. It sounded more like *fule*.

Watching her unpack her basket and litter his desk with the contents, Adrian couldn't help thinking how these rough, uncultured men had come to admire her, remarking to him time and time again what a woman she was, and how most civilized, cultured women wouldn't have tried to adjust to this rough life, let alone go to the lengths she did to involve herself in it.

He found himself thinking she was everything he had ever wanted in a woman. The next moment he understood why Ross had picked Maggie for his wife. Day or night, he couldn't get her out of his mind. It was always like that of late.

Maggie glanced up and saw Adrian's gaze locked on her. She smiled and went back to what she was doing, unwrapping a plate of blueberry muffins and placing them in front of him. She reached in her basket, taking out another plate, and began removing the napkin, humming a little tune as she worked. No matter how uninterested he looked, no matter how restless he acted, no matter how much he hinted for her to be on her way, she continued to hum and unwrap another plate.

Adrian had already learned that Maggie had the kind of patience that drove ordinary people insane. To make matters worse, she had the infuriating quality of self-control. Adrian could have dealt with a hothead, a woman who would have fits, scream, throw things—even one who would scream and kick and bite.

He hadn't the faintest inkling, however, about how to deal with a woman who remained cool-headed and calm, a woman who used logic and reasoning like a two-edged sword—it got you coming and going. He knew her most effective tool in dealing with him was a sort of quiet openness. She listened, and she did not judge.

She drove him crazy.

Adrian frowned and looked at the clutter of food she had spread over his desk. Knowing what would happen, the amount of teasing he would take if one of the men happened in and saw him picnicking with his wife at his desk, he stood up.

"Put that back in the basket," he said. "I don't have time to eat."

"Adrian Mackinnon, you don't know what you need."

"You've told me that before," he said, "lots of times." Taking his hat off the peg, he darted through the door, just as a loaf of bread sailed past him.

Adrian worked in the office all afternoon with his head bent over the ledgers. He was adding figures. He had added the last column three times. The lead broke. He tossed the pencil down and leaned back, crossing his feet on the desk, and his hands in back of his head. It was no use. He couldn't think. He couldn't concentrate. At least not on anything except Maggie.

Strange it was that, in spite of all the anxiety, the tension between them, he felt at ease, contented.

*Contented?* His feet dropped to the floor and he came to a sitting position so fast, the chair thumped him in the back. The shock of it hit him like the swift-kicking recoil of a rifle.

*Contentment.* It was a strange word for him. But if he was honest with himself, he had to admit that despite their differences, despite the occasional friction between them, he *was* content with Maggie.

Adrian found himself in a bemused state of disbelief and disgruntlement. He wasn't too happy with either one. The two seemed to feed off of each other, for when he found it hard to believe he enjoyed having Maggie for his wife as much as he did, the other part of him was consumed with desire for her.

He rubbed absently at the stubble of a beard on his face.

He had deliberately not shaved this morning, just as he had deliberately suppressed the knowledge that he was coming to care for her. Deeply. In the innermost depths of his being, he knew that his feelings for her had begun to change some time ago, but he had stubbornly refused to acknowledge the emergence of such new and tender emotions.

There was the sudden sound of stomping feet outside the door, and then it opened, Big John's large, hulking frame stepping into the room. His face didn't look as if it bore good news.

"Ship's come in," was all Big John said.

"Where's Maggie?" he asked, thinking she would enjoy seeing the ship dock.

"She was here earlier, in the medicine hut."

By the time Adrian reached the dock, Maggie was already there, standing on the dock, Israel sitting at her side.

Suddenly it seemed vital to him to know what Maggie thought, to know how she felt about him. Adrian opened his mouth to speak to her, but the words died in his throat.

He froze.

He had been so intent on what he wanted to say to her that he had not, until this moment, seen what was going on in front of him.

He looked up the dock to the plank, his expression blank as he saw a woman walking toward them. Two children gripped the folds of her cape; a third child was in her arms. *Who in the hell is she? What is she doing here?*

About that time Molly walked up, and turning to her, Adrian, still disbelieving what he saw, asked, "What in the name of God is that?"

"I believe they're commonly called children," Molly said. "Close your mouth."

"What are they doing here? Why are they getting off the ship?"

"I haven't any idea," said Molly. "Why don't you ask . . ."

Molly's words dwindled off to nothing as she watched Adrian turn slowly to look at Maggie.

Maggie stood trembling in silence, feeling as guilty as Eve must have felt after feeding Adam that fatal apple. All the color drained from her face. Adrian looked at her, his gaze scalding. She swallowed, opening her mouth, only to close it when no sound would come forth. Her heart sank like a lead weight in her chest as his puzzled gaze moved over her.

"Adrian," she said, "it isna what you think."

His gaze went back to the children, then came back to her. "They're your children," he said softly, his voice sounding flat and dull. Then, as if hearing his own words for the first time, he repeated the words with great emphasis. "They're *your* children." His hand shot out to grab her wrist, jerking her close to him, but his voice was loud enough to be heard all over camp. "Just when were you going to tell me?" He shook his head. "Jesus! Children. *Three* of them."

"You dinna need to shout. My *ears* are working perfectly."

"Your ears may be, but your mind sure as hell isn't. What's going on here? You've got some explaining to do, and you damn well better start talking. Now."

Her teeth chattering, she searched for the words to tell him how this had all come about, how she had always planned on telling him. But the right words seemed to elude her.

He gave her a shake. "Talk, damn you."

"What do you want me to say? They're my children . . . all three of them."

"Are there more?"

She shook her head.

"Are you certain there aren't a dozen more hiding out somewhere?"

"No, that's all."

"And I'm supposed to *believe* you? What else have you

kept from me, Maggie? How many more secrets are you hiding?''

"Nothing. There are no more secrets."

"And you expect me to believe you?"

"I ken you have a right to be angry, but it isna the way you think. I didna set out to deceive you."

"No?"

"No. I always intended to tell you."

"So why didn't you? You've had plenty of time. What prevented you?"

"I wanted more time. . . ."

"Time? You've ruined my goddamn life over a little time?"

"I don't blame you for being angry."

"Angry? *Angry?* I'm not angry. Angry is far, far too mild a word. Not even furious will describe what I feel right now." His eyes narrowed, but even that could not hide the pain in his eyes. "Damn you. I cared for you," he said. "I could have loved you."

The world that had seemed so bright suddenly shattered and fell in a tarnished heap at her feet. "It isn't too late for that." Her hand came out to touch his arm. He jerked away as if he'd been burned. "Adrian, please believe me. I didna intend for you to find out this way. I thought I had more time."

"Why?" he asked. "Why did you need more time?"

"Because I love you. Because I was afraid of losing you."

"I don't believe you."

"It's true. I do love you."

"That is your misfortune."

"Adrian, please, let me explain."

But Adrian didn't want to hear any more lies. He didn't want to hear anything. All he could think of was the way he had made a fool of himself the other night, and how she must be laughing at him now. Over and over, it echoed in his head. Maggie, sweet Maggie. She had deceived him again.

She turned away from him, and Adrian's anger exploded, white-hot. Having never felt such fury, he could barely choke out the word "Maggie!"

But Maggie was already running toward her children.

Adrian had never felt so alone, so left out. He hurt and he didn't know what to do. With a helpless look, he turned to Molly. Seeing no help from that quarter, he looked at John, who found nothing better to do than to shrug and look back at Molly.

He was too hurt and too furious to think straight; the only thing he thought to say seemed insignificant and rather stupid. "Who is that woman?"

"I suspect she's a nanny or governess or whatever they call a nursemaid over there," Big John replied.

"They can't stay here," Adrian said.

"You aren't going to make them go right back, are you?" Molly asked with disbelief. "They've been aboard ship for months, Adrian. They're just children. It would be inhuman to make them go right back."

"What in the hell do you expect me to do with them?" he asked.

"Well, I don't rightly know, but I'm sure you'll think of something unpleasant, although it seems a mite late to toss them overboard, seeing as how they're already on dry land."

"Don't be an ass," Adrian said. "It doesn't become you."

"Maybe not, but it sure becomes you, don't it?" Molly said, turning away to follow Maggie.

Adrian watched his wife greet her children with hugs and tears, but in spite of her apparent joy upon seeing them, something was missing. Her expression was sober as she spoke to the woman, and when Molly arrived, the two of them talked solemnly.

A moment later, Adrian watched Molly approach him.

"What's wrong? Have you invited them to stay?" asked Adrian.

"No, but I think you should. The child in the woman's arms is sick. She's burning up with fever. She would never survive a return trip—not even in good weather, and we know that isn't going to be the case this time of year."

Adrian felt trapped. He couldn't think. He couldn't speak.

"Well," Big John drawled after a long passage of time, "you can't exactly keep them standing on the dock until doomsday. Want me to drown them?"

"Don't be absurd."

"Does that mean you want me to drive them on up to the house?" Big John asked.

"Oh, no," Adrian said through gritted teeth. "I reserve that privilege all for myself."

Maggie sat in the wagon holding Ainsley, while Fletcher and Barrie sat beside her. Molly sat in the front seat, between Maude, the governess, and Adrian.

Pale and dizzy from the sudden loss of blood from her head, Maggie held Ainsley's burning body close. *Early*, her mind screamed. *They've come at least a month early.* She glanced at Adrian, seeing the frozen anger on his face. Dear God, she had only wanted a little time to set things right between them. She never intended for him to find out this way. But she knew, deep in her heart, this was all her fault— her fault for not sparing Adrian from discovering, in the worst possible way, the news she knew he would find so dreadful.

"It's all right, my little spunkie. Mama is here now. Dinna worrit," Maggie crooned, cuddling Ainsley's feverish body close.

When they reached the house, Adrian took Ainsley from Maggie's arms and handed her to Molly, then held out his hand to help Maggie down. Clearly furious, he squeezed her hand so tight, she thought he would crush the bones. His face contorted in grim silence, he did not touch her any more than he had to.

"Adrian . . ."

"Leave it," he said.

"I canna. I ken how you must feel."

"No, you couldn't. You can't possibly know."

"I'm sorry. I was going to tell you. I just wanted a little more time."

"We've been over all of this before."

"Was I so wrong for wanting you to care for me? For you to care enough to try to understand?"

"Everything about this has been wrong right from the start. I don't understand you or anything about you. I don't even want to anymore."

"Adrian, please try."

"I have no intention of trying. Ever."

"What do you want me to do? Leave? Is that what you want? Do you want me to take the children and return to Scotland?"

His face a frozen mask, his voice one she had never heard, he said hatefully, "Madam, I think that is an excellent idea. It can't happen soon enough for me."

Once she was on the ground, he took Ainsley from Molly, handing her to Maggie, without saying a word. Before Maggie know what he was about, he had turned on his heels, instructing the two men unloading trunks from the wagon to take them into the house.

Untying his horse from the back of the wagon, Adrian mounted, jerking the animal around in a wild spin, before taking off down the road at a dead run.

"Was that him? Was that yer husband?" Maude asked.

"Aye, that was Adrian."

"Friendly sort. Must be part Scot."

"He's all Scot, and he acts it." Maggie's eyes went to Ainsley, her hand coming out to touch the scorching brow.

" 'Tis shipboard fever. That's what the captain called it. Came on her all of a sudden, it did. She complained of a headache, saying her back and legs hurt. The next thing I ken, she's burning with fever. The puir little lassie has been awfully sick and calling for you."

"Come, love, Mother is here now," Maggie crooned, turning toward the house. Ainsley's tiny body was so hot. Maggie felt tears splash down her cheeks.

Turning through the door, she called to Molly.

"We need cold water and plenty of clean cloths. I need to bathe her and get this fever down."

"It willna come down," Maude said. "I've been bathing the puir little lassie for two days now. Her fever keeps getting higher."

"I'll get the water," Molly said. "If it won't lower her fever, maybe it will keep it from getting any higher. And we need to make sure she eats. She's going to need strength to fight this." Molly looked at Ainsley. "I pray to God that captain was right."

Maggie looked at Molly. "What do you mean?"

"I hope it's ship fever. Right now, judging from the way this thing hit her, it could be ship fever . . . or it could be typhoid," Molly said, heading for the kitchen.

"Oh, my God," Maggie said. Turning quickly to Maude, she said, "Take Fletch and Barrie with you for now. I dinna want anyone around Ainsley. Ship fever or typhoid, they're both likely to spread if we are no careful." She took Maude's hand. "I'm sorry, but you'll have to find your way around on your own for now, Maude. Try to explain to Fletch and Barrie for me. I have to stay with Ainsley."

Maude looked out the window, seeing Fletcher and Barrie chasing a large yellow dog. "From what I can see, there isna anything to worry about. They have enough to keep them busy. There's a whole new country to explore. I ken they'll be fine—a lot better than you. Dinna you worry about them."

Maggie carried Ainsley to the room she had always pictured her in, a cheerful, bright corner room on the third floor. She placed Ainsley on the bed and removed her clothes. When Molly came in with the basin of cold water, Maggie began bathing her, first cleaning her thoroughly with soap, then applying cool, wet cloths. She handed Ainsley's clothes to Molly. "Burn these," she said.

Exhausted, and afraid to leave her daughter's side, Maggie remained on her knees beside the bed, listening to Ainsley's rapid breathing. More for her own comfort than Ainsley's, Maggie held her tiny hand in hers and began praying.

It was dark when Adrian returned home. He found a cold supper and Molly in the kitchen. The nursemaid and the two older children were nowhere in sight. As if reading his thoughts, Molly said, "Maude put them to bed right after they ate their supper."

"And Maggie?"

"We put the little one in the big corner room on the third floor. Maggie is still up there with her."

Adrian nodded and left the room, lighting a lamp to take upstairs. He climbed the stairs to the third floor. Opening the door to the corner room, he held the lamp aloft and saw Maggie sound asleep and sitting on the floor, her head next to the little girl. He went to stand beside her, placing the lamp on the table. He stood over the two of them. Their heads were close, their hair so much the same color, it was difficult to see where Maggie's ended and the child's began. This little one of Maggie's was the spitting image of her mother. Without further thought, he went to Maggie and lifted her in his arms, placing her on the bed next to her daughter. Maggie stirred, but she did not wake up.

For some time he stood there, looking down at the two of them. He put his hand on the child's head. She was burning with fever. He removed the heated cloth and dipped it in the basin, wringing it out, and replacing it. Any fool could see the child was deathly ill. He was relieved that his initial anger hadn't removed all ability to think, as his anger sometimes did. At least he had sent to San Francisco for a doctor.

Looking at Maggie, he felt some of his anger drain away. He had come up here to tell her he wanted to talk to her, but seeing the exhaustion on her face, he decided it could wait. The damage was done. There would be time to talk tomorrow. He looked at the child. Tomorrow, or the day after.

He continued to look at her for a while. Maggie. His wife. His wife who had also been another man's wife. Maggie the wife. Maggie the mother. Maggie the deceitful one, the betrayer. His heart shattered.

How many other Maggies were there?

Adrian left them sleeping and went from the room. As he walked back down the stairs, he wondered what other secrets she had kept hidden from him. He rubbed his eyes, but the fatigue was still there. It had been a long time since he felt as if his life was out of his own control, a long time since he was so uncertain about what to do. He was a man of action, and one of his strongest attributes was the ability to see problems before they arose, and to act quickly. But ever since this strawberry-haired Scot had come into his life, he lived in a constant state of confusion.

Part of him wanted to bundle Maggie and her children up and send them packing. Part of him wanted to return the children and keep Maggie. Another part had the gall to suggest he keep them all. He wanted. He didn't want. He didn't understand how he could feel both.

But he felt the agony.

# CHAPTER
## ❧ FOURTEEN ❧

If it hadn't been for the high winds, the ship that brought Dr. Hiram Farnsworth would have never made it to San Francisco and back so fast.

Adrian brought the doctor up to the house, but he told Molly to show him upstairs. She made no effort to hide her disapproval. "Aren't you coming up?" Molly asked him, her eyes narrowed and pinning him to the wall, as if daring him to refuse.

"No," he said, "I'm not. I've been away from work long enough as it is. I've got a business to run, and I don't know a damn thing about medicine." He glanced at the doctor, and then back at her. "You've got all the help you need. I'd only be in the way. I've got to get back to the mill."

Molly grunted and led the doctor upstairs.

Adrian watched her go. Damn fool woman, snorting and grunting at him at every turn. It had gotten to the point that he wondered if Molly even knew how to communicate with words.

"Hell and double hell," he said, stuffing his hands into his pockets. He *did* have work to do. He *was* needed down at the mill. He *wasn't* . . . He paused in midthought, when something strange suddenly occurred to him. And the more he thought about it, the more he wondered why it was that he was always feeling guilty, or feeling he had to justify everything around Molly and Maggie. He wasn't the one who was deceitful here. He sure as hell hadn't betrayed Maggie. *There are too many woman in this house*, he told himself. He thought about Maggie's two little girls. *Now they're bringing in reinforcements*.

There were enough people up there fussing over Maggie's daughter without him planting himself in the middle of things. *Aren't you coming up?* Molly's words scampered across his mind like stones skipped across water.

He was on his way out the door when he remembered he left the accounts ledger in his study. He went back for it, and was almost to the door when he remembered that he had left his pocketknife on the bureau. He went upstairs for that.

Then he remembered he hadn't had any breakfast and more than likely wouldn't have any lunch either, so he stopped off by the kitchen, poking a couple of pieces of elk sausage in the middle of two biscuits when he noticed the coffee was still hot. He poured himself a cup and sat down at the table to eat his biscuits.

When he finished eating, he headed for the front door. He paused in the great foyer, looking up the great winding staircase. The doctor was still upstairs. *So, what concern is it of mine?*

*None*, he told himself, opening the front door. He stepped out onto the porch, casting an eye skyward. It looked like rain. Maybe he needed his other boots. He went back inside, returning to his room a second time.

He changed his boots, and went back downstairs. He almost made it to the front door. He stopped, thinking maybe he should go back upstairs for his slicker. Before he made up his mind, Molly came back down, her solemn eyes narrowed, accusing, as she regarded him steadily. ''What are you staring at?'' he asked, at the same moment she said, ''You still here?''

''Do you think you're talking to a ghost?'' he asked.

''No, I know you're no ghost; I'm just trying to decide if there are two of you. Seems to me one of you wants to stay, the other wants to go.''

''All of me wants to go.''

''Then what's keeping you? I thought you were needed down at the mill,'' she said. ''Are you sure you didn't change your mind?''

''I'm sure.'' Adrian regarded her for a moment, standing there like a blown horse, her sides heaving, her nostrils flared. ''I was detained,'' he said. ''It's as simple as that.''

Molly looked like she didn't believe a word he said, but she didn't mention it. ''Will you be going up now?''

Adrian hesitated. ''The doctor is there; what good would I be?''

''She might find it nice to have a little companionship about now.''

''If she wants companionship, she can call Israel,'' he said.

''Now, that was a clever statement,'' she said. ''When you get through being thoughtless, you might try thinking about how hard it is on a woman going through these things alone. I know how she feels. I would have never made it through the deaths of my two boys if I hadn't had that big old lout I'm married to. Big John Polly never left my side.''

''Big John never deceived you the way Maggie did.''

''Well, if he had, I don't think I would be too pigheaded to understand why.''

''Leave it be, Molly. Things were different between you and Big John than they are between Maggie and myself,'' he said.

''I don't reckon they were so different,'' she said. ''I think we just looked at it a bit more honestly.''

Adrian rubbed his hand over his eyes. He was tired, and he didn't want to go any more rounds with Molly. "Think what you like," he said.

"All right, I think you're a fool for refusing to listen to her. You don't even want to understand. Hasn't there ever been anything in your life you wanted so bad that you were terrified of losing it?"

"You seem to forget, Molly. All I've ever had in my life is losses," Adrian said, then started toward his study.

Molly had stopped on the bottom stair and was looking across the expanse of the foyer, watching him. "I thought you said you were going to the mill. The front door is that way," she said, pointing.

"I know which damn way the front door is," he shouted. "I decided to work here." His tone was lower now. "Do you have a problem with that?" Not bothering to wait for her to snort again, he gave her his back.

"*Humph!* Don't reckon I do," she said, smiling.

Adrian went down the hall to his study, but Molly's words followed him. He sat at his desk and picked up a letter and began reading, but the letters blurred like wet ink, the pigment rearranging itself to become not letters, but the likeness of a woman.

Maggie.

How could mere ink splotches capture the mystery of those eyes? Her eyes were the most dazzling and baffling ones that he had ever seen. They were eyes that looked at him now with pain and sorrow. He shook his head, feeling irritated with himself for such thoughts. He was a man grown, a man with work to do. Daydreams and fancy were for children.

Children. The word scraped like a knife across bare bones. Even the word terrified him. What did he know about children? It had been ages since he had even seen one. Of course, he wanted children, but they would be his—and they would be babies when they came, so he would have time to adjust to them before they turned into little people. It was too much too soon. He wasn't prepared for a full-blown family any more than he had been prepared for the shock of Maggie's betrayal.

Maggie. The very sound of her name hurt. His heart wrenched with the loss.

He forced his attention back to his work. It was no use. He couldn't work. He couldn't think. He couldn't get his mind on anything, save Maggie and that little girl up there. He remembered taking her from Maggie as she climbed from the wagon. The child didn't weigh more than a pound of feathers. And she had been so hot.

He shoved away from his desk and stood, going to the window, watching the rain splatter against the windowpanes. For the first time in years, a shadowy, blurred image of his little sister, Margery, shimmered in front of his eyes. He remembered that awful winter before she was kidnapped, when she had the croup, and how badly she coughed. He recalled how his mother and father built a tent over her bed with blankets, filling it with kettles of boiling water, hoping the steam would break the fever that accompanied her agonizing cough. He saw his father, his face drawn and haggard with worry, pacing the floor, while his mother sat inside the tent with Margery. But most of all, he remembered how his father held them both and cried when the fever broke and his mother said Margery was going to be fine.

A few minutes later, he strode rapidly from his study, his pace fast and brisk, his face set and composed, as he went upstairs, to the third floor.

Maggie was standing across the bed from Dr. Farnsworth as he examined Ainsley. She didn't notice Adrian when he entered the room and stopped just inside the door. Folding his arms over his chest, Adrian leaned against the wall and listened to the doctor, his eyes moving from the pale, concerned face of his wife to the pale, feverish face of the child who bore such a strong resemblance to her.

"Um-hmm, high fever, severe weakness." Dr. Farnsworth lifted the tiny gown, examining the bluish spots on her body. "When did these occur?"

"Three days ago," Maggie said.

"And you say she came down with the fever two days prior to that?"

"Aye, one day out of San Francisco."

"Unfortunate," he said. "Most unfortunate it didn't happen when you were there and much closer to a doctor." He lowered Ainsley's gown, then lifted each of her eyelids. "Have you noticed her tongue? Is it white?"

"Aye."

"Any delirium, talking in her sleep, restless movement, nervousness?"

"Aye."

He looked over his glasses at Maggie, giving her a severe look. "Well? Which one?"

"I canna pick one," she said, "since she has them all."

Dr. Farnsworth blinked and said, "Hmmm," but there was a glimmer of admiration in his eyes. "I suppose you can't."

"Is it bad, then? That she has them all?"

"It's both bad and good. Bad for obvious reasons, good in that it helps me with my diagnosis." Dr. Farnsworth then removed his eyeglasses, folded them, and put them into his pocket. "Well, God be praised, it isn't typhoid. It's typhus . . . or ship fever, if you prefer."

Seeing the stricken look on Maggie's face, he added, "But your daugher is young and strong, and otherwise healthy. That in itself offers much promise." He contemplated a moment. "If you're certain she came down with the fever seven days ago, then she should reach the critical point in three more days. After that, her fever should drop drastically."

Maggie looked down at her daughter, seeing the dusky skin, the deathly pallor. "Is there no anything we can give her? Any medicine?"

"Not really. Generally, typhus fever must run its course. She seems to be resting well, but I will leave tincture of opium drops for you to use if her delirium gets severe, or if she is unable to sleep. The delirium is a normal part of the illness. She will be restless and talk out of her head. Keep her calm and quiet. Give her soup broth when she's awake." He looked around the room. "This is a large, airy room. That's good."

"You ken she has a chance, then?"

Dr. Farnsworth patted Maggie's shoulder. "There's always a chance, Mrs. Mackinnon. I've seen people pull through things I never would have believed they would survive."

*And die from things they shouldn't*, Adrian heard himself thinking.

"Like I said, she's young and healthy. Now, don't go worrying yourself sick. You need to stay healthy if you're going to care for her properly."

Maggie felt the burn of tears in her eyes, but the urge to cry left when she glanced toward the door and saw Adrian standing there.

"How long," she said, pulling her eyes away from him, "before I can take her back to Scotland?"

Her words ripped at Adrian's heart, but he hardened himself and looked away. It didn't take a fool to know that question had been asked for his benefit.

Dr. Farnsworth's bushy gray brows lifted. "Back to Scotland? Didn't you say she just arrived?"

"Aye," Maggie said, unable to stop her eyes from drifting over to where Adrian stood.

Dr. Farnsworth glanced from Maggie to Adrian. "I see. Well, in that case, I would say a return trip would be out of the question for some time. She needs warmth and quiet and rest for at least three months. Six months to a year would be better. Typhus can reoccur, you know. To put her back on a ship at this time would be nothing short of murder, Mrs. Mackinnon.'' Maggie's eyes grew wider. ''I'm sorry to be so blunt, but you asked my opinion. I see no reason not to be completely honest with you when I give it. I daresay you wouldn't want it any other way. Not when the life of your child is at stake.''

''No, I wouldna. Thank you.''

Maggie changed the cloth on Ainsley's head, then walked Dr. Farnsworth downstairs, noticing as she left the room that Adrian was gone. When they reached the bottom of the stairs, Maggie said, ''If you can wait a moment, I'll find someone to drive you back to the dock.''

''Wong is waiting outside in the buggy. He'll drive Dr. Farnsworth.''

Maggie turned to see Adrian approach. He thanked the doctor and shook his hand, opening the door for him, stepping out onto the porch. She watched them walk to the buggy, their heads together, deep in conversation. For a moment Maggie stood there, watching from the open doorway, then went to find Molly.

After giving Molly the rest of the day off, Maggie was on her way back to Ainsley's room when she came around a corner and saw Adrian. He was standing beside the door, as if he were waiting for her. He stood tall and straight, his hands relaxed at his sides.

She gave a start when she saw him, her hand flying to her breast. ''You startled me. I didna expect to see you there,'' she said.

''Where are you going?''

''To Ainsley's room.''

Adrian stood unmoving and silent for a moment, then said, ''I think you should get some rest.''

"I canna rest now. I slept well enough last night."

"I mean real rest, Maggie. You won't be any good to Ainsley if you're too exhausted to keep your eyes open. Go lie down. I'll tell Molly to go stay with her."

"I just sent Molly home."

"Why?"

"She's as tired as I am. She was up most of the night."

"What about Maude?"

"I had her take Barrie and Fletcher on a picnic."

Maggie was not sure why her body began to shake and her knees threatened to give way. Perhaps it was shock, or jangled nerves, or perhaps just the release of tension, knowing now that Ainsley would probably survive. She stood there, feeling cold and insolated, as if winter had come and she was to go through it all alone. She thought she swayed on her feet, but she was not certain until Adrian spoke, coming toward her.

Adrian crossed to where Maggie stood. "You're tired. Go to bed," he said, "while you can still stand. I'll stay with the child." He started up the stairs, and for a moment, Maggie stared stupidly after him.

"Wait," she called. "You canna stay with her."

Adrian stopped and turned slowly. "And why not? You afraid I might smother her?"

Maggie blanched. "No, of course not, but she might wake up, and the cloths need changing."

"I am not an idiot, Maggie. I think I'm capable of wringing out a cloth."

Wearily she placed her hand on the banister and started up the stairs, intending to go to Ainsley's room, but when she passed the door to her own room, she stopped. Adrian had been right. She was too exhausted to think straight.

*There comes a time*, she told herself, *when sleep becomes inevitable*. If she didn't rest now, she would literally drop on her feet.

Upstairs, Adrian smoothed back the damp hairs that were plastered to Ainsley's forehead as he removed the hot cloth and replaced it with a cool one. Then he leaned back in the chair, his eyes going around the room, a room he had built, yet one he was completely unfamiliar with. *It's a good room for a little girl*, he thought, having a vision of what it might look like with toys scattered about a bright rug, a shelf of dolls, frilly curtains on the windows, and all those doodads little girls like lying about.

His gaze went back to the child. He knew nothing about little people like this. In his estimation, it had been at least two years since he had even seen one. So, what in the name of heaven was he doing with three of them under his roof? He studied the still, pale face, trying to remember when he was her age, then deciding that was just too long ago. Still, he didn't remember five or six being so small. Perhaps that was because she was a girl. Girls were smaller.

He studied the child critically for some time. Little people weren't such a wonder after all. They were just miniature adults. This child didn't look particularly terrifying. Of course, she was asleep. He wondered why he had always been just a little afraid of them.

Perhaps because they seemed to have a second sense that adults did not have, a sense that enabled them to know what was going on in your head. And they were frank. Painfully so.

Ainsley stirred and mumbled something Adrian didn't understand. He exchanged the cloth again, noticing how she had thrown one arm out, so that her hand dangled off the side of the bed. Adrian picked it up and was shocked to realize how small it was.

*Why, she's no more than a baby*, he thought, studying the tiny hand. He noticed a faint red scar on the palm and wondered how she had cut herself, when she began to grow restless.

"Papa," she called, whimpering. "Papa, where are you?"
She began to thrash and pull at her hair, and Adrian, fearing
she might pull it out by the fistful, gently held her down.

"Here now! Stop that," he said, then feeling suddenly
ridiculous, knowing his words were far too harsh and uncaring to be spoken to a child. But how did one talk to a little
person like this? He thought back to his own childhood, trying to remember his mother. He closed his eyes and could
almost hear her singing a lullaby in Gaelic. His mother was
gentle, and her words soft. Ainsley cried out for her papa
again, and Adrian held her hands down. "Shhh," he said.
"You're going to be fine."

She continued to thrash and talk incoherently, and Adrian
searched his mind for the memory of something to say to a
child, remembering only a ditty the neighbor girls used to
sing when they found a doodlebug's hole. With an awkward
glance toward the door, he began to chant softly.

> *"Ladybird, ladybird, fly away home.*
> *Your house is on fire, your children all gone.*
> *All but one, and her name is Ann,*
> *And I don't remember the rest of this stupid song."*

Ainsley settled quietly as long as he recited, but the minute
he stopped, she resumed her thrashing.

"Papa . . . Papa . . . Papa! Don't go away." As she spoke
through dry, fevered lips, she clutched Adrian's hand. "Don't
leave me, Papa. Please don't leave me."

"I won't," he said, feeling foolish to be so deceptive, even
to a child, but telling himself it was necessary to quiet her.

"I'm here, so sleep now," he said, smoothing his hand
over her forehead. Gradually she began to drift off to sleep.

Adrian must have dozed himself, for when Ainsley began
to stir in her sleep, he jerked full awake. The child was mumbling incoherently, but eventually she grew quiet, her hands

still gripping Adrian's hand firmly. Whenever he tried to pull his hand back, she would begin thrashing and talking wildly. With a sigh, Adrian left his hand in hers, wondering if it were possible for him to absorb some of the heat from a body that seemed too small to withstand such a high fever.

He was still sitting with his hand in Ainsley's when Maggie came into the room. He heard the door shut and pulled his hand away quickly, glancing up at Maggie as he did.

He shot to his feet. "I . . . uh . . . It seemed to make her sleep better," he said in a self-conscious way.

Maggie studied him for a moment. "Thank you," she said softly. "I'll stay with her for a while."

"You'd better see to dinner. I can stay here awhile longer."

"Molly is back now. She was starting dinner when I came up."

Adrian made it as far as the end of the bed, then paused, turning to look at Maggie in a strange way. "Tell me about her father," he said.

Maggie couldn't hide her look of surprise. "Bruce?"

Adrian looked at Ainsley. "She kept calling for him. She was out of her head. . . . She thought . . ."

"You were her father."

"Yes." Heat rose to his face and he looked off. "I was just curious; that is, I wondered if . . ." He ran his hand through his hair and looked away. "Never mind."

"You were curious to know if Bruce looked anything like you," she said, as if telling him, not asking a question.

"Yes, I suppose I was."

Maggie kept her eyes on Adrian. "Bruce was about your height, but thicker—more muscular—and his hair was much darker than yours, almost black." She was silent for a moment, then she said, "The two of you are nothing alike. Bruce was a tease and a talker. He never met a stranger. He had a Scot's brogue so thick, you could slice it with a dirk.

He joked a lot, and laughed a lot, and he adored our children.''

"In other words, he was everything I am not."

"I ken you could say that, but I dinna think you should think of it in a negative way."

Adrian's jaw clenched, and Maggie went on. "I would think you'd be glad you are so different from him. In time the children will come to love you for who you are, for a hundred reasons that are completely different from the reasons they loved their father. They will . . .'' She stopped suddenly, realizing how she carried on, what she was saying. *Foolish, foolish woman! You and the children won't be here long enough for those things to happen.* Her eyes flew to his. "I'm sorry. I didna mean to imply . . .'' She paused. "I ken what you must be thinking."

"To the contrary. I don't think you have an inkling of my thoughts, and as for your not meaning to imply . . .'' His voice faded away, then came back stronger than ever to say, "Don't think me so naive, sweet Maggie. I have a feeling you know exactly what you're doing. Just as you've known all along how to tie a man's guts in a knot."

# CHAPTER
## ❦ FIFTEEN ❦

Adrian went downstairs and strode briskly down the hallway to the library. Just inside the door, he drew up short. The other girl, the one called Barrie, was sitting in the rocking chair, singing to her doll. She looked up when he walked in.

The moment he stopped, she slid from the chair and made a wide circle around him, obviously heading for the door. Her look was wary and speculative, as if she were trying to decide something.

"Where are you going?" he asked gruffly.

Her face crumpled. "I dinna want to stay in here," she said, her voice soft, her hands clutching the doll against her.

"Why not? Because I'm in here?"

"Aye."

"Stay if you like. I won't bite."

"Aye," she said, "you willna if I'm no here," and she began inching toward the door.

"Stay," he said, turning away. "I'll go outside, where I can get a little peace and quiet."

Once out in the open, he heard Israel bark. He looked up to see the boy, Fletcher, running down the drive where it sloped down the hill. He was trying to fly a kite, but Israel kept chasing the tail, jumping into the air to grab it each time the kite lifted off the ground. Adrian paused for a moment, watching the boy scold Israel, feeling the urge to smile at the way Israel flattened himself and put his paws over his nose.

He turned off in the opposite direction and headed toward the stables, intending to saddle his horse and ride out some of his frustration. He got as far as putting the bridle on, and was just reaching for the saddle, when an authoritative voice behind him said, "Aren't you going to brush his back first?"

Adrian knew who that voice belonged to, but the resonance, the authority in it, surprised him. *Arrogant little bastard*, he thought, and turned to see Fletcher leaning over the gate to the stall, his brown hair wind-tossed, his eyes a deep blue and penetrating. He saw nothing of Maggie in this child.

"I thought you were flying your kite," Adrian said. "What are you doing in here?"

"I came to see what you were doing. I canna fly my kite with Israel along."

"You could lock him up in one of these stalls."

"I'd rather watch you," he said, his eyes going to the gelding. "What if there are burrs on his back? Aren't you going to brush his back before you put the saddle on?"

"You've already asked me that once."

"My mother says it's better to ask twice than to lose your way."

"Then go ask your mother. She's the one with all the answers."

"Why?"

Adrian scowled at him. "Why? Why are you so full of questions?"

"My mother says it's good to ask questions, then others won't think you know all the answers."

"Is there anything your mother doesn't know?"

Fletcher grinned. "Aye, she doesna know how to make

scones. Whenever she threw them out to our dogs, the dogs would bury them.''

The muscle in Adrian's jaw worked as the desire to ride drained slowly away. Was there no place safe from this sudden invasion of little people? Adrian removed the bridle and walked out of the stall.

''Change your mind?''

''Yes.''

''Want me to exercise him for you?''

''No, I do not. What I want is for you to stay away from me and away from this animal. He's too valuable for a child to ride.''

Fletcher grinned up at him. ''I ken how to ride and I ken a lot about horses. I ken that gelding of yours was blooded when I first rode him.''

Adrian saw red. ''When you first *what*?''

''When I first rode him.''

''And when was that?''

''This morning.''

''You will not ride this horse again. Is that clear?''

Fletcher looked around the stables, seeing the two carriage horses and no others, save the one he had ridden this morning. ''Then what will I ride?''

''Your imagination,'' Adrian said, and closed the gate, turning away.

Adrian looked behind him once to see if the boy, Fletcher, followed him up to the house. He didn't, and that made Adrian wonder if the boy was brazen enough to ride his horse after what he had just said. He decided the boy wasn't that stupid.

Adrian came around the corner of the house and saw a patch of red glinting in the sunlight. It was Barrie, the one with the flaming red hair and freckles. She was sitting on the back steps, singing to her doll.

*"Hush ye, hush ye, little pet ye,*
*Hush ye, hush ye, do not fret ye,*
*The Black Douglas shall not get ye."*

Barrie looked up and scooted over to make way as Adrian started up the steps. He grunted his acknowledgment and glanced down, seeing the small, pointed chin thrust out. He had almost reached the door when she asked, "Are you going to choke my mother?"

Adrian spun around, surprised, because that was remarkably close to the way he was feeling. *This* little chit had the guts to ask him that? "What makes you think I would choke your mother?"

"Molly Polly said you would."

About this time Adrian was thinking Molly Polly would be second on his list. "I haven't choked anyone as yet. I don't know why she would tell you something like that."

The small, freckled face relaxed somewhat. "She said we better stay out of your way, because if we gave you any trouble, you would choke our mother. I canna remember the rest of what she said."

"Good," Adrian said, and went through the door, calling Molly.

Molly, being wholly unflappable, took her time coming. "You called me?" she asked, stopping to look at him, leaning on her broom.

"Yes, and you damn well know it. I've got enough problems with my house being turned into a goddamn nursery without you making matters more complicated."

"And how am I doing that?"

"Don't act innocent with me. You know what you've done. Why would you say things to those two little distractions out there like I'd choke their mother if they don't stay out of my way?"

"That's what you told me."

"And what if I did? Do you find it necessary to repeat everything I say?"

"Only when there are three veins standing out on your forehead like they are right now. Otherwise, no."

"Molly, one of these days you're going to push me too far, and it's going to take half the men in this lumber camp to pull me off of you when I do."

"You wish," Molly said with a laugh. "You can bark, but you're like a dog with no teeth. It won't take those babies long to see that. You might as well admit it, you've been made a part of their lives whether you like it or not. Now, that baby up there is gonna be sick for a spell, and she's gonna need a heap of loving care before she's back to normal. You aren't going to lose anything by being nice, and that's much easier than working so hard to be the hind end of a jackass."

"Are you calling me the hind end of a jackass?"

"Do you see anyone else in the room?"

Adrian, his mind suddenly blank, could do nothing but watch Molly return to sweeping. A moment later she had swept her way around him and out of his sight.

Why he continued to put up with her mouthy ways was beyond him, but he had to admit that about one thing, she was right. He was drawn into the lives of Maggie and her little ones, whether he liked it or not.

And if he was going to be forced to be part of their lives, he damn well had a right to know more about what he was getting into.

After dinner he took Maggie by the elbow and guided her out of the room and down the hall to the library. "I want to talk to you," he said, glancing at Barrie, who looked at him accusingly.

"Don't worry, I'm not going to choke her . . . yet."

Once they reached the library and went inside, he closed

the door behind them. He gave her a leveling look. "I want you to tell me about your husband," he said. "I want to know everything and I want to know right now. I don't care if you want to tell me or not. I have a right to know."

"Aye, you do. I dinna ken why you didna ask before now," Maggie said softly.

Breathing heavily, Adrian clenched his fists and ignored that. "How did he die?"

Maggie's initial look was one of surprise, but the look faded to one of resolve. "He was run over a cliff."

"You mean he was murdered?"

"Aye." She nodded and looked away. "That wasna the official report, you ken, but Bruce Ramsay was too good a horseman and he knew the road to Edinburgh too well to simply ride to his death over the edge of a cliff."

"Why would anyone have wanted him dead?"

"It's a verra long story," she said, weariness in her voice.

"I'll tell you if I find it too exhausting," he said.

She sighed. She had spent so much time learning to live with Bruce's death. Now Adrian wanted her to open the wound. She looked at Adrian. He was her husband now, and the past had no bearing . . . or did it? With another sigh of defeat, she relented. He had a right to know, of course. This once, she told herself. She would talk about it this one time, and no more.

He was still silent, his look telling her he had all the time in the world and would not be put off. She found this sudden display of patience out of character for him, for if she had learned anything about Adrian Mackinnon, it was that he was not a very patient man.

She told him about Adair Ramsay, about his claim to Bruce's title, then went on quite calmly to tell him about Bruce's death, leaving nothing out.

"And your son was stripped of the title?"

"Aye."

"Do you think his life is in danger?"

"I did at first, and would now, if I had remained in Scotland. I dinna fret over it so much now that I've come to America."

"What has your being in America got to do with it?"

"It's verra simple. A matter of simple geography. It's a verra long way from Scotland to California. Adair Ramsay has what he wants. As long as I stay out of Scotland—as long as I keep Fletcher away—I ken we're safe. The distance alone would keep him away."

Adrian shook his head. "I can't understand how something like that could happen. You said the title had been in your husband's family for years?"

"Aye."

"Didn't you have good lawyers?"

"I did the best I could. You ken my husband was dead, and I feared for Fletcher's safety. I was afraid to fight too much, afraid something would happen to him."

"Didn't you have *anyone* to help you?"

She shook her head.

"What about your father?"

"My father is old and almost blind, and his funds are limited."

"What about Ross? He would have helped you."

"Aye, he offered, but I couldna let him become involved. I wasna certain that Adair wouldna take his wrath out on Ross and Annabella." She looked at him. "There wasna anyone I could go to," she said, her eyes filling with tears, her voice trembling.

It suddenly occurred to Adrian just how much Maggie had been through before she left Scotland. "So you accepted Ross's offer to marry me?"

"Aye. It seemed the perfect solution at the time, you ken."

"And now?"

She came to her feet. "Dinna ask me that now," she said, tears rolling down her face, "for I canna answer it rationally."

"Why not?"

"Because my heart gets in the way," she said, running from the room.

After she had gone, Adrian sat there staring at the last place he had seen her, his insides twisted with feelings that were at war. Part of him wanted to go to Maggie, to take her in his arms and comfort her. Part of him was afraid to try. Part of him didn't even want to try.

He still felt that way the next afternoon as he stood outside the camp office, talking to Clyde Bishop, when he looked up and saw Wong bring Fletcher and Barrie into camp with him, taking them into the washhouse, a bag of laundry tossed over his shoulder.

Once Clyde left, Adrian went back inside the office. Looking out the window, he saw it didn't take long for those two scavengers of Maggie's to become bored with the washhouse and venture outside. By the time Adrian left the camp office, John Archer was showing Fletcher how to throw a knife, and Hiram Curtis, who was leading a team of oxen, lifted Barrie up to ride on one of their broad backs. Both of them waved at him as he passed. Adrian didn't have much choice but to wave back. *This doesn't mean I've changed my mind about them,* he told himself.

His mind filled with thoughts about little people, Adrian called it quits. He met Molly coming out of the kitchen with a milk pail when he arrived at the house. "Go in quietly," she said. "Maggie fell asleep in her plate. I thought I'd let her rest until I finished milking. I checked on the baby. She's sleeping and quiet."

Adrian nodded, and stepped into the kitchen. Maggie was asleep, just as Molly had said, but her plate had been pushed away. The plate was full.

He walked around the table, to see her face. One hand was curled beneath her chin, her face streaked with the shadows caused by the late afternoon sun filtering through unbelievably long lashes. He dropped down beside her, his face level with hers. It was the first time he had looked at her—really, really looked at her up close. Tiny, feathery veins of palest violet crisscrossed her eyelids, and smudges of blue half circles lay beneath her eyes, but aside from that, she had the face of a child—morning-fresh skin, not more than a suggestion of a nose, and a full, pouting mouth. True, her nose was too small for her face, and her mouth too large, but oddly enough, in spite of the signs of weariness, today was one of the days he found her lovely.

He leaned forward, whispering her name softly. ''Maggie.'' He intended to tell her to go rest for a while, that he would watch Ainsley, but when she stirred and brought her face closer to his, he forgot what he had been about. She smelled like soap, and her breath was sweet and warm. He thought of what might have been and felt his heart wrench with the agony.

A moment later he stood, and taking her into his arms, he carried her from the kitchen. By the time he reached the stairs, Maggie, although still groggy, whispered his name once, then settled her face against his throat, her arms going around his neck. Adrian felt his mouth go dry.

He pushed open the door to her room with his foot, then kicked it shut behind him. He carried her to her bed. He stood over her for a moment, feeling dumbstruck when she opened her eyes.

''I want you,'' she said.

Adrian thought he had misunderstood her. Elegant, refined ladies did not say things like that. The daughers of earls did not speak that way. Nor did duchesses. He saw her eyes were bright and clear and staring right at him.

''Make love to me, Adrian.''

"You're tired. You don't know what you're saying."

"I ken what I'm saying. I dinna feel ashamed. I want you. I dinna want to think anymore about sickness and death. I want to feel alive. I want you to make love to me. I want to know that I can still feel."

The sun was setting, the last long shadows stretching across the floor and over the bed. His face was hidden in shadow, but she knew him well enough to know the look of resolve that would be on his face. Words seemed to desert her. She held out her hand to him, her fingers stretched out and trembling.

He stood stiff and silent, looking down at that hand for what seemed to be an eternity. He might have stayed there forever if he hadn't glanced at her face and seen the pain of rejection as she began to draw her fingers back. He dropped down on his haunches, taking her hand in both of his.

"I want you." She paused and swallowed. "I wanted you before the children came, but I didna know how to ask you. But now . . . Oh, Adrian, I want you so much, I canna think."

"Don't," he said, taking her in his arms and rolling over the bed with her, pinning her beneath him.

Adrian had never seen a woman look at a man with such honest need, and his entire body reacted to it with such violence, it unarmed him. He no longer wanted to resist her, for he knew he never really had. Desire for her had always been there. She was his and she wanted him. Everything else seemed to fade into oblivion.

She smiled up at him, her arms coming around his neck. Without speaking, he kissed her brow, then her eyelids. Her lashes fluttered, then her eyes closed. He heard her moan low in her throat as his mouth closed over hers.

Adrian groaned, kissing her deeply, his tongue seeking hers. He no longer had control of himself. The hunger in him for her was too potent, too strong, to call back. She wanted him, and he sure as hell wanted her.

Her hand slipped between them, touching, pressing, as he groaned with need. His body trembled, and his words, too. "Maggie, I can't . . . I can't hold back. I can't be gentle. Not now."

"Good," she said, helping him with his clothes before turning to remove her own. "We can be gentle after. . . ."

"Dear God," he said, parting her legs and driving into her, pressing himself until he could go no further. "You drive me and drive me until I'm insane with wanting," he said, his body coming against hers, again and again.

"I dinna ken insanity could feel so good," she said, groaning as she felt the heat of each stroke deep in her belly. Panting with exertion, she lifted her hips to meet each thrust, feeling as if her body no longer belonged to her. Again and again he drove into her, and mindless with the need to torture him as he was torturing her, she rose to meet him. Something wild was happening to her, something that teetered on the edge of pain.

"No," she cried out, pushing against him. "Stop, Adrian. Please. I dinna want any more."

A drop of his sweat fell from his face onto hers, his grip tightening. "You wanted it, Maggie, and I won't stop until you've gotten exactly what you asked for."

Her breathing was wild and out of control, coming in short, gasping pants, her body gripped in tension, trying to hold the invasion of its tender parts at bay. She had never felt like this, and fear gripped her. Was it possible to die like this?

She opened her mouth to deny him, hearing herself whisper as her mind spun away, "Yes, Adrian. My God! Yes!"

They were drenched in sweat, but he showed no signs of tiring, her words seeming to, if anything, urge him on. She felt her body twist in agony, and she knew she had crossed over the threshold of pain. Her body jerked, then opened to him, drawing him inside her. On and on the feeling went, past fear, past pain; gripping, convulsing, clutching in spasms that seemed to take her over the edge into another existence, a place of pure sensation and keen awareness. Agony. Ecstasy. She wasn't sure which. Perhaps it was both.

"You feel it now," he said, responding to her body and stopping her words with his mouth. His thrusting was harder, deeper, and she answered the fury of his passion with a fury of her own. Her teeth sank into his shoulder, her nails raked his back, as the exquisiteness of it gripped her. She felt wild, savage, desperate with the need to go beyond mating with him, to go beyond anything save the fusion of their souls.

Something shattered within her and she arched upward, a cry ripping from her throat.

Reality returned slowly, and Maggie found herself lying beneath Adrian's arm, his leg thrown over hers, his body limp and heavy in sleep. His breathing was steady and slow. She turned her face in to his neck, breathing in the smell of his flesh, his sweat, wondering as she did if this was the last time she would lie with him.

She remained there, without moving, afraid to do so, knowing it would wake him, and wanting to the point of desperation to prolong the closeness, to preserve for as long as possible the pleasure of lying with him like this.

At last she shifted her position.

He opened his eyes and looked at her. "Was this some sort of a contest?" he asked, his eyes as teasing as the smile on his face.

She smiled back. "I dinna ken. Do you feel like a contestant?"

"What I feel is exhausted. And I feel like I've run through a briar," he said, his hand coming up to his shoulder. "What did you do? Bite me?"

"Aye, and hard, too."

"You've got claws like a badger," he said, rolling to his back, cradling her against him.

"I didna want you to forget."

"Forget? Not damn likely. I'll carry these scars to my grave. Is this going to become a habit?"

Her fingers played with the hair on his chest. "I don't know," she said lightly. "Want to try it again and find out?"

"I couldn't move if you built a fire in the bed."

"I ken I could do that," she said, her hand coming from nowhere to close around him.

"Maggie . . ."

"Remember, if you canna take it, think of England," she said, laughing softly as her hand stroked and touched, feeling the gentle pulse of blood that made him grow large and hard in her hand.

"Liar," she said with a muffled laugh.

"That's the only part of me that wasn't tired," he said. "The rest of me is plumb wore-out. I couldn't, Maggie, no matter how much I wanted to."

"Then I will," she said, rolling over him, taking his face between her hands, and kissing his astonished mouth. "Don't worrit," she said softly, pressing her body against him, "I promise to be verra, verra gentle."

A moment later he said, "I feel sufficiently rested now." Then he rolled over and pinned her beneath him. "Don't say I didn't warn you," he said.

"I willna."

He made love to her again, and this time it was as easy and gentle as the first time had been desperate and wild. Drowsy and contented beyond belief, she closed her eyes, feeling she could sleep, really and truly sleep for the first time since Ainsley's illness.

Sometime during the night, she felt Adrian stir. A moment later he leaned over her and called her name.

"Maggie?"

"Aye."

"Are you awake?"

"I am now."

"Did you mean what you said?"

She stretched and looked at him. "When?"

"When you said you were in love with me."

"Aye, I meant it," she said. "Now, go to sleep."

"Not on your life," he said, rolling over her and searing her with a heated kiss.

"Maggie . . ." he said. "Sweet, sweet Maggie. Don't tell me you thought you could say something like that and have me fall asleep." He drew her against him; her palms flattened against his chest. Beneath them, she could feel the warm skin and hard, contoured muscle of his chest, the steady rhythm of his heart, which seemed to beat faster with each breath. She understood that, for her own heart was tapping out a song, and her love for him seemed to grow with each escalating beat.

His hands burned over her back, her buttocks, where his palm seemed to know instinctively just where to touch. His face nuzzling hers, she felt his lips seeking her own. She sighed, feeling his breath, fragrant and warm, on her skin. His lips moved softly, silently, over her, as if slowly searching for something too precious to miss.

His hands fanned over her breasts, his thumbs moving in scorching circles over her nipples. Her breath caught in her throat; her skin trembled from the gentleness of it. Desire swam in thick, gushing pools beneath the surface of her skin. Is this what it was like to die? Her hands dug into his hair, and she felt the hammer of his heart as she pulled him against her for a kiss. The languid warmth of his hand slid across hot, trembling flesh, moving around gentle folds, teasing, bringing the dull, throbbing ache to a consuming outburst.

"But what about you?" she whispered, when she found her voice.

"Maggie. Sweet Maggie. How like you to ask a question like that at a time like this. Can't you see that I get pleasure from just touching you?"

# CHAPTER
# ❧ SIXTEEN ❧

*Show him death, and He will be content with fever.*

Those words were Maggie's comfort and solace during the long days and nights of Ainsley's illness, and although it was difficult to forgive herself for leaving her children behind when she came to California, she wasn't so bent upon self-condemnation that she could not see that Ainsley's illness was not her fault.

There were many times of fear, moments of stabbing agony when Ainsley lay between life and death, times when her small body seemed so close to perishing from the prolonged high fever. And then there came that blessed moment, that beautiful, rain-drenched evening that reminded Maggie so much of Scotland, when Ainsley's fever broke.

When it was over, when the danger of dying was past, Maggie crumpled into a silken heap at Ainsley's bedside, her other children, Molly, and Maude standing at the foot of the bed, looking helpless and yet relieved.

"Sickness comes on horseback and departs on foot," Maude said.

"It comes on a *winged* horse," Molly added, "and it tiptoes out . . . barefoot."

"Is Ainsley dead?" Barrie asked.

"No, lambkin, she isna dead," Maude said. "She willna die now. She will only get better and better, you ken?"

"If she isna dead, then why is Mama crying?" asked Barrie.

"They are tears from the heart," Maude said. "Your mama is crying because she is happy."

"She doesna look verra happy," Fletcher said, narrowing his eyes in speculation.

"Weel, she is happy, and you can take my word for it," Maude said, taking Fletch and Barrie by the hand and leading them from the room, talking as she went.

"Off we go," she said, "to bed with you. We've an early day tomorrow. It's lax I've been with your studies and other things, but that willna be happening anymore."

"You mean we're going to have to do our studies tomorrow?" Fletcher asked.

"Aye, that's what I mean. Elocution and reading willna wait any longer. Did you finish reading James Thomson?" she asked, taking Fletch by the ear.

"Aye."

"And you remember the verses I told you to learn from 'The Seasons'?"

He didn't answer, and Maude gave his ear a twist, getting a yelping response.

"And your numbers, didna you study them either?"

"I studied, but I dinna remember," Fletch said.

"You've always the knack for studying and no remembering."

Leading Fletcher from the room by his ear, she said to Barrie, "What has your brother been doing while your sister has been sick?"

"Playing, mostly," Barrie said.

"And play will get him a fine education, sure enough. Weel now, my fine laddie, your life of leisure is over. Tomorrow it is nose to the grindstone."

"What about Barrie's nose?"

Maude gave Barrie a side look, then winked. "Hers, too, I ken, but it willna be easy to do," Maude said, "since she doesna have much nose to begin with."

At last Ainsley slept cool and peaceful, and the strain of it all finally caught up with Maggie. Like a crazed person, she ran through the house and down the stairs, yanking open the front door, inhaling the scent of a world washed fresh and new before rushing out into the rain, holding her hands out as she spun in a circle, the rain washing down upon her, drenching her hair and clothes, her slippers growing heavy with mud.

"Thank you," she shouted heavenward. "I had much need of a blessing." She spun around and around, faster and faster.

Standing in the doorway, Molly and Maude looked first at each other and then back at Maggie. "She's letting off a little steam," said Molly.

Maude watched Maggie, who by this time was soaked to the skin. "Aye, but she's taking on water." Without another word, Maude shook her head, and Molly shrugged. They closed the door.

Adrian, who was just riding up, pulled his gelding to a halt and watched her. Maggie stopped short when she saw him, looking up in astonishment. He was tall and erect in the saddle, his hands loosely holding the reins; the rain ran in rivulets from the brim of his hat and dropped onto his slicker. He simply stared at her for a moment, then grinned. "You'd better go in," he said, "or people will be thinking you don't have enough sense to come in out of the rain."

Maggie lifted a soggy wad of hair that had fallen across her face and peered up at him. "I dinna," she said, feeling delirious with happiness, her teeth chattering from the cold. "I ken if a Scot went in every time it rained, we wouldna get any exercise."

Looking at him, she saw Adrian's blue eyes look her over slowly, as if he liked what he saw. "Want me to join you?"

"This is a solo," she said, laughing when he urged the gelding into a trot. The heavens semed to open then, the rain coming down in cold, gray sheets, but Maggie didn't seem to mind.

When Adrian reached the stables, he dismounted and, with a laugh and a shake of his head, led his horse into the dark interior.

"And a good day to you, Your Holiness," Maggie said, giving a low-sweeping curtsy, losing her balance and falling face-forward in the mud. She immediately rolled to her back, flung her arms straight out from her body, and looking skyward, let the rain wash the mud from her face. "This," she said with soft satisfaction, "is what I call living."

When some semblance of normalcy returned, Maggie went inside, bathed and washed her hair, then changed clothes and hurried to Ainsley's room. Maude was sitting with her. After giving Ainsley a sponge bath, they had just put her into a clean gown when Molly brought her a bowl of potato soup.

Ainsley turned her head away.

"If you dinna eat, you canna see Barrie and Fletch," Maggie said.

Ainsley hesitated, the small, pale face contemplative, then she drew herself up, thrusting out her small chin. Determined blue eyes met determined hazel eyes. At last Ainsley opened her mouth.

When the soup was gone, Molly went after Barrie and Fletcher. When she brought them with her into the room, Maggie had just poured a spoonful of the opium drops and brought it up to Ainsley's mouth.

She turned her head away.

"Come on, my little silkie, take your medicine. You'll sleep better tonight if you do."

"She dinna like it," Barrie said. "It tastes bad."

"If it didna taste bad, it wouldna be medicine," Maggie said, smiling and caressing Ainsley's cheek when she swallowed it.

Maggie was sitting in a straight chair beside the bed, Barrie and Fletcher coming to sit on the floor beside her. Ainsley poked her thumb into her mouth as Maggie began to tell them a story of how the MacCodrums were descended from seals, nodding at Maude and Molly when they departed.

"From seals?" Fletcher asked, frowning as his mental gears cranked out the improbability of that. "They canna."

About that time, Adrian stepped, unnoticed, into the room, leaning against the doorframe, listening.

"Aye," Maggie said, "they can."

Fletcher looked skeptical. "How?"

"Well now, it isna easy, you ken, but fairies change themselves into seals—we called them silkies when I was a little girl. Now, these seals swim along the shore looking for a lad or lassie to steal for a mate. When they find one, they send something beautiful floating on the tide, something the person they have picked will admire. When the lad or lassie steps into the water to pick it up, the fairy seal pulls them beneath the water, ye ken?"

"And they drown?" Barrie asked.

"No, they marry the fairy and live in fairyland."

"What if the seal canna get the person to come into the water?" asked Fletcher.

"Then they take off their seal skin and change themselves into a beautiful human, so they can marry the one they have chosen."

"Do they live on land, like we do?" Barrie asked.

"Aye, just like humans."

"Do they ever go back?" Fletcher asked.

"Aye. It may be years and years, but sometime it will happen that the fairy will find his shed seal skin has suddenly appeared before him, as if by magic. The puir fairy is help-less and must put on the skin and return to the sea and fairy-land, to be seen no more.''

"Was Father a fairy?'' Barrie asked. "Did he change him-self into a seal and leave?''

"No, my little kelpie, he didna. Your father was a man. A real man,'' she said, looking up, her eyes locking with Adrian's, her face registering her surprise at seeing him standing there. Before she could say anything, he was gone.

After she sent Fletcher and Barrie to their rooms to get ready for bed, Maggie sat for a while holding Ainsley's hand, watching her eyelids droop as the opium drops took effect. When Maude came to check on them, Maggie kissed Ainsley and tucked the blanket around her.

"She should sleep through the night now,'' Maggie said.

"Just the same, I ken I would feel better sleeping in here with her.''

Maggie put her hand on Maude's arm. "I know you would, and it's probably best for you to stay with her some now that the worst is over. I ken I've neglected Barrie and Fletcher terribly. I need to spend a lot of time with them to make up for it.''

"They've been busy learning about their new home, and that yellow beastie, Israel, seems to have taken to them. Hout! I dinna think they have missed you all that much.''

"I'm thankful for that, at least,'' Maggie said. "I'll put them to bed now and see you in the morning.''

"Good night, ma'am.''

"Good night, Maude. Sleep well.''

"Oh, aye, I will do that, ma'am, now that the little one is doing ever so much better.''

Maggie nodded, then picking up her lamp, crossed the room, closing the door softly behind her.

* * *

"Was I ever sick like Ainsley when I was little?" Barrie asked when Maggie walked into her room.

"No, you were sick a time or two, but I dinna ken you were ever that sick." Maggie looked around the room. "Where is Fletcher?"

"Under the bed."

"I didna want you to tell her!" a disgruntled voice said from beneath the bed. "You said you wouldna tell," Fletcher said, coming out from under the bed.

"I dinna," Barrie said. "You asked me, but I didna say I wouldna." Leaning over, her hands on her hips, her face just inches from his, she wagged her finger and scolded, "Mama said we should always tell the truth . . . even if we have to lie."

A small mouse ran along the baseboard of the wall next to the bed, stopping and standing on its hind legs when it saw Fletcher, its eyes black and shining, its whiskers twitching.

"It's watching you," Barrie said. "I ken it thinks you're a giant mouse."

"It wouldna if you didna crawl around on the floor like one," Maggie said, leaning down and taking Fletcher by the arm. "Up with you, laddie. What were you doing under the bed?"

"I was going to scare you," he said, "but not bad."

The mouse ran when Fletcher came to his feet.

"I need to cut your hair tomorrow," Maggie said, giving Fletcher's hair a fluff or two.

"It's all right," he said, raising his shoulders, protectively drawing his head in, like a turtle, and tilting it out of the way.

"It is not all right," Maggie said. "It's too long."

Barrie laughed. "Aye. You look like a lassie."

Fletcher turned to Barrie and stuck out his tongue.

"I hate you!" Barrie said. "I don't want you in my room."

"There now," Maggie said. "You don't hate your brother."

"I do," Barrie said. "I do. I hate my brother. I want a different one."

Maggie smiled. "It willna do any good to wish for a different brother. All men are the same, you ken. They just have different faces so you can tell them apart."

"Do I *have* to have a brother?"

"No, you don't have to have one, but you do, and you should be happy for it," Maggie said for the tenth time since the children had come to California, and the hundredth time since Barrie could talk.


Over the next few days, Ainsley's appetite returned, and along with it, her color. Even her laughter returned.

But one thing did not return.

Since the onset of her illness, Ainsley would not talk.

At first Maggie thought this was something temporary, that her speech would return along with her health, but long after she recovered, Ainsley remained mute. When she wanted something, she would point or make gestures with her hands, and whenever Maggie asked her why she would not speak, Ainsley would simply look at her, a blank expression on her face, and turn her head away.

Maggie discussed it with Molly and Maude, each of them trying to think of ways to persuade Ainsley to talk. They tried not giving her what she wanted, but she would either get it herself, rely on Barrie, or do without.

"I ken the puir little lassie would starve herself to death," Maude said.

"Aye," Maggie said in agreement, "I ken she would at that."

"I've heard of things like this happening a time or two," Molly said. "I knew of a young girl what lost her whole family in a fire. She didn't say another word for almost ten years, and then suddenly one day she started talking.''

"It was brought on by some disturbance in her life, then?'' Maggie said.

"Yes,'' said Molly.

"If it's a reason she needs, Ainsley has plenty, I ken,'' Maggie said at last. "She was never as talkative after Bruce's death. Perhaps the close call with her own death affected her mind in some way.''

"Aye,'' Maude said, "if the wee lassie thought she was going to die, she couldna help but remember the day they brought her father home.''

Maggie's face turned white. She was suddenly remembering that day, and how Ainsley had been changed. Never would she forget Ainsley's face that day—the color of the whitest ivory, it was, and her eyes were so wide, they seemed too big for such a small head. She remembered, too, how long it was before Ainsley would talk.

That night, before she put Ainsley to bed, Maggie sat beside the window in Ainsley's bedroom, rocking her to sleep. Clutching her rag doll in one hand, Ainsley brought her thumb to her mouth.

"Ease your mind, my wee little one,'' Maggie said, kissing the delicate curls of red and gold. "Hush ye, hush ye, my troubled little mind. The Black Douglas shall not get ye.''

When Ainsley's thumb slid from her mouth, Maggie knew she was asleep.

Maggie wiped a ribbon of drool from Ainsley's mouth, glancing up to see Maude slip into the room. Maggie put Ainsley in her bed. Tiptoeing from the room, she closed the door as Maude said, "Take courage, ma'am, and dinna forget what Adam Lindsay Gordon said about life being most froth and bubble.''

Maggie regarded her with a puzzled expression for a moment, then with a deep breath, said, "Aye, I hadna thought of that for a long while."

> *Life is mostly froth and bubble;*
> *Two things stand like stone:*
> *Kindness in another's trouble,*
> *Courage in your own.*

Courage.

It did take courage to watch her child dwelling in a world of silence, seeing her brightness wasted. Because of Ainsley's affliction, Maggie was more devoted to her than ever, rocking her, reading to her, singing her songs. Sometimes Ainsley would clap her hands in delight, or collapse in a fit of giggles when Maggie said something funny, or tickled her out of her mischief. She was quick and clever, and Maggie noticed this more than she had before, when Ainsley could speak. Sometimes Ainsley would become serious and quiet; other times she was quite the prankster, and Maggie learned to recognize the spark of mischief gleaming in her blue eyes.

Ainsley seemed not bothered in the least by her own silence, but more often than not, Maggie went to bed with a pale, haggard face.

"You are trying too hard," Molly would often say. "She will speak when all things are right, and you will either accept that or kill yourself fighting it."

Maggie agreed, but as the days passed and Ainsley did not speak, Maggie grew more and more concerned.

" 'Earth hath no sorrow that Heaven cannot heal,' " Maude told her one night, but Maggie soon began to doubt even that, for added to her anguish over Ainsley was her distress over the way things lay between herself and Adrian, and the uncertainty of the future for herself and her children.

When night finally came, Maggie sighed wearily and climbed into her lonely bed. It took some time to rid her mind of its daily clutter, and when her mind finally did clear, it left her senses numbed. Everything around her, the chaos, the confusion, the disappointments, seemed strangely remote, as if her mind had a sanctuary of its own. She closed her eyes, seeking the blessed release of sleep.

*When sorrows come, they come not single spies, but in battalions.*

For days after Ainsley's recovery, Adrian did his best to stay out of Maggie's way, knowing she needed to spend time with her children. He felt so awkward around Maggie and the children. He didn't know how to act, or what to say to them. It amazed him how three little people could manage to be everywhere. He soon learned that children, natural eavesdroppers, had the uncanny ability to remember the most minute details when it suited them, and erratic memories when it didn't.

He once came upon Barrie and Fletcher in a heated argument over which one of them Israel liked best. Israel, ever the diplomat, remained perfectly neutral, sitting on the sidelines, his great yellow head tilted to one side as the argument grew more heated. At last, unable to win the argument, Fletcher called Israel to follow, and the two of them ran. Unable to keep up, Barrie returned to the house in tears.

Adrian learned that day that when a female cried, it bothered him, regardless of her age.

His hands thrust deeply in his pockets, Adrian had simply stared at Barrie's windblown red hair, listening to her sob, unable to believe he did not know how to talk to a child. At last, fearing Barrie would collapse from exhaustion, he suggested that she try to beat Fletcher at his own game.

"I dinna k-ken—h-how," she sobbed. "He's faster than me, and s-s-so is Israel."

"Carry a biscuit in your pocket," he said. "And the next time he calls Israel, take the biscuit out. Israel won't turn down a biscuit for any reason. Now, dry your eyes, and stop crying.'' He handed her his handkerchief. ''The first time you win Israel over with the biscuit, you'll forgive your brother and forget all about it.''

''I canna,'' she said, wiping her eyes, which he noticed were intensely blue. ''I canna ever forgive him.''

''Yes you can. It's not that hard. All you have to do is say it. Come on. Say you'll forgive and forget.''

Barrie looked at him, stubbornly thrusting out her chin.

''Come on,'' he cajoled.

''I'll forgive and I'll forget,'' she whispered at last. As Adrian turned away, she said more loudly, ''But I'll also remember.''

''I feel sorry for Barrie,'' Adrian told Molly one afternoon, immediately irritated with himself for saying it.

Molly had been washing down the cabinets in the kitchen with vinegar, and when Adrian spoke, she tossed the rag back into the bucket with a *plop*. ''You feel sorry for Barrie?''

Adrian shrugged in dismissal. ''Forget it,'' he said.

''Why do you feel sorry for her and not the others?''

''Because she's the one in the middle.''

''If it's any comfort to you, I felt the same way at first, but after I mentioned it to Maude, she set me straight. She said I shouldn't feel sorry for her. She said she pitied anyone who tangled with Barrie, because they would come out of it minced finer than a clove of garlic.''

After that day, Adrian began to observe Barrie a bit closer. Before long, he had a feeling Maude had been right.

Take, for instance, the afternoon he came upon Barrie and Fletcher in the stables. Upon entering, Adrian heard pint-sized voices coming from one of the empty stalls. Peeking over the boards into the stall, he saw Fletcher braiding a piece of rawhide while Barrie sat quietly petting the barn cat, her eyes fastened on Fletcher. Adrian watched Fletcher for a minute, noticing after the first three or four plaits, Fletcher had gotten off. The braid would not come out right. He wondered what the boy would say when he noticed it.

"Hellfire!" Fletcher said.

Barrie put the cat down and stood up. "Fletcher Ramsay, what would Jesus say?" She left Fletcher wide-mouthed and staring after her.

Unaccustomed to children, Adrian was perplexed by their multitude of questions, their relentless probing. Their favorite words seemed to be: Why? How? When? What? Only the youngest child, Ainsley, was quiet, for she rarely talked—come to think of it, Adrian could never remember hearing her speak at all. He pondered that for a minute, then dismissed it. More than likely, she was shy.

Children were such noisy creatures, clomping up and down the stairs, screaming as they slid down the banisters, running into the kitchen and slamming the back door, and it did little good to scold them. Even Israel had changed around them, for never could Adrian remember him running and barking in the house, and never, ever had he yanked the tasseled pillows from the sofa, to shake them until their stuffings fell out.

Whenever he scolded, Barrie would look at him with enormous blue eyes and would become contritely silent. Fletcher would simply give him an odd look and then walk away. Five minutes later, they would be at it again.

In all fairness, Adrian would have to admit there were times that he found the presence of children, if not uplifting, at least enlightening.

A discussion between Barrie and Fletcher was going on in the library, where Maude had sent them to locate Egypt on the globe. Adrian, who was on his way there, stopped just outside the door when he heard Barrie's voice.

"What is education?"

"It's what you find in books," Fletcher said.

"If it's already in books, then why do we have to learn it?"

"Because Mama and Maude say we have to."

"Why?"

"Because you'll be ignorant if you don't."

"What is ignorant?"

"It's when you don't know any of the things in books."

There was a momentary pause, then Barrie said, "I ken I like being ignorant better. It's more fun."

Another silence.

"Do you think Mr. Mackinnon has read all these books?"

"No."

"Then why does he have them?"

"Because he wants people to think he has read them. That makes him look smart."

"But he is smart."

"No, he isna. He just talks a lot, so you think he is."

Later that afternoon Adrian walked into the kitchen to find Maude standing over the bathtub with a towel in her hand, her gaze resting on a bright red topknot poking out of the bubbles. A moment later a face dotted with freckles appeared beneath the topknot.

"All right, enough o' that or you'll drown yourself, and you willna go to fairyland. Now, out wi' you," she said.

"Canna I stay in until my fingers pucker?"

Maude cleared her throat. "The only thing what'll be puckered is my temper if you dinna get out, *now*."

Wrapped in a towel and marching with indignation toward the door, Barrie mumbled, "I canna have any fun. Fletcher gets to stay in the bath until his lips turn blue."

"Changeling," said Maude, giving Barrie a swat as the two of them disappeared through the doorway.

If it was difficult being around the children, it was more

so being around them when they were with Maggie. Adrian had never seen so much hugging and touching in his life, nor had he seen Maggie as he was seeing her now—teasing, impish, and full of laughter and mischief. There was an element of loving and laughing together, a way they had of living that was warm and heartfelt, something that made him feel so many things—emptiness, anger, jealousy, and even envy. And the worst part of it was, whenever they reached out to him, whenever they tried to pull him into that tightly bound circle they called love, he felt threatened.

Bent over his ledgers in his study, Adrian calculated a row of figures and was about to put down the sum when he felt as if someone was watching him. Looking up, he saw Barrie standing in the doorway, in her nightgown, holding her rag doll by one leg.

"What do you want?" he asked.

"I'm going to say my prayers now, and I wanted to know . . ."

Adrian waited, then grew impatient. "Well? Out with it. You wanted to know what?"

"I wanted to know if you wanted anything."

"I can do my own praying," Adrian snapped.

"*You* say prayers?"

"I'm not a heathen. Of course I say prayers."

"And you go to kirk?"

"We don't have a kir . . . a church here, but that doesn't mean I don't know the Bible. Now, go to bed." Adrian began tallying the figures again.

"Do you ken the name of Jesus' mother?"

The pencil snapped. "Of course I know! What is this, the Inquisition? Will you go to bed, or do I have to send for Maude?"

"She's taking a bath."

"Why don't you go find your mother?"

"She's in Fletcher's room. They're waiting to say our prayers. Do you want to come?"

"No, I don't."

"Why? Because you dinna ken the name of Jesus' mother?"

Adrian placed both hands on the desk and stood up, leaning forward. "I *know* the name of Jesus' mother." He was almost shouting.

The redheaded imp standing in the doorway looked at him as if she knew something he didn't, but she didn't say anything. On the verge of a fit, Adrian took one look at that outthrust chin and knew it was what they called in Texas a Mexican standoff. If he had learned anything about these little people, it was that they were persistent. You rarely outwitted them, and never could you outwait them. Ready to have this over, he sighed and surrendered.

"All right. If I tell you the name of Jesus' mother, will you get out of here?"

Barrie nodded. "Aye."

"Mary!" he snapped. "Her name was Mary. Now, get out of here!" He sat down and picked up another pencil.

"That wasna her first name."

"She didn't have a first name!" he shouted, feeling something was close to rupturing.

Barrie stood there, the picture of patience, just like her mother. She was seven! Seven years old, for Christ's sake. What in the name of God would she be like in a few years? Adrian shuddered at the thought. He ran his fingers through his hair and tossed the pencil on the desk. It was no use. He came to his feet, crossing his arms in front of him.

"All right," he said at last, drumming his fingers against his arm. "*You* tell me. What was the *first* name of Jesus' mother?"

"Virgin."

"Out!" he shouted, coming around the desk. "Out! . . . Out! . . . Out! . . ."

Barrie shot from the room.

"And stay out."

A moment later, Molly poked her head in to see what all the ruckus was about. When Adrian finished telling her, all she said was, "Brute!" and left the room.

The next morning, Adrian came down to breakfast. He found a note beside his plate. "Women bend and men break" was all it said.

Adrian wadded it in his fist and threw it in the corner.

"What was that?" asked Maggie, looking up from the tea she was pouring.

"More torture," Adrian snapped.

# CHAPTER
## ❧ SEVENTEEN ❧

His home had been turned into a lunatic asylum, and Adrian wondered if he was the biggest lunatic of all for putting up with it.

The concept of marriage and family was a blueprint for self-destruction, a process so deeply ingrained into the minds of women and children that a man was helpless. Isolation and distrust had become his symbols, and as this increased, as he warred for power and control, his frustration and bewilderment increased. There were so many things he wanted to say to Maggie, but he didn't know where to start. He couldn't seem to express himself around them, yet there were things that needed settling. Did Maggie still plan on leaving? Did she believe he still wanted her to?

He was suffocating, and this made him afraid. He had to protect himself. He had to detach himself from this consuming family coliseum, where he was constantly thrown to the lions. He had to think. He had to find himself. He had to get away. He didn't tell her he was leaving until the night before.

Looking at Barrie, who was hiding her beets beneath her mashed potatoes, Maggie said, "Eat your beets so your cheeks will be pink."

"And your eyes, too," Fletcher said.

"They willna," Barrie said. "Will they, Mama?"

"No, they willna. Fletcher is teasing you." A quick look at Fletcher, and Maggie said, "Stop teaching Ainsley to put beans up her nose."

Ainsley sat silently at her place at the table, her eyes—too large and expressive for a child her age—resting upon Adrian. This child, Adrian feared most of all. There was something about her, something he could not put his finger on. He pulled his mind away. He did not want to think about children, or wives, or anything connected with family. A man needed room to breathe. "I'm leaving in the morning," he said.

Maggie's eyes flew to his, but she didn't say anything.

"Where are you going?" asked Fletcher.

"North, to our other mill."

To the children, Maggie said, "If you are finished, you may go."

After the three of them were gone, Maggie looked back at Adrian. "How long will you be away?"

"Just a few days," he said, looking off when Maggie gazed at him.

After saying good night, Adrian went to his room and spent a long, sleepless night, listening to the rain blowing against the window and wondering what he should do. *If you don't want her to go, you'd better tell her.*

*I will.*

*When?*

*Soon. I just need a little time to adjust to all of this.*

He was gone the next morning, before anyone in the house was up. But Adrian soon found removing Maggie from his sight didn't necessarily mean she was out of his thoughts. His purpose defeated, he returned home much sooner than he planned.

Winter had settled in with its full blustery force, and Maggie brought the children into the library with her before she sent them to bed. Fletcher sat on the hearthstones with Israel's yellow head in his lap. Ainsley was in the rocking chair, rocking her doll to sleep, while Maggie knitted, her yarn looped around Barrie's outstretched hands.

"Were you ever bad when you were a little girl?" Fletcher asked.

Maggie smiled in reflection. "Aye, bad enough, I ken, for a girl."

"Did you ever get a thrashing?" Barrie asked.

"Aye, I've plenty of encounters with the strap," Maggie said, laying down her knitting and opening her arms when Ainsley left the rocking chair and crossed the room to climb into her lap.

"Why did Grandpa whip you? What did you do?" asked Fletcher. His voice was louder now, and Israel raised his head and sniffed the air, then dropped it back into Fletcher's lap as he asked, "What was the worst thrashing you ever got?"

"For something I didna do," she said, her voice dropping as she saw Adrian walk into the room.

Fletcher and Barrie turned to stare at him; Maggie, too. Ainsley merely popped her thumb out of her mouth, looked at him, and as if she saw nothing threatening, put it back in her mouth and closed her eyes.

Maggie stared at Adrian. Impervious blue eyes stared back at her. It seemed more than just a few days to Maggie, but to the children, it was apparent time had no meaning. As if they had seen him only this morning, Barrie looked from Adrian to Maggie, asking, "How did you get thrashed for something you didna do?"

Maggie's eyes fastened upon Adrian. He lifted his glass in a toast. "Please continue with your inspiring revelations. Don't let me disturb you."

Maggie nodded. "I willna," she said, and began stroking Ainsley's head. "My cousin, Jane, and myself were playing in my mother's room, dressing in her long gowns, poking ostrich feathers from her old hats in our hair. Jane wanted to wear my mother's jewelry and asked me where she kept her jewel chest. I ken we weren't allowed to play in her jewelry, but I didna want Jane to be angry with me, so I told Jane where it was. She put my mother's pearls around her waist and tied them too tight. They broke and the pearls rolled all over the floor. We gathered them up and thought we had found them all, but my mother came home and found one of the pearls was missing. We never did find it, you ken, not to this verra day.''

"And your father spanked you for that?'' Barrie asked.

"Aye.''

"Why? You didna break the pearls,'' Fletcher said.

"No, I didna, but my father said I was getting three stripes, one for telling Jane where the pearls were, one for the pearl that was lost, and one for folding a bit of cloth and putting it in Jane's drawers, so it wouldna hurt when her father thrashed her.''

Fletcher laughed, and Israel opened one eye, then promptly closed it.

"But that wasna fair,'' Barrie said.

Her words were for Fletcher, but her eyes never left Adrian's face. "Sometimes we're punished for things we canna help,'' she said, her eyes moving to Fletcher now, "things we have no control over.''

When she looked back, Adrian was gone.


Half an hour later, Maude came for the children. Maggie put away her knitting, but she didn't go upstairs right away. She poured herself a glass of brandy and moved closer to the fire. She sat there, rubbing Israel's back with her foot, making a face when she swallowed the brandy, not realizing how badly it burned until it was too late. *Why would anyone find solace in torturing themselves like this?*

Soon the fire died down to gray ashes, and Israel left the room. Maggie knew it was time for her to go to bed, but she felt she could not sleep. She was apprehensive and wondering. Adrian was back. But for how long?

She had thought she would be able to win his heart and his love, but Adrian was more formidable than she had supposed. She could not go on indefinitely, no matter how badly she wanted this marriage to work. She would have to leave soon, as soon as Ainsley was stronger, and she wondered where she would go. Scotland was too dangerous for Fletcher as long as Adair Ramsay lived, and its close proximity to Scotland ruled out England as well.

Why not stay in America? she decided at last. There would be no long sea voyages for her or the children, no expensive ship fares to pay. Yes, she would stay in America. She lifted her glass. "To America," she said, and finished the last of the brandy, ending with a coughing fit.

Funny thing, brandy. It burned like hellfire, but once it was down, Maggie could see the reason for the torture. Feeling warm and infinitely better, she doused the lamps, save the one she took with her.

She wasn't sure what drew her to that room again, but tonight Maggie felt its inexplicable pull. Perhaps it was the sadness connected with it, the sadness of a love that did not work out, something she understood so well. She went down the dark hallway, following the long, stretching fingers of light that fanned out before her, as if pointing the way.

When she reached the salon, she walked to the fireplace and placed the lamp on an oval mahogany table, her eyes, as they always were whenever she entered this room, upon the ageless portrait of Katherine Mackinnon.

She found it odd that she still felt no jealousy toward this woman. Perhaps that would have been different if she had known Katherine, or at least met her, or perhaps she would have felt resentful and bitter if things had been different and Katherine had loved Adrian. But somehow, knowing Adrian's love for Katherine was all there was to it, that Katherine never loved anyone save the man she married, made it easier to swallow.

Like Adrian, Maggie had loved before. Loved, and loved deeply. The difference was that she was able to leave her love and memories of Bruce where they belonged.

In the past.

Maggie studied Katherine's face. This woman had known Adrian for most of his life. If she felt any jealousy at all toward Katherine, it was for that reason. *If I knew him better, I could help him.*

"Help me to know him. Help me to understand," Maggie whispered to the woman in the portrait, the woman who towered over her, bigger than life.

Yet, as she spoke those words, she knew it would do no good. The man Katherine had known no longer existed. It had been ten years since Katherine and Alex left for Texas, leaving Adrian behind. A man can change a lot in ten years. He can grow lonely.

And bitter.

Ten years of living with a memory can do strange things to a man, to his ability to live in the present, just as the ashes from a past fire can snuff out a new one.

She glanced at the portrait once more. Ten years was a long time to love a memory. How she wished he could forget that face, that hair, that smile. Forget, rather than remember and be sad.

She asked herself how she felt about this portrait, this link to Adrian's past that was like a wall between his past and present. Most women would have thrown a fit and demanded the portrait's immediate removal. Most women would have refused to spend another night in this house, as long as that portrait hung there.

*And most women would be out of his life by now.*

Maggie thought about that. Yes, most women would.

She took one last look at Katherine's portrait, knowing,

as she had always known, that Adrian was using Katherine, using this portrait as a weapon, using it to drive her away.

That ploy would work only if she allowed it to. But there were times when it was hard; times when she wanted nothing more in her life than to rip this shrine from its throne and beat it into oblivion with a poker.

In his study, Adrian had finished three drinks when he heard Maude come down the stairs and take Barrie and Fletcher up to bed. A little while later, Israel stopped in the doorway and looked at him for a moment before padding away.

Adrian had two more drinks after that, then left. Passing the salon, he saw the pale glow of lamplight reflecting long shadows down the hall, and he paused in the doorway and saw her.

Maggie.

He had thought her upstairs sleeping. He looked at Katherine's portrait, and then at Maggie standing beneath it, still as a statue, and he felt his heart contract.

*Tell her*, a voice said.

*I will. Give me time.*

Maggie was staring up at Katherine, looking as luscious as she had earlier in the library. She was wearing a gown of deepest gold, low-cut and edged with cream lace, her shoulders gleaming pale and lovely in the candle's saffron light.

"You dinna have to stand there all night watching me," Maggie said without turning around. "I willna destroy her portrait. I dinna ken lashing out at objects is a way to deal with a problem."

"And is it a problem?"

Maggie knew what he was hoping. That she would say yes, so he could tell her the portrait stayed, and if she didn't like it, she could go. *Lord, give me strength. I canna do this alone.*

"No," she said softly, then turning to look at him, "it isna. Should it be?"

He ignored her question. "I suppose you want me to take

it down,'' he said, readying his breath to tell her it was a waste of time.

''No, I willna ask you to do that,'' she said.

For a long time neither of them said anything, as if they were both using this silent stretch of time to regroup their thoughts. Maggie smiled wistfully, knowing the kinds of things that must be going through Adrian's mind. *He's fighting me*, she thought. *He's puzzled and surprised and just a little angry that this isn't going the way he planned. God grant me patience . . .*

*And a gilded tongue.*

''You like the portrait where it is?'' he said at last.

She almost smiled. ''I wasna the seventh child of a seventh child and born no canny, so I canna go so far as to say I like it here,'' she said frankly, ''but I willna ask you to take it down.''

''Why?''

She shrugged. ''You will take it down when you are ready, when you no longer see the present as a threat against what you cherish from the past.''

''I find that a little odd,'' he said.

She looked at him steadily. ''Do you?'' she asked. ''I wonder why.''

She saw the furrow of bewilderment between his brows, seeing, too, even from this distance, the way the lamplight brought out the vivid blueness of his eyes. His mouth was sensual and full in its relaxed state. *That* was the mouth she wanted to kiss her.

She remembered the way they had made love the last time. She had been satisfied as a woman, but she hadn't felt *beloved*. She realized then that that was what she wanted. She wanted him to love her freely, without holding anything back. Even as she thought it, she knew that kind of love would only come with trust. *And I havena given him much reason to trust me.*

God help her, she was more in love with him now than

before, and she wasn't even certain as to when it happened. She was less certain as to what she should do about it. *Talk to me. Tell me you don't want me to go.*

His eyes were on the portrait. "I suppose I should feel guilty and take it down," he said.

He watched her turn toward the portrait, amazed at her strength of purpose. He knew he should take the portrait down, but he seemed to have no control over it. It was as if this portrait was his defense against being hurt again. Maggie had deceived him. Not once, but twice. Nothing she said could be trusted. Still, the turn of events tonight, the things she said, made him curious. He wondered what kind of woman he had married. What kind of woman was kind enough, patient enough, to live with a man who kept a portrait of a past and perfect love over the fireplace?

Maggie spoke without turning back to look at him. "I havena asked you to take it down," she said, "out of guilt or otherwise. I willna."

Something about the tone of her voice touched him. This woman puzzled him. This woman was different. This woman was soft and tender, patient and understanding. This woman suffered no loss because of it. If anything it made her stronger.

It also gave her more power over him.

Anger, he could control. Words, he could shrug off. But patient understanding weakened him. He had no defenses against it. He didn't understand why. "I know you *willna*," he said at last, feeling some strange force drawing him forward. He stepped farther into the room, coming to stand behind her. Close enough that he could smell her. She smelled of jasmine and roses, and warm, willing woman.

"If you keep your head tilted back like that for too long, you won't be able to move it in the morning."

She smiled. "Good. Maybe that will give me an excuse to stay in bed."

His voice dropped. It was softer now. Lower. "Is that what you want to do? Stay in bed?"

*Aye. With you.* "Rest is a precious thing," she said. "It's every mother's wish, I ken."

His hands came up to massage her neck. Maggie did not move. He felt her body tremble at his touch. His breathing was rapid. He saw nothing but this woman. "Tired?"

"Aye, I'm tired," she said, "but happy."

"Happy?"

"Hmmmm. My children are safely here, and Ainsley has been given back to me." She raised her arms and pushed the tiny tendrils of hair up, and off her nape. "Aye, I'm happy."

Adrian looked at her bent head, the pale skin of her neck glimmering in the lamp's pale light. She seemed infinitely lovely to him now, lovely in a way he could only call sad. His hands left her neck to drop lower, caressing her arms, then pausing momentarily, only to slowly inch forward, his fingers close enough now to touch her breast.

The moment he touched her, she groaned and her head fell back against him. "Dear God," he whispered as he lowered his head, pressing his lips to her shoulder.

"Adrian . . ."

"Don't," he said like a command. "Don't say anything." He kept kissing her shoulder, moving across it to her neck, then to her ear. His breath was warm and steady, coming in quick flutters across the skin of her shoulder. She was as still as the flame of a candle where there was no wind.

His blood stirred. For days he had done nothing but dwell upon her, the bits of her he called to memory—the hair between her legs, golden red, so like the hair on her head; her whimpering cries when she came—and the things he hoped for, like the feel of her mouth on him, warm and wet.

He closed his eyes, remembering what it felt like to be inside her. A sort of tense anticipation gripped him, as in the moment before ejaculation.

He wanted her.

But desire caused him pain. He threw back his head in agony. She was everything he scorned—wanton, brazen, unrepenting. She was everything he admired—honest, straightforward, dependable. She had accepted him, made herself a part of his life, opened herself to him in all the ways a woman could. He was so immersed in her, so weighed down with her body, the way it felt, the scent that marked her, her sound, her look, and what it was like to be with her, that he seemed unable to reason. Maggie . . . Maggie . . . Maggie . . .

He wanted to love her, and his refusal to do so was willful. It was his habit to be hardest upon himself. His secret yearning gripped his insides like a fist, his desire for her dwelt in a dark, secret place, and his revenge was to reject her, to send her away.

How could he? She was everywhere. His house breathed of her, her smell, her touch—her reminders were all about. When he was with her, his eyes drank in the sight of her; when he was away, his mind provided the memory.

And when there was no memory, he would call one forth, dreaming.

Iron bands of need closed around him. He was motionless, frozen, his hands filled with living warmth. Slowly, tentatively, bound by something stronger than himself, he began to caress her. Lightly.

Completely possessed now, his fingers found the pearl buttons beween her breasts.

"Dinna," she whispered.

"Why?"

"The door is open."

He laughed softly. "It's all right," he said. "We're alone. Everyone has gone to bed."

Now she laughed, low in her throat. "We're *never* alone."

"We're alone now," he said, and his tongue traced the curves of her ear, and she felt him tug at her dress. It fell to the floor with a golden whispering of heavy fabric against bare, naked skin.

Startled to feel nothing but skin, he let his hands sweep over her. *Dear sweet God!* "You're naked," he whispered, his voice breaking.

"I was afraid you wouldna notice."

"I noticed," he said, his voice low.

"Aye, you noticed," she said, her head falling forward as he began kissing his way from one shoulder, across her back, to the other one. Ripples of pleasure shot through her, making her toes curl in delight. She felt as if she had been running, until she was weak and breathless, poised on the lip of a precipice, wanting to leap, to feel herself weightless and floating, but terrified of hitting the ground. What was wrong? What was happening to her? It had never been like this before. The world around her was dissolving, the perimeters melting and running like ink in water, leaving nothing behind but a murky blur.

"Why?" he whispered. "You had nothing on beneath your dress, sweet Maggie, and I can't help wondering why."

"You wouldna believe me if I told you."

He chuckled. "You are probably right, for knowing you as I do, I know the answer isn't a simple one."

His words were light and his hands were gentle, seeming to know all the sensitive points of her belly, her breasts, and she moaned, barely able to whisper, "It isna what you think."

He drew her back against him, his hands caressing her, touching, exploring, learning. "No?"

"No."

"And what was I thinking?"

"That I left my underthings off deliberately."

He drew circles on her skin with his nose, and she shuddered. "And you didn't?"

"No. I didna know you were back."

His breath fluttered like a moth's wing over her sensitive

skin. "Even the most absentminded lout has sense enough to remember something as basic as undergarments."

"I wasna absentminded. I didna have any to wear."

"What?"

"Everything was wet. Molly was too energetic today when she did laundry. She washed . . . *everything*. I only had the underthings I was wearing, and those were drenched when I gave the children their bath. They were too wet to wear under this dress. It was either come like this, with nothing, or not come at all."

"I'm glad you came," he whispered. "I could find myself getting used to this." His hands were rubbing now, low on her belly.

"The door is open," she reminded him again. "I dinna ken what to say if someone walks in."

"They wouldn't believe you, anyway. But don't worry. I'm behind you, blocking the view. No one will see you around me. You aren't big enough."

She laughed, her hand coming around to touch him. "*You* are," she said, and laughed softly. "I canna help thinking I'd like to see the look on Maude's face if she came in here and caught you with your arse bare."

"If she comes," he said, his hands moving down to touch the tender skin at the top of her thighs, "I'll wager she won't stay long."

"Aye," she said breathlessly, "not long."

"I want to touch you. Move your legs," he whispered, and her bones turned to jelly, leaving her limp and breathless against him.

"More," he said.

"I canna. My legs are too weak. I'm going to fall."

"You won't fall. I'm holding you."

She opened to him and his hands came between, one touching her, the other easing inside. She groaned and moved with him, her sanity shattering a moment later when her body convulsed, yet he still did not release her.

"No more," she whispered. "Please. I canna."

"Yes you can," he said, and he showed her.

When her body convulsed again, he lowered her to the floor, leaving her only for a moment to release himself, then he covered her completely.

As he murmured his desire, his hands moved over the velvet of her skin. Need for her went through him like a fire fanned by high winds. With a tenderness, a patience, he didn't know he possessed, he touched her, telling her with his hands the things he could not say. He prayed as he touched her—prayed that she would understand, that she would realize he hadn't meant the things he had said, that it was only his hurt talking, his pain. *Help me, Maggie. Help me to show you how I feel.*

"Please," she whispered against his sweat-dampened skin. Her body moved beneath him, restless and impatient. Distraught sounds came from her throat.

He eased himself into her, feeling her warmth surround him. He paused for a moment, giving himself time to gain control. He did not want to spill himself inside her until she had found her own release. He moved slowly, thrusting again and again against her hips, until she shuddered and called out his name.

At last, when he did roll away from her, he kept her against him, throwing one leg over her possessively, his hand curved beneath her breast. They remained that way, neither of them talking, until he wasn't sure if she slept. Raising himself on one elbow, he looked down into her face. She wasn't crying, but her eyes were bright and banked with tears, fastened upon the portrait.

His hand came out to cup her face, but before he could speak, she closed her eyes and turned her face away.

"Don't cry," he said, "and don't hate me."

"I dinna hate you," she said, turning against him, "and I havena cried yet."

"I'm glad," he said. "I would hate to think what we just shared made you sad."

She knew he meant it, and she felt comforted. He drew her closer as the chill of the room began to creep into her bones; she couldn't help wondering how a man could make love to a woman like that if he truly intended for her to go away.

# CHAPTER
## ❧ EIGHTEEN ❧

Molly was standing at the stove the next morning, lost in a swirl of steam and stirring a pot of grits, when Maggie walked in. It wasn't in Maggie's nature to be wildly euphoric, but today she was happy—happier than she had been in years—and that made everything about her seem brighter.

"Good morning. It's going to be a beautiful day, I ken."

"It's going to rain," Molly said.

Maggie drew up short. She looked toward the window, seeing the sun was out. "Rain? I dinna want to believe that," she said.

Molly shrugged and whacked the wooden spoon on the side of the pot, loosening a clump of grits that fell back into the pot with a *plop*. "Believe it or not—that won't change the facts."

"What facts?"

"The fact that every jackass in camp this morning—the four-legged kind, mind you—was rubbing against the fence with its ears forward. And Clem Burnside said the oxen were licking their feet."

"And that means rain?"

"It does."

"Then I'll be prepared for rain," she said, and went to

kiss Barrie, Fletcher, and Ainsley on top of their heads. She started to say something else, but found herself distracted by Barrie's plate. "What is that?" she asked.

Barrie looked down at her plate. "Flapjacks," she said in a way that made Maggie think she was sounding more like Molly every day.

Maggie looked at Molly, then back at Barrie's plate. "I ken flapjacks to be round. Why have you cut them in such big squares?"

Barrie looked a bit put out, as if she could not believe her mother could be such a thick-wit. She licked the milk mustache over her lip. "Because," she said heavily, "Molly said."

Maggie looked at Molly, who exchanged accusing looks with Barrie. "Don't be dragging me into this," Molly said. "I don't care if you cut your pancakes into curli-cues, but I never told you to cut them into squares. Now, you best be telling your mother the truth of it."

"Dinna look at me," Barrie said to her mother's stern look of reproof. "It's her fault," she said, pointing at Molly. "You canna blame me! She told me to do it. She did!"

Molly shook her head and laid the spoon down, clamping her hands on her hips. "And when did I tell you that, Miss Troublemaker, and what exactly did I say?"

Turning her fiercest scowl upon Molly, Barrie said, "I canna remember when, but I ken you said growing children need to eat three *square* meals a day."

"Aye," Fletcher said, "I heard her."

One thing about Molly; no matter what happened or what was said, she remained unflappable.

"Some people are resourceful at being remorseful," Molly said with a snort. "I'm not. But I reckon I'm caught, nonetheless. 'By thy words thou shalt be condemned.' "

And that was the end of that.

\* \* \*

While Barrie ate her square pancakes, Maggie poured herself a cup of tea, noticing that Adrian's place was still set at the table. Her heart thumped with renewed excitement over the tiny reminder of him and last night. "Where is Adrian?"

Molly went back to stirring. "Outside, talking to Big John."

Maggie looked surprised. "Big John? I canna remember him ever coming up here this time of the morning."

"He don't—usually. I think there must be some problem down at the mill. That's the only thing I know that would bring John up here like this."

Maggie smiled and winked at the children. "Perhaps he came up here to tell us the oxen had stopped licking their feet."

Molly snorted. Then Adrian walked into the kitchen and poured himself a cup of coffee.

"Your breakfast is on the table," Molly said, ladling the grits into a lopsided crockery bowl.

Adrian looked preoccupied, and Maggie wondered if he had heard Molly at all. Apparently he had, for his next words were, "I don't have time to eat it now. I've got to get down to the mill."

"Is something wrong?" Maggie asked.

"It's nothing that I can't handle. I don't want you to worry about it."

"Canna you tell me what's the matter?" He smiled, but she knew it wasn't a real smile, that it was only one to put her at ease.

"If I tell you, then you'll worry," he said.

She started to open her mouth, but he shook his head. "I can't tell you any more right now. Trust me in this, Maggie, and don't worry. I've got to go now."

Before Maggie could respond, he was gone.

Maggie gazed off, losing herself in thought for a moment,

then she put her teacup on the table and started from the room.

"Don't you want something to eat?" Molly called after her.

Maggie paused. "I'm not hungry." She felt slightly more than curious about what was going on down at the lumber mill. Adrian was not very adept at quelling a woman's natural thirst for information, she thought, remembering the way his face had resembled a blank piece of paper with a secret code scatched across it.

Molly's brows went up. "Made those plans to go out early, did you?" she asked.

Maggie mumbled something sassy under her breath.

Molly shrugged. "Curiosity—now, that's the thing! The best way I know to make a beeline straight from the path of wisdom." She shot Maggie a surreptitious look. "Now, a little curiosity can be a good thing at times, but you don't want to overdo it, you know. One shouldn't be too inquisitive about the workings of fate, or God's secrets, or one's mate."

"I—" Maggie started to speak, but was unable to say more when Molly interrupted.

"He who asks questions cannot avoid the answers. Ask too many and you'll be feeling like you poked your head into an adder's basket—all darkness, but you can feel the bite."

Maggie smiled and quoted Burns. " 'Auld Nature swears, the lovely dears, Her noblest work she classes. Her prentice hand she tired on man, And then she made the lasses.' Dear Molly, havena you heard, a woman's wiser because she knows less and understands more?"

Molly snorted her opinion of that. "I still say you better ask yourself if you're sure it's the mill . . . or are you just wanting to know why Adrian left in such a big hurry?"

Maggie laughed and blew her a kiss, whistling a little Scottish ditty as she danced from the room. "I canna say."

A faint look of amusement settled across Molly's face.

"Whistle before breakfast, cry before noon," she said to Maggie's retreating back.

There wasn't much stirring around the sawmill when Maggie arrived. Seeing Adrian's horse tied outside the office door, she stood there for a moment, staring at the door, debating whether or not she should go there first. *Indecision*, she thought. *If you don't wash your hands, you're dirty. If you do, you're wasting water.* After a bit, she shrugged and turned away. She would stop by later.

Finding nothing else about camp to distract her, Maggie made her way to the medicine hut.

The inside was dark and dreary when she arrived, but soon she had the shutters thrown back, the lamps lit, and the room dusted and swept clean. Two boxes of supplies that had been ordered were stacked near one wall, and after cleaning a place on the glass shelf of the medicine chest, Maggie busied herself with sorting and labeling the supplies, stacking them neatly on the shelf.

She worked uninterrupted through the morning, and once she had the hut in order, she spent the next hour or so flipping through the new *Carlisle's Complete Medical Journal*, taking notes. Absorbed in the most up-to-date medicines, she read about the multitude of plant and mineral drugs available—quinine for malaria, digitalis for heart failure, colchicine for gout, and opiates for pain—finding she was more interested in the latter.

It was while reading that she came across the name of Dr. Crawford W. Long, a Georgia doctor who performed three minor surgical procedures using sulfuric ether, which she promptly wrote out an order for. She did not like the cartoon labeled "Prescription for Scolding Wives," which showed a husband forcing his wife to inhale laughing gas so she would laugh hysterically when he punished her.

So absorbed was she in what she was about, Maggie did

not at first notice the growing sound of voices coming through the window—until Clem Burnside thrust his head inside the door, looking for Big John Polly.

"He isna here," Maggie said, conscious now of the commotion going on outside. Before she could ask him what was happening, Clem was gone.

Maggie soon followed.

The camp was a cluster of gathering men, whispering, offering speculation, but none of it loud enough to make much sense to Maggie as she stood on the porch of the hut. A moment later, she crossed the grounds to stand near the men, going up on her toes, yet still unable to see more than a gathering crowd outside the door to the bunkhouse.

She saw Big John standing a few yards away and made her way toward him, knowing he would tell her what was happening. Before she reached him, the bunkhouse door crashed open with such force, it slammed against the planked sides with a loud *thwack*. Maggie's eyes were accustomed to the bright sunlight, and that made it difficult to see into the dark interior of the bunkhouse. A moment later, two men wrestled a third, trying to get him outside, but the man, who looked both frantic and desperate, fought them wildly, bracing both of his feet on either side of the doorjamb.

*This*, Maggie thought, feeling a moment of excitement, *is nothing more than one of those rituals men seem to have a fondness for, one where some poor, unsuspecting soul is made a laughingstock of the rest of the camp, much as was done the day the men bathed poor old Dirty Shirt.* She smiled to herself, remembering how Dirty Shirt had taken off for parts unknown the next day, and hadn't been heard of since.

She was about to turn away when something she could not describe detained her.

As quickly as it had come, her smile faded, and with it, the sense of excitement. There was something else going on here, something that was neither humorous nor amusing. The man wasn't just protesting a little brotherly fun. He was screaming and kicking, a look of stark terror on his face. The others in the crowd were subdued, not shouting and laughing, or taking jabs at the man being wrestled through the door. It was clear that these men had gathered here for another purpose entirely.

Surrounded by the crowd of men, Maggie could only follow along with them as the poor man was forced through the door, then pushed, wrestled, and led—stumbling and falling—over the rough, deeply rutted ground. They had no more than reached the center of the camp when Adrian stepped out of the office.

His face was white, his lips held in a tight grimace. She reluctantly realized that Adrian had something to do with all of this. Her mouth open in silent denial, Maggie began to back away, her movement halted by a scream of bone-chilling agony.

"Please," the man yelled. "You can't let them do this to me. Someone help me. Clem! John! Elijah!" he screamed, desperately looking from man to man, finding no support.

"Don't let them do this!" the man shouted again. "For the love of God, somebody help me!"

He began crying, his words no more than incoherent babbling. Transfixed, Maggie stared as drool began to dribble from his mouth. A moment later he wet his pants. She had seen such fear only once before, when she saw a man hang.

A low, rumbling whisper spread through the crowd. The men began backing away, as if they were afraid.

The thought of such cruelty made her stomach heave.

There was no clue as to what was going on here, no more than she knew before—that Adrian lay at the center of it.

*Trust me in this, Maggie.*

Dear God, she wanted to, she wanted to. Her gaze drawn to her husband, she looked at him with eyes that were hazy and yellow-green with confusion. Eyes that ,questioned. Eyes that doubted.

If he saw her in the crowd, he didn't let on.

"Lock him up," Adrian said, his voice loud and in control. His eyes scanned the crowd for a moment, then rested on the man, but they did not soften as he spoke. "I'm sorry," he said. "There's no other way. If there was, you know I would do it."

"Liar! Bastard!" the man screamed. "Cold, unfeeling bastard! You'd find another way if it was your hide that was being locked up like this . . . to die like an animal."

Maggie saw the muscle in Adrian's jaw work. "Put him in the shed. I've had a bed set up in there. . . ." He paused a moment, then said, "Tie him to it."

*"Nooooo,"* the man screamed. "For the love of God, no!"

Maggie looked at the man straining with every muscle, struggling against the two others leading him away. He was barefoot and thin, his face covered with a dirty black beard. His hair was long and unbrushed, adding to his wild look. Unable to pull her horrified gaze away from him, she couldn't believe anyone, especially Adrian, could be so cruel. No matter what the man had done, to tie him to a bed in a tiny shed was, as the man said, inhuman.

*Woe to them that are wise in their own eyes, and prudent in their own sight.*

The words of Isaiah came to her, words she knew were meant for Adrian. *Righteous, pompous fool*, she thought. *How could he?*

So overwrought was she by the sight of this man's misery that she was barely conscious of the warning that seemed to come to her in the guise of her father's voice, a past prophecy she thought to bear witness to Adrian's wrong.

*My son, these maxims make a rule, and lump them aye*

*tegither; The Rigid Righteous is a fool, the Rigid Wise an-
ither.*

She was trembling with anger at the rigid righteousness of
her husband, and the sound of her own voice at first took her
by surprise. "Stop it!" she screeched. "Stop it this instant!"

She stepped quickly around the man standing directly in
front of her and began pushing her way through the crowd,
her hands shoving angrily at the broad backs that stood between her and her husband. "Get out of my way," she said.
"Let me through."

Her blood pounding like a fist against her temples, she
could see nothing but backs and heads, and then she stepped
out of the crowd into a clearing. Adrian turned toward her.
His face was no longer pale. Now it was dark and furious. For
a moment she felt as if she were the condemned man, stepping
out alone against a crowd, faced only with her courage, which
seemed to be more cowardly than she. An ice-cold chill passed
over her, and she suddenly felt alone as if she were standing
in the dark.

*Then I saw that wisdom excelleth folly, as far as light
excelleth darkness. The wise man's eyes are in his head; but
the fool walketh in darkness.*

Were these words from Ecclesiastes for her? She stared
stupidly at Adrian for a moment, wondering what she had
done. She swallowed hard and forced herself flat up against
the wall of determination. She had come this far. She could
not back down now. She started to speak. The look on
Adrian's face stopped her.

Maggie had seen many faces on this man she had married—cynical, hard, aloof, accusing—but today his look was
one she had never seen before. It was a look that pierced her;
a look that was both determined and painful, a look that,
while not pleading, begged. *Humbled* was the first thing that
passed through her mind. The thought that this proud, self-

made man would beg, even if it was only with his eyes, was silencing.

"Go back to the house, Maggie. This doesn't concern you," he said. His voice was no longer angry, or even explosive.

Maggie's face, which had lost all its color, was suddenly suffused with red. His gentleness made her feel more the fool than his fury ever could.

"What in the name of all that's holy is wrong with you?" she asked angrily. "How can you tell me this isn't my concern? Someone is being mistreated."

Turning to glare at the men standing around them, she said, "How can you call yourselves men? You disgust me!" Turning her anger back to Adrian, she continued, "You can't lock this man up like an animal and tie him to a bed. It's inhuman."

Adrian swiftly crossed the few feet that separated them, taking Maggie by the arm, and walking her back toward Big John. His voice was low, ominous, and throbbing with anger. "I said this is none of your concern."

She was so astonished that her mouth gaped open.

"None of my concern? How holy you sound. Never mind that I'm your wife! Go ahead! Bruise my arm! Push me about! I'm only something you want to rid yourself of—any way that you can!"

As if they had some magical power, her words seemed to drain his face of color, turning it fish-belly white. "And I *will* rid myself of you," he roared, taking both of her arms in his hands. His fingers gouging into her flesh, he shook her hard. "Whether you want to go or not!" He shoved her toward Big John, who caught her as she fell against him.

"Get her out of here," Adrian said.

Maggie twisted and pulled away. "Aye . . . get me out of here! Send me away! That's the easy way to deal with everything! I'm not Katherine, so get rid of me!'' she said, deliberately trying to hurt him.

''Is that what you think?'' he said.

''It's what I know. Since the day I came here, you haven't been able to forgive me for not being Katherine.''

''You're wrong. I don't expect you to be Katherine any more than you expect me to be Bruce. But unlike you, I don't expect you to care for me simply because I've willed it.''

''Willed it? You think that's what I've done? That I've simply willed it?''

''I do. You came over here determined to make this marriage work, regardless of how I felt. You didn't just want to be married, to give me children—which is what you knew I wanted from the first. You wanted it all—love, devotion, commitment—and when I didn't give it to you, you set out to make me pay. I may not have loved you, Maggie, but at least I've been fair—and I've been honest. Which is more than I can say for you.''

''Och! Aye, you've been honest!'' she shouted. ''You kept her portrait up, and you didna care if I ken all about her. At least I was kinder. I didna tell you about Bruce and the children and try to rub your nose in it.''

''No, you kept it all to yourself. That part of your life was too precious, too beloved, to share, wasn't it?''

Maggie was chilled by his words. While keeping it from him had not been her intention, still, she had not made any effort afterward—after he found out—to ease his fears.

She was panting now from exertion and anger, and in spite of her new awareness, she was unable to back down. Bruce and Katherine belonged in another war, one that still had to be fought. Later.

This battle belonged in this war. ''If you want to tie up someone,'' she said, ''tie me.''

Adrian stood stock-still, looking down at her for a moment, wearing an expression she had never seen before—a combination of disbelief, anger, embarrassment, and uncertainty. At last he gave her a dismissing look and said, "Go home, where you belong. I'll handle this."

"I won't let you do this, Adrian."

For a moment she thought he might strike her. Then, grabbing her arm and looking over her head, he said roughly, "John, get her away from here . . . and keep her away. . . . I don't care if you have to gag her."

When John reached for her, Adrian shoved Maggie forward to meet him. Without another word, Adrian turned away, going back to where the two men stood, still holding the third, who by now had fought himself into a state of exhaustion.

"What are you waiting for?" Adrian said to them. "I told you to lock him up, didn't I?"

"Come on, Mrs. Mackinnon. You shouldn't be here," Big John said, holding her by the arm.

"He was right," Maggie screamed over her shoulder at Adrian as John led her away. "I ken you are a cold, unfeeling bastard."

The expression on Adrian's face struck terror in her heart. It wasn't a look of anger, but of abject pain. He watched her, then his gaze flicked over to Big John before he turned away.

"You shouldn't speak to him in front of his men like that," Big John said grimly, taking her to the buggy and helping her into it. Maggie stopped midway, turning back to glance down at him. She was unable to ever remember Big John looking at her as he did now, with contempt and hostility.

"Surely to God you dinna agree with what he's doing? You canna think that kind of treatment is right—no matter what that poor fool has done."

Big John didn't answer. He simply snorted, putting his big hands on her fanny and shoving her upward, into the seat of the buggy.

"Hout!" Maggie said as she fell forward, catching herself

with her hands. She didn't hurt herself, but the impact sent her hat shooting over her face.

Coming to a sitting position, she righted her hat and straightened her skirts. She was trying to subdue a hopelessly broken feather that persistently flopped in her face. At last she broke the feather and tossed it to the ground, then turned to Big John. "I dinna understand why you are acting like this to me when it's Adrian you should be concerned with. Didn't you see what he was doing?"

Walking to the hitching post, Big John untied the lead. Only when he climbed into the seat next to her did he speak. "I saw, but that isn't what I'd be concerned with, if I were you."

"What do you mean?"

"It ain't so much as what he's done, as it is what he's liable to do. I'd be a mite worried about that, missy, if I were in your shoes right now." They had pulled out of camp by this time and were headed up the road that ran up the hill to the big house. It was usually at this point that Maggie felt sorry for the horse, straining to pull the buggy up such an incline, but today she had her mind on what Big John was saying.

"Adrian may seem cold and cruel to you, but he was acting in the best interest of every man in this camp. It takes a man of strong conviction to do what he did this morning. The men know that. That's why none of them intervened. It's too bad you couldn't trust him a little more."

"Trust him?" She snorted. "Trust is the virtue of an ass. I'd sooner trust the gentleness of a wolf, the soundness of a horse, or the oath of a whore."

Big John gave her a look that made her feel three inches high. "Trust," he repeated, "such a big notion for such a little word. Still, I wouldn't think that would be so hard. Considering."

"Considering what?"

"You're his wife, aren't you?"

"Aye," she said slowly, remembering it was with wits as with razors—they were never so apt to cut those who used them as when they had lost their edge.

She remembered Adrian's words this morning. *Trust me in this, Maggie.*

Adrian's words echoed in her mind, but she was too furious to listen. "Trust him?" she scoffed. "You make it sound so easy, but I know how Adrian's mind works. I'd sooner trust a rabbit to deliver a head of lettuce." With a look of contempt, she said, "If you had an ounce of decency in you, you wouldn't let something like this happen. I'm disappointed in you. I didna know you could be as cruel as he is."

Big John was clearly angrier than she had ever seen him—furious even. She felt her own anger rise against him. "If you were any kind of a man, you would have stopped it."

"I was never one to listen to an egg trying to teach a chicken," he said. "And since you're so fond of advice, you'd best be remembering some I gave you a while ago. You'd be smart to stop worrying about what don't concern you, missy, and worry a little about what Adrian is liable to do to you."

Maggie felt a knot form in her throat. "What do you mean, what he's liable to do?"

"You'll find out soon enough, although I'd be highly in favor of his tanning your bare arse, like he would any snotty-nosed youngun bent on rebellion."

"Rebellion!" she sputtered. "I'm not the one in the wrong here. He is!" Even to her, those words had a false ring that left the taste of tin in her mouth.

"I always thought you to be a sensible lass," Big John said, "but when you get all riled, your head swells up and your brain stops working."

"Och! *My* brain? What about his?" she shouted in a roar

of outrage. "Why must you overlook what he's done in order
to castigate me?"

"Because you don't know what you're talking about. Do
you think that's all he's got to do—run around trying to decide who he's going to be cruel to next? Did it ever occur to
you that he might have to do something cruel to one man in
order to save the lives of the rest?"

Her mind went blank. Her mouth fell open.

She bit her lip, thinking. "To save lives? Of the rest of the
men?"

"That's what I said, missy," Big John said.

Maggie sighed and closed her eyes, pinching the tension
that seemed to gather at the bridge of her nose. When she
opened her eyes, she said simply, "I'm sorry I lost my temper. . . ."

"And your good sense along with it."

She was silent for a moment. "Tell me what you meant,"
she said at last, "about saving the lives of the rest."

"A mad wolf was spotted in the higher elevations—up
where the men were felling trees a few weeks ago. One of
the lumberjacks shot it, and before anyone could caution
him, Baxter drew his knife and went running to where the
wolf had dropped. He wanted the pelt. The wolf wasn't dead
yet. It bit him."

"That was the man," she said softly, "the one Adrian
ordered locked up."

Big John nodded. "He has to be locked up until we know
if he's going to go as mad as that wolf."

"Hydrophobia," she said slowly. "You mean the wolf
was rabid?"

"Yes, as mad as they come. Adrian let the man go as long
as he could. We thought Baxter might be lucky enough to
escape having hydrophobia, but this morning he woke up
complaining of a headache and numbness in his arm where

the wolf bit him. There was nothing else Adrian could do. He had to be locked up."

"But why tie him to the bed?"

"Convulsions." Big John turned his head to look at her. She had never noticed how blue his eyes were. "Have you ever seen a man go mad, Maggie?"

"No," she whispered, unable to think of anything at this point except the look on Adrian's face when she called him a cold, unfeeling bastard. It wasn't so much the way he looked at her, but the regret she saw in his eyes when he looked at Big John. She had humiliated him in front of his men. He would never forgive her for that.

Never.

"A man in convulsions . . . well, it ain't a pretty sight. After the numbness sets in, the throat begins to lock up, and they become terrified of water. Convulsions usually follow, and by that time they're out of their head and dangerous. Quarantine is the only way to keep a man with hydrophobia from attacking and giving it to the others."

"How long will it take for him to die?"

"Four or five days."

Maggie's stomach lurched. She felt nausea rise in her throat. She turned her head away.

When they reached the house and Big John helped her down, Maggie looked at him, placing her hand on his arm. "You're his friend," she said softly. "What should I do?"

For a big man, Big John looked rather helpless. "I don't know," he said. "I honest to God don't know. But I can tell you this much; I wouldn't want to be in your shoes."

"Aye," Maggie said, turning away slowly. "I ken I dinna want to be in them either. They're feeling a mite too big right now."

She stood in the doorway and watched Big John drive away.

*A sadder and wiser man, he rose the morrow morn.*

* * *

Shortly before dinner that same day, Maggie left her room and went down to the kitchen. Molly was industriously tackling a shank of ham with a dirk large enough to be called a first cousin to a claymore. She looked up when Maggie walked in. "You through sulking?"

"What makes you think I was sulking?"

"Your face is as white as a candle in a holy place."

That drew her up short. "I wasna sulking."

"What were you doing in your room all afternoon? Having tea?"

"I was thinking."

"Thinking . . . sulking . . . The difference will never be noticed on a galloping horse."

Maggie picked up a small sliver of ham and put it in her mouth. "You heard about what happened? At the mill, I mean?"

"I heard. Big John told me."

"I made a fool of myself today. What's worse, I made a fool of him in front of the men, and I canna say that I would blame him if he never spoke to me again."

"You can't make a fool out of someone else. People only do that to themselves. He was probably embarrassed as all get out, and rightly so, but the men don't blame him none. But *you* might find their reception a mite chilled the next time you see them."

"Aye, I ken it's already happened," Maggie said, rubbing her arms. "Just riding home with Big John has given me frostbite."

Molly took one look at Maggie's pale face, her look of pure misery, and laughed. "Well, cheer up. Big John isn't a man to stay unforgiving. It simply isn't his nature to stay that way for long. He'll thaw out."

Maggie shrugged and pulled out a chair, sitting down at

the table, looking as miserable as before. "I dinna remember ever jumping to conclusions as I did this morning."

"You didn't have any right to fly off the handle like you did, I'll hand you that much. It's women like that who make life hard for the rest of us."

"What do you mean?"

"Most men think women should be seen and not heard, just like children. When something happens like it did this morning, men are convinced it's so. Sets us back, is all I can see it does."

"I've never noticed you being afraid to talk," Maggie said crossly.

"And you won't, but we aren't discussing me. I'm not the one in hot water here." Molly shook her head. "I have to hand it to you, though. You certainly jumped in the well with both feet—shoes, too. Question is, how are you going to get out?"

"I dinna ken, but I'll think of something." Maggie drummed her fingers on the table. "I ken I should have done my thinking first."

"Afterthoughts are always so much wiser."

"Aye, it's a bed of briars I've made for myself."

"I don't suppose you're going to appreciate me heaping more briars on your bed, but I noticed something this morning that I wish you had seen before you left. I started to tell you, and decided not to, because I thought you'd like to discover it for yourself."

"What was that?" Maggie asked.

"The portrait," Molly said. "The minute I went into the salon to dust, I noticed it."

"Noticed what?"

"The portrait over the fireplace . . . the one of Katherine . . . It's gone."

\* \* \*

Fletcher was waiting at the stable door when Adrian rode up that evening, pulling Loner to a halt.

"Need any help?" he asked. "I can unsaddle Loner for you."

Adrian dismounted, pausing for a moment to look down at the boy. "What you can do is stay out of my way," Adrian said, leading Loner around Fletcher and into the barn. "Go on back to the house."

Fletcher followed.

Inside the stable, Adrian unbuckled the cinch and the girth strap. "Mother told us about the sick man. She said what you did was right," Fletcher said, coming up behind him.

"Did she?" Adrian said, clenching his jaw against saying more.

"Aye. She wasna too happy when she came home. She said she was sorry for what happened."

"Sorry doesn't mend it, but that's of little importance. It's a little late now to talk about. Go to the house."

Adrian pulled the saddle off and carried it to the rack. When he returned, Fletcher was brushing the horse. Adrian stopped short, his hands on his hips. "I thought I told you to go inside."

The thrust of Fletcher's jaw was both stubborn and familiar. "I'd rather be out here with you."

"I didn't ask you what you'd rather do. Didn't your mother tell you about obedience?"

"Aye, and my grandfather said the man who obeys is bigger than the man who commands."

Adrian gritted his teeth. "Your grandfather was probably right."

"My mother said it was important for a boy like me to be around a man sometimes. I was glad she said that, you ken? I get awfully tired of being with girls all the time."

"I can understand that," Adrian said, opening the stall door and slapping Loner on the rump. He removed the bridle and stepped out of the stall, closing the door. The boy was still there.

"If you want something to do," he said gruffly, "give him some water and two measures of oats. No more."

"Aye, sir."

When he reached the house, Adrian went to the kitchen. Molly was up to her elbows in piecrust. "I'm making fried pies tonight," she said, looking as if nothing out of the ordinary was going on.

Molly was a woman who knew when to talk and when not to. Now, if that had been Maggie . . . His lips compressed into a thin line. He didn't want to talk to Maggie right now. He didn't even want to see her. "I've a lot of work to do tonight," he said. "I'll be taking my dinner in my study."

He had almost reached his blessed sanctuary when Maggie's voice rang out softly behind him. "I'd like to talk to you."

"I don't have time," he said curtly, not stopping, not even bothering to slow down.

"It willna take a minute."

"I have nothing to say to you, Maggie."

"But I have something I want to say to you."

"I don't want to hear it."

"Why?"

He stopped, but he didn't turn to look at her. "Because I don't want to get started thinking about what happened today. If I do, they may have to call in help to get me off of you."

"Are you *that* angry, then?"

He started walking again. "I'm sure as hell *that* goddamn angry," he replied.

"Can you stop a moment, or at least *look* at me? I'm trying to apologize."

He stopped, but, as before, he didn't turn to look at her. "I *know* what you're trying to do, but the problem is, you don't seem to understand what I'm trying to do."

"And what is that?"

"I'm trying to avoid you, Maggie, simply because I don't want to see you and I don't want to talk to you. And I hope to God that is clear."

"It isna," she said. "Why don't you want to talk to me?"

"Because I want to stay angry at you, and I can't if we talk." He opened the door to his study and went inside, shutting it behind him.

Following close behind, Maggie almost thumped against the door. Putting her hand on the handle, she stood there a minute and debated opening the door. Should she? Or shouldn't she?

Part of her wanted to apologize and resolve this.

Another part wanted to leave well enough alone.

For a long time she stood there, staring at the closed door, her hand still on the handle, wondering what Adrian was doing on the other side. Then, with a sigh of defeat, she shook her head and turned away. It was best to let boiling water cool a bit before plunging one's head into it.

On the other side of the door, Adrian poured himself a shot of whiskey and then went to his desk, sitting down behind it. He opened an envelope and began shuffling through the papers inside, but before long, he dropped his head into his hands.

Wearily rubbing his eyes, he lifted his head and returned to work, reading several letters from his contacts in the ports where he sold his timber. Almost to a letter they were all the same. Someone working for Pope and Talbot was contacting his buyers, trying to undercut him and drive him out of business. He wrote five letters, instructing his representatives to cut his timber prices beneath the prices quoted by Pope and Talbot.

He started a sixth letter when he heard the door open. Looking up, he saw Ainsley standing in the doorway. He scowled at her, expecting to see her shrink and flee, but she only stood there, one small hand fingering the ruffle on her white pinafore, the other hugging the same rag doll she always carried.

He ignored her and went back to work. After a minute or

two, he tossed the pencil on the desk and glared at her. "Are you lost?"

She shook her head.

"Looking for your mother?"

She shook her head.

"Your brother?"

She shook her head.

"Your sister?"

Again, she shook her head.

"Well, what are you doing in here then?"

She pointed at him.

"Me?"

She nodded.

"You came to see me?"

She nodded, and stepped into the room.

He watched her. She went to the large leather chair, going at it twice before she was able to climb into it. On her way up, her pantalets were visible, the white lace and pink ribbon that edged the ruffle around the knees showing.

Once she had settled herself in the chair, she cuddled her doll and poked her thumb in her mouth.

"Are you planning on bedding down in here for the night?"

She shook her head. The thumb stayed where it was.

"Is this a visit then?"

She nodded.

"Does your mother know you're here?"

She shook her head.

"Does that thumb taste good?"

She nodded.

"Can't you talk?"

She shook her head.

"A silent woman," he said, throwing up his hands. "There must be a God in Heaven after all."

# CHAPTER
## ❧ NINETEEN ❧

Maggie was not a woman who found solace or even relief in crying, but she cried that night, and once she started, she could not seem to stop. How could this happen? How could fate be so cruel as to make the time she had made a complete fool of herself the same time Adrian had taken Katherine's picture down? And why couldn't she do anything but cry about it? Perhaps it was because the unfamiliar sound of her own weeping was so desolate, making her feel lost and abandoned; perhaps it was because there were so many things she had kept inside for too long—things that needed to be washed away by the tears that rose from her heart.

Katherine's picture was gone.

It wasn't fair that she should gain so much ground with him; that she should learn he had removed the portrait *after* she had humiliated him in front of his men. *Why?* she wondered. *Why did God hand me something with one hand, if He only intended to take it away with the other? Oh, misery, misery, misery.* She would have rather not known about the portrait's removal. There was, after all, a tranquil sense of survival in remaining ignorant about some things.

She sat in the window seat of her bedroom, knowing the room had grown cold, yet refusing to call for Wong to light the fire, as if, by staying cold, she could somehow right the wrong in her life. She leaned her head against the pane of glass, tears rolling down her face. She could feel the eerie silence, the terrible loneliness of the northern woods closing in around her, and her weeping increased.

After a while, the sobbing, so connected with deeply felt grief, subsided, but the tears did not stop. She didn't know what she was going to do. There seemed to be no place for her, no place that she could go. She was running out of time, for Ainsley was recovered, and before long it would be warmer weather around the Horn.

Did Adrian really want her to leave?

*Yes*, her heart cried, *he would*.

A jagged flash of lightning lit up the midnight sky, followed a second later by a crash of thunder that rattled the panes in the window. Raindrops, hard and fat, pelted the thin sheets of glass like a wall of never-ending water.

Outside, the trees beat against the house, and the sound of the wind echoed in the chimney, flooding the room with a cold draft. Another clap of thunder, and the house shook. Suddenly Maggie found herself frightened and alone, overwhelmed by her own sadness, and the vengeance of the elements outside. She felt alone in the world, a single, solitary being without friend, without mate.

Unaware that she had moved, she suddenly found herself at her door, flinging it open without conscious thought. The sound of her own feet was something strange and foreign, and she knew she was running—running down the hallway, her dressing gown flowing out behind her, her hair streaming down her back.

It wasn't until she reached the corner that she stopped, running smack against Adrian. His arms came out to grab her. For a moment she stood still, looking up at him with her chest heaving and her eyes wild.

"Maggie," he said, giving her a light shake. "What is it?"

She shook her head, pressing her face against his chest, clinging to him, crying softly. She felt his lips in her hair, his arms around her gently, and her misery became a living thing that stretched its great dark wings and took flight, freeing her heart from shadow, and flooding her soul with light. She shuddered, as if the last of the despair was finally leaving her.

Then he was pulling back from her, and lifting her chin with the curve of his finger, his eyes soft and gentle on her face, his lips curved in a smile. "So," he said, "you're a real woman after all. For a while I wondered if Ross hadn't married me to a water fairie." He drew her against him, pressing her head to his chest, his hands infinitely gentle against her back. "It's all right to cry," he said. "It only proves you're human, that you can feel."

"If this is being human," she said with a sniff, "I dinna ken I like it."

"Well," he said with a laugh, "it does take some getting used to."

He drew his head back and looked down at her. "Are you feeling better now?" he asked.

"Aye," she said, and made a move to pull away, but he held her fast.

"Tell me why you were crying. Was it because of Ainsley?"

"Aye . . . partly."

"And because of what happened at the mill?"

"Aye . . . partly."

"Just how many parts are there?"

"Too many," she said, sniffing.

He handed her his handkerchief.

"Thank you."

"You're welcome," he said.

"I'm sorry about what happened down at the mill," she said. "Verra sorry."

"I know, but I don't want to talk about that right now. I'm more interested in knowing why you were crying."

She sighed. She was feeling better now, and a little ashamed that he had seen her like this. Perhaps it was best to answer him and get it over with. "I cried for a lot of reasons."

"Name one."

"Because I'm alone."

A ghost of a smile lingered about his mouth. "In this house? With all of us here?"

"One can be alone in a crowd," she said.

He laughed. "That's a bit melodramatic, isn't it?"

She looked up at his face, more alive with humor and understanding than she had ever seen it. She felt its pull. "Aye," she said, smiling, "I ken it is."

Over the next few days, things seemed to be going so much better between them, but still Adrian did not ask her to stay. Worry over his failure to put her mind at ease seemed to rob her of her vitality. Another ship would drop anchor soon. Unless Adrian said something, she would have to be on it. She felt pressured, thinking that once again, time was her enemy.

"You look like someone died," Molly said when she saw Maggie coming down the stairs the next morning.

"Someone did," Maggie said. "Me."

The dustrag stilled in Molly's hand, and she had a faraway look in her eyes. "Lord, Lord, I can remember those miserable nights—crying my eyes out, bellowing like a sick calf, thinking Big John would be won to my cause by a bucket of painfully shed tears, only to find the big oaf had slept through it all."

Then, suddenly conscious of how she was going on, Molly

changed the subject and spoke in cheerful tones. ''Well, you don't look so far gone that we can't get some color back into that pale face.''

Maggie wasn't so optimistic.

After talking to Molly for a few more minutes, she left to visit the salon to see for herself if Katherine's portrait had been restored to its proper, shrinelike place.

She had not gone to the salon last night, when Molly first told her about the portrait, because she was certain after what had happened at the mill that Adrian had wasted no time in replacing Katherine's portrait.

Maggie came to a slow stop outside the massive doors that opened to the salon.

What if the portrait was back up?

What if it wasn't?

She opened the door, keeping her eyes on the floor. Stepping inside the room, she closed the doors behind her, her eyes still on the floor. She leaned back against the door, bracing herself against her hands. Slowly, and with great purpose, she lifted her head, her eyes going to the space above the fireplace.

The portrait was still gone.

She thought about Adrian and the two things she had most wanted out of his life: Katherine and chewing tobacco. ''Chewing tobacco,'' she said, with a slow shake of her head. *Would he ever give that up?*

*Probably not.*

But then she remembered how she had said the same about the portrait, and her heart lifted.

*One down, and one to go.*

It was raining when Adrian came home, a little earlier than usual. He was just coming in through the back door when he met Maggie going out. Even before he spoke, she knew the gentle Adrian she had seen last night was gone. In his place was the familiar Adrian, the one she knew, the rigid, stiff one, the cynic.

"Where are you going?" he asked.

"To the stables to find Fletcher. It's time for his lessons. He isna too easy to find when it's time to study."

"You'll need an umbrella."

"Why?"

"Because it's raining."

Maggie harrumphed. "And will taking an umbrella make it stop?"

After Maggie left, Adrian turned around to find Molly standing behind him. "Was that a bit of Scots logic, or simple feminine wit?" he asked.

In answer, he heard Molly's trumpeting laugh.

The rain stopped, collecting in little puddles. Evening was nearing as Adrian made his way down to the cliffs for his walk.

He called Israel to his side, then seeing the dog's mud-caked legs, and the clumps of mud hanging like jet beads from his belly, he wondered if that was such a good idea. Even so, they walked along the jagged edge of the cliffs, toward a gentle slope where a narrow trail forked off to the left, winding and dipping its way down to a narrow strip of beach below.

Israel ran ahead of him now, with his great tongue hanging to one side. For a moment he stopped at the junction of the trail, looking back at Adrian, barking and wagging his tail. Too impatient to wait for someone moving slower than winter molasses, he turned toward the beach, disappearing between the rocks. It was only after Israel ceased his infernal barking that Adrian heard the soft pad of footsteps following him. He turned, looking back, half expecting to see Maggie.

It was Ainsley.

"What are you doing out here?" he asked gruffly.

She pointed at him.

"I don't want you coming with me. I came out here to be alone. Go on! Get back to the house."

She stood there looking at him for a moment, with those eyes that seemed too large and too knowing for such a small head. "Go on," he said. "Scat!"

She didn't scat, exactly, but she did turn back toward the house. Adrian watched for a moment, then turning, he continued on his way down the trail to the beach, his thoughts returning immediately to the thing that concerned him even more than Maggie's outburst in camp.

Someone was out to destroy him.

He walked on, remembering how he and Alex had come out here over ten years ago to build a lumbering empire. At first it had been a fragile beginning; a seasonal undertaking where lumberjacks and mill workers could only work during the six warm, dry months. He remembered how they had risked every penny they made in the gold fields to hire larger crews, and how they were laughed at for working around the clock to stockpile a large supply of logs. He remembered, too, how those who laughed never mentioned it the next spring, when he had proven that stockpiling had given him enough lumber to keep the big saws running not only during the winter months, but often for twelve hours a day, six days a week.

He had been here first, and had carved this place out of nothing but primitive, raw forest, knowing that there would be those who would come later.

And they had.

But some of those latecomers weren't content to carve their own place as he had done. Adrian paused, looking out over the water, watching a group of sea otters playing among the sea stacks just beyond the surf. He wondered if the gray whales had come yet, and if Maggie had seen them.

Adrian sat down, his gaze on the sea otters, his thoughts

on Maggie and his business. He thought about the large fleets of schooners he had ordered, schooners designed and built by his brothers, Tavis and Nick, and how those very schooners, with the addition of several new ones, would plow the seas in good weather and bad, carrying his lumber to exotic ports. He remembered that it had been Maggie's suggestion to have his brothers build his ships.

He had been first to come this far north, first to stockpile, and first to own his own fleet and market his own lumber. There was no reason for anyone to try to take or destroy what was his. The forests were too large, as were the foreign markets, for anyone to ever try to form a monopoly and take over. So why would anyone even try? Adrian could only imagine that it was simply easier for some people to take over what others had built.

Big John and Adrian were down at the mill office before daylight the next morning. The office was small and rustic, the walls no more than raw, unfinished redwood planks, the same as the floor. Two enormous maps were pinned to the walls, one of the western coast of America from Mexico to Canada, the other of the northern California area, carefully detailed as to where the California Mill and Lumbering Company was logging.

The windows were uncovered, Adrian having vetoed Maggie's offer to make curtains. He remembered his words to her that day. "This is a lumber mill, Maggie, not a tea parlor." When she had tried again, he had stopped her by saying, "It's *my* office and it's the way *I* like it."

And that was true. The office *was* exactly the way he liked it: two desks, five straight-backed chairs, one spittoon, a stand holding a collection of rolled and labeled maps, a coat rack, and a potbellied stove with a coffeepot on top in the wintertime.

Adrian was sitting at his desk, his chair pushed back and

balancing on two legs, his own legs crossed and placed on the desk in front of him. He glanced across the room at Big John.

"If I were going to throw a log in the gear works, this would be the time I'd do it," Big John said. "Over the past two years we've been growing much faster than in the past. We've got four lumber mills operating now; thirty-eight saws at one mill alone. At that rate, one mill can fill a ship in two weeks—that's sixteen million feet of lumber a year. The bigger we get, the harder it is to protect our flanks—and a hungry wolf is desperate."

"I know, and I want to get a grip on this thing. I've been thinking we should start shipping venture cargoes—we've got the lumber to do it, or we will have, as soon as that new saw is installed."

"Venture cargoes? You mean to sell in cities where we have no agents?"

"If we get to the root of the trouble we've been having, that's what I mean."

"And if we don't find a buyer?"

"We unload it, divide it into smaller lots, and auction it off."

"As soon as we get to the bottom of these accidents," Big John said.

"Exactly," said Adrian.

"Do you think Matt Greenwood should still be a suspect? Burt Haywood has been keeping an eye on him, but he's come up with nothing. Maybe we should just fire him and see if the accidents stop."

"I told you before, I can't fire a man on suspicion alone," Adrian said. "He could be innocent. He did discover that cut cable in the logging lines."

"And he could have done it to make himself look good, to throw us off," said Big John.

"Yes," Adrian said, contemplating. "He could." Adrian

came to his feet. "We'll put another man on him; with two watching, maybe they'll come across something."

"Who do you suggest?"

"Put Mose Whittaker on the same crew with Greenwood. Tell Mose to keep him in his sight. Watch everything the bastard does. If he so much as pisses crooked, I want to know about it."

It was past ten o'clock when Adrian came home. Maggie was waiting for him in a dressing gown of saffron velvet that set fire to her hair.

She looked up when he walked into the bedroom, and saw the troubled expression on his face. "Is something wrong?"

"No."

"You look worried."

"I'm tired," he said.

"Come into the kitchen," she said. "I'll fix you something to eat."

"I ate with the men at camp."

"Adrian, you've got to slow down. You're killing yourself."

He gave her a cold look. "Did you wait up to tell me that? If you did, you should have saved yourself the trouble."

"I waited up because I want to talk to you."

"Not tonight, Maggie. I'm too tired."

She winced at his indifference, longing for the softness she had seen the other night. "I ken how you feel about me, Adrian, but I'm not asking for me. It's Ainsley."

"What about her? Is it the fever again?"

"No, she's fine in that regard." Maggie looked at him, her eyes never leaving his face. "I'm worried about her not talking."

Adrian was watching her, but he didn't say anything. "She hasn't talked for some time. Why all the concern now?"

"Because I wrote Dr. Farnsworth about it. I just received

his reply. He said it happens sometimes after a child has suffered some illness or trauma. Perhaps it was too much, losing her father, then my leaving her—all of that added to her own illness. It was much harder on Ainsley when Bruce died, because she was too young. She didna understand death. She wandered around the house for weeks calling 'Papa, Papa.' ''

''Did Farnsworth say what could be done? Did he have any suggestions?''

''No. He said sometimes this lasts only a short while, in other cases he's heard of it going on indefinitely.''

''If Farnsworth can give you no help, what makes you think I can?''

''She seemed to respond to you during her illness, you ken. She . . .''

''She didn't respond, she thought I was her father.''

''There had to be something about you that made her feel you fit the role. I ken it's only a gamble, but it's the only thing I've got. I was hoping you might spend some time with her, to see if she will respond to you . . . perhaps then, she might talk.''

He frowned. ''I don't have time, Maggie. There are problems—big problems at the mill. Everything I have worked for is at stake. You don't understand.''

''No,'' she said softly, ''you are right. I dinna understand. I dinna ken how anything could be more important than a child.''

Maggie spent the next morning in the kitchen with Barrie, Fletcher, and Ainsley. They were making gingerbread men. Molly helped Barrie mix the dough, Fletcher cut them out, Maggie and Ainsley put on the raisin faces and buttons, while Maude was in charge of baking.

Ainsley was standing in a chair, taking the raisins that

Maggie handed her and pressing them into the gingerbread figures Fletcher had so carefully cut.

''Where will you put the nose?'' Maggie asked.

Ainsley's chubby finger came out to point, then she looked at Maggie for approval.

''How many buttons on his coat?''

Ainsley held up three fingers.

''And how many gingerbread men are you going to eat, you little scamp?'' Maggie asked, grabbing her and giving her a profusion of kisses. Ainsley giggled. ''Come on,'' Maggie said, ''tell me how many you're going to eat.''

Ainsley held up ten fingers and giggled.

''No fingers,'' Maggie said, closing her eyes. ''I canna see your fingers, so you will have to tell me.''

Ainsley looked at Barrie.

''She dinna want to,'' Barrie said.

Maggie opened her eyes. ''Why?'' she asked Barrie. ''Why doesn't she want to?''

''She canna,'' Barrie said.

Maggie looked at Maude, but Maude dabbed at her eye with the corner of her apron and looked away.

Everyone teased Ainsley after the cookies were baked because she ate only three cookies, not ten. While Maude took Barrie and Fletcher into the bedroom they had converted into a schoolroom for their studies, Maggie washed the crumbs from Ainsley's face and hands and, taking her by the hand, led her to her room, putting her down for a nap.

She gave her a kiss, and had almost reached the door when Ainsley made a whining sound. Turning, Maggie saw her point at her, then point at the bed. ''What?'' Maggie said. ''Do you want me to read to you?''

Ainsley shook her head, pointing at the bed again.

''Do you want me to lie down beside you?''

Ainsley nodded.

Maggie lay beside her, stroking the long, rosy curls until Ainsley's eyes drifted closed and she had fallen asleep.

After she left Ainsley's room, Maggie went to her own room, threw herself across her bed, burying her face in the pillow, and cried. She had always thought herself a strong woman, capable of handling whatever came her way, but she had too many things weighing her down at once. She couldn't deal with the problems between herself and Adrian and deal with Ainsley and the gloomy future that awaited herself and her children back in Scotland.

She cried herself to sleep. It was dark when she awoke. She went downstairs.

"Do you want some soup?" Molly asked.

"What time is it? Did I sleep through dinner?"

"Dinner and the dishes," Molly said.

Maggie looked around the room, still feeling a bit groggy. "Where is everyone?"

"Maude is getting Barrie and Fletcher to bed."

"Ainsley?"

"Adrian took her up to her room after dinner."

Maggie looked astounded. "Adrian?"

"That's what I said, and I didn't stutter. Now, do you want that soup or not?"

"In a minute," Maggie said, and left the room.

When she reached Ainsley's room, the door was ajar. She stood in the hallway looking inside. Adrian was tucking her in. He started to leave, and Ainsley whined. Adrian turned toward her, and she pointed to her doll sitting on the chair.

"You want the doll?"

She nodded.

He picked up the doll and handed it to her. "What's the doll's name?"

Ainsley shook her head.

"She doesn't have a name?"

Ainsley nodded.

"She does have a name?"

Ainsley nodded.

"She has a name, but you won't tell me?"

Ainsley looked at him for a moment, as if she were considering something. Then she pointed to the curtains at the window.

"You want the window open?"

She shook her head and held up her doll, then pointed at the window.

"You want me to put the doll on the window?"

Ainsley looked really frustrated now. She shook her head and pointed at the doll, then crawling across her bed, she picked up the lace curtain and waved it.

"Lace?" Adrian said.

Ainsley nodded and pointed at her doll.

"The doll's name is Lace?"

She nodded, then shook her head.

"It is, but it isn't," Adrian said, then paused a moment. "This is asinine," he said, then staring at the little rosy-headed mite looking at him, he sighed. "Okay, you win. I'll play one more round. You mean the doll's name is something like Lace?"

Ainsley nodded.

"Ace . . . Base . . . Case . . . Dase—*that doesn't make sense*. E—*why am I doing this?* . . . Grace . . ."

Ainsley whined, nodding her head, pointing at her doll.

"Grace," he said at last. "Your doll's name is Grace?"

Ainsley nodded.

"Well, then, it's time to tell Grace good night." He blew out the lamp and left the room.

"Thank you," Maggie said when he closed the door.

He looked at her, and the mask slipped into place. "No need to thank me. Molly and Maude had their hands full, and you looked like you could use some sleep." Then his face hardened. "Don't expect me to make a habit of it," he said, and turned to walk away.

When Fletcher and Barrie came running into the house, they were screaming as if banshees were after them. "Hold on now, Miss Ruckus," Molly said, grabbing Barrie by the collar as she streaked by. Fletcher dodged and started up the stairs, only to find his way blocked by Maude. "I dinna see your britches on fire, so why are you running in the house?"

"Where's Mother?"

"I'm right here," Maggie said from the top of the stairs.

"Come quickly," Fletcher said. "Come and see. . . ."

"Ainsley has a burro, and it's the most precious thing you ever saw. Come and see," Barrie said.

"*I* was telling her," Fletcher said, turning and coming down the stairs in a hurry, his eyes hot and locked on his sister.

Barrie shrieked when he drew closer, breaking loose from Molly and running out the front door, Fletcher dead on her heels.

"Merciful heavens," Maggie said, rushing down the stairs and following Maude and Molly outside. When they reached the front yard, they saw the burro, a long-eared melee of brays and hoofs with a tufted tail and a ruffling of hair for a mane. It was adorable, and that must have been what Ainsley thought, for Grace had been ignominiously dumped in the dirt and was lying on her side. Ainsley had her arms around the burro's neck. It was then that Maggie noticed the burro was attached to Adrian by a length of rope.

Maggie looked at him, a question in her eyes. "I brought it for her. I thought maybe if she had a pet, something of her own . . . well . . . I . . . I thought it might help."

"I dinna ken what to say," Maggie said. " 'Thank you' doesn't seem to be enough." Dropping down beside Ainsley, she said, "Do you know if it's a boy or a girl?"

Ainsley pointed to Barrie.

"It's a lass," Maude said.

"What do you suppose we should call it?" Maggie asked.

"She wants to call her Heather," Barrie said.

"How do you know?" Maggie asked.

"Because I asked her if she wanted to call her Heather or Hortensia, and she picked Heather."

"I dinna say I can blame her," Maude said, and everyone laughed.

Molly turned her head to one side and studied Heather. "She's a cute little moocher."

Maggie looked at Heather, taking in the long, brown, shaggy coat, the way the color grew lighter at the nose and beneath the belly, only to turn darker around her eyes, as if someone had drawn circles around them.

After a minute, Adrian said, "I'll put her in the barn for now. Tomorrow I'll have one of the men build a pen for her."

Adrian started away, and Ainsley ran after him, taking his sleeve in her hand and giving it a yank. She pointed at herself and then at Adrian.

"She wants to know if she can go with you," Fletcher said.

"I know what she's asking," Adrian said, then, to Maggie, he said, "She can see the burro tomorrow," and he turned, leading the burro away.

Maggie picked Grace up and handed her to Ainsley. "Why don't you go give Grace something to eat. I think she's awfully hungry. You can see Heather tomorrow. Would you like to watch the man build her pen?"

Ainsley nodded, and taking her mother's hand, followed her into the house, her head turned in the direction Adrian and Heather had taken.

# CHAPTER
## ❧ TWENTY ❧

Maggie awoke to the most dreadful noise.

She opened one eye and heard nothing. *I must be dreaming.* She rolled over and pulled the blanket over her head.

There it was again.

With a disgruntled sigh, she climbed from the bed and went to the window, drawing back the drape. She looked around the yard for a full minute before the dreadful noise drew her eye toward the stable.

There in the doorway stood, or rather sat, Heather. Sitting on her haunches, her forelegs stretched out in front of her, Heather scratched her back against the rough planking of the stable and gave a tremendous yawn, before letting go with another braying blast. *"Eeeee—awwwwww . . . Eeeee—awwwwww!"*

Maggie turned away as Maude burst into the room. "I ken you've heard it then," she said, coming to stand beside Maggie at the window.

Maggie laughed. "How could I not?"

"Aye," Maude said, "How could you not? Wake the dead, that one would."

They laughed together, the two of them turning to watch Heather come to her feet, shaking the dust from her soft coat, then taking off to run in a zigzagging motion, braying and kicking, ears flopping and tail swinging to and fro. "If that doesna make Ainsley talk, nothing will," Maggie said, falling suddenly silent, and praying with all her heart that it was so.

For the third morning in a row, Heather had everyone awake before daylight, and for the third morning in a row, Maggie staggered down to the kitchen earlier than usual.

Molly showed Eli into the kitchen about the same time Maggie stumbled in. Adrian was just sitting down to his breakfast.

"The saw is down," Eli said.

Adrian put the biscuit in his hand on his plate and looked at Eli. "What do you mean, *down*?"

"It won't work. We tried to crank her up this morning and she wouldn't come around. She's been tampered with. Big John and Nicholson are looking her over. Seems there are some parts missing."

"Parts?"

Eli nodded. "That's what Big John said."

Adrian stood, his chair scraping across the floor. "I'll come with you," he said, taking his hat and jacket from the rack.

"You gonna eat first?" Molly asked.

"No time," Adrian said, casting an eye at Maggie, then motioning for Eli to follow him.

"Nice to see you again, ma'am," Eli said, nodding to Maggie.

"You coming?" Adrian asked, careful not to look at Maggie.

Maggie nodded and said, "Nice to see you, Eli," then looked at Molly. Molly shrugged and said, "What about you? You have any breakfast?"

"No," Maggie said, "just tea."

Molly watched her go. "At the rate everyone keeps going off their feed around here," she said, "I'll soon be out of work." Molly eyed the food she had just cooked. "Might as well eat it myself," she said.

And she did.

Adrian stood beside Eli as Big John and Shorty worked on the gang saw. One of the flywheels was missing, as well as two of the vertical blades.

"We'll have to get another flywheel out of San Francisco," Big John said. "As for the blades, we've got plenty of those."

"I thought we had extra flywheels," Adrian said.

"We do. At least we did. We used two last week," said Eli.

"Two in one week?"

"They were broken, but who's to say they weren't helped a little?"

"The bastard didn't bother to break this one," Adrian said. "He simply took it."

"It isn't easy to break a flywheel by hand," Big John said. "He might have started out to break it, then heard someone coming and decided to take it with him. Probably tossed it in the river somewhere."

"Get Mose Whittaker," Adrian said. "I want to talk to him."

Eli looked at Big John. Seeing their looks, Adrian said, "Now what? Don't tell me you've misplaced Mose Whittaker?"

"Almost," Big John said. "Mose disappeared sometime during the night."

"What do you mean, disappeared?" asked Adrian.

"He went to bed in the bunkhouse with the rest of the men, only when they woke up this morning, Mose wasn't there."

"Get some men out looking for him," Adrian said.

"I already have," Big John said.

Adrian went on over to the office, but the day was plagued with misfortune. There were three injuries in the logging area, a small fire in the sawdust pile, and later on in the day, someone found Mose Whittaker's body floating in the river.

It was a warm and sunny afternoon, rare for the time of year. While the children played outside with Maude, watching a man called Ben build a pen for Heather, Maggie went looking for Molly. She found her stripping beds.

"Molly, who would you say knew as much as anybody about the lumbering business—not someone like Big John or Eli, but someone with less responsibility, someone who might have a little more time?"

Molly didn't have to think. "I guess that would be that big blond giant they call Nor."

"The big Swede?"

"Norwegian. Nor is short for Norway."

Maggie was heading out of the room. "Thank you," she said.

"Hold on now. You've got my curiosity aroused now. What are you up to? And don't you go saying 'nothing.' I know better."

Maggie shrugged. "I dinna ken much about things here. I want to learn something about this country, about running a mill."

"Why?"

"Molly, I dinna know the first thing about running a mill or the work Adrian does."

"You've been spending a lot of time in camp for a woman who don't know much about it."

"Yes, but not in the main office. You know that. It isn't the same thing."

"Then why don't you ask . . ." Molly caught herself.

"Oh, never mind. Ask Nor. He's as friendly as a basket of kittens."

Maggie did ask Nor the very next morning. Nor was a little shy, but agreeable. The following Sunday she slipped out of the house and met Nor on the trail that led up to the logging area. For over two hours they walked along the trail, Nor pointing out the different trees, and what their lumber was good for. Once they reached the logging area, he showed her how the trees were cut and felled. When they reached camp, he showed her the various tools the loggers used. "I'd like to take you up to the logging area myself, but I think it'd be better if you asked Big John to do it," he said.

Big John took her to the logging area a few days later. It was here, in the higher elevations where the timberbeasts worked, as the loggers were called, that Maggie began to understand Adrian's love for the forest and the work that he was doing. It was quite a job to topple the tall redwoods, get them down the mountain to the mill, then make them into lumber and get them into the hands of the selling agents.

Men were needed for all kinds of jobs: There were fallers, who cut the trees; and peelers, who peeled the bark away; and buckers, who sliced the logs and split them into "shingle bolts," to be shaved into redwood shingles at the mill. There were choker settlers, who hooked the logs to cables; and river pigs, who herded the logs downriver. And as always, there was Adrian.

"Adrian works right along beside the men," Big John said. "One day he's in the mill, the next day he might be cutting or felling, or helping the bullwhackers. That's why he gets so much out of his men. He doesn't ask any of them to do something he doesn't do himself. He's a fair man, and honest, and he isn't afraid to do a hard day's work. Some of the men may not like him, but they all respect him."

Maggie didn't say anything, and Big John went on. "I best

be getting you back to camp. Tomorrow I'll take you to see the flume.''

The flume was unlike anything Maggie had ever seen. It was nothing more than a water-filled trough used to move roughly cut wood from the mountains down to the mill. But there were places where the flume had to cling to walls of canyons and bridge deep ravines, like a crudely constructed Roman aqueduct. Many times this required a grid-work of lumber that far surpassed any bridge she had ever seen.

It was also dangerous, for logjams or water leaks could prove disastrous, causing the entire flume to collapse. On Maggie's third visit to the flume, she watched a man called Jem Johnson ready himself to travel the catwalk across a deeply scarred ravine to free the logs that had jammed in the middle. The tension in the air was something Maggie could feel as Johnson started up the flume, the men gathered around growing oddly quiet. Adrian, who had been watching from Loner's back, suddenly dismounted, calling Johnson back. A moment later, Maggie watched breathlessly as Adrian made his way up a catwalk no more than six inches wide, walking parallel to the flume, inching his way forward until he was in the middle of the ravine, three hundred feet in the air.

Maggie held her breath, watching Adrian shove the one log that jammed the others with his foot. With a loud crack, the jammed log shifted and the logs began to make their descent as Adrian made his way back to his horse.

That night after dinner, Maggie found him reading the San Francisco paper beside the fire in the library.

She crossed the room to her chair and picked up her knitting. After a few minutes, she stopped, and the sudden silence, after so many minutes of hearing her needles click, must have distracted Adrian, for he glanced up.

''Why didn't you let Johnson free the logjam today?''

"Because he has a wife who's quite sick, and thirteen children, back in Minnesota. He's all that stands between them and starvation."

"You're a strange man, Adrian Mackinnon."

"According to women, all men are strange."

She laughed. "Not all, just some. But I ken you're strange in a different way."

"Am I supposed to ask how?"

"Only if you're interested in knowing."

Adrian shrugged and returned to his paper.

"You aren't as uncaring as you'd like me to believe," she said, "but you're still too quick to anger and too slow to forgive."

He sighed and lowered his paper. "Is that why you came in here? To interrupt my reading with all these revelations about what is wrong with me?"

"No, I didna. I came in here because I wanted to be with you."

"Well, I came in here to be alone."

"Aye," she said softly, "I ken."

In comtemplative silence, he watched her put away her knitting. This woman was his wife, he was married to her, but they were like strangers—no, worse than strangers. At least strangers would be cordial to each other—kind, considerate—but they were none of these things. His eyes swept over her. She was wearing blue tonight, and it suited her, for there was a bit of melancholy to her, something that touched him, as mournful as the plaintive song of a mourning dove. He studied her, finding it strange that he was still having the devil of a time deciding if she was pretty—not that it mattered any, for he found he desired her, and his desire had nothing to do with the way she looked.

As if they had been out of focus, his eyes suddenly fixed on Maggie, her image coming sharply into his mind. She was standing with a ball of yarn in her hand, two knitting needles jabbed into it, pressing the yarn against her stomach, as if she were trying to ward off pain. "You got a belly-ache?" he asked.

"No."

"What ails you then?"

"Nothing. I just realized something that I ken I should have realized before."

"And what is that?"

"That you're afraid of me."

"Have you been filling the kerosene lamps?"

"No, why?"

"Because you must have been breathing too many fumes. It's addled you. I'm not afraid of you."

She smiled. "Aye, you are, and it willna do any good to deny it."

"I don't have to deny anything," he said. "I came in here to get some peace and quiet, and I sure can't get it with you around."

"Why not?"

"Because you bother the hell out of me, if you want to know the truth."

"How bad do I bother you, Adrian?"

He came out of the chair, tossing the paper aside as he did. Two swift strides brought him to stand just inches away from her. "Bad enough for me to put a stop to it."

"Go ahead," she said. "Show me, Adrian. Show me how you'd put a stop to my bothering you."

"Damn you," he said, his hands coming out to jerk her against him. "Damn you," he said again, his mouth coming down hard, closing over hers.

He broke the kiss. His breathing was rapid and rasping. "Get out of here," he said. "Or you'll be sorry."

She came up on her toes and wrapped her hands around his neck. "I canna," she said.

"Why not?"

"Because you're standing on my skirt."

Before he could say anything, before he could step away, she brought her mouth against his and whispered, "Kiss me, Adrian. Kiss me like you want me."

"I do," he said. "God help me, but I do."

He followed her down to the floor, peeling out of his clothes, helping her out of hers. She could smell the scent of wood shavings and redwood on his skin. He pulled away the last bit of her clothing, then rolled over her, covering her with his body, drawing her hands up, over her head, holding them pinned against the floor.

"I'm no afraid of you," she whispered.

"You should be," he whispered back, spreading her legs apart with his knee and fitting himself in between. Before she could reply, he drove into her with a single thrust that made her gasp, sheathing himself as deep as it was possible to go.

"You should have run when you had the chance, lass," he said softly, withdrawing and then pressing himself deeply into her again. "You're going to find out what happens to women who hang around places where they have no business."

She gasped, sucking in her breath hard as he pushed himself deeper. "Frighten me some more."

"You may not say that when this is over," he said, "for I mean to ride you harder than you've ever been ridden before." He wasn't able to say anything more, for his body seemed to take over, driving into her with hammering strokes.

Maggie couldn't speak. Her body trembled as she gave in to the gripping spasms that twisted her, and still he hammered into her, again and again. He seemed to be driven by demons.

"You wanted it, didn't you?" he said, his voice strained. "You wanted it and you begged for it, and by God, I intend to see you get exactly what you've been after. There'll be no quarter given between you and me, Maggie. Now now. Not ever.''

He thrust into her harder and harder, pounding repeatedly until she thought she would be ripped apart. The weight of his whole body rested on her now, pinning her against the floor as he drove against her, his hands coming down to slide between them, then gripping her buttocks and lifting her, making his penetration even deeper.

''Yes,'' she cried. ''Yes, love. Yes. Oh, God! Adrian! Yes!'' She screamed then, and he stopped her with his mouth, but even then he did not stop.

After a long while, when their breathing had returned to normal, Adrian rolled from her, just enough to lie next to her. She cradled her head against his shoulder, her hand trailing in the thick mat of hair on his chest.

''This is becoming a habit,'' he whispered, groaning as he stretched the kinks from his legs. ''I don't think we've ever made love on a bed.''

''Is that what we were doing?'' she asked, unable to suppress a smile. ''Making love?''

His chin was flattened against his chest when he looked down at her. ''You're a pain in the arse,'' he said, mussing her hair, then in a muffled tone, he added, ''but I've had worse pains.''

''That's good, because I have something I want to ask you.''

''What?''

''I was wondering,'' she said, laughing, ''if you would mind my bothering you some more.''

He laughed. ''Be my guest,'' he said, sucking in his breath as she rolled over him.

# CHAPTER
## ❧ TWENTY-ONE ❧

Adrian felt like getting drunk, and he probably would have if he hadn't realized he needed his wits about him if he was going to resolve things between himself and Maggie. It frustrated him that he had let things go for as long as he had. It wasn't his nature to let things bump and slide along in a haphazard manner without any direction. He would never consider allowing his mill to run itself . . . so why had he been guilty of such with his marriage?

*You get out of things what you put into them.* There was little wonder, then, just why it was that Adrian didn't feel as if he was getting as much out of his relationship with Maggie as he should. How much more obvious could it be that there was something missing? She was open and receptive when it came to making love. She was gentle and considerate whenever they were together. She had even told him she loved him that fateful day her children came. She was all-giving, and it shattered him to know he had accepted something he did not deserve. Maggie's most outstanding trait was her forgiving spirit. She was like the sandalwood tree that perfumes the ax that fells it.

Yes, something between them was missing. Things were not normal. He still felt reserved and shy around her—when he wasn't bumbling and ill at ease. And Maggie? He hated to admit that she didn't act like a woman in love. She didn't have the look of a woman in love. She did not look happy—and because of that, Adrian could not be happy either. Strange how his own happiness seemed to rely upon hers.

True, Maggie had deceived him; she had withheld information he had every right to know. Yet he couldn't help thinking the mess that had been made of things was more his fault than hers. The reality of it ate at him.

So did one question. Was Maggie leaving him? Surely she couldn't be, for there were too many signs that she was entrenching herself into his life and home and business like a rodent that burrows deep into the earth. Couldn't she see that he had come to care for her? Didn't she understand that what he called desire was, in fact, love? Wouldn't she realize these things, knowing that the words he had spoken so hatefully that day were only his reaction to pain, and the anger that follows betrayal?

But what if she didn't?

*Are you willing to risk everything on that gamble?*

"Damn you, Maggie," he said to an empty room. "You said you were going to tell me about the children before they came. Why didn't you? Why did you wait too long? I don't understand."

*Don't you? Maybe it was for the same reason you keep waiting to tell her how you feel. Maybe she was afraid. Just like you.*

The more he mulled that over, the more he became convinced that he was guilty of the same thing he had criticized Maggie for. Why did it seem such a crime when Maggie did it, only to be perfectly understandable when he did?

He went in search of Molly. He found her in the laundry, folding clothes with Wong. "I want to talk to you, if you have a minute," he said.

"Didn't want to fold clothes anyway," Molly said. Giving Wong's pigtail a yank, she followed Adrian from the room.

Back in his study, he poured himself a glass of claret, pouring another one for Molly. "We may need this," he said, picking up the bottle and carrying it back to his desk. He took a seat behind the desk, indicating a chair for Molly.

"Tell me something," he said. "Is Maggie still planning on returning to Scotland?"

"Why don't you ask her?"

"Because I'm asking *you*. Is she?"

"I sure wouldn't blame her none if she did."

"A direct answer will do. Is Maggie leaving?"

"Why wouldn't she? If I remember right, you sure as fire liked the idea when the children came."

Adrian clenched his fists. Why was conversation between a man and a woman so difficult? He took a deep breath. "Molly, I am not trying to force you to tell me anything you don't want to tell me. I've come to you because . . . because I need help."

It was the first time in months that Adrian noticed Molly's features soften toward him. "Well," she said, "I suppose— considering how hard that confession had to be for you—that the least I can do is offer to help."

"Thank you."

"You know, I had a similar conversation with Maggie."

"You did?"

"Yes, not over her leaving, mind you. It was long before that, right after you found out about her being married and all."

"She told you about that?"

"She did. Told me she had younguns, too."

Adrian came out of his chair. "*You* knew? You knew all along?"

"I did."

"And you didn't tell me?"

"Wasn't my place to tell you."

Adrian sat down. "Go on."

"She told me about her children, asking me what she should do."

"And you advised her to tell me," he said.

"No, I advised her to wait awhile, to give the two of you a little more time together. I can see now that I was wrong. *That's* why I'm not going to give you any advice." Molly came to her feet. "Thanks for the claret."

Just as she reached the door, Adrian said, "Molly, if you were me, what would you do?"

She turned back to him. "If I were you," she said, "I wouldn't let any dust gather under my feet. If you love her. If you want her and the children to stay. You'd better tell her."

"I had hoped she could tell that I wanted her to stay. Damn," he said, staring up at the ceiling, his face twisted with indecision. "I know I could make her understand. If I only had more time."

"'Had I fish' is good without mustard, I hear."

"You aren't much help."

"There are some things a body has to do for themselves." She shook her head. "I don't reckon I'll ever understand just why it is that the good Lord made a man so strong in so many ways, only to make him weak when it comes to baring his heart to the woman he loves. A woman isn't like parched earth. Just because you've sprinkled her liberally with droplets of information doesn't mean she is going to know a man loves her by soaking all those droplets up. If you want Maggie to know how you feel, you're going to have to tell her."

She left the room. A moment later she poked her head around the door.

"Change your mind?" he asked.

"No, but I have something that might change yours."

"And what is that?"

"Something my pa used to say."

"Wonderful. That's just what I need. Family wit." Seeing the curve of a smile on her face, the twinkle in her eye, he said, "All right. What is it?"

" 'For want of a nail, the shoe is lost; for want of a shoe, the horse is lost; for want of a horse, the rider is lost.' If I was you, I wouldn't wait too long. The way I see it, you've already lost the shoe and the horse. You're down to where the water hits the wheel, as Big John says."

"I've been such a fool," he said. "A stupid, inconsiderate, blind fool."

"Well, I don't think you should go blaming yourself too hard. Lord knows, if every fool wore a white cap, we'd all look like a flock of geese," she said, and then she was gone.

For a long time after Molly left, Adrian leaned back in the chair with his eyes closed, contemplating what Molly had said. He was filled with regret and relief. Regret for all the wrong that had passed between them, the misunderstandings, the lack of communication. Relief that he had realized his mistake in time. Maggie *did* love him. She had told him so. *But you never told her. I will*, he thought. *I will.* His last thought before opening his eyes was that he'd like to get his hands around the neck of the man who first said, "Actions speak louder than words."

In this particular case, actions weren't worth a bucket of warm spit. Maggie needed words, and lots of them. And that was what Adrian dreaded most. He was not a man of words. But for Maggie, he would learn.

His mind made up, he began to think about Maggie. To his amusement, he had spent, if not an informative, at least an entertaining half hour with Maggie only this morning at breakfast. He smiled and shook his head, remembering how she seemed bent upon telling him everything she had recently learned about redwoods.

Did he know they were resistant to fire, disease, and insects?

*Yes.*

Did he know that they were nearly always protected—when they grew close to the coastline—by a stand of Sitka spruce?

*Yes.*

Did he know that they were closely related to the giant sequoia?

*Yes.*

Had he ever seen a sequoia?

*Yes.*

Would he take her to see one sometime?

*If she behaved herself.*

To which she replied, "Oh, well, we canna always see everything we want, can we?"

To his amazement, he found himself laughing harder at that now than he had this morning. She amazed him with her knowledge, her understanding of his business, her interest in it, her ability to talk intelligently on subjects he thought of interest only to a man.

He realized then just how much he looked forward to coming home each day, to listen to her excitement over telling him what she had done that day, her questions about his business, her wise counsel. But, as usual, she had surprised him.

Of late she hadn't been around when he came home, and whenever he asked about her whereabouts, Molly would simply say, "She's around here someplace."

That bothered him. He found himself thinking about his feelings for Maggie, how bright and shiny and new his love for her seemed. Oh, he supposed he had loved her a lot longer than he knew, but the realization of it—it was like holding a rainbow in your pocket.

Had it truly been recently that he had come to love her? *And yet, when she wasn't here, I always felt her absence.*

*And I remembered the way her skin felt, the smell of pine in her hair.*

He hadn't loved her.

*And yet I would find myself listening for the sound of her footsteps outside my door, the sound of her laughter when she puts the children to bed.*

He didn't love her.

*Yet I would find myself remembering how her step falls in so well with mine, and how my eyes seem to seek her out, even in a crowd.*

He didn't love her.

*Then I wonder why it was that whenever she came and went, I would find myself staring at the place where she had been.*

Maggie, Maggie, Maggie. Desire for her filled his day. Thoughts of her kept him awake at night. Night, ever the mother of counsel. Night, when he could get in touch with feelings he could not show. At night there was the nagging fear that he might wait too long, that she would leave. And that always brought up the question, if she did leave, where would she go? She couldn't go back to Scotland.

The reminder of Scotland brought up another point. Fletcher. Treachery of any form didn't sit too well with Adrian, and when it was committed against his own, it stirred his ire. He might be isolated here in the woods of northern California, but he knew what was going on in the world— enough to know crimes rarely came singly. If this Adair Ramsay had the guts to plan this flamboyant hoax, if he had the audacity to even think about stealing a title from a duke, then he was a man to be reckoned with.

Adrian leaned back in his chair, whirling it away from the desk, to gaze out the window. From where he sat, he could see Fletcher grooming his gelding. The lad had an eye for horseflesh. He also had the confidence and the bearing of a young duke. You could see good breeding in his features as well as his manner. It occurred to Adrian just how well

Fletcher had adapted to his new life here. And Adrian was going to make sure the boy remained safe, no matter what.

Needing to clear his mind, Adrian went outside, intending to go for his walk along the cliffs, but when he stepped through the door, he saw Ainsley trying to tie Heather to a cart.

"Here now," he said, walking toward her. "You can't tie her to a cart with just a rope around her neck. You don't want to choke her, do you?"

Ainsley shook her head.

When Adrian took the rope and loosened it around her neck, Heather's ears went up in greeting and she let out a loud bray. *"Eeeeee—haaaaaaw."*

"Look at her now," he said to Ainsley. "Do you see how she put her ears up? That meant she was glad to see me. Now, if she ever puts her ears down, that means she isn't too happy, and if her ears are laid back along her neck, she is telling you she is angry and might be tempted to bite you."

Adrian ruffled Heather's mane. "If you want her to pull this cart for you, I'll have you a harness made."

He looked up at that moment and saw Maggie standing a few feet away, looking at him in an odd way that made him self-conscious. "She was choking the donkey," he said hoarsely, then turned away.

Thrusting his hands deep into his pockets, Adrian wandered along the path that wound through the rocks that lined the cliffs. The sun was setting, a mirror of glaring white on a backdrop of deepest blue.

He heard a rock fall, tumbling and bouncing over the rocks to splash into the surf below. Turning, he saw Ainsley and Heather following him.

"Go away," he said. "You shouldn't be out here. It's too dangerous." When that didn't have the desired effect, he said, more gruffly, "This is no place for children. Go back to the house."

He started back down the trail, turning to look a moment later. Ainsley and Heather were still behind him. "You heard me," he said. "Get on back to the house before I tan your backside. This is no place for you."

Ainsley stood looking at him, the same way she always did. And as he always did, Adrian turned away, walking a few more yards before stopping and turning back to look.

Ainsley and Heather were gone.

# CHAPTER
## ❧ TWENTY-TWO ❧

Adrian had always been a thinker, but today he was doing some *serious* thinking. He decided that standing here, looking out over the point that stretched out over the Pacific, was a good place to do it. He was contemplating Maggie: how pretty she always looked when he came home each evening; what an effort she made to be cheerful and good-humored, even when he was cross as a bear fresh out of hibernation. He recalled the way she looked in the library in the evenings when she gathered Barrie, Fletcher, and Ainsley there to read them stories, and how he was always distracted by it—for how could he help watching the wealth of expressions that came and went across her face, or the dozen or so ways she had of changing her voice to suit the characters in a book? How could he forget those incredible eyes that seemed to change color with her mood, and the flame-kissed highlights of her hair that made him think she was born of fire? Most of all, he thought about the way she made him feel whenever he was around her.

Maggie, with her pedigree all the way back to Charlemagne. Maggie, with an education any man would covet. Maggie, with her feminine ways, her Scots logic, her dry humor, and her infinite patience. Maggie, slow to anger, quick to forgive. Maggie, who must know him better than he knew himself. Maggie, the woman he was going to lose if he didn't tell her how he felt. He closed his eyes and prayed.

*God, give me the right way to tell her. Give me the words she wants to hear. There have been so many losses in my life. Don't let me lose Maggie, too.*

As an afterthought, he added: *And don't let me make a fool of myself.*

He returned to the house and poured himself a glass of claret. Then he went to find Maggie.

"She's taking a nap with Ainsley," Maude said. "Want me to fetch her?"

"No," Adrian said. "I'll see her at dinner."

Seeing Maggie at dinner didn't work out the way he wanted it either, for Adrian had no more than dressed for dinner when Eli came to tell him that someone had tried to break into the mill office.

Grabbing his coat, he followed Eli out the door.

"Was anything taken?" he asked, running to the stables.

"No, I don't think so. Big John happened to notice a lamp on in the office and thought it had been left on by mistake. He headed on over to the office to turn it off, and when he opened the door, the culprit climbed out the back window."

Adrian saddled his gelding, letting Eli fill him in on the rest of the story as they rode down to camp. Big John was in the office when they arrived.

"I think there were two of them," he said, "although I only saw one go out the window." He walked over to the window. "They broke the bottom pane of glass. That's how they got in."

Adrian looked around the room. Everything seemed in place. His gaze rested upon a stack of ledgers. He frowned. He was certain he put those ledgers back in the drawer. And what was that can of coal oil doing on the table next to them?

"By God," he said, "whoever it was, they were going to burn the ledgers. . . ."

"And probably the office with it," Big John added, coming over to the table where Eli and Adrian stood.

Adrian looked around the room. "Well, there's nothing we can do now. You two might as well go home and get some shut-eye."

"What about you?" Eli asked. "You going home?"

"I'll put some boards over the window and put things away, then I'll head on home."

Adrian boarded up the bottom half of the window and returned the coal oil and ledgers to their proper place. When he had finished, he stood at the window, staring out over the campsite, seeing the faint glow of lamplight from the bunkhouse. A gust of wind rattled the front door, but Adrian barely noticed. He was feeling his life had forked in two directions—his lumber mill and his wife—and he was stranded somewhere in the middle, standing on the lunatic fringe.

Adrian turned away from the window and turned out the lamp. A short while later, he was back home. He ate a cold supper of salmon and potatoes, then went to find Maggie, only to discover her door was closed. He knocked softly, but Maggie did not answer. For a long time he stood outside her door. *Wake her up and tell her,* a voice said.

*She needs her sleep.*

*Are you stalling again?*

*No, I'll tell her in the morning,* he thought, suddenly recalling something engraved on a scrimshaw paperweight on his desk. *Defer not till tomorrow to be wise, Tomorrow's sun may never rise.*

He turned away from Maggie's door. His footsteps were slow and heavy as he went to his room.

* * *

For the rest of his life, Adrian would think of that next morning as the most fateful day of his life.

Upon arising that December morning, Adrian made his way down to the kitchen, where he was greeted with two bits of news: one, that a ship had docked, and two, that they had found Clyde Bishop with his throat cut.

Hearing the news just as she was about to enter the kitchen, Maggie paused outside the door. The ship was in. The time had come.

Her appetite suddenly gone, she turned away from the door, making her way silently up the stairs, going to her room and closing the door behind her.

Some time later she heard a soft knock. "Maggie, are you awake?" It was Adrian's voice.

On the other side of the door, Maggie clutched her dress to her bosom, her heart beating frantically in her chest. He did not knock again, nor did he call out her name. Wiping tears from her face, she turned away from the door, walking with slow, plodding steps back to her bed, where her clothes lay scattered. With a ragged sigh she folded the dress and placed it in the trunk, on top of the others. It seemed such a short while ago that she had folded these very same clothes to come to California, and now she was leaving. She picked up her muff, rubbing her hands over the soft fur, her mind wandering back to a moment ago. She could not help wondering what might have happened if she had opened the door when he knocked, if he had seen her packing. *No*, she told herself, *it is better this way. Better that he does not know. You are'na as strong as you think, Maggie. A strong woman would have opened the door.*

On his way to camp, Adrian became aware of a deep, aching pain that seemed to squeeze the breath from his chest. The pain wasn't from his procrastination as much as what it had resulted in. He realized that Maggie was the reality that shaped him, but when that ship docked before he had a chance to tell her what was in his heart, he felt that he and Maggie were like grain that had been ground into flour, grain that would sprout no more.

He was trapped now, between the decisions of his past and the reality of the present, and there was agony there, knowing he could neither go back to the past, nor leave it behind. So many memories rushed before his eyes, and nothing . . . *nothing* gave him a deeper feeling of loneliness and regret than treading the silent and deserted hallways of former times. He didn't know what he should do. He shoved his hands deep into his pockets, thinking, knowing it was too late for that.

After going over the details about Clyde Bishop's death with Eli and Big John, Adrian stood at the window of his office, looking at the ship.

"Maggie and the children are leaving. Did you know that?" Big John asked.

Adrian whirled around. "Leaving? Why didn't you tell me before now?"

"I thought you knew."

Adrian turned back to the window. Maggie was standing on the dock, now, two men stacking her trunks around her, Israel standing at her side. The children were nowhere in sight. Her face was turned away from him, and as he watched, her hand came up to touch the collar of her dress, a winsome expression that was also sad. Recriminations jammed his mind.

As swiftly as a mule's kick, he realized she was leaving, and he considered what he had done. Joined, first by marriage, then by lust, finally settling into a comfortable friendship, he had acted in anger, then he had been content to let it ride.

He left the office quickly, walking toward the dock. As if sensing his presence, she turned and stood silently, looking at him. He swallowed hard. He had wanted nothing more for the past several months than to tell her how he felt, and now it was too late. The ship had docked and its masts were bare and stripped of all canvas, like a grisly reminder that reached out to him, an omen of what his life would be without her: bare and stripped of its brightness.

A loud thudding noise distracted him and he looked away, seeing the plank had been lowered. The captain would appear at any moment. She did not look at him, but he saw her reach down and pick up her wicker basket. How much she looked like Ainsley. His heart wrenched at the thought. His gaze rested upon her basket. He remembered it sitting beside her chair in the library, skeins of yarn spilling out, her knitting needles jabbed into the shawl she was knitting for Molly. He remembered it, too, crammed with food and loaded in the wagon for a picnic.

He could not let her go.

His mind searched for a way to stop the madness he had put into motion as his gaze took in the men who had gathered around the dock. Hostility and contempt seemed to rise from the group of them like pointing fingers of accusation.

His gaze came back to her. She was wearing a dress he had never seen before, one that was so dark a blue, it was almost black. It was a somber dress, and grave. It fit the occasion.

He walked up to her, stopping at her side. "What are you doing down here, Maggie?"

"I'm doing what you wanted. Leaving." She was looking at him now. "Dinna worrit. I brought the children with me," she said. "Ainsley wanted to see Heather one last time, so Maude took them to the smithy. Emmitt was making a harness for Heather. He's been keeping her in a stall until he had it fitted and made."

Adrian's heart cracked. He opened his mouth to speak, when she looked off and said, "Dinna say anything, Adrian. Please." She looked at the group of silent men. "I dinna want them to see me cry, and I canna keep from it if you start talking. It's over. You have what you wanted. Please leave me with some dignity.''

It was the first time he could remember hearing so much anger, so much hurt, in her voice. "I had hoped . . .''

She whirled, her face inches from his now. "You had hoped what? That I would leave laughing? That I would thank you for not wanting us? Or were you hoping we could part friends? Well, we canna.''

"Maggie, love, don't be angry.''

"Love? Don't call me that. You wouldna understand love if someone whacked you over the head with it. Aye, you wouldna understand it if it were sitting on the tip of your nose. You are a blind man, Adrian. Blind and stupid.'' She stamped her foot. "Why?'' she asked, looking heavenward. "Why did I have to fall in love with a stupid, stubborn, blind man?'' Then looking back at him, she added, "And dinna tell me not to be angry. I have a right to be angry. . . . I want to be angry. I *have* to be.''

He had never seen her this mad. He had never loved her more. "You don't have to be angry.''

"Aye, I do. It will be easier for me to go if I'm angry at you.''

His hand come out to touch her sleeve. "Don't go.''

"Why?''

"I don't want you to.''

"You will have to do better than that,'' she said, and he suddenly knew he would.

It was now or never. *Speak up. Tell her, or lose her. Swallow your damn stupid pride. She loves you. Can't you tell her what she wants to hear?*

It was the most difficult thing he had ever done. "Maggie.'' When he spoke her name and saw the way hope sprang into her eyes, it all became easy. "I love you.''

The moment he spoke the words, a million pounds of

doubt and frustration fell away from him. He felt as if he would float away. He felt like a new man. His heart pounded in his chest as he saw her anger was slowly melting. To love and be loved. Was there anything better than this?

His arms went around her and he kissed her, full upon the mouth—and in front of every logger in the camp.

A loud cheer went up, and laughing, Maggie pushed him away. "The children," she said. "I need to find them, to tell them."

"I'll come with you," he said, reaching for her hand.

"No, I ken it would be better if I talk to them first. They are no verra happy with you right now, you ken."

"Aye," he said, "I ken." He tried to imitate her burr and failed, but he could tell from the warm look in her eyes that it didn't matter that he had failed, but that he had tried.

He walked with her as far as the office, then stood on the porch, watching her cross the camp, walking toward Maude and the children—who looked, just as she said, no verra happy with him.

Happiness inflated him. He felt ten times his size. He was a strong man. He could walk through fire. His woman loved him, and somehow that made the world seem right.

He went inside. The office was deserted. He poured himself a cup of coffee and went to stand at the window, looking out at the ship that would soon sail without its precious cargo—*his* precious cargo.

A moment later, the door opened and Maggie walked in.

She came to the window where he stood. He put his coffee cup on the windowsill, and moving behind her, wrapped her in his arms, his chin resting on top of her head. "Do you want some coffee?"

"Do you have any tea?"

"No, but I will from now on."

She closed her eyes and sighed, leaning closer against him. "I love you."

"I love you more," he said, "for there are more of you to love." He turned her to face him. "I love you, Maggie . . . *all* of you."

"Even Maude?"

"*Especially* Maude," he said, drawing her against his chest.

She burrowed closer against him, releasing a thin little sigh. "I heard about Clyde Bishop," she said. "Big John said that man you suspected was no here."

"Greenwood," Adrian said. "No, he's gone. Disappeared."

"You think he's dead?"

Adrian snorted. "I doubt it. Off on a holiday spending his newly acquired wealth from Pope and Talbot is more like it."

"I'm sorry about poor Clyde. He was a kind man. He didna deserve what happened to him."

"No, he didn't," Adrian said, his eyes going over her. He started to say something, but at that moment Eli burst through the door. Before he could say anything, the fire bells began to clang.

"Fire!" Eli shouted. "There's a fire in the sawdust pile behind the mill. The wind is picking up. It looks like the fire could spread to the mill or the blacksmith's shop."

Both Adrian and Maggie ran outside. Already the sky was filled with thick, choking clouds of smoke. Adrian took off running in the direction of the men who were forming bucket lines, desperately trying to douse the campsite with water, before the wind-whipped flames that were already roaring like a hungry beast could ravage the tiny camp. Leaping from tree to tree, the flames gobbled the dry grass, racing along the gentle slopes toward the scattering of small wooden buildings, and the larger one that housed the mill saws.

Wind-whipped herself, Maggie began to search for the children as her eyes began to tear. Already the smoke obscured the tops of the trees in the background, blocking out the sun and turning the sky to a dull, dark gray. All about her, she could hear the popping and crackling of burning brush and trees, then one of the small wooden buildings burst like an exploding teakettle, hurling flaming darts of burning wood into the air.

Maggie saw the children with Tom Radford, and shielding her eyes, she ran across the camp to where they stood. "You'd best be getting yourself and the children out of here, ma'am," Tom said. "The way this wind is fanning the fire, there may not be much left of the camp."

Maggie watched Tom limp off, then she turned, herding the children in front of her as she searched for the buggy, seeing the last of it as it disappeared down the road that led to the house.

"The horse ran off," Fletcher said. "How will we get home?"

"We'll walk," Maggie said, suddenly feeling herself whipped around and yanked up against Adrian.

"Come with me," he shouted, grabbing her and taking Ainsley by the hand. "Hurry! We haven't much time."

"Where are you taking us?"

Clouds of smoke billowed around them. Somewhere nearby a loud crack erupted like rifle fire. Another shower of sparks. Maggie beat at a glowing cinder that stuck to her skirts.

"I'm taking you to the ship."

Maggie jerked to a stop. "Please," she said. "Adrian, please dinna do this."

"It isn't what you think, Maggie. I'm not sending you away." He put his arms around her. "Don't you understand I could never send you away? You're part of me, but the ship is the only safe place to send you. You can be away from here before this place becomes a death trap."

Maggie pulled up sharp. "You can't send us away now,"

she shouted, trying to be heard over the loud roar. "Look!" she screamed. "Look around you! If you send us away, they won't stay," she said, watching Adrian as he began to look around him at the men, who already had begun to slow down, many of them just standing there with pails in their hands, looked at Adrian, waiting, watching, to see what he would do.

"If you put us on that ship, they won't stay. You need them, Adrian. And you need us. You'll never stop this fire if they go."

Adrian's eyes swept over her, and for a moment she thought he was angry with her. "I'll be back," he said, giving her a quick kiss. "Wait for me over by the docks. If the fire gets worse, put yourself and the childen in that rowboat and get the hell away from land. Do you understand?"

"Aye," Maggie said, then she watched him run across the camp toward the area where the fire seemed the worst. The wind whipped the flames out of control now, and it was dangerously close to the sawmill and the blacksmith shop nearby.

Soot-streaked and soaked with water and sweat, Adrian shouted at Maggie to get the children back. "Come on," she said to Fletcher as she took Barrie's hand. She reached for Ainsley, only Ainsley was not there. Looking up, Maggie saw Ainsley's bright head, her curls bouncing as she ran toward the blacksmith's.

Maggie screamed and took off running. Hearing her, Adrian looked up, seeing Maggie running toward the blacksmith's. A moment later, he saw why.

He dropped the bucket in his hands, running toward Ainsley, reaching her just before she reached the blacksmith's. Scooping her into his arms, he headed toward Maggie, putting her squirming, kicking body down, telling Maggie to get her and the other children out of here.

Taking Ainsley and Barrie by the hand, Maggie turned away, freezing in place when she heard a piercing cry.

"Heather!" Ainsley screamed. "Heather is in there. Dinna let Heather die."

Dropping down in front of Ainsley, Maggie started to cry. "What did you say?"

"Heather," Ainsley sobbed, pointing to the smithy's.

Adrian looked at Maggie, then at Ainsley, before his eyes went back to the sawmill. There weren't enough men to douse both the sawmill and the smithy, and he had already given the order to save the mill.

His heart felt as if it were being torn from his chest. He saw Maggie looking at Ainsley, and the way Ainsley, her face streaked with tears and soot, looked at him in a way that said she did not understand. "Heather," she sobbed softly. "Heather."

"Eli!" Adrian shouted. "Get the men over to the blacksmith's, and hurry!"

"The blacksmith's?" Eli questioned with a surprised look.

"Yes, and hurry."

"Do you realize what you're saying, man?" Big John said, running up to Adrian, his large frame heaving from exertion. "You pull the men off the sawmill now and you lose it. Think, man. You can't save both the smithy and the mill. You have to choose between them."

Adrian's eyes flicked to Maggie. "I already have," he said. "Let the mill burn," he shouted, running toward the blacksmith's. "Save the smithy's."

Fortunately, the building was small and the wood dry, making it easy to douse with water. When the flames were somewhat under control, Adrian grabbed a tarp, and dousing it in a water barrel, he wrapped it around himself just before running into the building. Coughing from the thick smoke, he searched the row of stalls, finding the donkey. Sticking a burlap sack over her head, Adrian led her from the stall and outside.

Ainsley ran to them, throwing her arms around Heather's neck. For a moment he stood there, watching her hug the small, singed donkey who picked the most god-awful times to bray.

*"Eeeeee-haaaawwwww . . . Eeeeeee-haaaawwwww."*

"She's happy," Barrie said.

"No, she wants me to thank you," Ainsley said.

Adrian swallowed hard. He didn't know what to say, how to talk to Ainsley. He glanced helplessly at Maggie.

"Why?" Maggie asked, her eyes going over to the mill, which was now engulfed in hungry flames. She put her hand upon his arm. "Oh, Adrian, why . . . when you might have saved the mill?"

"I'm not sure," he said, looking at Ainsley, then at Maggie. "Perhaps it's because I'm crazy," he said, and smiled, his voice sounding hoarse and full of feeling. "Or maybe I realized there are some things that are more important than money."

Hours later, when the fire had burned itself out, Adrian stood with Maggie and the children, looking at the smoking remains of what had been the California Mill and Lumbering Company. There wasn't much left now, save the smithy, the bunkhouse, and part of the office. The medicine hut, the cookhouse, the mill, and several outlying buildings were all gone.

Big John and Eli came to stand beside Adrian, and like him, their arms glistened with sweat, streaked black with soot—their faces, too.

"Did you find anything?" Adrian asked Big John.

"Enough," Big John answered. "We found Greenwood."

"Just the bastard I want to see," Adrian said. "Where is he?"

"Dead."

"Another happy bit of news," Adrian said. "We'll never know who was behind this now."

"Oh, we know, all right. Seems Greenwood's killers were in such a hurry, they didn't wait around to make sure he was dead. He didn't have much time left, but it was enough to scribble two words on a tree stump with his own blood."

"What two words?"

" 'Fire' and 'Talbot.' "

"It's not enough to stand up in court," Adrian said.

"Why not?" asked Eli. "We've got plenty of witnesses who saw Greenwood and what he wrote on that stump. We've got the stump, too."

"Yes, and all those *witnesses* work for us. Besides, we don't have a thing to connect Greenwood to Pope and Talbot."

"I wouldn't go so far as to say that," Big John said, taking a small black notebook out of his pocket. "Seems Greenwood kept a pretty good record of his pay from Pope and Talbot." He opened the book and showed Adrian. "See? Here it is, neat as you please—date, amount paid, and every blessed one of them shows he was paid by Pope and Talbot, right up until last week." He closed the book. "It's right here in black and white, and in Greenwood's own hand. He was working for them or they wouldn't have been paying him."

Big John handed the book to Adrian.

"I'll put it in the safe in my study," Adrian said. "At least there's one thing around here that's fireproof."

Big John looked around. "Seems like your house is about the only thing you've got left," he said.

"Oh, I don't know," Adrian said, his eyes on Maggie.

"I don't understand it," Eli said, unconscious of the look

that passed between Big John and Adrian. "If you hadn't pulled the men off the mill and put them to work saving the smithy's, we could have headed the fire off before it reached the mill." He let his eyes roam around the blackened remains of their camp. "I know for a fact that if we'd saved the mill, it wouldn't have spread to the rest of the camp." He looked at the three remaining buildings and shook his head. "Now you've lost everything."

Adrian looked from Eli to Big John, then to Maggie. He watched her put the children in the wagon, sending them home with Maude, before crossing the camp yard with Molly, ready to tend to the injured who had gathered around a small tent hastily erected to serve as a medical facility. Most of her supplies had been burned in the fire, but her spirits were high, and her gait as determined as ever.

As she walked, the wind whipped around her skirts, and something about it reminded him of the first time he had seen her, standing on the point, and Adrian couldn't help asking himself: *Was everything lost?*

He had Maggie. And he had her children as well. He realized then that that was enough. He smiled, never taking his eyes off his wife as he turned toward Eli and Big John. "Was there never anything in your life that was worth risking everything for?" he asked.

He stood there, amid the charred remains of his lumber mill, his hands thrust deep in his pockets, his face blackened and streaked with sweat. Then he did the strangest thing. He threw back his head and laughed.

# CHAPTER
## ❧ TWENTY-THREE ❧

Adrian spent the rest of the day taking inventory of what remained of the California Mill and Lumbering Company. In places, the mill still smoldered, bits of twisted metal sticking out here and there, like the bones of some prehistoric mammoth.

"What now?" Big John asked.

"We rebuild," Adrian said. "We've got plenty of lumber."

"You can thank your lucky stars that the new saw we ordered was delayed. It should be here just about the time we've got the mill rebuilt and are ready to install it," Big John said. "But it's still a shame we lost the building."

"Oh, I don't know," Adrian said. "I never was too happy with the design of that mill." He threw one arm across Big John's shoulders, and the two men walked off.

"Now, let me tell you about my plans for the new one," Adrian said. "I thought we'd . . ."

The two men went into the office and their voices faded away, but the sound of Big John's laughter could be heard everywhere. A moment later, another burst of laughter blended with Big John's.

The men around camp stopped working, and some of them

scratched their heads and stared. Others were simply wondering what was going on. But whatever they thought, there was one thing they agreed upon:

How could a man who had just watched a large chunk of his fortune burn to the ground laugh about it?

After he arrived home, Adrian was impatient for dinner to be over. Once the meal was finished, he was going to make love to his wife.

To kill a little time, he made his way down to the study, passing by the salon and continuing on his way, when something drew him up short. He whirled around and walked back to the salon, his eyes going immediately to the place above the fireplace, the place where Katherine's portrait had been before he had taken it down.

Hanging there, where the space had been bare, was another portrait, and although it wasn't as large as the one he had painted of Katherine, it was infinitely more dear.

He knew immediately it was Maggie's work, for no one but she captured the essence of her subject with such simplicity. The painting was of him and Israel, perfect in form and balance—but what he found that drew his attention most was the strange emotion he felt, seeing himself through her eyes.

"It's my way of saying thank you," Maggie said, coming up softly behind him.

He turned to look at her. "It's remarkable," he said. "I had no idea you were doing this." His eyes softened. "I don't know what to say. I can't remember anyone ever giving me anything before."

She laughed. "Aye, you can. Ross gave you a wife and three children, only I ken you werena so grateful for it."

His arms went around her. "I'm grateful now," he said.

"Are you?"

"Do you doubt me?"

"You couldna blame me if I did. You fought it long enough."

"But I've learned the way of it in time." His hold on her tightened and he drew her against him more firmly, his jaw resting on her head, sending tingling vibrations through her body as he spoke. "When I think of how close I came to losing you . . . If you had gotten on that ship . . ."

She began to laugh softly. "I wouldna have gotten on that ship, Adrian Mackinnon. I'm far too stubborn to do that."

He drew his head back to look at her. "Oh, you wouldn't have, would you?"

"No, I wouldna. The only way I would have gone was if you carried me aboard, and you no would have done that," she said, coming up on her tiptoes to kiss him.

"And why not?" he asked, his words no more than a croak.

"Because I ken how much you loved me. You just didna know it."

"I know it now," he said, kissing her back.

"Aye," she said softly, "and I mean to see you dinna forget it. Ever."

The sound of shouts and running feet told them Barrie and Fletcher were at it again.

"I ken our days of lovemaking on the floor all over the house are finished," she said with a slow laugh, then kissing him lightly once more, she turned away, and going to the door, caught Fletcher by the ear, just as he dashed by.

"Why didna you grab her?" Fletcher wailed, glaring at Barrie as she skipped down the hall out of sight.

"You were closer," Maggie said.

Dinner was a long time coming that night, and Adrian decided to take a walk along the cliffs.

Israel the Faithless was nowhere in sight, so Adrian struck out alone, following the winding path that led to the point.

When he reached the bluff that overlooked the rolling swells of water that crashed into foam against the rocks below, he paused and stood for a moment, looking out over the water. Then, with a sigh of resignation, he took something out of his pocket. He opened his hand and stared down at the pouch of chewing tobacco, remembering that Katherine had once told him that a woman for him would come along someday; a woman who would make him forget all about chewing tobacco.

With a shake of his head, Adrian thought how wise God was to sometimes give us, not what we want, but what we need. Then he took a step back and hurled the pouch of tobacco off the bluff, and watched it sail out, out over the water in a slow-descending arc, before disappearing into the deep blue water of the Pacific.

Thrusting his hands deep into his pockets, he stared out at the water for a spell, then turned down the path to finish his walk.

He hadn't gone very far when he heard something behind him, and turning, he expected to see Israel. Instead, he saw Ainsley. "This is no place for you to be," he said. "It's dangerous out here. Go on back to the house."

The two of them stood, each one looking at the other, a showdown of sorts.

Stubbornly, Ainsley made no move to leave.

Just as stubbornly, Adrian didn't either.

"Go back to the house," he said, and started off, but after a few minutes, his curiosity got the best of him. He stopped and turned.

Ainsley stopped as well.

Adrian felt his anger rise. No matter how much she looked like her mother, she had to learn obedience. "I'm not going to tell you again," he said. "Go back to the house."

He started off again.

After a few minutes, the same thing happened. His curiosity pecked at him until he stopped and looked. Sure as the sun was shining, there Ainsley was, following him.

She was wearing a blue dress and a dark blue velvet coat, and her shoes buttoned right up under it so you couldn't see the tops. But it was her face that held him. It was such a queer little face, he thought, a face that was both young and old. He never thought to see such expression on a face that was so young, for truthfully, it would have seemed too old even for a child of ten, and Ainsley was much younger. She was an odd little creature, he thought, with her intense eyes and her watchful, silent ways. She reminded him of himself when he was a boy.

"I thought I told you to go back," he said gruffly. "Don't you ever mind?" He turned away and started down the path that slowly angled down to the beach.

"I want to come with you," a soft little voice behind him said.

His heart thudding in his chest, Adrian turned slowly. For a long while he stood there looking at her, the little girl with the small cherub face, and the huge blue eyes that looked back at him.

An eternity seemed to pass, and then at last he spoke. "Well, come on, then," he said brusquely, and turned away, walking briskly down the path, feeling a moment later the warmth of a small hand slipping inside his.

Adrian stopped and looked down at Ainsley; then he gave her hand a squeeze, and the two of them walked on.

# ❈ EPILOGUE ❈

Fletcher sat straight in his chair, as still and solemn as a man. Barrie undressed her doll for the sixteenth time. Ainsley did what she always did whenever Adrian was sitting in his favorite chair. She climbed all over him, dropping cookie crumbs in his shirt pocket and giving him wet kisses, asking him to sing a song to Grace. The only song Adrian knew that was appropriate for a doll was "Rock-a-bye Baby," and he had already sung that five times.

He was praying for a miracle when he got one.

The wailing squall of a newborn pierced the air. In unison the four of them sprang to their feet and rushed out into the hallway to look at the top of the stairs. A moment later, Molly came out. "Well? What are you waiting for? You want to see your baby brother or don't you?"

The children shrieked and dashed up the stairs. Adrian followed them, then stopped outside the door as they hurried through, uncertain for a moment as to what he was supposed to do.

"Go on in," Molly said, giving him a nudge. "A newborn is just a smaller version of these little people you were so afraid of. It won't bite you," she said with a laugh.

Adrian stepped inside the room, standing in the doorway,

and looked at Maggie propped up in the bed, his newborn son cradled against her breast, Fletcher, Barrie, and Ainsley clustered like peeping chicks about her.

Maggie looked up, and seeing the lost look in his eyes, she smiled and patted the bed beside her. In three swift strides Adrian crossed the room, sitting down beside her on the bed. His gaze traveled over three young faces before going to that of his wife, and finally that of his newborn son, and he felt humbled to the depths of his soul. He looked at his family, feeling his heart flood with warmth.

"So this is love," he whispered, and he took the five of them in his arms.

## Here's a sample from
## HEAVEN KNOWS,
### next year's historical romance by Elaine Coffman.
### Coming from Fawcett Books in 1994.

He dismounted, walked around the buggy, and then he stopped. Tall and slim-hipped, he stood with his profile toward her, the sun catching him from the back. When his horse noticed her and snorted, he looked up.

It was hard to ignore those sensual features, the promise of that experienced mouth and softly arousing gaze. Oddly enough, his expression was, for a change, one she could easily read. It was the same sort of expression her father had often worn when she was a child—whenever he was trying to decide between punishing her or giving her a hug.

He was wearing a dark blue shirt that made his hair look blue-black. His face was as beautiful to her as it had always been, his thick black brows curving almost wickedly over the intense iron-blue eyes, whose gaze never left the scrutiny of her face.

"This is an unexpected, but pleasant surprise," he said. "I was thinking that perhaps this horse had run away with the buggy."

She gave him a curious stare. "Run away? Why would you think that?"

He looked back at the horse hitched to the buggy. "Because he wasn't tied."

"Grandpa is getting a bit forgetful," she said.

His gaze traveled over her slowly. "He isn't the only one," Tavis said. "Every time I look at you, I find it hard to remember that the Lizzie I recall, and the Elizabeth I see, are actually the same person."

She laughed. "Good. If I remember right, you were never too enamored with Lizzie."

He smiled. "I don't think I can honestly say I was ever en-

411

amored with you . . . you *were* nothing more than a child, you know. But there was always something—something about you that never let me be quite as angry at you as I led everyone to believe.''

If he had come right out and told her he had designed a ship that could fly, she couldn't have been more astonished. "You could have fooled me,'' she said.

He smiled again, flooding her soul with sunshine. "Apparently, I did just that.''

"And you fooled a lot of other people as well,'' she said. "Like everyone else in Nantucket, I thought you hated the sight of me.''

"Hate never entered into things,'' he said, his voice strangely soft. "You irritated the daylights out of me on occasion, but even then I'd go home at night, and, more often than not, I would find myself lying in bed, thinking about something you had done, and laughing.'' He raised a brow at her. "I was always curious to know, just how you got the red dye out of your hair.''

"It wasn't dye. It was henna. It washed out . . . eventually.''

"You see? I do remember things about you.''

"But you always seemed so angry.''

His hand came up, brushing over the hollow beneath her cheekbone. "Sweet Elizabeth, I had to. How else would I discourage you? You were a child. I was a man full grown. People talk about a man with interests like that,'' he said, his voice light and teasing. "They won't allow him to come in their homes. They say prayers for his sinner's soul at church. They take their children by the hand whenever he passes. They think he should be locked up.''

She knew he was making light with her, but all of this was simply too much for her to absorb quickly.

Before she could think further, she felt his hands, warm on her shoulders. He drew her toward him, nestling her gently against the hard lines of his body, an act that was neither forced nor suggestive. In truth, it struck her more as a token of affection than anything sensual. His chin resting on the top of her head, he spoke to her, and she could feel the vibrations of his words against her cheek, which harbored in the curve of his throat.

"Don't be so quick to condemn yourself,'' he said. "You will never know how much you brightened a world that seemed terribly dull after you were gone.''